TIDDLYWINKS

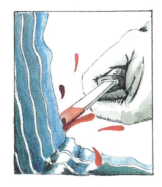

[In *Tough Tiddlywinks*] Christopher Nowlin gives us a true sense of place and time; he transports us to the gritty streets and building sites of Vancouver, made grittier by an economy in freefall in recent years.

— Anne Emery, award-winning author of *Sign of the Cross* and *Children of the Morning*

Chris Nowlin's second novel creates a vivid, lively portrait of contemporary life in Vancouver, from street artists to greedy developers out to make a big buck. His large cast of characters displays a host of contradictions, passions and drive – just like real folk. Best of all, his story is a grabber. A fine follow-up to *To See the Sky*.

— Jon Redfern, Arthur Ellis Award winner for *Trumpets Sound No More*

Tough Tiddlywinks

an illustrated novel

by

Christopher Nowlin

A Picture's Worth Press

Copyright © 2014 Christopher Nowlin

All rights reserved. Printed in the United States of America. No part of this book may be used or reproduced in any manner whatsoever without written permission except in the case of brief quotations embodied in reviews and critical articles.

Designed by Anna Shvets at Neshama Books

For information, contact A Picture's Worth Press.

1 – 139 West 11 Avenue
Vancouver, B.C. V5Y 1S8
www.apicturesworthpress.com

Library and Archives Canada Cataloguing in Publication

Nowlin, Christopher, 1964 –
Tough Tiddlywinks / by Christopher Nowlin.

ISBN 9780987726841

To the memory of Hazen Stuart Pingree

All of the characters in this novel are fictitious. Any resemblance they might bear to actual persons, living or dead, is purely coincidental.

Acknowledgments

I hereby wish to acknowledge all those individuals who so generously took their time to read my manuscript and to offer their thoughts. These people are Jon Redfern, Anne Emery, Carellin Brooks, Jeffrey Oh, Sarah McLeod, Sylvia Eastman, John Ryan, Nada Jurišić, Katheryn Petersen, and Donna Hall. I also want to thank Trysh Ashby-Rolls and Eroca Dancer for their weekly input into my story as it emerged on Pender Island. I am indebted to Bill Milnes and Sylvie Bordelais for their French translation assistance. Any errors in that regard are definitely mine. I thank Addison Lanier for his helpful thoughts about the interior design of my book. I am grateful to Julian Lawrence for being an inspirational cartooning instructor. I am indebted to Anna Shvets for the passion and skill she brought to designing this book. Finally, I offer my heartfelt thanks to Gordon Thomas, whose unflagging belief in this project pulled it into the light of day.

3rd Quarter 2007

Ryan Ghostkeeper was still on probation as he sat crossed-legged against the polished stone of the Hudson's Bay Company department store, the cool sun hitting his face and steel-toed boots before dipping behind the Hollyburn mountains. Three completed carvings – painted plaques – were laid out before him as he worked intently on a fourth, the steel blade of his knife occasionally flashing a white beam. Indeed, that was one restriction the judicial system had yet to impose upon him – a prohibition against possessing knives. Although he had built himself a criminal record over the years, including a conviction for assault causing bodily harm, he had yet to brandish a blade at anyone.

...A shadow blocked out the fading sun and scarcely moved.

"How much?"

That is how Ryan understood the question, though his ear heard, "Ouw much?" He detected a strong French accent.

A tall, well-built man in a leather bomber jacket and designer jeans had made the query. He carried a small, crisp paper shopping sac containing a watch purchased only blocks away.

"Tw – Fifteen dollars a piece," Ryan informed him. He had almost quoted his usual price of twelve dollars, but given the man's apparent capacity to pay more, and the real sense of interest in his voice, Ryan decided to gamble.

"Fifteen?"

"Mm-hmm. That's original Native carving," Ryan confirmed.

The man kneeled down to take a closer look and Ryan smelled a pleasant fragrance come off his jacket or neck. His skin was dark too, a different hue than Ryan's. He picked up each carving in turn and studied it.

"I think I like this one," he said, picking up the middle one a second time, and holding it out toward Ryan. "My fiancée likes turtles, so it is good." *Ahh.* They had something in common, Ryan realized. Canadians, but begrudgingly so. He had placed the accent. *I tink I like dis one*, with the "one" being bent deep like a blues note. The man was from Québec. Just possibly his ancestors had bartered with Ryan's own.

"Does it mean anything, like, to you?" Frank Belleveau asked. The plaque he was holding depicted a raven with a salmon's eye. The bird was paddling a canoe atop a turtle.

Every now and then a curious onlooker or a prospective buyer asked a similar question. What did his images mean? He was always happy to make something up.

"It's about a wise old bird. A *tricky* woman. She tricked a salmon and stole its eye, then tricked some humans and stole their canoe."

"What about the turtle?" – or *de turdle*, to Ryan's ear.

"That's North America."

"America? The turtle?"

"Yes sir. We call it Turtle Island, but it's a long story."

Francois Belleveau looked at his watch and then reached in his wallet.

"Do you have a five?" he asked, now holding out a twenty dollar bill.

Ryan dug into his pockets, pulled out various coins, and counted them. Frank could see there was less than five dollars and said, "That's great. That's enough. Here." He handed Ryan the twenty, received his change and the carving, then made his way to his Ducati motorbike.

Frank almost skidded out when he first saw his fiancée that large, and he had plenty of time to stare at her. Cambie Bridge traffic had come to a standstill because of a conglomerate of bicyclists moving westward along Broadway. It was about 6:20 pm, on Friday, October 26, and the monthly "critical mass" ride was making its rounds through the streets of Vancouver, with a police escort no less. On this autumn evening the multi-wheeled Leviathan was about 800 pedallers strong.

"Fuck this," Frank muttered to himself before pulling out of his lane and slowly riding southward past the stopped vehicles. When he got to 7th Avenue he turned right and went westward, thus avoiding a delay of about ten minutes on the way home.

Hannah Verso saw it too, not the mass bike ride, but the billboard, from the bus window. There she was, larger than life, smiling, arm-in-arm with a confident male model, strolling along the boardwalk east of Granville Island, condominiums gleaming in the Pacific Boulevard background. The billboard for Pacific Tides Trust mortgage specialists had been mounted that afternoon. "Realize Your Dreams with a Risk-Free Monthly Flex®," it advertised.

Hannah had to look away a few times before the bus passed by. A knot had formed in her stomach and her hands shook slightly, as they did when she drank too much coffee in the morning, which wasn't too often.

"It's vain to stare at yourself in the mirror," her mother had told her when she was a young girl, upstairs in her parents' bedroom, reveling in her beauty in front of a full length mirror. She was used to hearing how pretty she was, from relatives and friends, so she had taken to checking herself out when opportunities arose. To dissuade her from this tendency, her mother had even told her the story of Narcissus.

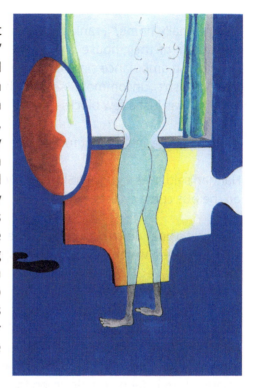

"Never again," she now thought to herself with pursed lips.

People stared at her enough as it was anyway, men and women alike – either at her 'big hair,' her large eyes and lips, her pronounced cheekbones, or hourglass figure. Some compared her to Sophia Loren, others to Rosario Dawson. She was 'a looker,' she had been told, so people looked at her by definition.

Even now, she noticed a middle-aged passenger lift his eyes from his paper – he did it a couple of times – just to have a look at her, so she stared ahead and wondered what Frank would think about the ad.

A few more minutes passed before she pulled the cord. The

driver stopped at 14th Avenue and she headed west through a comfortable residential district called Fairview.

"You're finally home," Frank said when she pushed through the front door of their house on 15th, between Laurel and Willow Streets. An ambulance siren could be heard in the background, which wasn't uncommon, as the busy Vancouver General Hospital was just a few blocks north.

"Did you get caught in that fuckin' bike ride thing?" Frank asked.

Hannah said, "Yes, I guess." She had overheard some passengers on the bus curse cyclists.

Frank set a beer down on a coffee table, got up from his armchair – he had been watching a television sportscast – and extended his arms.

"You got it," she blurted.

He beamed and leaned back slightly, to show it off. She clasped his wrist and studied his new diver's watch, with its numbered, rotating bezel, deep aquatic green face, chronometer and other gizmos she did not understand.

"Pretty fancy," she remarked.

He embraced and kissed her, then she asked, "What is this bike ride thing anyway?"

"You know. Those crazy assholes who ride their bikes all over the place on the last Friday of each month."

"Oh. I didn't see them. I just stayed a little late at the library."

"But you've seen it, right? Tell me you saw it."

She nodded.

"And?" He pulled back and looked squarely into her eyes.

She shrugged.

"Oh Hannah. It's great. Really. You look great."

"Thanks."

She hung her jacket up and headed into the kitchen.

"That's all? You got that kind of exposure and you're not excited?" Frank asked, following her with his beer in hand.

"It's all right. It's a billboard, for a bank, or credit union, or whatever." She was pulling food from the fridge. "They chose me because I look ethnic, no big deal."

"Unh unh unh. No they didn't. They picked you because you're beautiful."

"We've got enough stuff here for burritos. Does that sound okay?"

Hannah laid out some cheese, olives, spinach and red peppers on the counter, then reached into a cupboard for refried beans.

Frank shrugged before saying, "Sure. That's fine with me."

Hannah pulled a wine glass from a different cupboard and picked up a bottle of Pinot Noir from the kitchen table.

"Hey, what's this?" she asked, putting down the bottle and picking up Frank's carving.

"Oh. I bought that from a guy on Granville Street, an autochth...

a native guy in front of the Bay there."

"It's got a turtle on it."

"That's why I got it."

Hannah looked at her fiancé skeptically.

"Okay. I don't know why I did it. I felt a little guilty. I just looked down, saw the carvings, and the steel toe of his boots. He had construction boots on, like we all wear, but he was obviously out of work and I had just bought a brand new watch for four hundred and sixty bucks."

"Why didn't you just ask him if he needed work?"

"Han*nah*. What do you mean by that?"

She leaned against the sink with a glass of wine in hand and said, "I don't know. You're always complaining that you guys can't get enough labourers? The demand is too high. The market's gone crazy."

She took a sip of her drink and Frank said, "But I didn't know anything about the guy."

"What did you need to know? Ask him if he was out of work, if he could swing a hammer, carry two by fours. I don't know what these guys do, but he had the boots on, you said, and he can obviously use his hands." She picked up the carving again and waved it lightly in front of Frank, who shook his head slightly before opening the fridge door and reaching for a beer.

Hannah set down her glass and began to open the can of beans. Frank returned to the television news.

🚲 🚲 🚲

Over the next few weeks Frank Belleveau rode his Ducati to work as usual, to THE MANNA site on West Broadway, between Granville Street and Burrard. It was one of CanCon's many developments, a mixed-use project that was well underway. Frank was a professional and experienced tradesman who had been in charge of the interior wall frames and now supervised the insulation and drywall installation.

Each afternoon he returned home, helped himself to a beer, checked out a few men's sites on his computer, which linked him to NSFW sites if he was so inclined, which he usually was, then he watched hockey highlights and the news on the television. Next to the magazines on the coffee table the wooden, tricky raven stared at him, vying for his attention. He and Hannah had not yet agreed on where to hang it.

Hannah tended to be away during the day. Even when unemployed she regularly attended pilates and yoga classes, and spent two or three hours at public libraries or in cafés, usually reading best sellers. She shopped a little for herself, ever-drawn to sales, and she made a daily groceries run, to top-up fridge and cupboard supplies, and get whatever was needed for dinner. Although she wore the chef's apron at home, make no mistake, she was no foodie. She just got the job done.

In the last few days Frank had taken an unusually circuitous route home from work. He rode his motorbike around the downtown area where he had seen the Native fellow who sold him the carving. He went first to the Bay, then through Gastown and the downtown eastside, but with no luck. The fellow was a transient, Frank figured. The chances of bumping into him again appeared to be virtually nil.

Frank was naturally shocked, therefore, to see the elusive carver in a hard hat and carpenter's belt at THE MANNA job site a week later. Ryan and another fellow were carrying plywood sheets past the foreman's office.

"Eh there," Frank said, having approached the Native man on his lunch break.

Ryan looked up, squinting.

"Do you remember me?" Frank asked.

"Uh – yes, yes sir, I do. You bought my canoe."

"You have a good memory. Umm, I'm Frank, by de way."

"I'm Ryan." The men shook hands. "You're not here for a refund, are you?" Ryan asked. "I don't give refunds."

Frank grinned and Ryan chuckled.

"No, I'm not here for a refund. I really like your carving. I just wanted to say Hi. I'm so surprised you are here because I had been looking for you, to see if you might want a job."

"I came to the site first thing this morning. I need the money, and my probation officer's gettin' on my case 'cause I'm supposed to be seeking gainful employment. I think that's what it says, one of my conditions."

"Oh." Frank was surprised by Ryan's

candid disclosure, which was made right in front of a few co-workers who were eating lunch.

"The guy hired me right away," Ryan added. "He said a couple of guys quit last Friday."

"Oh, I see…So you've had a little run in with the law, eh?" Frank asked.

"Causing a disturbance and assault police officer. Down near the Skytrain there. Waterfront. Yeah. I was drunk, out of my head."

"Sometimes shit happens when we hit de booze too hard," Frank said. "But good luck on the job, okay? I gotta run."

The two men shook hands and Frank left to have his lunch, in an office trailer perched on stilts.

🚲 🚲 🚲

"I'll take a run at it," Donald Dickerson told his friend and banker Sam Rickels over a cocktail at the Wedgewood Hotel piano lounge, a popular meeting place for the professional set in Vancouver's downtown shopping district. Ceiling fans spun unnecessarily, as the air conditioning kept the room cold enough to store vegetables. The place was mostly empty anyway. A well-polished baby grand sat mutely nearby, waiting for someone to sit on its bench and warm things up, but neither Don nor Sam planned on staying past the rush hour, so Sam wouldn't be asked to play it once, or even again.

"But it's right in front of the shops. Where are the patrons going to park?"

"That's just the point." Don wrapped his torpedo-cigar fingers around a Canadian Club and Coke, and lifted the drink. "Jeezus, Sam, when are you gonna' get with the program?" He took a hefty sip of his juice but didn't return it to the table. Rather, he held it aloft, like a magician who's got something else up his sleeve. "It's all about getting people to stop driving everywhere. I put a multi-use in there and bingo bango, the grocery store's right in your backyard. Stick in an accountant, an insurance broker, a pizza parlor, and one of those, those fuckin' bronze-tanning places. Denise loves 'em. Put all that on the main floor, and who needs a car?"

Sam swirled his swizzle-stick around the mint leaves of his mojito, a drink he'd discovered on a recent trip to Cuba.

"You forgot the liquor store," Sam Rickels added.

"Oh you're right there! We can't do without that, especially the elderly. The discount crowd needs easy access to the sauce."

Sam smirked before sipping on his drink. "How many lots?" he asked.

"Six."

Sam put his glass down. "How many stories?" he asked.

"Same."

Sam raised an approving eyebrow. "Square feet?" he queried.

"About forty thousand."

"And the FSR?"

"Just one right now, but it can go as high as three."

Don leaned to his left and waved his big arm affably at the predictably attractive server. She was chatting with the bartender but peripherally noticed the realtor and instantly walked toward him. Don lifted the stainless steel bowl and said, "We're out of nuts." She spun smoothly on her heels and dutifully returned to the bar.

"But you know your credit is stretched to the limit," Sam said.

Don shrugged just as the waitress returned. She set down another bowl of squirrel food. "Another round?" she asked. Don lifted his glass and shook it slightly, exposing his gold-plated watch band. "For me, of course, but you never know with lightweight here."

Sam chuckled, then rubbed a hand across his forehead. "Okay. One more. Please." The waitress left.

"So what?" Don asked. "Tell me something new. Am I really in trouble?"

Sam shifted in his chair. "You're stretched pretty thin and you need rent just to pay the huge interest that's building on your debt. Manna's behind schedule. Nirvana's behind schedule. And so is The Temple."

"That is not my fault, as you know. Now we're goddamn held up waiting…"

"I know that," Sam interjected. "But still, you're stuck with the problem, and we are not getting the money upfront that we need. It's making your creditors nervous."

"But this deal will be a winner all around."

The waitress arrived from behind Sam as he shook his head. "I'm not so sure," he said.

She put the drinks down.

"You've already applied, haven't you?" Sam asked.

Don grinned deviously and lifted his fresh elixir. As the waitress crossed the floor Don watched her rear-end get smaller and smaller, evanescence being such a cheeky thing at times.

Sam reluctantly raised his own drink and said, "People are getting tired of seeing condos go up on every vacant lot or corner in the city. I mean, how many have there been in the last month alone?"

Don sat back and opened his arms, as if to say, "search me."

"There's been at least a half dozen downtown – on Georgia, Thurlow, a couple on Granville. There's a brand new one at Main and Kingsway."

"That's downtown to you?" Don asked.

"No, sorry, pardon me, but there's two along the Canada Line and I just saw an ad for one in Kits, at MacDonald."

"What do you care?" Don swiveled his drink and took a sip before adding, "No one's making any applications in your neighbourhood, as far as I know."

"That's not the point. The point is that this boom is gonna' go bust soon. We're reaching a critical mass. Credit's drying up, all around the world. Didn't you read the paper today?"

"Which one?"

"The Times."

"No, I'm up to my ass in..."

"'Markets plunging globally.' That's the headline," Sam interrupted.

"Maybe they are down south, in Asia, in Europe, but not here they're not. No, this is the moment. I've got the council eating out of my hands." Don took a fat sip from his chilly glass. "Sure, old people are complaining," he remarked after a second-thought, "but not the young. They buy all this densification crap. It's about affordable new homes for them, nice homes, modern homes, but with smaller footprints – Christ, they call them "footprints" – and fewer cars, if you can believe it? Fewer cars? Thank God for the young and idealistic, is all I can say."

"I can't believe that you're actually *supporting* these bike nuts. Some of them are demanding that Commercial Street become car free."

Don leaned back in his chair with a grandiose smile on his face and opened his arms.

"What did I just say?" he asked, and after a few seconds of awkward eye contact with Sam, he said, "That I got the council eating out of my friggin' hands. This is a biggy, as you can imagine. It's radical to the Jethros on council. They don't want to do it, but I come in there and tell 'em, 'Lookit here. Close off Commercial Street, say, from the park there, 1st Avenue, all the way to Venables. Shut it down for vehicular traffic. Let it become car free.'" Don made finger quotation marks around "car free." "Shit, they have one in Calgary and in Ottawa," he continued. "Lots of places have them. 'You don't have to be scared', I told 'em. 'The sky won't fall. You know what I mean?'"

Sam was sipping from his drink but he managed to nod his head ever so slightly before putting his glass down.

But the key, Don emphasized, was to rezone the area to allow for higher density, multi-use projects. "That way the *need* for cars in the area is dramatically reduced," he explained.

"And they bought that?" Sam queried.

"Well shit." Don took a quick sip of his whiskey. "They're gonna' buy it. I'm positive, 'cuz it's the perfect solution. It's win-win. It's the way of the future. And when they got money like me backing it, who's gonna' turn their nose up."

"Ben Anderson will object, I'm sure," Sam replied, treating the rhetorical question as a real one.

Don laughed out loud, so that everyone in the room – a handful of patrons – could hear how jovial his life was. "Yeah," he said after. "That commie nosepicker'll put his finger into it, like he does to everything else."

Sam chuckled against his will.

"Goddamn it, I bet I've got Ford rolling over in his grave," Don mused.

"Let him roll, the son-of-a-bitch."

Don raised his eyebrows.

"What?" Sam asked. "The guy was an anti-Semite, and more or less retarded."

"Retarded? The guy who invented the model T? A self-made billionaire?"

"He could barely even read, or spell," Sam explained.

Don paused on the thought, then said, "I did not know that, but it says a lot about the value of higher education, and I guess it explains why you've been driving Buicks your whole life."

Sam grinned and said, "I've never driven a flivver in my life."

Don chuckled and added, beaming, "What was that line from *Public Enemy*? You know. Where James Cagney..."

"Never saw it," Sam said as Don wracked his mind.

"Well, he calls this guy a stooge and then says something like, 'This one's got gears. It ain't no Ford' – you know, belittling how shitty the Ford was back even then."

Don's cheeks were pink with mirth when Sam said, "Well, you've got no quarrel with me, and like you say, the guy was a billionaire."

"Fuck." Don shook his head, then said, "And the first guy to pay five bucks a day. *Five bucks a day.* In *1914*."

"Not true," his friend hastened to point out. "That's the legend. In point of fact he paid the same lousy wage as everyone else but topped it up to five dollars a day if you lived like a dutiful Christian. I'm telling you, the guy was twisted."

"Agh. So what. You and I couldn't have carried his jock if we tried." Don popped a couple of cashews into his mouth, chewed them up and washed them down, then paused before saying, "but I will give you this much, he didn't take the long term into account."

"No question," Sam agreed. "Michigan's a mess. I just read somewhere that Detroit has the second highest foreclosure rate in the U.S."

"Yeah, well until anyone has the slightest clue of where that dump's headed – and I'm talkin', Will it recover or is it headed straight for the shit can – I'm not touching real estate there with a 10-foot pole."

🚲 🚲 🚲

That's my biological dad: Donald Roy Dickerson, or DeeDee, Donald Dick, Big Dick, or "Densification Don" as he was variously known, but in all cases a gregarious, big-bellied bullshitter. Well, okay, "bullshitter" is a bit unkind, even disrespectful, but Don definitely had the gift of the gab, which he used along with his gold cards to entice a Torontonian named Denise Nora Laylock into holy matrimony.

Their courtship began 11 years ago, in the lounge of the Jericho Tennis Club. Denise was wearing a white top and shorts, displaying mildly weathered and deeply tanned skin. Her graying, dirty blonde hair was dyed just enough to give the appearance that it had been bleached by the summer sun. She was seated next to her older, shorter and less attractive sister, Louise Talbot.

Don had a full head of natural, wavy blonde hair. His teeth were ivory white but his face, arms and legs were burned badly, salmon pink.

"You've gotta put on some lotion, or ointment. Jesus, I never go out these days without lotion," his friend, business associate, and tennis partner, Marv Goldfarb, informed him.

Denise walked by, primarily to use the washroom, but also to create opportunity, and her ploy must have worked, because en route Don asked her if she might have some skin cream for his burn.

"Oh my goodness. Look at you," she replied, gawking at his arms. "I'll see what I have."

Denise obtained a tube of salve from Louise and encouraged Don to apply it liberally; and that brief introduction – one might say that simple act of salvation – was sufficient to bring the two tables together for drinks and idle chatter, during which it became apparent that Don and Denise were the only two single parties at the table. Marv left first, to go home for dinner, then Don invited Denise and her sister for a ride around the bay in his sailboat.

"Tonight?" Denise asked.

"Sure. It's Spain, I think."

"Spain?" Denise looked at her sister.

"The fireworks. Festival of Fire or whatever it's called. Tonight it's Spain's turn to light up the skies."

"Seriously!" Now Denise's eyes were bright, though her sister's were ambivalent. Louise looked intently at Denise, with a view to sobering things up, or at least slowing them down.

"Come on, Lou. Let's watch fireworks on the water. I'm sure it'll be amazing."

Don leaned back in his chair, gave Louise a seasoned salesman's smile and opened up his arms as if he were stretching the bellows of an accordion, to show his cordiality, and to challenge Louise to spoil her sister's fun.

"Well. When in Rome, as they say," Louise replied, referring to the fact that she was visiting from Toronto, a fact Denise had already brought to light.

The expression was only partly apt, as when on the water Dee Dee the sailor man liked to picture himself as Anthony Quinn in *The Greek Tycoon* – wearing shades, white boaters, or pinstripes, charming and smooching the likes of Jacquie Bisset – not as a dusty, sandal-wearing Roman with a bowl cut.

That evening, the trio stepped onto the sailboat – a 42 footer with a movie projector inside, and all the other mod-cons, including a dry sauna – and drifted not too far out from the Royal Vancouver Yacht Club's marina at Jericho Beach.

"Oh my God. Wouldn't Bernie just love this!" Denise exclaimed from the helm. She sported a cranberry-coloured sleeveless summer dress. Two finely gathered lengths criss-crossed her back, came over her shoulders and crossed over her breasts to her navel, amplifying her cleavage.

"Well, he'd love the view, the spectacle, for sure, but you've forgotten: he's a little wary of water."

"Oh gosh. I forgot that."

Both ladies sipped on champagne, a clear violation of boating rules, but DeeDee was prepared to take the risk that the boat police would leave him alone. His party was subtle in comparison to some of the revelries floating around the bay.

"So he's stuck in the big smoke while you two lovely ladies get to cruise around the coast. That's a trustworthy guy, I'd say."

"Oh Bernie," Louise said, "he loves his Toronto, and he always reminds me: 'I love my solitude' he says. I'm no fool, though. He's happy to get rid of me for a while. But hey – it works. He knows how close Denise and I are. When we travel together, it gives Bernie and me just enough distance to keep things healthy."

The fireworks began to explode to the opening strains from Carmen.

"Oh-my-god!" Denise exclaimed.

Don anchored the boat and poured his guests more champagne. "Do you mind if I smoke, a cigar?" he asked. "I was in Cuba recently and brought back a few."

"Oh – oh no," Denise replied, looking at her sister.

"It's your boat," said Louise.

"Be honest now."

"No. Really. I love the smell of a good cigar," Denise said.

"Well then, I'll be right back."

"Since when?" Louise asked her sister, under her breath, after Don descended into the cabin.

"I'm not as fussy as you and Bernie," Denise replied.

"Well I think they stink."

"Too bad."

Don reappeared, with a Cohiba and a snifter of Courvoisier. The sisters smiled, though only Denise's was genuine.

"Have either of you ladies ever been to Cuba?" he queried, fireworks and opera dazzling the sea.

The sisters shrugged before saying No, as if they did not want to admit to having a crack in their worldliness.

"Well, they know how to dance, those women do. That Tropicana is something else." Don removed his cigar from his lips and looked at it, then said, "Those commies make one helluva cigar, too."

"I didn't think you could bring those back," Louise noted.

"Not if you're American, but for us Canucks it's okay." He grinned before saying, "We don't have the same problem with commies I guess."

"But you've seen the showgirls in Vegas, haven't you?" Denise asked.

"Of course."

"And how do they compare?"

"With the Cubans?"

"Yeah."

Don scratched the back of his neck before saying, "I've never thought of it...They're all beautiful women. Half-naked. Sequins. Big feathers. What's the diff?"

Louise rolled her eyes. "Denise is a pretty good dancer."

Denise looked at Louise with big eyes. Don looked at Denise the same way.

"Well. I have been in a couple of dance championships – swing, you know, Benny Goodman songs, Chattanooga Choo-choo, In the Mood..."

Don raised an eyebrow.

"She's won," Louise informed him.

"No I haven't," Denise quickly corrected. "But I've placed, 3rd and 2nd, 1990 and 91, Toronto city-wides. That got me to the regionals, for the 25 to 35s..."

"That's winning, by my books," Louise jumped in, lest her sister Denise become too literal. After all, she was ostensibly on a date. A little bluffery was fine. The sky was brilliant with light and sumptuous music.

Don had done the math: 25 to 35s in 1990 and 91 put Denise anywhere between 31 and 41, *and a champion swing dancer.*

"Have either of you ladies been to Seasons in the Park?"

"Uh..." Louise looked apprehensively at her sister.

"Do you mean your Shakespeare thing, the one on the beach?"

Don smiled, let out a puff of smoke, then said, "It's a restaurant, up on little mountain."

"Little mountain?" Louise had obviously never heard of it.

"Queen Elizabeth Park."

"What's it like?" Denise wanted to know.

"The park?"

"No. The restaurant."

Denise rolled her eyes after she said No, to be flirtatious.

"Well if you're still here on, on Sunday night, I'm inviting you both. Second to none, the most spectacular view in all Vancouver, and more fireworks – the grand finale, I think."

The two sisters looked at each other again.

"Well…" Louise was deciding quickly whether to admit that they were scheduled to fly back to Toronto on Sunday afternoon.

"We've got a flight on Sunday," Denise said, "but we can always change it. That's not a problem."

"You sure you know what you're doing?" Louise asked her, back in their hotel room at Coal Harbour. She was staring at herself in the bathroom mirror, wiping make-up from her eyelids. "What's wrong with Toronto men?"

"Nothing, but we don't get views like this in Toronto, do we?"

The sisters now had a panoramic view of the mountainscape behind North and West Vancouver. Reflections from lights along the Longsdale Quay stretched across the water.

"No, we certainly don't. I'll grant you that. But this is summer, and you shouldn't forget that." Louise rinsed her face with a terry cloth. "Apparently it rains here for months on end," she added.

"I just want to see him one more time."

"He's not a bad lookin' guy for his age."

"Oh come on. You don't want to compare him to Bernie, do you?" Denise asked with a mischievous smile on her face. She was looking at herself in a wall mirror, holding in front of her chest a summer blouse she had bought that afternoon.

"Hey, watch it there. I didn't marry Bernie for his looks, and beauty's in the eye of the beholder anyway."

The sisters chuckled as Denise tucked away the blouse in her luggage.

"Well you go back, to your beauty, and I'll go for dinner with mine. Let him wine me and dine me. I want to see if this Seasons in the Park place or whatever it is is all he says it is."

"Enjoy the fireworks," Louise kidded, putting another smile across her sister's face.

"I'll be home Monday night," Denise said, entering the bathroom to brush her teeth.

The dining experience at Seasons in the Park was even more luxurious than Denise had expected. The expansive view of English Bay, and of The Lions and Cypress mountain tops, further impressed upon her the desirability of Vancouver as a place where she could see herself living, despite Louise's cautionary note about the rain.

Don learned that Denise liked to do beautiful things and places

– that she "did" the Statue of David, the Sistine Chapel and the Tower of Pisa while she "did" all of Italy, just as she did the Mona Lisa while she did Paris – and "to wait in line for an hour for that!" she exclaimed when the waiter brought her a dish of crème caramel. "It was so small, and I don't know, so *plain*."

Just to check his date's sense of humour, Don said "I did Wayne Newton last time I was in Vegas," but "Ohhh," Denise quickly and eagerly replied, "We did too. Louise and I. Wasn't he great?"

Don smirked as Denise lightly hummed "danke schoen, danke schoen." He was liking her more and more. Not the quickest doe in the woods, which is how he preferred it, but she was full of life, and attractive.

After signing for the exorbitant bill without a second glance, Don brought Denise back to his sailboat to watch the grand finale of the fireworks.

Or maybe not.

They started out with good intentions, sitting on the deck with snifters of cognac in hand before the fireworks had yet to spray into the sky, and then Don said, "Would you mind showing me a move or two, you know, of that swing dance you're so good at? I'd really like to see it."

"Are you serious?"

"Sure. Why not?"

"Well then. Here."

She stood up and held out her hand. Don put down his drink, clasped her hand, and she helped pull him up and out of his chair. A warm feeling raced through both of them.

"So…" Denise shivered slightly. She was nervous. "You've got to put this hand here. Yup, right here," she said, placing Don's right hand just above her left buttock. Oh God, she thought. She felt good. "And this one goes here," she said, placing her partner's left hand on her right shoulder.

Now we're getting' somewhere, Don thought. Denise was wearing a spaghetti strap one piece dress. Black. Rayon. Micro-knit, with a bell shape toward the knees, ideally suited for a little sashaying.

"Now, there's a simple rhythm that you've got to keep, and it never changes."

"Okay. I'm all set," Don confirmed.

Denise eased him into a few patterns of rock steps and basics, humming Chatanooga Choo-choo as she did, and then the fireworks began.

Don caught on quickly as the pair rocked and twirled. Denise was excited to be dancing with a new "man," and to be touched again in a romantic way. Don pictured all the lifts and throws he had seen in archival footage, and wished he could already do them, to impress Denise, and himself. After ten minutes or so, however, he grew tired of bouncing around while a heavy orchestral cadence blared from the shore. He thanked his partner for the lesson, offered to replenish her drink, and invited her downstairs, ostensibly to choose from his bar selection. Denise cheerfully accepted, though she looked him directly in the eye before descending, as if to say, "I know what you're doing here."

As the Captain mixed his guest a drink in the forward cabin, port side, she used the secrecy of the washroom to text her sister, "This man can dance! Under the stars!" She then found her suitor in the aft cabin, sitting in a pre-fab love seat with a drink.

His stocking feet were resting on an oval coffee table. A fresh drink sat only a foot or so away. Slices of fireworks could be seen from generous portals on either side of Don's head.

"Gin & Tonic, as you ordered," he said, gesturing with an open hand to the drink. "And don't be shy. You've earned it. You've actually made me feel twenty years younger, something I didn't think was possible."

Oh shit, I don't look twenty years younger, Denise thought.

"C'mon. Join me. This is a great night, isn't it?"

Denise nodded. "It sure is. I'm having a lot of fun, and boy, you can dance." She picked up her drink and sat next to the Captain, as she was willing to have even more fun if it all felt right.

Don made the first move, after talking about Vancouver real estate and the forthcoming Olympics, especially about his role as a local consultant to IOC brass; after slipping in the expression, "I'm not getting any younger," to signal that he was ready to settle down; and after dispensing another round of G & Ts. That's when he ventured to kiss his date, and she was fully responsive. She was willing to take a chance because that's how it had to be with men, so she had learned. Louise had once pointed out to her, "They call it trial *and error* for a reason," conceding immediately that Bernie was an exception to the rule.

No matter how sincere men might seem, no matter how 'together' they might appear, they could not be trusted, Denise realized. That was life: unpredictable, plain and simple. The alternative was to be a shrew, or to marry a guy like Bernie – nice, fair, and supportive, but not manly enough for her desires.

So she kissed Don on the lips, and in short order the sailors' lips moved to one another's necks. When Don placed his hand on Denise's lower back, just above her butt cheeks, she confided,

"I've got a tattoo there," and after a couple of seconds pause, she added, "I hope you're not offended."

"Offended?" Don said, but he thought, *You kidding?* In truth, he was more surprised than anything. From the little he had observed, his date didn't seem the type.

"Here." Denise sat up, with her back to Don, and slowly pulled her dress down, until it got to her coccyx.

Don squinted and said, "I can't read it."

"It says, *la dolce vita*."

Don leaned toward the tattoo and examined it. In elegant, fine calligraphy he could make out the expression, all lower case letters, in red ink.

"I like it," he said. "When did you get it?"

"Just last year, after my trip to Italy with Louise."

That was true enough, but Denise was content not to say why she went to the Boot, which was to get over a painful split with a Toronto stock-broker named Turner. He had a new woman on the sly.

"But what does it mean? Something about the good life, right?" Don was now surveying her entire back, and the elegant black bra-straps that were holding her in check.

"It's the sweet life, and the name of a famous movie, I guess, that Bernie took us to."

That too was true, but again Denise was reluctant to say why she got the tattoo, being that she was feeling old and unattractive upon being dumped for a younger woman. Imagine that. She was only thirty three at the time, but in her vulnerable condition she decided to do something "on a whim," something modern and youthful, and sexy. Louise was against it, but she would be, Denise reasoned, being happily married as she was to Bernie. Half-consciously, Denise wished to be as desirable as Anita Ekberg in Fellini's movie, and for no intelligible reason, thought a tattoo across her backside would help to make her so.

To her good fortune, Don really did like it. He didn't just say so to be nice. Having pulled down his lover's dress enough to see her panties, the artful saying across her skin did indeed draw special attention to the dimples on her buttocks, which were still in fact young and nicely shaped.

"Of the sweet life."

She brought her mouth to his ear and whispered, "I'm all yours."

So it was that Don and Denise passionately commingled right there and then. The Greek tycoon and the Roman Sylvia rocked the boat only slightly as symphonic music blared from English

Bay and bright red, green, pink, and blue streams of light pop pop popped high overhead.

🚲 🚲 🚲

'Til death do us part.' That is what Don and Denise told one another a year later in a summer wedding fit for royalty, and they meant it at the time. They uttered those words with all the romanticism of 17-year-old boys who couldn't wait to battle Germans in 1940. Only death would part them, Don and Denise imagined, and so it did, the year they would have celebrated or at least noted their steel anniversary.

To explain: On the last Friday of 2007 Frank Belleveau held a New Year's party for his fellow workers at THE MANNA. Don's appearance was unexpected because Big Dick was brass, not a bee, and bees get careless with their stingers when they're drinking; but it was a party after all, and the boss suspected that intoxicated female plumage would be on proud display.

Indeed, Don had arrived without his wife or his wedding ring, as the marriage was exactly how Denise liked her Gin and Tonics: on the rocks. Denise had grown weary of Don's roving eye and how easily he was led by the leash of temptation. That shouldn't seem too surprising. My dad wasn't a profligate – it's such a tongue-twister – but he was perfidious, and he didn't deny himself the pleasures that profit brought his way. He was a free marketer, after all.

After saying hello to Frank and finding a beer in the ice-filled bathtub, Big Dick surveyed the scene. Lively chatter emanated from loose clusters of guests, their cheeks rosy from drink, the anticipation of a few days off, and the optimism brought naturally with a new year ahead. A modest but actual fir Christmas tree stood in the corner of the living room. Only a few strings of delicate coloured lights, a collection of small silver bells and plum-size glass balls, and a handful of miniature wooden figurines adorned it. Occasionally a raucous laugh ripped across a room.

Hannah Verso was leaning against the living room wall, nursing a beer, and listening intently to what a young woman named Cactus Delaine was telling her about Vancouver's critical mass rides.

"So you need corkers, riders who stop at the intersections and block the cars from entering," Cactus explained.

"Is it scary? Like do the cars actually try to get through?"

"Some do, fer' sure." Then Cactus chuckled. "It actually looks pretty funny when a driver goes mental," she said. "They lay on the horn, but sorry sucker. You ain't gettin' nowhere." Cactus chuckled more boisterously and hiccupped at the same time.

"And no one gets hurt?"

"I've never seen it, but I dunno', maybe it's happened."

"Good evening, ladies."

Hannah and Cactus turned toward the source of the greeting. Don Dickerson stepped toward them and extended a hand. "I'm Don."

Both women shook his hand, introduced themselves, and sized him up, though his eyes tended to lean toward Hannah's own, which were large and ocean blue – unusual, he thought, for a woman with skin the colour of a new penny and puma black hair that hung in rich, snake-like coils.

Don was a big man, not fat, though his protruding belly showed an unapologetic appetite for luxury. His skin, well-tanned from a recent trip to Cancun, complemented his gold watch, and his well-trimmed, wavy hair was gradually turning a distinguished meringue white. The pressed casual beige pants he wore concealed prominent veins along his calves, suggesting that his youth was fast becoming a fading memory.

"Great party, isn't it?" he remarked.

"It sure is," Cactus replied. She brought her free hand around her waist.

"Do you ladies work for me?" he asked.

Both women flushed, looked nervously at each other, then toward the ceiling.

"At Manna, I mean," he clarified.

Cactus shook her head. Hannah said, "Not me, but my man does."

"Oh, and who's the lucky guy?"

"The host of this party, don't you know?" Hannah replied.

"Frank?"

"That's right," Hannah replied with a tinge of haughtiness, then she looked at her acquaintance and the pair smiled.

"Well isn't that something. He's been working for me for some time now and I never knew. Ah...wait a minute...ah, yes, now that

I think about it, he did mention once – we were in the office – we were going to…well, yeah, I just remember him saying he had to get home. He and his fiancée, I guess, had plans."

"So there you are," Hannah said. A broad smile appeared across her face.

"And now you know," Cactus added, lifting her glass up. She winked and looked at Hannah when Don met her glass with his bottle of beer.

"To Frank," Don said.

Hannah lifted her glass in response. "To Frank," she and her acquaintance echoed.

"What kind of work are *you* in?" Don asked Hannah.

"Well…normally I'm in film. I do bookkeeping and administrative stuff, but there's been no work for months."

"That's our goddamn government for you. Taxes are so high right now that they're scaring good business dollars away. Jesus, it makes me wanna' – but hey, I'm sure that if I dig around I could find room for an able bodied bookkeeper like yourself. Why don't you come down to our admin office on Hamilton Street on, uh…how about Wednesday?"

Hannah brought her left arm across her belly and Cactus looked at her.

"Here…" Don fished into his back pocket, pulled out his wallet and a business card and handed the latter to Hannah.

"Just call that number on Wednesday morning, and I'll see if we can't set up something for you. Maybe not full time, but something. We're going pretty full guns at the moment."

"Oh, thank you," Hannah said. She rubbed her right arm and looked at Cactus, who returned a cautious smile.

"Well, it's been a pleasure to meet both of you," Don remarked, giving both women a one-over with his eyes one more time. "I'm going to get myself another drink and mingle a little."

On the back deck, under the light of a nearly full moon and a patio lantern, Frank was busily preparing burgers and ribs on his propane Bar-B-Q, and chatting with Ryan Ghostkeeper.

"It's perfect there," Frank said, having just informed Ryan that his carving was tacked above the toilet. "I get to see it every time I take a piss."

"I don't know if I like that. It's like you're pissing *at* it."

"Well if that really bothers you then I'll move it. I didn't mean any disrespect. Like I say, I like looking at it when I piss...Whoa dere."

Ryan wavered slightly as he pushed himself from the porch railing. With a drunken grin he said, "You're all right, man. I guess I'm gonna go see my carving again, 'cuz I gotta take a piss." When he reached for the knob on the back door he suddenly got whacked in the forehead.

"Oh fuck!" he blurted, staggering back.

"Sorry, man. Jesus, are you all right?"

Don grabbed Ryan by the arm, to steady him. Frank could not stop himself from chuckling.

"I'm okay, I think. Jesus, man. Just watch where you're going."

Don grinned and said, "I'm sorry. Seriously."

Ryan boat-walked into the house and Don asked Frank, "Who's the injun?"

"One of your employees, at Manna. He's a hard worker actually."

"A hard drinker too, so it seems."

"It's a party," Frank reminded his boss.

"So it is. I've just been talking to your fiancée."

"Oh yeah."

"Goddamn, Frank, you won't hit me if I mention she's beautiful, will you?" Don clasped Frank's shoulder in one hand, but Frank didn't stop flipping burgers. He looked up with a mildly soused smile and said, "No, sir. I know that."

"Jesus, where'd you find her?"

"Right here."

"Jeee-sus. So it was worth coming West?" he asked.

Frank dobbed barbecue sauce onto the patties, then paused and appeared to be lost in thought.

"From Québec, my boy. Lighten up."

"Oh yes," Frank said. "It was definitely worth it."

"But French women are beautiful too. I've seen 'em," Don added.

"Yes they are. That's for sure. I got lucky here, I guess."

Don heard "lucky ear" – such was the nature of Frank's accent – and Don thought, *Your ear has nothing to do with it, you dumb*

Frenchman, but he said, "I'll say. Keep a good eye on her."

Don then released his friendly grip on Frank's shoulder, patted it a couple of times and said, "She told me she's looking for work. Is that true?"

"Uh, yes. It is. The film industry has cut back. The contracts are not coming in."

"And she does *books*, right?"

"That's right." Frank stopped pushing meat around the grill, stepped back and looked Don in the eye. The host was pleasantly pickled.

"Tell her to be on site Wednesday morning."

"You're kidding me."

"No, my boy, I'm not." Don gripped Frank's shoulder again and pinched it a couple of times, not hard enough to hurt, but hard enough to let him know he meant what he had just said.

Frank told Hannah the good news late the next morning, over a tall Bloody Caesar. He was leaning back in a kitchen chair, rubbing his temples.

"Seriously?" she replied.

Frank winced. His hangover was actually painful.

"It's up to you. I think he likes you. He told me how beautiful you are, how lucky I am to have you."

Hannah saddled up to Frank and put her hands softly around his face. "You are, aren't you," she said, smiling.

Frank looked up into sparkling eyes. "He's a dawg. Isn't that what you say out here? A man that keeps his eyes on women all de time?"

"He was a little forward, but he won't step out of line, would he? With you so close-by?" Hannah sat at the kitchen table, across from Frank, and laid her bare arms across it.

"Sometimes I'm at other sites. It depends on what we're doing, what stage of the building we're on, but he's all right."

"Well...What do you think? Should I take it?"

"It's up to you, Hannah. You choose."

Frank got up, slowly, and yawned widely. "I think there's a race on today," he said.

"Did he say how much he'd pay me?"

"No, he didn't. Jesus. Ask him yourself, on Wednesday." Frank was now in the living room.

"Okay, I will, grump. Maybe don't drink so much next time, okay? You're not too pleasant to be around when you do."

Frank replied by turning on the television and surfing from one sports channel to the next before settling on the French CBC. His native tongue was about all his mottled brain could process at that time.

1st Quarter 2008

To Don Dickerson's great delight, Hannah Verso showed up at THE MANNA construction site on Wednesday, January 2, 2008 at 10:00 am. Dressed in a stylish, contour-hugging, mid-length dress, and a light, lambs-wool cardigan, she ascended the stairs leading to a pre-fabricated trailer on stilts. Frank did not notice her as he was installing wall frames a couple of hundred metres away, but other, nearer hardhats tilted upward as her shapely form passed by.

"You're here," Don said when she walked through the office door. The excitement in his voice was obvious to all in the trailer.

"I am," she replied nervously.

"Henry, this is Ms. Hannah...uh..."

"Verso. My last name is Verso."

"She's Frank's fiancée. Frank Belleveau's old lady."

The office manager – Henry – nodded Hello.

"She was an out-of-work book keeper, but not today. I've got some work for her," Don explained.

Hannah blushed.

"Well let's get going," he said to her. "I'll be at the admin office if anyone's looking," he told Henry.

"All right."

The pair left THE MANNA and Don drove Hannah to Yaletown.

"How do you normally get to work?" he asked.

"I take the bus, or sometimes a taxi. The bus is becoming a real pain these days. They're always crowded, so you can never sit down, or they're too full, so they go whizzing by you half the time. Frank says it's the price of gas. We're at peak oil or something."

"Don't believe 'em. It's all politics – *geo*-politics," Don said.

"Well – anyway – more and more people seem to be taking the bus. I'm seriously thinking about getting a bike."

"Like Frank?"

"Oh no. A bicycle. Motorbikes scare me."

"But Frankie loves 'em. He rides one almost every day."

"I wish he wouldn't."

"Oh come on. He's never taken you for a ride?"

"Sure. At first. I wanted to get on with him, and I did like it until he almost got me killed."

"Showing off, I bet," Don guessed.

"I guess. I kept asking him to slow down, like on the corners, and he wouldn't, and then he lost control for a second and the bike warbled and I thought we were going to crash."

"You're bloody lucky he didn't."

Hannah made no comment as she recalled the intense quarrel she and Frank later had about the episode.

"You know how to dress," Don remarked as they exited the Cambie Bridge and entered Yaletown. "It's not a prerequisite for the job – dressing that well – but it's not discouraged either, so take it as a compliment."

"Thank you. I brought you a resumé, in case you needed it."

"Well, we'll see. Frankie says you're good at your job, and I trust him completely. He's one of my top contractors."

Hannah offered no reply.

"He says the film biz is leaving town. It's our almighty dollar, isn't it?"

"I guess so. I'm not sure."

"Ahhh, who is? Who *really* understands the mysteries of economics, eh? If there's one thing I know for certain, it's that economists can't surf a supply curve." Don chuckled in a low register, then paused before asking, "Why haven't you taken up acting yourself?"

Hannah flushed and cast her prospective employer a surprised look.

"You never considered it, being around all those stars?"

"Uh, not really. No." Hannah did not want to admit that she had once desired that kind of attention.

"If I may say, you got what they're lookin' for," Don said.

"I'm sure it takes a lot of nerve to get in front of those cameras," Hannah mustered.

"Ahhh. I'm sure it's a cinch – here we are." Don pulled into a parking space along Hamilton Street, technically a back alley, but one of the hippest places to park in all of Terminal City.

🚲 🛴 🚲

Over the next few weeks Don found plenty of opportunity to visit his Yaletown administration office. He flattered and flirted with his new bookkeeper, and boldly took her out for the occasional lunch. These dalliances made Hannah feel special, as sophisticated servers with forced smiles bowed to her passing fancies and well-heeled patrons at nearby tables discreetly eyed her with secret musings of jealousy. At home, however, Hannah's life remained quotidian, until her betrothed got some very bad news.

"I'm going home," Frank said in a raised voice. He was staring at the television screen, having inserted a DVD into the player a few minutes earlier – *Once Upon a Time in the West*, by Sergio Leone, the man who made Clint Eastwood famous, so he believed.

"You're what?" she called out from the upstairs bedroom. She was pinning her hair in preparation for a Saturday evening bath. A satin, solferino robe with an exotic bluebird sewn onto the back covered her naked body. The belt was undone.

"I'm going back to Québec," he said. Again, he spoke over the sound of the television. On the screen, three menacing-looking, rugged gunfighters wearing dusters had taken over a one-room train station, silenced the attendant, and appeared to be waiting for a train.

"What for?" She sounded a little worried.

"My mom just had a brain aneurysm."

"Your...what? A brain..."

Hannah left the bathroom and went to the top of the stairs.

"My mother suffered a brain hemorrhage last night. I'm going home tomorrow. Will you come with me?"

"Why didn't you tell me this when I got in?"

"I thought I would wait until..."

"What does that mean? What happens when...?"

"I'm no scientist, Hannah. My sister says my mom suffered a mild hemorrhage in her head – it is bleeding, around de brain. She was rushed to de hospital last night. They think that she might have suffered a stroke, a small one."

"I am so sorry, Frank."

"You didn't answer me. Will you come home with me?"

"Ah, I will have to see if I can get away on such short notice. Maybe I can. We're so busy right now, but I could probably get away in a few days. I'm sure."

"It might be too late then."

"It sounds really serious."

The three gunfighters appeared in close-up. They were now on the railway platform. A metallic, foreboding sound emanated from somewhere and a stagecoach departed the station.

"When do you think you'll come back?" Hannah asked.

"I don't know. I've got to phone Marlene, to find out what's happening."

A zoom-in showed a weathered Charles Bronson wearing a cowboy hat and playing a harmonica he carried on a string around his neck. Frank sat forward.

"What if Don doesn't let you go? I thought you guys were behind," Hannah queried.

"It's my mom, *tabarnak*. Don can fuck himself."

Hannah was used to Frank's preferred profanities, such as his disrespectful reference to the tabernacle itself. "What?" she asked.

Frank did not respond right away. He was listening to Charles Bronson exchange tough words with the gunmen. Evidently Bronson had expected to meet someone named "Frank," and he made a tough-guy remark about there being 'one horse too many.' Frank Belleveau thought the line was clever but he did not smile. "We *are* behind, but Don will manage," he said.

"I'm sure he will."

Frank did not hear Hannah because a shot rang out from the television speaker.

Hannah re-entered the bathroom, slipped out of her robe, and tested the water in the tub with her toes. It was hot, but not too hot, so she stepped in. The bathroom door remained open.

"I hear he really likes your, uh, your company," Frank said.

"What's that? I can't hear you over the t.v."

"I hear my boss likes your company," Frank repeated, louder.

"Oh honey. He's a flirt, just like you said. He treats me for lunch now and then. Who am I to refuse?" She lifted her left leg onto the rim of the tub, shot some shaving foam onto her shin and rubbed it around her lower leg, front and back, down to her ankle.

"You just tell him that you can't have lunch. It's as simple as that."

"And that's what you would like," she said. She began to gently and firmly stroke her calf with a razor. "You want me to say no, I'm Frank's girl, and I can't be bought that way?" Hannah used a supercilious tone for that last clause, mimicking the sound of a high-principled Southern coquette.

On the t.v. screen a young, red-headed and freckled woman in an off-white country dress came out of a ranch house. Her arms were wrapped around a large basket of food. A chorus of rubbing insect wings could be heard but then suddenly stopped, causing a farmer, a very young boy (another ginger), and the red-headed young woman (the farmer's daughter) to look warily across the semi-desert landscape.

"Do what your *heart* tells you to do then," Frank Belleveau replied, "but I'm going home to see my mother." Hannah had just slid under the water for a few seconds, to wet her hair. She didn't hear him.

The farmer smacked an adolescent boy, yet another carrot-top, on the face before sending him to a train station. Both boys were the farmer's sons, and the elder of the two was supposed to pick up the man's wife, a pretty woman wearing black, so his father told him.

Hannah pulled herself into a sitting position, reached for some shampoo, and said, "I bumped into Cactus today, that woman I met at our New Year's party, you know the one I was telling you about, who rides in those critical mass bike rides?"

The crickets had resumed their shrill song, but then ceased it abruptly, again. The farmer, who was now standing at a water well, looked around, as did his daughter. Wind whistled through the hills.

"She wants me to join her on the next ride, and I told her that I would probably do it. It sounds like so much fun."

With a beatific smile, the daughter watched a small flock of black birds fly up from the brush, but just then a rifle report was heard. As the camera panned back the girl fell to the ground. She was dead.

"I think they're assholes, but if you think blocking traffic on Fridays is a lot of fun, then go for it." After a pregnant pause Frank asked, "Do they allow motorbikes?"

"No, they...God, what are you watching?" Hannah asked, for she had just heard a man yell and the sound of more gun shots.

"Just another Western I picked up," Frank replied, "but it's good."

He was fixated on the screen, as the father, his oldest boy and the daughter had all just been shot by a lone gunman or a group hiding in the distance. The youngest boy came running out into the yard, only to behold with wide, innocent eyes, the strewn bodies of his family. A haunting score commenced.

"Oh shit," Frank said when cowboys in dusters emerged from the brush, with rifles in hand. As they approached the youngest boy it became clear that Henry Fonda was their leader. He stopped just feet from the child and stared into the transfixed child's eyes with his own marble blue pair. When one of the men accidentally mentioned his boss's name – "Frank" – it became painfully clear what Fonda had to do next.

Hannah descended the stairs in her robe, which was now fastened at the waist. Frank caught a whiff of the sweet scent of her shampooed hair.

"Uh, I don't think you should watch this," he warned.

In a split second, the menacing Frank shot the boy at point blank range.

That is where things started to get messy – for everyone.

Frank went to Québec City to visit his mother in hospital. She was in critical care, having suffered partial paralysis.

Don Dickerson didn't waste a minute of the precious reprieve. He pressed Hannah for more lunch and dinner dates. After making excuses for the first few days Hannah succumbed on the rationalization that supper with her boss, in public, would be "harmless."

Don decided he would lay his cards on a reserved table at the

Water Street Café, a restaurant in the heart of Gastown with enough chic for the middle-class and just enough class for the petite bourgeoisie. Starched waiters attended dutifully to patrons at white-linen tablecloths and could recite their red and white cellar stock off the cuff. Large modernist but soft paintings subtly reminded all occupants, 'be gentle.' And expansive windows allowed diners a sumptuous view of the well-preserved mercantile remnants of port life during Vancouver's rail and mining heyday.

"It's over," Don assured his date over a candlelit plate of P.E.I. mussels and a regional Pinot Grigio. "That's why she lives in Toronto half the time. We do our own thing."

Hanna looked out at the charcoal-blue sky, alit by faux antique street lamps, then slumped in her chair. She stared at the napkin on her lap and Don stayed silent, nervously so. Suddenly she leaned forward, looked her boss in the eye, and said, "What do you mean, you 'do your own thing?'"

"She does hers. I do mine."

"And what is it, exactly, *her* thing, and *your* thing? Don't tell me you're swingers? I find that disgust..."

"No, Goddamn it." Don looked around, to make sure Hannah had not drawn unwanted attention.

"I don't know what she does, okay? I don't wanna' know. She goes to Toronto every now and then and stays with her sister and brother-in-law. They try to convince her to divorce me, but she won't do that because she wants my money, which I *generously* allow her to spend, almost at will, and she can't prove that I'm doing anything anyway."

"Anything like what?"

"Like fooling around."

"So you admit it?"

"What?"

"You do, you fool around!"

Don shook his head, having no immediate words for reply. Perspiration was penetrating the threads of his Brooks Brothers pin-stripe collar, which he had worn open, no tie.

"My fiancé's in Quebec, visiting his sick mother, and you try to take advantage of the situation?" she asked.

Don now sat back and raised his arm, but not up high; more like a schoolboy who is unsure he wants to answer the teacher's question. When the waitress arrived he ordered a Canadian Club and Coke. "A double," he emphasized.

"And anything for you, madam?" the waitress asked.

"Yes. I think so. Uh...an Irish coffee, please."

"You see," Don said when the waitress had departed, "it's nice to enjoy life when the good things in it are offered up to you; but no, I'm not trying to take advantage of any situation. I've been doing my damnedest lately not to shoot myself in the foot, not to cause a stir between you and Frank, but yes, I should admit here and now that my heart damn near jumped out of my skin when I first laid eyes on you – I'm not kidding – and I've been doing my damnedest to get you to feel anything like that about me, *without* stepping on Frank's toes, if you know what I mean."

Hannah blanched and looked thoughtfully into her bowl of emptied mussel shells.

"Frank's my fiancé," she said, and she was about to say more.

"But he doesn't know what a prize he has, and you don't know what a prize you are," Don interrupted.

"You don't know that," Hannah countered.

"Oh yes I do," Don replied. "Frank's one helluva worker. He's one of the best, and reliable as hell, but he's immature." Hannah's eyes widened and Don sipped his drink before saying with a slight hitch in his throat: "How do you know he doesn't like that bike of his more than you?"

Hannah took a deep breath of air into her lungs and looked like she was about to rail into her host, but she fell silent.

"C'mon. I've seen his tattoo, but I haven't seen your name etched into his arm, unless it's somewhere more – more intimate."

"So what? He had that tattoo when I met him."

"And what did he tell you about your ring there?"

Hannah's eyes widened again.

"I can tell you about that ring."

Hannah reflexively touched the diamond on her ring, then nervously moved it back and forth on her finger, as if it were a tiny lever. Don looked probingly into her eyes but kept silent.

"I don't think I want you to." Hannah was on the verge of tears, just as the waitress set down the drinks. Don waited for the latter to leave before he said, "Hannah, I'd leave my wife for you, Goddamn it, and I've never thought that about anyone I've met since I've been married."

Don then reached out to grasp Hannah's left hand, which was clenching a napkin on the edge of the table. She pulled her hand back. Her body trembled slightly. "You're being silly," she replied, "and besides, Frank can be dangerous. I don't think you know that."

"Oh I'm sure he can be," Don replied airily.

"I know that," Hannah said, "but you don't."

"What? Has he ever hurt you?"

"He's hit me, but just once. He was drunk and I spoke my mind to him. But it's different with him. He's…"

"He's out of step, it sounds like."

"No. He's just…"

"Ahh. You're protecting him. Stop protecting him. I told you, he doesn't know what a prize he has."

☙ ☙ ☙

The next day, after the dust of that little tablecloth tango had settled, Frank called Hannah from Québec.

"It's really bad," he told her, struggling to hold back a well of tears. "She's in a coma, and the doctor says…" He started to cry.

"Oh honey…I…I don't know what…"

"You don't have to say anything," Frank interjected. "There's nothing you *can* say. She's done, and that fucking bastard won't even come to see her – to see us even."

"Does he…"

"Of course he fuckin' knows. He just don't give a shit."

"What is the doctor saying, about her situation?" Hannah asked very softly.

"Marlene called him. I've called him, but he won't answer. He's chicken shit."

"But how is your mom..."

"Her situation's critical. They can do surgery on her, but it's high risk, really high risk. That's what he said. Because of her age, there could be complications."

"Does she have anything to lose?"

"Her brain's damaged because of de rupture, so it might not be worth even operating on her."

"Who has the say?" Hannah asked.

"I don't know. I don't know if I have any say. They might just start to operate on her, whether Marlene or I agree, or disagree."

"So you're going to stick around with your sis for a while, I take it?"

"Of course. What do you think?"

"Okay okay...I didn't mean anything. I just want to know when you plan on coming back."

"All right, but if you find some time I'd like you to get out here. Please, Hannah, I need you right now. My mom might not live much longer."

"Do you want me to tell Don what's going on, just in case this gets worse and you can't come back for a while?"

"Fuck, Hannah, stop worrying about Don. He'll take care of himself. Just get him to give you a day or two off, or come out on de weekend. I'll pay for your flight."

The next afternoon Hannah flew to Québec City. As she passed over southern Ontario Charlie Raymond Menz was quickly pedaling his bicycle northward along Commercial Street. He was a few minutes late for a public hearing at Brittania Secondary School, a stalwart institution whose student body proudly hailed from the ethnically diverse and economically challenged community of East Vancouver. The school also had the distinction of being the Home of the Bruins, a fancy name for brown bears based on an old story about a fox.

As soon as Charlie entered the gym from a large steel back door he heard a woman in the middle of the crowd yell out, "Don't give us bullshit!" She got a boisterous round of applause for doing so. Charlie chuckled, as he was slightly drunk, having just come from a pub on Granville Street.

A conservatively-dressed man on stage waited for the din to quiet down, then said, "You can see on this plan the area under application." He drew attention to it with his hand.

"It is currently zoned at an FSR of 1, which means the owner can build as many square feet on the property as the property has. This property is approximately 20,000 square feet, and about half of that is used for parking, which means..."

"About 10,000 square feet can be developed," a hirsute man in the crowd shouted. "I learned math, right here in this building, about 30 years ago."

"Okay. Stylist," Titely replied, and he half-heartedly laughed. "My point, of course," he continued, "is that the closer you are to your amenities, the less need you have for a car. The broader aim of this rezoning application is of course to create even more community than currently exists. Available space for accommodating everyone is dwindling. Let's face it. We all have to reduce our..."

"You're full of shit," a lanky young man barked, causing many heads to turn his way. His friends knew him as Slim Jimmy. Perspiration beaded across his brow and a "Density is a Mental Problem" button was pinned to a canvas bag slung over his shoulder.

"This is all about developers like fuckin' CanCon and whoever else they're called, filling their fat pockets with more and more dough. Don't any of you kid yourselves," Slim Jimmy advised.

No one, including the CanCon rep, interjected, so he continued.

"More units – more *multi-use* units, to use the buzzword – equals more rent for the owner. That's more money owed by the tenants. More profit for the developer. No rocket science in that. The increased rents go directly into some fat cat's bank account so he can buy yachts and grease the palms of our caring city councilors. Yes, I mean you, Titely. Don't be deluded," Jimmy said, turning to face the people gathered in the room. "This whole fuckin' process is a scam!"

"Here here," a few attendees shouted in support, but Jimmy, feeling a little overheated, lowered his head and hastily pushed his way through the crowd to the exit door. The applause for him grew louder, but Charlie and a few other persons he passed on his way out heard the rabble-rouser mutter, "Somebody should shoot the fuckers." Jimmy knocked Charlie off balance and offered no apology for doing so.

Lou Reed's lyrics, *Different colors made of tears*, ran through Charlie Menz's mind as he stood at Hawks and East Hastings, waiting for the bus to take him up Burnaby Mountain to Simon Fraser University. Almost 24 hours had passed since the Brittania School meeting, and Charlie taught an evening class at 7:00 pm. Light drops of rain dotted his head and shoulders, and as traffic whizzed by he thought about Detroit and an ex-girlfriend from there, Cleo, who dumped him for the bright lights of the Big Apple. She loved Lou Reed.

Charlie had resolved to begin his lecture by talking about the community meeting on the weekend. He was disappointed that none of his students had attended, as he had encouraged, but it wasn't in their neighbourhood, he rationalized, stepping off the curb to see if the bus was coming.

There we go. He could see one in the distance, just emerging from the heart of the Downtown Eastside – the *infamous* DTES. I know that sounds like a bad medical condition, and it almost is. The poorest postal code in Canada. Charlie had heard that more than once. Drugs, mental illness, HIV, welfare – all characteristics routinely associated with the district.

If you don't like it, you can always bulldoze it, he thought sarcastically as the destination name on the approaching bus became legible. *Just lay down a highway and voila, it's all gone*. That's what they did to his hometown. No more Paradise Valley. *No more Leland Bar. No more Corner Bar. But if you have the money, you can now watch the Lions play on Ford Field and the Tigers right next door.*

That's what he did last summer, Charlie recalled as his bus pulled up. He watched the Tigers with Treat Dufraine, a childhood friend who complained about the thirty percent depreciation in his home's value. That was until Monroe smacked that grand slam. Then the crowd went wild and Treat cheered up, but just for a while.

Charlie flashed the driver his monthly pass and proceeded to the back. A few curdled faces – no blacks, as usual – either momentarily glanced up or remained lost in thought.

Charlie settled into an empty double-seat near the back. Directly across from him on a long side-bench two young Aboriginal men chatted, sniggered, and drank beers. One of these was Ryan Ghostkeeper. He gripped a white plastic bag containing a few cans of beer.

A young Chinese man and his girlfriend, so Charlie presumed, sat directly across from the Aboriginal guys.

"Hey you," Ryan said to the Chinese couple. The boyfriend looked at Charlie, who shrugged, and then looked at Ryan.

Ryan was now holding out a fresh beer to the Chinese fellow, who nervously pointed at himself, as if to say, "Do you mean me?"

"Have a beer, man," the other Aboriginal fellow said.

"No, no." The Chinese fellow replied, shaking his head. "It's not allowed."

Both Aboriginal men laughed reflexively.

"Not allowed? We're not allowed," the one closer to Charlie said, then he turned to Charlie and asked, "Why did the White Man fly to the moon?"

After about twenty seconds of reflection Charlie replied, "Uh… beats me."

"Because he thought Indians would be up there with land to sell!"

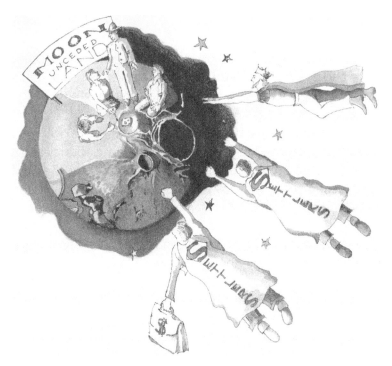

Charlie laughed, sincerely, but not as loud as Ryan, who pulled out another beer and gave it to his friend.

The Chinese couple did not laugh at all, but looked rather apprehensively at Charlie and the Aboriginal men.

"That's good," Charlie said, "but I couldn't believe what I learned at the aquarium the other day."

"What's that?" Ryan asked.

"I was standing in front of one of those huge tanks, you know, the ones with the octopi, eels, and all kinds of fish swimming around."

The Aboriginal pair nodded and drank their beer. Charlie saw one of his students enter the bus. He nodded in recognition and so did she, before sitting down near the front.

"And then a big school of fish went swimming by," Charlie continued. "I had to look twice because the fish in the very front of the pack looked like a nasty bugger; all black, except for a little white spot under its gills and a small crucifix hanging from its pectoral fins. Several of the fish in the pack were holding up small signs. 'Help Us!' 'Please Help Us!' Stuff like that.

The Native guys were grinning. Hannah was smiling from a billboard the bus just passed.

"So I turned to one of the guides who was standing there, and I asked him, 'What the hell is that?'

"'Oh,' he said, 'that's a residential school.'"

"Ohhhhhh." The two Native guys groaned. Ryan said, "pretty lame, man," but with a big smile he offered Charlie a beer.

"Sorry, man, I'm going to work," Charlie said.

"That's never stopped me," Ryan said, and he and his friend started laughing again.

When the bus got to S.F.U. at the top of Burnaby Mountain – the founders of the institution took their commitment to higher learning literally – Charlie was craving a beer, but he repressed the urge, walked to the quadrangle and gave his lecture.

🕭 ŏ ŏ

Always keep your eyes on the prize. When Don Dickerson's uncle Rodney was drunk at family gatherings, he liked to stoop down and whisper such words of wisdom into his nephew's ears. As a wet tongue does to a frozen sign pole, they stuck, and in fact became Densification Don's own philosophy of life and the key to his success, but Hannah had knocked the real estate guru off balance.

"He has sent flowers *every* day for the past week," she exclaimed on the phone to her mother, Rosetta, who lived in Kelowna.

"That's not good. You mustn't accept dem."

"Well you can't re*turn* them. It's not like he would get his money back."

"You must tell him, stop. You're engaged to Frank. Didn't you tell heem?"

"He already knows that. Frank works for him."

"That's not gooood."

Hannah sighed, then said, "Frank never sent me flowers."

"He's busy, like your father always was."

"But dad sent *you* flowers, and played music for you."

After a pause Rosetta said, "You stick with Frankie. Hees a hard worker. Hees handsome, and...."

Hannah interjected with, "He never cleans up, or does dishes or laundry. He spends all his free time riding his 'crotch rocket,' or fixing it, and when he's not doing that he sits in front of the t.v. drinking beer. He *always* expects me to cook for him."

"I tried to *teach* you, but you were never interested. A good wife needs to know how to cook," her mom noted.

"Oh *mother*."

After a few seconds Rosetta replied, with some hesitation in her voice. "You're not having doubts, are you?"

"Yes, mother. If you want to know the truth, yes, I am, but it's not just Frank."

"How is his mother?"

"I'm not sure, but it's bad, I think. I don't think she's going to make it."

"God bless her."

"Mom, you were so pretty when you met dad. Did you have lots of boyfriends?"

"It was different. You know. You could date boys, but you had to be very, very careful, you know?"

"And you chose a farmer."

"Well yes, but he was so passionate, about me. I can never forget *that*."

"But you knew he was a farmer, and you still picked him."

"I didn't mind. Your father was a very hard worker."

"You guys had to clean rooms when you came here."

"That was no problem. We were young. We had our dream."

Hannah paused before saying, "He's taking me out for dinner tomorrow."

Her mother paused again, then said, "He should not be doing that." She drew out the word "that," then said, "Hee's a married man."

"It's just dinner. There's no sin in that."

It takes two to tango across the lurid but well-waxed dance floor of fertilization, to swivel while staying stiffly in sync with the fluid rhythm of the pulsating bandoneón, to tickle those big buttons and tease and inflame with a little corte interruptus now and then; for even the most artful partner will turn out to be a prick. But abracadabra! With a lot of sweat and hard work (the breast stroke works admirably) at least one of the wriggly but single-minded spermatozoa will swim his way into his partner's ovary, butt heads with an awaiting oocyte and wear down her zona pellucida with his special organelle.

And alcohol helps.

"*Kriek*, sir, is a sour cherry beer. It is made in a cask, just like wine," so the waiter explained to Don at *Chambar*, Vancouver's slick, contemporary simulation of a Belgian drinking establishment. Stout white candles flickered on square tables lined neatly along exposed brick walls. The ceiling lights were dim, not to conceal the quality of the cuisine, which was always exquisite to the local palate, but to create the spiritual aura of the very abbeys that made Belgian beer famous around the world. And if "location, location, location" was truly everything, it could be no coincidence that *Chambar* was situated in Crosstown, a meandering European groove in Vancouver, only a stone's throw from Abbot Street.

With childlike enthusiasm in his eyes Don said, "I'll try that," and invited Hannah to have the same, so she did.

For dessert Don requested "the plum flan for me and a peach Frangipani for the lady," and when the lady's dish was served to big eyes and the waiter departed, Don pulled out two tickets from a small envelope in his shirt pocket, and Hannah's eyes widened again, with excitement and nervousness.

"What are they for?" she asked. She had become mildly drunk

and was feeling ebullient.

"Have you ever heard of Toots Thielemans?" Don asked her.

She chuckled. "Of course."

"Oh really?"

"Yeah. He's my dad's favourite."

"Your dad listens to Toots Thielemans?"

"Yeah. He has some of his records. He loves the harmonica. He still plays them now and then."

"Is he good?"

Hannah chuckled again. "No. Not quite. But he's not bad."

"I mean Toots," Don said, as he in fact had only a cursory knowledge of the man, despite his familiarity with other jazz greats.

"He's brilliant, jazzy, I'd say, but I don't really know technical things about music. I just remember hearing him on records as a kid."

"Well he's playing with the VSO."

"Seriously? Our symphony plays with harmonica players?" Hannah asked.

"I assume they'll play with almost anyone these days," Don replied. "Let's face it, these classical guys are a desperate, dying breed. They need to make money and this guy Toots, he's a legend, right? Or what's the word? A *virtuoso*?"

Hannah smiled a tipsy smile.

"It's in a few weeks, so you're gonna' have to make a decision soon."

Don reached his hand across the table immediately after saying that, and with some trepidation his date met it halfway.

"Would you like to hear some jazz tonight? Some live jazz," he asked.

"Uh, sure. Why not?"

So, after the bill was paid and the duo returned to the open night air, Don hailed an approaching taxi.

"Hey."

Don looked south and saw a First Nations man almost upon him.

"Oh Jesus," he said, and ushered Hannah into the cab that had just pulled up.

"No. I'm Ryan. I'm not askin' for..."

"Well take it anyway. Buy a chaser," Don offered, pushing a $5 bill into the young man's hand before sliding into the cab and closing the door.

Ryan Ghostkeeper had called out simply because he recognized Hannah and Don from Frank's New Year Party. He was returning home from the Stadium-Chinatown Skytrain station, where he had unsuccessfully tried to sell carvings. His destination was ultimately the Portland Hotel, where he rented by the month ever since getting hired at CanCon, but with the five dollars he had just received he intended to make a pit stop at the Cambie Hotel for a pint of draught, a potential breach of probation be damned.

Don and Hannah went west, to the grandiose Hotel Vancouver lounge. There a dolled-up, fleshy and aging entertainer in a strapless red-satin dress played honey-coated Gershwin and Berlin favourites, intermingled with popular ballads by Neil Diamond, Lionel Ritchie and Billy Joel. The emotive lyrics, the syrupy passion in the singer's dulcet voice, combined with the bubbles from the champagne that Don had ordered, served to intoxicate his dreamy guest. Hannah fell into a romantic mood, and just like the horns did for Jericho, her wall of restraint came a tumblin' down.

"I've got to go to the boy's room," Don told her after handing the waiter his credit card, but that was untrue. He went to the hotel's front desk and ordered a room.

Hannah chuckled but looked to the floor when Don showed her the key-card. "Hey. You tricked me," she said. Indeed, he had escorted her to the hotel elevator, not an exit, and he now stood waiting for the door panels to separate. With his right hand firmly clasping her shoulder, he glowed when passers-by turned their heads to glimpse his trophy.

"Hannah," he said under his boozy breath. "We can do this. *You* can do this. It's your future. It's *our* future."

To her inner ear these words sounded wrong but titillating. Hannah was emboldened by the influence of a good alcoholic high. She lowered her eyes, lightly poked at the marble floor with her right foot, and dropped her head into Don's chest.

"Please, Hannah. Let's just do it." This time Don's plea had a little more intensity to it, like a weak growl, just a few inches from her ear. "I'm madly in love with you," he said.

Please. Stop, she thought. She had heard those words before, from younger guys, even Frank, and she was feeling the pull again, just like on the Lake Okanagan dock. How could she forget? It was a scorching day, shared with friends and a cooler full of drinks. She was tipsy. They all were. And they pulled her right off the dock into the cold, refreshing lake.

Holding her breath, she swam below for several strokes, emerging only a few feet from Buckley Cairns, just as she had hoped. They smiled at each another, and she soon wrapped her arms around him and straddled him because he had used those words all summer, in notes sent through her girlfriends, and he was cute and athletic. It was now time to show her appreciation, she decided, by impetuously lowering her bikini bottom and helping him get inside. That was some four minutes or so. Probably quite a show for passing trout, but she had no regrets.

Her toes were now on the edge of the dock again. The lake was inviting, but darker than before. It would take more courage – but *if you love to climb a mountain*, and *want to reach the highest peak* – she hadn't heard those wonderful words sung for so long, and she did want to reach the highest peak. *How late was it anyway?*

Hannah lifted her crown off her proud suitor's chest and looked into his eyes. Don responded with a wide smile before kissing her on the cheek. The elevator doors opened and a patron exited. "C'mon," Don urged under his breath again, then he reached down, put a broad palm across one of Hannah's buttocks, and gently squeezed.

The elevator whisked the couple to their expensive suite, wherein Don quickly went to the bar fridge and made a couple of drinks.

Hannah sat nervously on the edge of the King-size bed. Don sat down right beside her and handed her a rum and Coke before delicately touching her – her hair, her thighs, the back of her neck and shoulders. He strained not to go straight for the deep cleavage on display. After a few minutes she reached up and lightly caressed the back of his head and neck, so one-by-one Dee Dee unhooked the small, bulbous buttons keeping her bosom in check.

A sheer black brassiere shaped her bosom into a couple of Fat Boy bombs. Don could barely cap the pressure mounting in his crotch as Hannah caressed his neck and shoulders. He pulled the right, short sleeve of her dress gently down, and then the left. Now he saw her stupendous figure in the near raw – as tantalizing as a minnow to a bull trout. Don reached down and put his drink on the carpet, then reached for Hannah's.

"Just a second," she said, before finishing it in one gulp.

Don put her glass down and stood up. She followed his lead and the top of her dress fell around her hips. Don reached out and pulled the folds down, as he had done to Denise's summer dress while anchored on English Bay, but his wife was in Arizona now, fast asleep or doing whatever she pleased. Don started undressing himself while Hannah removed her brassiere and shoes, a pair of crimson high heels she wore very rarely, only when she wanted to be both hunter and hunted.

She giggled when she lifted her head and saw the isosceles

branch extending from Don's ragged tuff.

Don chuckled drunkenly and said, "God*damn*, your beautiful – the sexiest woman in this entire city."

"You're not so bad yourself," Hannah replied softly. "For an older guy," she teased, her blue eyes visible in the dark.

"C'mon. Let me feel you," Don said. He brought his catch close, then maneuvered her deftly onto the bed, where he caressed her entire body, sucking and fondling her breasts, kissing her stomach, her ribs, her hips, and knees, passionately and vigorously – accidentally kicking his drink over in the process. Frank had not shown her such a love of foreplay for months, and her body responded favourably. Don turned her over and kissed her shoulders, back and buttocks. He touched behind her knees with his tongue. He even sucked on her toes. How fantastic she was in comparison to Denise, he thought. Hannah just closed her eyes and let the drunken affection overtake her, and when Don finally dipped his striving, weathered root into her salty rill she suddenly pictured Frank's mother lying in a hospital bed, hooked up to an intravenous drip tube.

"I think so," she told Don when he asked her the next morning if it had been "safe".

"Well good," he said. "I trust you, of course, but do you mind if I take a little run downstairs. I know where I can get some protection, and if you're willing, it'd be great to have a replay. Don't you think?"

"Seriously?" she asked.

"Sure. You were terrific. And you're more beautiful this morning than…"

"But my head hurts."

"Ah, c'mon. It's nuthin' that a tall glass of OJ or a strong cup of coffee won't cure. We can have a nice brunch later. At Tony's."

Hannah wearily acquiesced, so after a quick trip to the main floor men's room of the Vancouver Hotel, Don returned with a blue-tinted condom in his pocket, which he gleefully placed atop his circumcised knob before rolling down the rim to win, again.

The next afternoon Denise returned from Phoenix, deeply-tanned.

She relayed how the capitol itself was flat busted, so "there are golden opportunities there, commercial and residential," she advised. "But hon, you definitely need to have the long term in mind down there. Seriously," she added.

"What about Maricopa?" Don was anxious to know.

"Oh God. It's yours for the picking if you want, but I don't know. It's pathetic, and a mess. I'd be careful. A problem that big has to have consequences, you know. Like legal consequences. People fighting to get their homes back, in the courts, that kind of thing. We heard talk like that over breakfast just yesterday."

"Chandler the same?"

"Yeah. Pretty much. You could buy up a whole development there."

"At least you look good."

"Well thank you. You look rested yourself."

"How's your back swing?" Don asked.

"Better, I think. At least Lou thought so."

With energy to burn and a guilty conscience that needed burying, Don shagged Denise after dinner, thus deftly managing a weekend hat trick. No one in the NHL could say they achieved that much that week.

🚲 🚲 🚲

Arthur P. Connelly, Esq., made time in his busy Monday schedule to fit Don in on short notice.

"I'm telling you, Don, you want to think long and hard before you do this," he said from the 15th floor of his West Georgia Street office.

"But why? What's the point of waiting?"

Don was leaning over the client's side of his lawyer's desk, his knuckles pressed onto the shiny mahogany top. He didn't even know I was already a zygote. He had no idea that in her drunkenness Hannah had screwed up. She didn't do the math about her periodic cycle. She had begun to ovulate hours before the cork of the champagne popped at the Vancouver Hotel to "Help Me Make It Through the Night."

Arthur was seated, looking up at Don and slowly stroking his Italian silk tie as if he were trying to extract a few last drops of goodness from it.

"For starters, there's a lot of money at stake, as I'm sure you know, and she's entitled to half – but she can ask for more. She probably will when she finds out what this is all about."

"Will she get it?"

Arthur shrugged. "I don't know. It's hard to say. She's certainly not your average housewife, you know, the middle-aged mother who has slaved away to build her husband's career, you know, keeping her own opportunities on hold."

"Just the opposite," Don concurred, wrapping the desk with his knuckles a couple of times. "I fucking taught her how to make money – real money – buying and selling, leveraging."

Arthur nodded.

"Surely to Christ that's gotta count. Can she get less than half?" Don asked.

Arthur pushed his lips together and shook his head. "She's gonna get half. For starters. That's the law, but second – "

"God damn it anyway. She's no gold digger. I'll give her that," Don interrupted, "but why she should get half of everything I've sweated my bag to earn I'll never figure out. We don't even have kids!"

Little did Don know. And I wasn't the only puck he shot on the weekend that stuck to the net. He scored on Denise, last night, without even any tape on his stick, so now I had my very own half-sister taking shape. Ravens can make sweet hat tricks too.

"Well, I was going to say that it's my duty, whether you like it or not, to advise you that the law expects you to make efforts at reconciliation, if there is any reasonable prospect of that whatsoever."

"What?"

"And I'm supposed to advise you of the kind of counseling services available to effect reconciliation, if that's in the realm of possibility."

"No. It's not. Jesus, Art, are you working for me or against me here?" Don removed his knuckles from the lawyer's desk and sat down.

Arthur's face was now pink. He asked, "Are you actually planning on moving in with, with this Hannah? I mean, have you even discussed any of this with…"

"What do you think?"

Now Arthur looked stymied.

"Of course not," Don said.

"You don't want to move in with her, or…"

"No no no. God damn it. I haven't discussed it with her. The whole plan is to surprise her."

"But you've only known her for….."

"For what? What does that matter?"

Don cast his lawyer the hairy eyeball, then said, "Take one look at her and you'll understand."

"Yeah. You said. She's beautiful, I take your word for it, but..."

"She's Spanish, or Brazilian...or Indian or something. Picture Marilyn Monroe, but with caramel skin, black hair."

Arthur shook his head and said, "I'll draw up a petition and get John to give it a look-see before filing."

"When'll that be?"

"Possibly tomorrow, or Wednesday. Do you think you can wait that long?" Art's question had an affably sarcastic tone.

"Watch yourself," Don replied, grinning. The two men had done a lot of business over the years and were comfortable kidding one another.

"Will we see you at the game on Friday?" Arthur asked.

"Uh, no actually. Other plans." Don stood up.

"Let me guess," Arthur said, grinning again, and standing up.

"I said watch yourself." Now Don was grinning as Arthur shook his head. The two men shook hands over the table, then Don let himself out.

🚲 🚲 🚲

Frank would be back tomorrow evening, "so only if you really must," Hannah told her mother over the phone.

"Not *must*, dear. Your father and I *want* to do this. It's the right thing to do, no?"

Rosetta had phoned to ask if she could send flowers to Frank in Québec – and to get a mailing address.

"I just...I just...I don't know what to say, really." After a pause Hannah confided, "I'm really torn, mom, about Frank..."

"And that *man*?"

"No mom. Stop about the man, please," Hannah pleaded. "It's not about him. It's about me."

"What dear? What are you..."

"I'm just...I'm just..."

Hannah leaned against her sofa, put her feet on the edge of the coffee table, her left arm across her stomach, and said, "I'm just not feeling too good right now, about myself." She had taken a bath and was in her robe. The room was cool.

"Well you shouldn't work for that man. How many times should I say so?"

"Okay okay. So maybe you were right. Maybe I shouldn't work for Don-fucking-Dickerson – pardon my language, mom – but I never wanted to be a book-keeper in the first place. So I'm good at math. So what? When I was a kid I actually dreamed of being a scientist..."

"I *know*. So why didn't you..."

"I just didn't, mom. I don't know why." Hannah sighed deeply, then explained, "I know you and dad wanted it, but I got sidetracked. I got lulled in, by all the compliments, by all the attention paid to me. By *beauty*. Photographers – creeps, I realize now – paid me a lot of money for pictures, and I was happy to take it. I wanted to be in magazines, in bikinis, underwear. I thought it was really cool, at least better than studying for university. Better than being a farmer, I'm sorry to say."

After a pause Rosetta said, "But you have been successful. We saw the billboard on the Internet."

"God I hate that billboard. Every time I pass it I regret doing it."

"Well sweetheart, I don't know what to say then. Go back to school."

"You mean university?"

"Sure, why not?"

"I think it's a little late for that. I'm not even sure I would have the stomach for some of that stuff anymore, cutting open frogs and things, all that formaldehyde, you know what I mean?"

Her mom chuckled lightly and replied, "Oh yes, I do."

"I've been thinking about seeing a life coach," Hannah reticently ventured.

"A life coach?"

"Well, yeah. I've seen ads for them. They're like career experts, I guess, but they look at who you are, as an individual. Your strengths. They help you...I don't know, really...I've just..." Hannah fell to silence.

"I don't know what is troubling you, sweetheart, but please, quit your job if that feels right. Do whatever. Frank must make enough money to..."

"But that's just the point, mom. I know he does. I know I don't *have* to work. When I quit a job, or get laid off, I just sleep in, go to the library, drink coffee, do yoga, and come home and feed Frank on his credit card. I'm only 36, mom. I think I should be doing something a little more meaningful with my life, but I just don't...."

After a pause Rosetta said, "I don't know what to say, sweetheart. I'm sorry, but maybe you are overtired right now, feeling the pressure of Frank and his mother, and..."

"*Don't say it*, mom," Hannah urged.

"Okay. Okay." Rosetta sighed, then said, "but I am going to send flowers. It's the right thing to do."

"Okay. You do that."

Hannah gave her mother Frank's mailing address, then got off the phone. Either the room temperature was dropping, or her robe was not thick enough, but she shivered and her hands were cold. She decided to make a cup of tea.

🚲 ⏲ 🚲

"I'm leaving you," Don told Denise a couple days after visiting Art Connelly. His lawyer had agreed to file divorce papers, but not to serve Denise quite yet.

Denise was seated in her dining room, about to sip from a glass of rosé, but she paused. Her back twitched and she clutched her drink. A half-eaten serving of chicken cordon bleu and steamed vegetables sat warmly in front of her, a BlackBerry to the left of that. A wine bottle chilled at arm's length to the right.

Don appeared in the doorway, smiling grimly. He held a ring of keys at his side and shook it a few times, like a Salvation Army Santa Claus with a yuletide bell.

Denise put her glass down and looked at him.

"I know," he said. "I've never talked about it. *We*'ve never talked about it, but we both know it's the right thing."

Salt water formed on Denise's lower lids.

"Whoever said it was a wise, wise man, so maybe we're just a pair of fools. But money can't buy love," Don said.

Denise had another sip of wine, then hurled her glass at her husband, who blocked it from hitting his face.

"Fuck you, fuck you, fuck you!" she shouted. "Can't buy love. Don't fucking insult me. My *love* was never for sale."

Don's arms were still up. "I wasn't saying it was."

"But you've finally found someone whose is, right?"

"What?" Don pulled his head back and sneered at the suggestion, lowering his arms.

Denise got up from her chair, retrieved another wine glass from the sideboard, and poured herself a fresh drink. Then she sat down again.

"I'm gonna get myself a drink," Don said, and he walked into the adjoining kitchen. Fixing himself a Scotch and soda he called out, "I've finally had it with the charade. You see more of your sister than you do of me, and it's no big secret that she and 'Bernie the Bureau Cat' think I'm a proper asshole."

Denise's tears had resurfaced. When Don reappeared in the doorway with his drink his wife said, "Leave them out of it. They've never said any such thing."

"Shut up," Denise replied as Don sat across the table from her. "You must have a really bad conscience if you've gotta bring them into it," she added.

Don had a gulp of his whisky. "I was just saying, we live separate and apart for days, sometimes weeks. You're either with her in Toronto, or Arizona, or..."

"Tending to *your* real estate concerns," his wife interjected.

"And *yours*," he snarled.

"But you're missing the point," she rejoined.

"Oh am I?"

Don sighed before saying, "Lookit. I don't see what's the big deal. The passion's gone. The…"

"Didn't seem like it the other night," Denise jousted.

Don rolled his eyes. "Okay, okay, but one night in what? A month? Two? Longer?" He paused before saying, "We've never wanted kids. You've become a successful realtor in your own right, and I helped you do that. I want to stop pretending. Let's split the property and go our separate ways."

After a pause Denise said, "So, what? I guess you've had this all planned out? You're going to stay at the Wall tonight? Or maybe you've already bought yourself a new penthouse?"

Don frowned. "I'm not going anywhere right now," he said. "I'm gonna sleep in the den, on the foldout. You're still going to Toronto Friday, right?"

Denise nodded.

"So I'll arrange something by the time you get back."

🚲 🚲 🚲

Preferring a little turbulence above clouds to serious marital discord on turf – and rarely one to cancel travel plans – Denise did fly toward the welcoming arms of her sister, and on the evening of Friday, March 28th, she sat only eleven rows up from the lip of the broad stage of the Prince of Wales theatre, Louise and Bernard flanking her to the right. She was being treated to *The Life and Adventures of Nicholas Nickelby*, but the magnificent set, costumes, voices, moral ups and downs of Dickens' plot, as well as the rich forms of Frank Stella's murals, all had to compete for her attention, which drifted in and out of recollections of her husband and their happier times together.

At least Louise and Bernie got Denise to the show on time. The same could not be said for Hannah's chaperone. The 8:30 pm start time for the VSO concert was fast approaching and Hannah was still watching for Don to arrive.

Like a blue heron among crows, she stood slightly apart from the Deutsche Grammophon crowd outside the plush Vogue theatre on Granville Street. Once a star attraction unto itself, a glowing example of Art Moderne, this party lane was now a dirty artery of narcotic and nicotine dreams, inked necks, skull rings, pierced nipples and stale pizza slices. Drug traffickers and underemployed denizens crawled around the area like spiders on the prowl for the best places to spin traps of sex, drugs and rock and roll, but Hannah and those who had paid handsomely to hear the aging yet mellifluous Toots Thielemans bring an ailing symphony to life were dressed superbly, in the style befitting the traditional predilection of their class.

In a low-cut manganese summer dress and silver heels Hannah was distinctively easy on the eyes. Her lithe stems were well-preserved and her buoyant bosom showed contempt for the laws of gravity, both Newtonian and Einsteinian. Large, circular handles of a black patent sac were looped over her right shoulder, and her naturally shimmering locks were pulled back and pinned to foreground her strong cheek bones. Her azure pupils gave the overhead theatre bulbs something worth lighting up. She was so pretty there were butterflies in her stomach, but every few minutes their flapping wings caused perspiration dots across her forehead. She was feeling a little queasy.

When the crowd around her dissolved she was nearly alone but for the energetic youngsters who passed by, en route to the next spliff, pint of beer, strip show, or other such entertainment. Some of the less inhibited males couldn't resist a double-take or a gawk at her magnetic form.

Her date was late and he had the tickets. Though she was sorely tempted, Hannah Verso knew better than to pull her cell phone from her handbag and phone him. It wasn't worth the risk. The call might be traceable. Instead, when she felt sure the houselights had been lowered inside and the spotlight had been cast upon the Belgian harmonica virtuoso, she quickly crossed the street, nearly bumping into Ryan Ghostkeeper, who offered under his breath to sell her a knife – though she thought he was selling drugs – and she entered a moribund taco joint. In the bathroom she slipped out of her dress and pulled on the light sweater and skirt she had worn to work.

∿∿∿∿

"I got your message," Frank said before she even entered the living room. Hannah removed her shoes at the front entrance. Frank was sitting in his favourite armchair, staring at the television in near darkness, as the lights were dimmed low. He took a sip of beer and released a flatus just before his fiancée appeared in the doorway. "Pardon me. I add sausages for dinner," he said. Hannah threw her bag onto the floor next to the sofa and plopped herself down.

"You had the sausages?"

"Yeah. Workin' late again eh?" Frankie asked casually.

"Yeah, but I left you a message." Hannah's tone was slightly anxious.

"Yeah. I know. I'm just checking." Frank smiled at his fiancée, to let her know he was being light hearted, but she did not see it.

"This time of year's crazy, as you can imagine," Hannah said. "It's year end. Everybody wants their T-4s, and more bullshit on bullshit." Hannah's voice trailed off as she swiveled onto the sofa supinely.

"So you didn't go out with the girls, or did you?"

Hannah sighed. "No. Not tonight. No one was up for it, and besides, I'm not feelin' too well. I'm feeling a little nauseous, actually."

"Do you want a Tylenol?"

"No, Frankie," she said to the ceiling. "I'm all right. I'm gonna' make a cup of tea. I'll go to bed soon, if you don't mind."

Frank shrugged. "My day was great. Mom's still a vegetable if you care to know, and Dad hasn't gone to see her yet."

"Oh, I'm sorry. That was inconsiderate of me." She got up from the sofa slowly and walked into the kitchen, catching Frank's eye as she did. "What are you watching there?" she asked. Guns were firing left and right on the screen.

"Oh, I rented a DVD. *100 Rifles*. It's just about over. I can tell."

Hannah put water on for tea.

"You would have liked it. Raquel Welch is in it. She looks kind of like you," Frank said.

"You'll never read a book, will you?" Hannah asked.

"I've told you before. Why read when I get all the information I need on the net and tv: news, sports, weather. It's 24-7 these days."

"But I mean stories. Fiction. You know what I mean."

"I just told you. I just watch – I just *watched* a good movie. We only go around once. I don't wanna' waste time turning pages when a filmmaker tells the same story in two hours, with a lot more excitement in it, cutting out the crap."

A couple minutes passed, then Hannah entered with her tea. She sat down on the sofa and said, "some people *like* the crap. They think movies are crap, not the books."

"I don't know what your problem is. You worked in the industry."

"I'm just sayin." She lowered a tea bag gently in and out of her cup.

"You don't like it when we go to the movies?"

Hannah sighed, slumped her shoulders, and dropped the tea bag into her cup. "Yes. I guess I do. I'm just...oh forget it. I don't even know how we got onto this topic…"

"You started it! You asked me why I don't read."

Hannah had to strain to see Frank's eyes clearly. The lights were too low. From what she could see, however, they looked a little wired.

"I didn't mean anything by the question," she said. "It sounds like things are pretty awful, with your mom and everything."

"My father's such a prick. I'm probably going home again."

"For how long?"

"I don't know yet."

"Well…let's do something together tomorrow, like something we wouldn't normally do. I don't know. We could go to Granville Island or something like that. I haven't seen the turtles for ages. What do you think?"

Frank pulled some of the label of his beer bottle off before replying, "Sounds a bit boring but yeah. Sure. Why not? I'm gonna' hit the sac early tonight, as you English say."

"Will you give me a tummy rub?"

Frankie yanked more of his beer bottle label off when she asked that question.

"Well?" she asked after a pause. "What do you say? I'm not feeling very well." Her tone was friendly and warm. Frank clenched his beer bottle and took a deep breath. After exhaling he relaxed his grip and said, "Of course, but what's the matter with you, anyway? Just last week you were threatening to call off the marriage."

Hannah shrugged from across the hardwood floor. Frank couldn't see her eyes. "I'm under a lot of stress too," she offered up. "I'm working too hard. I can't wait 'til tax time's over with."

Frankie did rub Hannah's stomach later that night as they lay together in bed, but he was in no mood to take the intimacy any further, to rub above or below – to rub her the wrong way.

Denise Dickerson awoke the next morning from under an 800 thread-count Egyptian sheet on a queen-size bed. She had slept well – heavily, that is – breathing slow and deep, as if from a scuba regulator 50 metres below sea level.

"Well good afternoon, party girl," Louise greeted her as she entered an immaculate kitchen. "What can I get you for a kick-start? A regular coffee, cappuccino, Americano? What pleases you?"

Denise wore a pair of pink silk pajamas. Her hair was tussled. She looked older than her 45 years. "Oh, an Americano would be nice. Thanks, Lou," she replied, before picking up her BlackBerry from the bar and checking it for messages.

"Bernie and I were thinking about taking you to the islands today. It's a bit cloudy, but it should clear up."

"We don't get many opportunities to take ferries out here, not like you west coasters," Bernard piped up. "And you know how it is. You're never a tourist in your own town."

"And we're talking an actual island," Louise chimed in. "Not like that one you guys have, uh, what's it called again?"

"Granville Island," Bernard replied, before looking at Denise with a raised brow.

"Well. Not so fast there," the transplanted West Coaster admonished. "We *do* have a real island now, not far from Granville. A tiny one built for the Olympics Games. You know where the Molson Indy used to be?"

Bernard looked at his wife.

"No, hun, I don't," Louise said, looking at her sister.

"Well, it's just a tiny little thing. A couple of hundred square feet, but really cute. I think it cost about a million dollars."

"Please tell me *that's* not a CanCon," Bernard said without batting an eye.

"No. Not that one. He's always got more projects on the go than he can handle."

"And a lot of good it's done you two," Louise remarked, then she looked her sister in the eye and said, "Oh, come here."

Louise gave Denise a warm embrace. When she let go Denise sighed and said, "Oh well, do I need to get dressed right away, or…"

"No no. Relax and have your coffee," Louise urged. "I'll make you some toast and eggs if you like. There's a…Bernie…what's the ferry schedule?"

"Hang on. I'm just checking here." He was scrolling through a website.

"Now smell this," Louise told Denise, handing her a cup of coffee. "Really *breathe* it in," she said.

Denise obliged her sister, closing her eyes and breathing through her nose, as if she were holding a glass of 12-year-old Lagavulin.

"Oh, it's wonderful."

"At 40 dollars a pound it better be," Louise said with unabashed pride in her voice.

"Oh heck, ladies, we can go pretty much every 45 minutes or so, so..."

"All right," Louise interjected. "So there's no panic, but let's not leave it too late."

"No, I agree. I'll get dressed, but I would love a couple of scrambled eggs if that's no trouble," Denise said.

Bernard swiveled around in his chair, away from his computer monitor, and said to Denise, "I heard on the radio this morning that Ottawa is going to shorten amortization periods; maybe even prohibit zero percent down mortgages. Apparently we're heading into a bit of a credit problem, just like our friends to the south. What does Don think?"

"I don't know, Bernie, but God knows it could only do him some good. Seriously, he needs to slow down, for his own good. I have no idea where he gets his money from anymore. He's got creditors starting to squeeze him but he keeps making one rezoning application after another, as if he's untouchable – as if people don't care – and the city's right in there with him, eating out of his hands, as he always says."

"Well, it's the same here," Bernie replied, and just then Denise's BlackBerry rang.

"Oh that's mine."

Denise picked up her phone. "Private caller," it told her.

"Hello. Denise Dickerson speaking."

"Hello Mrs. Dickerson. My name is Constable Juanita Barclay. I'm a member of the Vancouver Police Department."

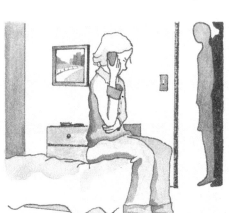

"You are a police officer?"

"Yes I am."

"Okay." Denise looked at her sister and brother-in-law and shrugged.

"You are the husband of Donald Roy Dickerson, am I correct?"

"Yes."

"And your address is #405 – 2210 Hamilton Street, right?"

"Yes. That's one of them."

"Do you have a private place where we can speak, madam?"

"Uh…" Denise cast Louise and Bernard a worried look.

"Yes. I do," she said. "It's the police," she mouthed to her hosts and walked into the guest bedroom where she sat down on the edge of her bed.

"Well, Mrs. Dickerson, unfortunately I have some very bad news for you."

Denise twitched and brought her left arm across her chest.

"Okay."

"Your husband was killed last night."

Denise gasped. Louise and Bernard appeared outside the bedroom door with drawn, inquisitive expressions on their faces.

"I'm very sorry, Mrs. Dickerson. Your husband is dead. We've been trying to obtain your number."

Denise blanched and began to cry. Louise stepped in, sat beside her sister, and put her arms around her trembling shoulders.

"But how?" the satin-clad widow whined.

"We can talk about that in person. That's what we prefer, for you to come home, as soon as you can, so we can tell you everything we know."

"Well can't you just tell me how?" Denise pleaded.

"No, Mrs. Dickerson. He was killed. We believe he was murdered."

Upon hearing that last word Denise went limp. Her phone fell out of her hand and she stared dully into her lap.

Louise picked up the BlackBerry and said, "Hello. This is Louise Talbot, Mrs. Dickerson's sister. Can you tell me what's going on please?"

"My name is Juanita Barclay, ma'am. I'm a Constable with the Vancouver Police Department, and I've just informed your sister that her husband was killed last night."

Louise looked aghast at Bernard, who was standing at the foot of the bed. Denise was now pressing a clenched hand against her lips. Tears streamed lightly down her face.

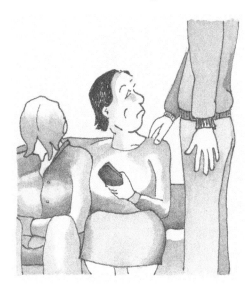

"Can you put your sister on a plane, ma'am?" Constable Barclay asked. "It's important that we speak to her as soon as possible."

"Uh…" Louise looked up at her husband, who lightly touched her shoulder. "Can you arrange a flight home for her?" she asked him softly. "The police need to speak to her in Vancouver."

"Of course," he replied.

"Yes of course," Louise told the officer. "We can do that and anything else you need from us right now. What should we do?"

"Just comfort her, I think. That would be best right now," Constable Barclay said. "Take care of her. Make sure she is okay to fly before you send her home. These matters are traumatic. We know that. If necessary, we can wait a bit, until she is emotionally ready to return home."

A veteran postal employee found him, dressed all smart like he was going to a hipster's ball, but he didn't look very bright, lying all sprawled out on his back across the painted concrete. His convertible Mercedes, with its CanCon vanity plates, was parked a few feet away.

Mrs. Carmella Lepont had just returned home, parked in the underground lot, and walked a few yards from her vehicle when she saw him, about 15 minutes after he had stopped breathing. She tried to steady her fluttering heart before moving closer and studying the scene – a modest blood pool around her neighbour and a bag of groceries spilled all over. Then she hightailed it to her suite and called 9-1-1.

The police cordoned off the area and did not let anyone in or out of the building without questioning them first. The paramedics went through their motions too. They gave Don the 'trapezia squeeze,' not a high-flying circus hug, but a hard pinch in the neck. He didn't flinch, so the attendant cut off his shirt and hooked him up to a set of battery cables – automated external defibrillators or AED in their lingo. They tried to jump start his heart but to no avail. The machine didn't recognize a re-startable rhythm so "Donald Dick" was now a dead duck. He was quickly carted off to St. Paul's trauma room, where he got his very own crypt.

While Don was being examined at the hospital, Sergeant Sandra Wolychenski seized his wallet and searched his pockets. Woolly, as she was commonly known, was a chunky police officer with glacial eyes, a low centre of gravity, and an even lower tolerance for due process violations, as her fellow officers had come to learn. Don's driver's license informed her that he resided just a few floors up from where he was found, at #405 – 2210 Hamilton Street, surrounded by other concrete condos, slick restaurants and cafés.

She also found two tickets for a Toots

Thielemans concert that was underway at that very moment. "Date: Friday, March 28. Door time: 8:30 pm." That's what the ticket said.

Common sense told Woolly that one of the tickets was for the deceased and the other was for his wife, or a date, or just a friend, whoever that might be. She returned to the crime scene with her partner, Constable Clyde Sorenson, a lanky, opal-faced brunette with not much in the attic except an adolescent desire to drive through red lights, sirens blaring, and to handcuff long-haired potheads, thieves, and "recidivists," a word he first learned in a criminology class.

The pair went up to the manager's suite and knocked on the door. Dancing With the Stars was on television, and Jersey Steinbauch and his wife were intently watching a couple of C-list celebrities tango across a stage.

"Coming," the police heard a gruff voice say.

The door opened and the officers were greeted by a wan, graying, slump-shouldered man. "We'd like to see Mr. Dickerson's suite," Woolly told him after introducing herself and Sorenson.

"This is God damn awful, isn't it?" Steinbauch said.

"Yes it is," Woolly acknowledged.

"In all my years I'd never thought I'd see anything thing like this. Here, in my building. Have you caught the son-of-a-bitch already?" he inquired. The bittersweet odour of spirits wafted from his cake hole.

"No, sir," Woolly replied. Steinbauch closed his door and escorted the police to Dickerson's suite.

"Did he live with anyone else?" Woolly asked.

"His wife."

Steinbauch knocked on Don's door. No reply came. "Maybe she's not home," he said. "She's away a lot."

"Try again," Sorenson said.

Steinbach knocked a few more times before Constable Sorensen asked, "Can you please let us in, sir? This is important police business."

"All right, all right," he replied nervously, unlocking the door with his master key.

🚲 🚲 🚲

Late the next morning Ryan Ghostkeeper was having a cup of coffee at the Aboriginal Front Door on Main Street – "If you want coffee, bring your own cup", a sign on the front door said – as Leonard Jordan reviewed photo ballots laid out for him at the Vancouver police station, just east of the Cambie Street Bridge on False Creek.

No matter how much Mr. Jordan wanted to identify the native man who tried to sell him a knife the previous evening, he could not do so. Mr. Jordan was a bartender at the Yaletown Brew Pub.

"I think it's 'cuz of that hard hat he was wearing," he explained to an officer.

"Shit, I even lost my fuckin' helmet," Ryan told Robbie, a regular at the AFD. Ryan sat at a table. Robbie reclined against on a pine green vinyl sofa across from him.

"You lost it?"

"Oh fuck. I gotta stop drinkin'. I'm gonna get breached."

"How much longer?"

"About six, yeah, six more months."

"Now you gotta get another job."

Ryan shrugged. "I'll find something. In the meantime I'm self-employed."

"Do they count that?" Robbie was referring to Ryan's carvings and his obligation to seek employment.

"They should." Ryan had a sip of coffee.

"Did you hear about the murder last night?"

"What murder?"

"Big Dick. Didn't you hear?"

"Big Dick?"

"Yeah. That Dickerson guy, the one who owns all the condos."

"Fuck, no. Do they know who did it?"

"If they do, they're not sayin."

"Oh my God! Frankie! Oh my God!" Hannah yelled out as Frank came downstairs, pulling a sweatshirt over his head. She was in the kitchen, visibly trembling and clenching the handle of a full pot of coffee. Frank had just taken a shower, following his Saturday morning run. It was one o'clock in the afternoon in Vancouver, four o'clock in Toronto, March 29. Denise Dickerson had just been notified of her husband's death, so the press had the go-ahead to publish the fact but not any details of the high-profile homicide.

"Put that down, Hannah, before you scald yourself," Frank ordered.

Shaking, Hannah placed the coffee pot on the kitchen counter. The breaking news from the radio about Don Dickerson's death had temporarily passed. Frank stepped toward Hannah and hugged her.

"What's the matter?" he asked in a surprised tone.

"D-Don. Don Dickerson…"

Frank pulled back and looked her in the eye.

"Your boss. He was murdered last night."

Frank tightened his grip on Hannah's arms and looked intently into her eyes. "What the hell?"

Louise Talbot had booked her sister a flight for Sunday morning – business class – and supplied her with a couple of sedative tablets, one of which knocked her out for most of the westward trip.

Within a few hours of Denise Dickerson's arrival in Vancouver, Sergeant Wolychenski and Constable Sorenson interviewed the widow in the comfort of her condo living room. She was the prime suspect, as spouses tend to be, especially when a lot of money is at stake.

Woolly noticed that everything in the home was shiny clean and colour-coordinated. Denise wore a form-fitting black knit sweater and charcoal knee-length skirt. (*Nice legs*, Sorenson mused). Her streaked-hair was lifted in lolling waves by Ammonium Thioglycolate and the burning kiss of a curling iron. She wanted to look presentable to the officers, despite everything, but even her judicious applications of Clé de Peau and L'Oréal could not reduce the puffiness of her lids or brighten the whites between them. Her sedative had not entirely run its course, leaving a wayward fatigue in her eyes.

"If you don't mind me asking," Woolly asked, "do you know if Don was planning on going to the symphony on Friday night?"

Denise's eyes suddenly opened wide and she clenched a tissue in her hand. She thought of the play she had seen at the Princess of Wales that night. "No. I had no idea."

"Seriously now," Woolly urged.

Both officers studied the suspect's face, her eyes, looking for a furtive gesture. Denise studied theirs too for a few seconds, before asking, "Seriously?"

"Seriously, ma'am," Sorenson said. "When your husband was found there were two tickets in his pocket for a concert that evening at The Vogue."

Denise looked at both officers with surprise and even a hint of embarrassment.

"I have no idea why he would have those tickets," Denise said.

"He bought them about six weeks ago, through Ticketmaster. We already know that. He didn't tell you?" Woolly asked.

"No he didn't."

"Are you surprised?"

Denise thought about it for half a minute. "Yes and no," she decided.

"Can you..."

"Yes, I can explain. I've just learned that he bought concert tickets behind my back – probably for him and Sam, maybe Marv – and no, he was not always frank with me...about personal matters."

Sorenson scribbled down "Sam" and "Marv."

"I know this must be very painful for you," Woolly added, "but it's very important for us to know that, okay? If it's true."

"Have you spoken to any of his *jazz* friends?"

"No m'am. This is the first I've heard of them. Can you tell me their phone numbers? Or last names?"

"Sure."

As Denise identified Sam Rickels and others perspiration beads formed on her forehead and her pale skin turned a luxurious porcelain, almost pearl white.

"Are you okay, ma'am?" Woolly inquired.

"Actually, if you may excuse me. I'm not feeling well."

Denise quickly got up and rushed to her washroom. A door down the hall closed and within seconds Woolly and Sorenson could hear violent retching. The crime busters eyed each other with a sense of sympathy, mild embarrassment, and even a hint of guilt at moving in so quickly.

After a few minutes Woolly walked to the bathroom door and rapped lightly on it. "Denise, we're going to help ourselves out. We'll return at a more suitable time, okay," she said.

"With a search warrant," Sorenson said out of earshot as Denise replied, "okay, thank you."

The Leonard Jordan lead was helpful, but the police got another one, an equally compelling one, as far as they were concerned, from an East Vancouver citizen who had been at the Brittania School gymnasium the evening "Slim Jimmy" ranted about CanCon's local mixed-use application.

"He was really angry, really steamed," the caller said. "Before he left he said something like, 'I'd like to shoot the fucker' – pardon my language – or something like that."

"Do you know this fellow's name?"

"Yeah. Everyone knows him as Slim Jimmy, but his actual name's James Bridges. The guy's got a real fuckin' chip on his shoulder."

"James Bridges, a.k.a. Slim Jimmy?"

"Yeah. That'll work."

"Can you describe him, sir?"

"He's pretty tall, about five foot ten, I'm guessing, and skinny, pretty skinny. He's a fixture on the Drive, usually in a green jean jacket. It's got a sign on the back, you know, like a name on the back of a sports jersey. It says "The Resistance," you know, like The Clash, a punk rock group or something. If you're interested, look for him at the park, on a weekend. He hangs out there with his friends, smoking pot and whatever else those type do."

"What does he look like?"

"He's got black hair. Not quite shoulder length, and – oh yeah – he's got buttons on his jean jacket, like political buttons."

The tip was passed along to Sergeant Woolly, who asked Constable Sorenson to "book him." Sorenson grinned. He liked her term for Facebooking someone. "Either that," she said, "or Google 'The Resistance – East Vancouver'."

By now Hannah realized she had two secrets to keep from Frank and the world at large, as long as possible, and that doing both would not be easy. Not only had she missed a VSO concert on account of Don's untimely death, she had missed her period, which meant that technically I had already been conceived.

I'd like to say that I was "alive," but that would cause a big debate about *what* was actually alive. The law would say I was just a "potential" human being – a being *in posse* – which sounds a little rough, like I was a member of a vigilante group. It's nicer to think that I was *en ventre ma mere*. French is so much more pleasing to the ears.

And mom wasn't the only one harbouring a couple of big secrets. Denise too was in a pretty pickle when her time of the month passed by without the usual headaches, cramps, and insertions.

Maybe I'm just late, the widow prayed before self-administering the test at home, the afternoon before Don's funeral. She burst into tears as a blue cross appeared in the window because now she had a bun in the oven. But I don't know why she was so sad. I had a sister in the making. A real sister. What could there possibly be to cry about?

The very next morning multi-coloured light rays filtered through the marvelous stained-glass windows of the Holy Rosary Cathedral while a somber organ filled wandering imaginations with thoughts of the after-life. A plaster replica of the saviour from Galilee hung from wires on a cross above Denise, who sat veiled in the front pew. He was tilted forward slightly as if he were an Olympic athlete about to perform an incredible feat of strength on the rings.

Denise wept openly, but not because of him, her ol' money belt. She wept for herself and the baby growing inside her, the new 'significant other' in her uterine life.

The who's who of Vancouver's FIRE scene were present at the memorial – that's the Finance, Insurance and Real Estate scene – as were many of the deceased's personal friends, including Marv Goldfarb and Sam Rickels, who were accompanied by their wrinkled wives and clinging children. That French-cuffed pair of jazz aficionados had already been interviewed by the police, to determine if either of them were an intended beneficiary of the second ticket for The Vogue on March 28, but they were not. Such news left Denise embittered with the presumption that, while she was visiting Louise and Bernard in T.O., home of the decaying Maple Leafs and a rather dead but honest Ed, Don was intending to see a concert with a younger woman.

That's why Don had made love so intensely to her the night before she flew to Toronto, she was sure: to ease his guilt and give her the same lovin' stuff he had given his mistress. If so, it was karma. Big Dick deserved it. He had it coming.

Hannah did not want to attend the funeral, that's for sure, but Frank would have none of it. "I've worked for Don for ten years," he shouted in exasperation from the kitchen when Hannah expressed her reluctance, "and goddamn it, it shouldn't be too much to ask my fiancée to go to the man's funeral with me."

Frank had a point. Appearances are everything for some people. So Hannah begrudgingly attended that most sanctimonious of sianoras, the final salute of a man who had been her fiancé's meal ticket for years. And she dressed appropriately, in an unrevealing black jacket, blouse and mid-length dress.

Sam and Marv were sitting side by side as the mayor eulogized the great realtor. Sam shook his head when Marv asked in a whisper, "Do you think it had anything at all to do with him bangin' that Spanish broad."

After a pause Sam leaned toward his friend's right ear and replied, "Maybe, but I've heard through the vine that they're looking into some guy who worked for him, who he axed. An Indian."

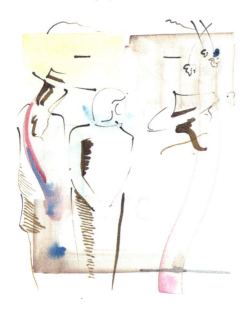

"What – so the guy tomahawked him back?" Marv asked in a whisper.

Sam winced.

"Kidding. Denise might have set it up. He was about to call it off, and she was plain sick of his adultery. Now she's sitting on a gold mine."

Sam shook his head and leaned in close to Marv's ear again. "She was in T.O. You're not seriously suggesting she hired someone? Are you?"

Goldfarb shrugged, then put his index finger to his mouth and said "later."

"This was the man who really pushed for densification across our great city," the mayor impressed upon the mourners. "And we were reluctant at first, but it was he, not us, who saw the direction in which the 21st century is heading. As revolutionary as it may seem, the parkade is becoming a thing of the past, and he saw that with crystal clarity."

Many other redeeming qualities were ascribed to the man who had worked hard to keep his right hand from getting caught in the cookie jar.

Hannah's own palms went clammy when the silken sentiments from the pulpit were over, the mourners had started to mingle, and Frank introduced his fiancée to Denise. He gave the widow a firm hug, and expressed his most sincere condolences. "It's a great, great loss," he said.

Louise Talbot stood by and watched as Frank whispered into Denise's ear, "And don't worry, whoever did this, they'll nail the son-of-a-bitch to a cross." He then looked up at the tilted crucifix and crossed-himself. Hannah shook Denise's hand, weakly, and said, "I'm sorry for your loss."

Don's confidantes who suspected that Frank's pretty companion might have been the dead man's final conquest had the tact to keep Denise in the dark.

"That's her, I'm sure," a senior partner at McNolton, Skiddu, & Bentley said under his breath to a merely salaried lawyer in the firm. The two men were standing side by side, sipping apple juice as many guests loitered around the front vestibule, waiting for some word as to how to the procession would form and begin. The gray-haired partner tipped his head in the direction of Hannah.

"Oh, yowza," the underling said in a whisper. "From what I can see, he must've died with a smile on his face."

🚲 🚲 🚲

"Look at that," Woolly said to Sorenson.

"Fuckin eh."

"Watch your mouth," the superior admonished.

> Down with Don Dickerson – The Resistance – Din
> 30 Mar 2008...Ding Don, the King is Dead, the King is Dead, the King is Dead...
> Follow The Resistance on Facebook || Twitter ||
> http://www.stopdondickerson.ca/ – cached

"Look. There's even a blog," Sorenson pointed out as Woolly absorbed the find.

"Where?"

"Right there." Sorenson put his finger right in front of the link, so Woolly double-clicked.

> Ding Don, the King is Dead, the King is Dead, the King is Dead; Ding Don, the Condo King is Dead – and in the sagacious words of the immortal Nietzsche, "we have killed him. How shall we comfort ourselves, the murderers of all murderers? What was holiest and mightiest of all that the world has yet owned has bled to death under our knives...Is not the greatness of this deed too great for us?"
>
> Make no mistake, Dickerson is dead and condomania is temporarily six feet under too – at least until the next Mandarin rides into town on a gilded saddle, dreaming of penthouse suites, champagne for corporate comrades, and rose-scented whores.

Woolly didn't need to read further, except to note the author, James Bridges, on behalf of The Resistance. She returned to the "Stop Don Dickerson" website, opened the "Contact Us" window, identified herself as a VPD officer, and asked Mr. Bridges for an interview as soon as possible.

☥ ☥ ☥

"No. It's not a fucking confession. It's not to be taken literally. I was spouting off, all right?"

Slim Jimmy had sprung forward in his chair, his arms lifted in frustration. Woolly didn't budge. She was seated at the corner of the desk in the police interview room.

"Well who in his right mind would take responsibility for something like this if he didn't do it?" she asked him.

"I was trying to make a point, for Christ sake – using a literary allusion. We, the Resistance, did not kill Don Dickerson. *Someone* out there did, and it doesn't really matter who, because the point is that Don had it coming one way or another. I just happen to relate to whoever could be so angry as to do it. That's what I meant by 'we' – we the angry, we the frustrated, we the sick and tired of being subjugated by corporate power. The little guy is always steamrolled."

"Is that what this Nietzsche person meant?"

"Of course not. He was talking about religion, theology, the death of religion through science, rationality, the Enlightenment, *et cetera*. We invented God, a figment of our imaginations – that's a no-brainer – and we destroyed him. The implications are huge, and we're not even ready to accept them. That's what he suggests."

"But you specifically say something here…" Woolly leaned forward and picked up the printout from James' website – "Yeah," she said, "this part here about bleeding to death under our knives. Why did you include that?"

"Because it's part of the quote," James snapped. He perched forward and put his elbows on the desk. "Seriously, ma'am, I have no bloody clue who murdered the guy, or how, all right?" His tone was now pleading. "If a guy wants to build an empire at the expense of others, then go ahead, I say. There's nothing new in that. It's how nations are built. But Kings tempt fate when they piss off their subjects. We're all made of flesh and blood. The evil eye is always watching, and someone was obviously watching Don."

"You obviously watched him, and pretty closely it appears from your website."

James slumped in his seat and rolled his eyes. His fingers trembled. The audio tape continued to run. He had declined the invitation to speak to a lawyer beforehand. "My last one was an idiot," he had remarked.

"I want to run through your whereabouts on March 28th one more time, if that's okay?"

James shrugged, then looked at Woolly directly and said, "Go ahead."

"You went to the Cinematheque for the seven o'clock show."

"The double bill," he replied.

"Okay, the double bill. Do you have your receipts?"

"Who keeps film receipts?"

"Is that a yes or a no?"

"A no."

"But if you did, would it show you attended a double bill?"

James nodded, then said, "Yeah. The *Bicycle Thief* was first, then *Blow Up*, by Antonioni, if those films mean anything to you."

"They don't. Do you make a habit of going to movies by yourself?"

"Sometimes, sure. But it's not what you think, like I'm making this up for convenience. I'll say it again, I'm no criminal. I'm an activist, an anarchist, and unlike most suck-asses I know, I actually exercise my constitutional rights to free speech."

"Wow, an anarchist with constitutional rights," Woolly remarked before picking up the printout again. "'And we have killed him?' Referring to Don Dickerson. The day after he was murdered? That's free speech to you?"

"I've explained that, and too bad, but I thought Dickerson was a destructive prick. I'm not sorry someone did him in."

"But you can't tell me where you were that night except to say you were at a double bill, by yourself."

"That's right."

"The Cinematheque. That's on Howe, right? Around, uh, Helmken?"

James nodded.

"Not too far from Yaletown."

"So what?...Hey..."

James pulled out his wallet and shakily pulled out his Cinematheque membership.

"Here. Here's my membership," he said, handing it to Woolly. "Everyone needs one to get into that theatre."

Woolly looked at his card. It was date-stamped months before Dickerson's death.

"You can check their fuckin' calendar," James said. "It's not like I memorized it before I got here so I could fabricate a defence. Fuck. I was actually supposed to meet Gurdy, my friend, but she texted me at the last minute to say she was going to a burlesque show or something. A friend of hers called her at the last minute. I didn't care. She's not big into film."

"And she'll confirm this."

"I swear it. Go ahead. Call her. I actually met up with her after *Blow Up* got out, down on Alexander Street somewhere."

"And when was that?"

"I don't know. Probably around quarter to twelve or so."

Woolly stared at him.

"Jesus, if you want her number, I'll give it to you. I've got nothing to hide from you."

"How did *you* get there?"

"To the party, or the film?"

"Either."

"I biked."

"Bicycle or motorbike?"

James shook his head and rolled his eyes. "A bicycle."

Woolly paused before saying, "You said you're not a criminal, but you've got a couple of priors. You haven't mentioned those."

James shifted in his seat.

"So what." He looked into his interrogator's eyes, searching. "Like I said, I exercise my constitutional rights. I protest. I fight against abuses by the state, against abuses by cops just like yourself who think they can get away with beating protestors, pepper-spraying them, tasering them. The world's a lot fucking bigger place than this Shangri La. Why don't you go fishing somewhere else?"

"Are you going to take your website down?"

"What for?"

"Try respect. Mr. Dickerson's dead."

"Don't talk to me about respect."

Woolly flinched, then said, "May I ask you, and you don't have to answer, certainly not without consulting a lawyer first, but have you ever considered that The Resistance might be viewed as a criminal organization?"

"Ohhh shit." James slumped back in his chair. "You're kidding me, right? This is a joke."

Woolly eyed him steadily, then said, "We're done, for now. I appreciate you coming in to talk to me, but think about what I said."

🚲 🚲 🚲

Dee Dee had been laid low before the 2008 post-season got underway, before the icy battle to win Lord Stanley's shiny Grail had begun. The Canucks had yet again managed to squeeze into the fray, and courtesy of CanCon, Denise got a great view of the stick handlers and one-timers from box seats. Don's friends and other FIRE set patrons treated her like tinsel, and she found it hard not to indulge in the free wine and beer being swilled by her associates.

"No, no, no. I wish I could, but I just can't. I'm driving," she'd say to anyone who would encourage her. She knew better than to commit capital crime number one: getting the foetus tipsy, an act punishable by ostracism, stoning, and possible litigation down the road. Besides, Denise was a light sleeper. She reached out and popped a sedative whenever the problem became too acute, so she had an additional reason not to drink.

I had a more naturally relaxing time in the slowly-stretching expanse of my mother's saline hull. Cactus had been encouraging my mom to "get with the program," specifically the program of using only two wheels and old-fashioned muscle power to get herself from point A to B throughout the day. Hannah decided to give the pastime a try and bought herself a mauve cruiser with a wide springy saddle, white wall tires, and a steel mesh basket over the front wheel.

On the last Friday of April, just after 5:00 pm, Hannah headed north, over the Burrard Bridge, to the rich green lawn behind the Vancouver Art Gallery. She was excited to see a gathering of hundreds of cyclists of all shapes, sizes, and fashion-senses. The playful spirit of the riders was matched by the personalities of the bikes that would be the highlight of the ride, for she was about to participate in the monthly critical mass ride.

Two hands waved in the distance and she spotted her friend.

"You made it," Cactus called out.

Hannah waved back and carefully walked her cycle through the crowd, stopping here and there at the sight of unicycles and a couple of custom-made high-rise machines with extra sprockets, chains and gears.

Cactus was wearing a black skirt, fishnet stockings, black boots, and a bleached white jean jacket over a shiny silver t-shirt. For accent, she wore a hair band with a cloth red rose sticking out of it. Hannah had no such costume, not knowing in advance that the group thrived on expressive clothing and bicycles. She wore jeans and a slim, form-fitting long sleeve t-shirt.

"Barely," Hannah replied, when she was in earshot. "I had no idea what an effort it would be to get up hills on this thing."

"Oh, but it's pretty," Cactus said. The friends hugged each other, then Cactus introduced Hannah to a couple of her friends – "fellow members of The Resistance," she called them. "This is Jimmy, or Slim Jimmy." He smiled, nodded, and shook her hand.

"Hey, you've got those flappy things," Hannah said to him.

"Just hockey cards."

"Hockey cards?"

"Yeah. I don't like the game so I love the thought of the players getting slapped in the face thousands and thousands of times by my spokes."

"Ohh-kay."

"At least he gives me the gum from the pack," a young woman said, extending her hand. Her grip was stronger than Jimmy's. "And he calls me Hurdy Gurdy, but you can call me Gertrude if you like."

Gertrude Kepfeldrummer was a rosy-faced, bright-eyed young woman with Henna-dyed hair, tattoos down her back, a flabby midriff, a peasant dress, and black police boots like Cactus's.

"Okay. So – when does it all begin?" Hannah asked.

"It won't be long," Cactus assured her. "Nobody's in a hurry here."

But suddenly there was movement, and like a motley school of truant tropical fish, the crowd of smiling pedal pushers slowly funneled onto Howe Street. The cyclists shouted out whoops and yelps, whistled and rang bells, much to the delight of pedestrian onlookers, who pulled out their cell phone cameras to catch a lasting record of the curious parade.

"Oh my god, this is so amazing," Hannah gushed. She peddled slowly alongside Cactus, about midway in the pack, which was about five or six bikes wide with lots of room in between shoulders and tires. Jimmy and Gertrude went together near the front of the pack.

Charlie Menz was up front too. *I've seen that guy before*, he thought, as he recognized Jimmy from his Brittania School outburst. *I hope no one pisses him off today.*

Music blared from sound systems rigged onto bike racks and handlebars, and a trail scent of marijuana wafted by every now and then.

"Wow, what freedom!" Hannah exclaimed. Indeed, the cyclists ruled the road. No cars came near her, and she almost never had to stop, even at red lights.

"Thank you, corkers!" Cactus said as she passed a few cyclists who were blocking vehicle traffic at the Davie Street intersection.

Others in the school expressed the same sentiment.

"What are they called again?" Hannah asked.

"They're the corkers I told you about. Do you want to do it?"

"No thank you. Not this time. I'll just enjoy the scenery."

"Fer sure. Maybe next time."

The spokes spun over the Granville Street bridge, again occupying all southbound lanes. Hannah felt elated. A few northbound drivers honked happily in support. When those at the front of the pack got to the apex of the bridge they stopped and waited for the rest to catch up. Several cyclists lifted their bicycles high in the air. Many riders whistled, let out more whoops, and honked bike horns.

"They always do this on bridges," Cactus explained. Hannah was impressed. She even felt a rush at the solidarity and passion of it all.

After five minutes or so the group turned east onto West Broadway, past the Dick Building. Frank had once drawn her attention to the fleurs-de-lis adorning that structure. The pack cruised for several blocks, curtailing eastbound traffic all the way to Commercial Street. It turned left there, at the busy Broadway-Commercial Skytrain junction, where lower middle-class commuters stiffly awaited for the next bus to arrive and take them away from the jumpy, sweaty paupers who were busily pushing drugs and passing around bottles of beer, wine and spirits.

About ten minutes of rolling northward brought Hannah and Cactus to Parker Street and a small string of colourful business fronts on the south side. These extended north to Venables.

"You see those shops there," Cactus said, tilting her head left.

"Yeah."

"We'll next time you ride by, they'll probably be gone."

"Let me guess: another condo."

"Close, but no cigar, sugar. They're slated for *mixed-use*. Remember? I told you about them already when I was giving you shit for taking that job with that Dickerson dildo. I couldn't believe it, and you wouldn't listen. No. You needed a job, you insisted, as if you're the only one. We all need jobs at some point or another, sister, but some of us have our principles."

Hannah's stomach quivered.

"Actually, I can't believe I'm still your friend." Cactus chuckled after saying that and reached her open hand out to Hannah, to show her that that remark was in jest.

Hannah's cheeks flushed.

The shops that Cactus and Hannah had just passed were in fact those that CanCon wished to demolish and replace with a denser, condo-business mélange. They were the heated subject of the Brittania School meeting that Don Dickerson made a point of avoiding.

"Rosie's makes the best burritos in town, easily, and The Vintage Point is my favourite retro store. Or was. I got this jacket there for four bucks," Cactus said, holding open the flap of her fraying jean jacket. "But soon they'll be gone. They won't be able afford the rent increases."

Okay, okay. Enough already, Hannah silently wished. She did not need guilt heaped on regret.

"I know you're not supposed to speak ill of the dead," Cactus remarked, "but I'm glad someone capped that greedy bastard. Fuck, they suspect Jimmy, if you can believe it 'cuz he went and wrote some stupid shit on his site."

Hannah did not know what to think about Jimmy. Her mind was stuck on the fact that she had actually had sex with 'that greedy bastard,' behind her fiancé's back, no less, and as a result got pregnant. So she assumed.

As she and her friend pedaled along, slowly, very slowly, the timing of Don's killing troubled her deeply. She could not shake her feeling of guilt for having betrayed Frank's trust that very evening.

"Should we speed up?" Hannah asked. She and her friend had inadvertently found themselves near the back of the pack.

"No. Go as slow as you want. Don't let those dicks behind you spoil your ride."

By 'dicks,' Cactus meant the police officers at the tail end of the ride. One was on a motorbike. A couple of others were on bicycles. They kept a soft hand of control over the ride, making sure that the pack did not stretch itself out too thin.

"Frank must have been freaked out by the murder," Cactus offered. "They worked together for a long time, didn't they?"

"Yes. They did, but Frank's coping okay. He's mad as hell, of course. He's dying for the police to find out who did it….I told you about his mom, right?"

"Oh yeah. She's in a coma or something?"

"Yeah. She had a brain aneurism, so Frank's been going back and forth."

"He what?"

"He goes back and forth, from here to Quebec."

"Oh. That's gotta be really shitty. My grandma's on her last legs right now, from leukemia. She gets lots of help – like lots of care – cause she's loaded, but she could pass any day."

"Oh. I'm sorry to hear that."

"Well, I will miss her, sorely. She's been my inspiration since childhood, but I wish she could just die gracefully."

"Yeah. I think that's what Frank wants for his mom now. He's been really on edge and honestly? We're not doing that great lately."

"Oh. Do you want to talk about it?"

"Uh…no. It's okay."

Hannah and Cactus entered onto East Hastings Street and Hannah could not help but gawk at the grubby sidewalk theatre. Rickety drug addicts argued with each other in front of shop windows and on corners as others huddled or slept in doorways. She noticed a guy wearing two fedoras stacked on top of each other. Another fellow wore orange soccer socks, a sandal on one foot and a jogging shoe on the other. A couple of zombies walked right into the cycle path and everyone had to swerve around them.

"There's a party tonight at the Arts Club, if you want to come," Cactus said as they pedaled past Main Street and into the slipstream of West Hastings. "It's to raise awareness about our rivers being sold to the States."

"What do you mean? Who's selling our rivers?"

"Our government. They're selling licenses to American private hydro-electric companies so they can come up here and build power plants along our rivers. They bulldoze, cut down our trees, cut access to public roads and build generators that will transmit electricity to Americans and eventually – get this – to us."

"Really?"

"Yes. Of course."

"I've never heard of that."

Why does that not surprise me?"

"What do you mean by that?"

"You and thousands of other people. You gotta read if you wanna learn about this stuff, sister."

"But I *do* read."

"Like what?"

"Novels."

"Any good ones?"

"Sure. Best sellers."

"Oh gawd. Airport filler. You're not gonna learn what's going on in your own backyard by reading that stuff."

"I learn lots."

"Do you know about the Tar Sands?"

"A bit."

"Like what?"

"Well…come on. You're making me nervous."

"All right. You're a newbie, so I'll tell you straight up. They're a fucking nightmare."

"How so?"

"Almost every oil company in the world is there right now, in Fort McMurray, mining the hell out of the place, dredging bitumen from the Boreal Forest."

"Bitumen?"

"Yeah. Tar. Glue. It's like pitch in the sand. Dirty oil. Miles and miles of it; the size of Florida. Poisons from the extraction process get in the Athabasca River and mutate the fish. Native people around there are sick as hell. I'm not shitting you."

At Bute Street a driver got out of his car and approached the corkers.

"I'm gonna be late for the Canucks game, you fucking goofs!" he shouted. Hannah heard every word, loud and clear. "Do you know how much tickets cost? More than the cost of your shitty bikes!"

The few cyclists blocking his car simply shrugged. A few more pulled aside and joined them, to make a show of solidarity.

"Wow. Those guys are courageous," Hannah remarked. "I'd be too scared, I think, to stand my ground like that."

"Oh no. You could do it. Really," Cactus said. "You just stare the fuckers down." Then she chuckled. "Everyone's got your back. You're not gonna' get hurt."

"Why do you and Slim Jimmy, and Gertrude call yourselves The

Resistance?"

"Either you're part of the resistance, or you're an accomplice. It's that simple."

"An accomplice to what, though? I don't get it."

"To what I've just been talking about: the rape of our natural landscape."

"But how am I an accomplice to any of that?"

"'Cuz you do nothing about it."

"But I didn't even know it was happening!"

"Well now you do. Jesus Christ, girl. You've got to get informed, and stay informed. Did you vote in the last provincial election – and be honest?"

"Uh...no."

"Well why not?"

"I don't know. It just doesn't seem important."

"Hannah, that attitude is precisely what makes you an accomplice. If it doesn't matter to you what's happening around you – to those people back on Hastings Street, to our forests, or our rivers – then you're not off the hook when all these things are fucked for good."

As the pack passed Denman Street, en route to the Lion's Gate Bridge, a few drivers laid heavily on their horns – in anger, not in support. The difference was obvious to the cyclists. Happy honkers honked in quick bursts. Angry ones drew out the noise.

"This is where things get really testy," Cactus said. "We're gonna block off the northbound lane of the Lion's Gate Bridge. It's the only way to get to the ferry, so some people really lose it."

"Really?"

"Yeah, and to make matters worse, when we get to the top we take our sweet time coming back down. I love it. 'In your face, suckers!'"

When Hannah finally returned home, about an hour later, feeling confusingly weary and elated, Frank was watching the Canucks game.

"Hi," he said, getting up to give her a kiss. "How was the ride?"

She kissed him before saying, "It was really wild; really, really fun…and weird."

He had turned his head to the television set. Hannah's shoulders sunk.

"Oh sorry, honey," he said. "It was a power play dere, and I wanted to…"

"It's all right, hon," Hannah said. "I'm all sticky and sweaty. I'm going to take a shower."

"Okay," he said, staring at the television screen. "The game'll probably be over by then."

⌛⌛⌛

The next morning Frank finally took notice of the distinctively convex shape of Hannah's typically taut tummy. After all, four months had passed since I was conceived – a curious expression, as I wasn't really thought out at all – and now I had stretched

Hannah's well-honed mid-riff into a mixing-bowl sized bump.

"Sweet-art, you're getting a little rotund in the belly there – a little, what do you English call it? A pot belly?"

Frank was lying in bed, lazily watching his fiancée step through a leg hole in her panties. A narrow but generous ray of morning light cut between half-open shutters on two large bedroom windows. The beam warmed the shiny hardwood floor and revealed dust bunnies that had gathered mutely here and there. In the middle of the room Hannah was stooped over in profile, entirely naked but for the thin fabric between her hands. Her shiny black locks concealed her face.

When she stood up, with her sleek underwear now snug around her svelte hips, she crossed her arms below her breasts and faced her fiancé.

"I haven't smoked pot for a while now, in case you haven't noticed?" she replied diffidently.

"Oh ho." Frank reflexively pushed himself up and sat against the bed's headboard. His face flushed. "What's this? You've been hiding something from *me*?"

"Well, yes. I wasn't going to hold out forever. I couldn't anyway. But I am a little surprised that you didn't notice 'til now."

"Did not *notice*?"

"Yeah."

"You're pregnant?" Frank sat straight up.

Hannah curled her arms in, lowered her head and nodded.

"Jesus! Frank jumped out of the bed stark naked, went to his fiancée and put his arms awkwardly around her. She weakly resisted by crossing her forearms in front of her breasts, and she started to cry.

"Jesus Christ, Hannah. We're having a baby?"

She neither nodded nor shook her head, but tried to stifle her tears, so Frank stood back. Hannah averted his gaze.

"For Christ's sake Hannah, what's got into you?"

She faced the open window and trembled as a couple of rivulets flowed down her cheeks.

Frank plunked himself onto the edge of the bed and put his head in his hands. All was still for a moment, then Frank lifted his head and asked in a doubtful tone, "It's mine, right?"

Hannah took a deep breath, shrugged, wiped tears from her face with the back of her hand, and went to her dresser. She pulled a pretty,

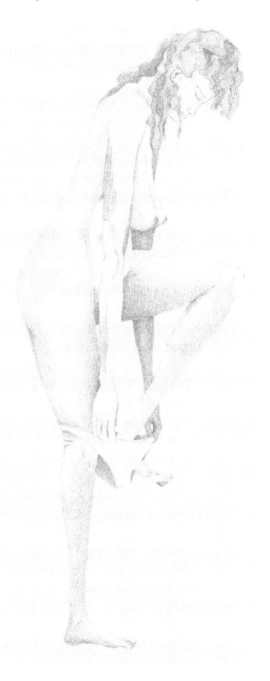

pink brassiere out of a drawer and looped it across her chest.

"Fuck, Hannah! Tell me who you've slept with!" Frank jumped up from the bed again and approached her with a raised hand. "Don't make me get like dis!"

"Really, Frank," she said, facing him with moist eyes, "I'm a little surprised by your sudden concern."

"My sudden concern! *Saint-crime!* You're my fuckin' fiancée. We are supposed to be getting married." He grimaced, clenched his fingers into a fist and breathed deeply.

"I don't know, Frank," she said, looking him straight in the eyes. "I don't know whose child it is."

"You do too!" he barked.

Hannah cowered slightly. "Don't yell at me, Frank. Please don't yell at me," she pleaded.

"Well you know what you better do, and don't think twice. *Tabarnak!*"

Frank stepped past Hannah to the dresser, pulled open a drawer, and grabbed a pair of briefs.

"I am going to have it," she informed him. "I want to have it. I was raised to believe…"

Frank was pulling on his underwear. "Oh fuck you. 'I was raised to blah blah blah.' So was I, fuck, but that Catholic bullshit didn't stop you from opening your legs for me without a wedding ring, did it?"

Hannah turned her back to Frank and sifted through clothes hanging in the closet.

"Did it?" he repeated louder.

"Don't talk to me about rings," she said.

"What do you mean by that?"

Hannah turned to face her fiancé. "I have never considered it my business where you got my engagement ring, but maybe now would be a good time to tell me."

Frank stood just a few feet away from her. His body was tense. Angry colour had filled his cheeks and he stammered slightly before saying, "So it's about the ring now."

"No. It's not about the ring, or where you got it, though some honesty about that would be appreciated." Hannah let a few seconds pass in thoughtful silence before saying, "You can do what you want, but I'm going to have this baby."

"Do what I want? Do what I *want?*" Frank returned to the edge of the bed and angrily put on his socks. "What the fuck does that mean? You've been cheating on me and you tell me, do what I want! Hannah, look at me!"

Hannah slipped a paisley-print cotton-knit dress over her head and shoulders, then pulled and plucked it into place in front of a vertical mirror.

"Oh nice. Real nice, Hannah. You're not being smart. This isn't right. If you're trying to punish me for something then fuck you. I don't deserve it." Frank stood up again.

"It could be yours," she said to the image of Frank in the glass's background.

"I fucking hope so, but that's not the point. For Christ's sake, you're a salope!" Frank put his hands to the side of his head and pressed his temples.

Hannah turned around and said, "I'll spare you the pain, Frank. I'm moving out."

"Jesus no. We're supposed to get married!" he shouted, grabbing her by the elbow. She looked at him, his face drawn and desperate, and jerked her arm from his grip. Then she stepped back and sat down on a chair in front of the window.

"I have to, Frank. You don't want the baby, but I do. You've told me you're not ready, and I know you're not. And you're not going to change. *We're* not going to change. You know it."

"Well what's wrong with us?" he rejoined. "What's so fuckin' bad?"

An impulsive, one-note chuckle pushed out of Hannah, like a burp, and she stared at Frank coldly.

"I could get used to having a kid," he said. His eyes had the expression of a dog watching a visitor eat something he cannot have.

Hannah sighed and dropped her shoulders. "I don't know about that," she said, "but I'm not going to wait around to find out." Then she stood up, looked at herself in the mirror, and pulled and twisted her hair up high. While holding it in place with her right hand, she inserted pins with her left.

"No Hannah! No no no," Frank pleaded. "This is a mistake. You'll fucking regret this. I'm gonna' take de test."

"What test?"

"Le paternité."

"Ah, of course, but you can wait till I've had the baby." She turned around to face him. "Our relationship is done," she said, "and I've lived with it long enough. I'm going now, Frank, really. I've made up my mind. And I've gotta get going now. I've got some apartments to look at."

"Well fuck you," he rejoined, shaking his head in disbelief. As she left the room he grabbed the small digital alarm clock from the bed table and hurled it against the wall. It broke into a few pieces. "You fucking salope, méchant," he moaned to himself, his head buried in his hands.

🚲 🚲 🚲

As Frank sat angrily on his bed in his tighty-whiteys and cotton socks, Hannah headed for the South Granville Street area, between 16th and 12th, to meet a few apartment managers. WASPS buzzed all around the boutique-lined neighbourhood, shopping for epicurean delicacies and boxed silverware, dining out or chuckling at a clever line from Stanley Theatre thespians.

After observing a few rental suites Hannah walked into Ouisi's, a slender bar/restaurant with a high, exposed ceiling and fans, big oils on the walls, of Louis Armstrong and other jazz greats honking their horns, and lots of wood around – trim, tables and bar cabinetry – to put one at ease. The aura was notionally New Orleans although Hannah was greeted by a young, blonde, frizzy-haired waitress in a tartan skirt. "Sit anywhere you like. I'll be right with you," she said with a home-grown Irish lilt.

Two men at the bar nodded at Hannah and smiled. She reciprocated the greeting and sat at a deuce a few feet away, just across from the bar. They returned to their discussion.

Americans, their accents told her. One was a wiry fellow in a worn blue and black button-up shirt. He was Charlie Menz. With his straw-like hair and bony shoulders he looked like a living, breathing scarecrow. The older fellow next to him, with his doughy wattle, graying silk hair and turtle-shell glasses, looked like an owl, maybe crossed with a rooster. He was Victor Pavlenko.

"What can I get fer you today, ma'am?" the waitress asked her.

"Just a cold beer to begin with. What do you recommend?"

"There's Bass on special. It's lowvly railly."

"Then I'll have that. Thank you."

Hannah perused the menu – Alligator sandwich, Jambalaya, et cetera – and while she did so Victor Pavlenko raised his left eyebrow and nodded ever so slightly in her direction. Charlie raised both eyebrows to acknowledge that he got the picture. He had noticed her, but sure, periscope up: a beautiful, possibly single woman, was on the horizon.

Hannah decided upon a spinach salad and carrot soup that were advertised on the Specials blackboard, then pulled a newspaper from the abandoned table next to her. "G<small>LOBAL</small> M<small>ARKETS</small> O<small>N</small> B<small>RINK OF</small> C<small>OLLAPSE</small>," the Business Section headline announced.

She pulled out the Art and Culture section's "Weekend Review" and half-heartedly began to read the reviews under "Hot Picks for Summer Reading", but her attention was disrupted when a female patron on the other side of the floor exclaimed, "Oh my God! You did not!"

A couple of other patrons turned their heads and the waitress, who had just put down Hannah's beer, could not stifle a grin.

"You are crazy, woman!" Louise Talbot declared to her sister, who stared back from across the table with a screwed up smile. Denise Dickerson clung to her Cran and soda. "You only live once," she said. "And besides, there's a lot of movie stars doing it too."

"Oh la la," Louise replied. "Do you know if you'll get to fly with any?"

"I have no idea." Denise shrugged. "I hope so. For 200 grand that would be a nice perk."

"Oh – my – God." Louise put her hand to her mouth when she said that. "What about the baby? She'll be born by then, right?" she asked.

"Of course, but don't worry, I don't even think it would be legal to be pregnant in outer space."

"Do you actually go into orbit?"

"No. No you don't. The flight is called sub-orbital because you go just below the perimeter of outer space, but I will get to see the curvature of the earth." Denise was referring to Sir Richard Branson's commercial space venture.

Suddenly Victor Pavlenko imitated the ominous, pounding sounds of Richard Strauss's *Also sprach Zarathustra* — the ones everyone associates with Stanley Kubrick's *2001: A Space Odyssey* – nicely out of earshot of Denise and her sister. Charlie strained to see the two women past the bar.

"I think the blond is going into space," Victor told him, just as Denise said, "Come on Lou. Join me. Pleeez."

"She's an astronaut?" Charlie asked.

"Not on *your* life. I'm – I'm content with inner space. I think," Louise told her sister.

"If she's an astronaut," Victor said in a lowered voice, "I'm a

Huguenot."

"A *what* not?"

"God. What would Don have thought?" Louise asked.

"A Huguenot."

Hannah missed the thrust of the space travel conversation, but her ears picked up at the name "Don."

"What's a Huguenot?" Charlie asked.

"He would have gone with me. I'm sure of it," Denise said.

"It's the kind of knot you find yourself in when you're both French and Protestant," Victor quipped.

"Oh, always so cheeky," the barmaid said to Charlie, winking and nodding toward Victor as she did.

"Well, I don't know," Louise challenged her sister after a pause, "but this is all so exciting! *You* can't wait to see outer space, or sub-orbit, or whatever it's called, and I can't wait for the arrival of my first niece."

Hannah caught herself staring at the affable trio at the bar, the two Americans and the barmaid, so she looked away, out the front window.

"Well, shall we?" Louise asked.

Denise checked her watch. "Yes. I want to step into Edward's before it closes."

The sisters slid out of their booth and walked toward the bar, but Denise froze upon seeing Hannah. The grapevine, a much more primitive but enduring form of telecommunication than the BlackBerry, the Smartphone or even the Android could ever hope to be, had informed Denise that Frank's fiancée – the very woman she now recognized from her husband's funeral – was the most likely object of Don's final affections and infidelity. Denise stopped her sister and nodded in Hannah's direction.

Oh shit, Hannah thought, instantly lowering her eyes to the newspaper in front of her, but within seconds she felt the presence of a body looming next to her table. She looked up and without warning was slapped hard across her left cheek.

"You horrible slut," Denise said, delivering the blow. Hannah recoiled into her seat, holding her left hand in front of her face. The few other patrons in the pub turned their heads. Charlie jumped off his stool and strode toward the women.

"Could you please bring us the bill?" Louise called out to the barmaid. She was shaking slightly and holding Denise back. The barmaid nodded and anxiously rang up the bill.

"Are you all right, miss?" Charlie asked Hannah after eyeing Denise and Louise scornfully.

Hannah nodded while keeping her hand over her cheek.

"Don't be alarmed," Louise said to Charlie. "She knows exactly what that's for."

"That's an assault," Charlie emphasized.

"C'mon, please," Louise said to Denise, tugging on her sleeve. "Let her be."

The waitress appeared with the bill and Louise handed her a credit card.

"Do you want me to call the police," Charlie asked Hannah, who calmly shook her head. She was staring at Denise's midriff, which was flabby but not obviously incubating a child, and yet Hannah certainly heard Louise refer to a niece. Tears trickled down her cheeks.

"Get the hell out of here before I throw you out on your ass," Charlie told the sisters, who were waiting for Louise's credit card.

Denise was gawking with watery eyes at Hannah.

Who's the horrible slut here? Hannah wondered silently. *You look pregnant too, so soon after your own husband was murdered.*

But then another, darker possibility occurred to Hannah: that Denise had become pregnant by Don shortly *before* he was killed. If that was so, and if Don's murder was in any way connected to her affair with him – a possibility Hannah took seriously – then Hannah was indirectly responsible for bringing a second bastard into the world.

Louise held Denise by the arm. "Don't worry yourself over this little piece of trash. She not worth it," she said to Charlie, then she pulled Denise away and the sisters left the premises.

The patrons stopped rubbernecking and returned their attention to their own plates.

"You sure you're okay?" Charlie asked.

"Yes. Thank you," Hannah assured him.

"That's an assault, ma'am. You can report it to the police."

"No. Thank you. It's between her and me." Hannah actually believed she deserved the slap. Retribution was bound to come in some form or another. The man she had betrayed had come close to striking her that very morning. He had done it before, but apparently it took a woman to deliver the blow this time.

Charlie stared intently at her, desirous to know the cause of the violent scene.

"Would you still like your meal, love?" the waitress asked upon appearing at Hannah's table with a soup and salad.

"If it's okay with you, I'd rather not."

"Of course it is. I feel awful for you, ma'am. Wendy says you can have the beer on the house. We'd like you to come back."

The waitress left Hannah alone with Charlie.

"Thank you," she said to him again.

"Absolutely not. I have no idea what you did to get walloped like that, ma'am – and it ain't any of my business, so I'm not prying – but I didn't hear any argument, and I just can't see how a fine woman like yourself could possibly deserve that."

Hannah looked him sincerely in the eyes but was reluctant to reveal her situation to a stranger, even such a kind one as he appeared to be.

"Well, my name is Charlie Menz," Charlie said, extending his hand. Hannah shook it. "And if you are okay for now, I'm going to get back to my friend Victor there. We're regulars here, so you know where to find us if you ever need a couple of American avengers."

Charlie shook his head and smiled at Hannah before turning toward the bar. Hannah took one last, big swallow of beer, then picked up her coat and purse and returned to the street.

They found him, finally; or Leonard Jordan did, to be precise, on a Saturday evening, but it was the busker who gave him away.

A skilled, bearded banjo player in a Hawaiian shirt, sunglasses and crumpled straw cowboy hat had drawn a semi-circular crowd of about a dozen people in front of the Waterfront Skytrain station. Ryan Ghostkeeper was squatted just a couple metres away, trying to sell his carvings.

The Yaletown bartender stopped to hear the music en route to the Sea Bus and his meandering eyes suddenly noticed the carver. Mr. Jordan was not entirely sure it was him, but he dialed 911 anyway, stepped away from the group, and explained himself to the dispatcher.

The crowd was now singing along to a tune they obviously liked and knew.

*...Down the track came a hobo hiking
And he said, "Boys I'm not turning...*

"Yeah, I'll be right here," Jordan said.

*Where the handouts grow on bushes,
and you sleep out every night...*

Two cruisers pulled up in tandem. The officers from one car got out and approached Ryan, who dutifully stood up. He believed that his probation breaches had finally caught up with him.

All the cops have wooden legs....

A light burst of laughter came from the busker's audience but abruptly stopped when one officer shouted, "Drop the knife and whatever else you're holding. Put your hands in the air."

Ryan let his carving knife fall to the ground. "It's just..." He wanted to say "a carving," what he held in his left hand, but the officer pulled out a Taser and shouted, "drop it!"

The busker was being seriously upstaged but in his experience public arrests of panhandlers and other riff-raff in the Gastown area were not uncommon – titillating to some, perhaps – so he carried on.

*There's a lake of stew
and of whiskey too*

The gawkers, including Leonard Jordan, watched Ryan's carving splinter as it hit the sidewalk.

"Now turn around and put your hands against the wall. Spread your legs out."

The jails are made of tin...

The two officers advanced until they were immediately behind their suspect.

"What's your name, sir?" the taller and bulkier of the two officers asked him. His name was Balwinder Rarru.

No axes, saws or picks...

"Knock it off, sir. Police business!" Rarru's partner barked at the busker.

"Ryan."

"Ryan *what*?" Rarru asked.

"Ghostkeeper."

"Do you have any i.d., sir?"

"A status card, in my back pocket."

Constable Rarru's partner removed that as Leonard Jordan approached. "I'm the one who called you," the bartender said.

Rarru's partner returned to his cruiser to run a computer check as two others approached the scene. One stopped to talk with the witness Jordan. After a minute that officer approached Ryan. Jordan was in tow.

"You may turn around, sir," the officer told Ryan.

Ryan faced the policeman, and Jordan looked up and down at him.

"To be honest, I can't be completely certain, but I'm almost a 100% sure that's him."

Rarru's partner returned from his cruiser and shrugged. "He's on probation, some priors, but nothing outstanding," he told Rarru. Nodding at Jordan, he added, "This fellow says he's 99% sure it's the guy."

Rarru frowned, then said, "Mr. Ghostkeeper, give me your hands."

Ryan offered his hands to the police bracelets.

"You are under arrest for the charge of first degree murder." A few bystanders gasped. "I am going to take you to the police station now," Rarru continued, "to process you, but you must know right now that you have the right to obtain legal advice and the right to remain silent from this moment forward. You do not have to say anything to me or my partner here, or to any other police officer, but anything you do say can be used in evidence against you. Do you understand?"

"I am being charged for first degree murder?" Ryan asked, putting an emphasis on the word "murder."

"That's right, sir. It's a very serious offence, as I'm sure you can appreciate, and I just said, you have a right to obtain legal advice and to remain silent, but if you do say anything, that can be used as evidence against you. Do you understand?"

"Of who?" Ryan asked.

"Sir. I won't answer that question here. It is better for you to refrain from speaking at this point."

Rarru's partner nodded at Rarru to take the prisoner to the car.

"What about my..."

"I'll retrieve your belongings, sir," one of the other officers said. "We'll bring them to the station."

"Fuck. That guy just got charged with first degree murder," one of the bystanders told his friend.

卌 卌 卌

At least Charlie Menz had something to celebrate. Not the arrest and detention of Ryan Ghostkeeper for the murder of the Condo King, but the fact that the Red Wings had just ousted the Penguins for their eleventh Stanley Cup. Some feat, if you ask me: besting penguins on ice.

And with the hockey season now over, finally, Vancouverites happily sank their entertainment dollars into another favourite pastime – real estate tiddlywinks. Grown men and women across the Lower Mainland returned to the exhilaration of flipping properties, one after the other – pop pop pop, goes the weasel – just like that. And the market responded joyfully. It floated higher and higher into the clouds like ten thousand helium-balloons unleashed from a child's feckless grip, but it had to pop sometime. It just had to, and imagine the sound; the sound of 10,000 balloons bursting in unison. BOOM!

Ryan Ghostkeeper didn't have to concern himself with such a frightening prospect. Though he vigorously denied having anything to do with Big Dick's murder, the Crown prosecutor believed that the circumstantial evidence strongly incriminated him, as did the judge at the bail hearing. He was therefore remanded into the grey bar hotel and could now expect to live rent free, courtesy of the State, for several months to come. Some might consider him rather lucky. After all, his new Surrey Pre-

Trial Centre quarters had 100 square feet of floor space, painted concrete floors, and a 6-inch by 12-inch plexiglass window on the front door. And he got free board – three squares a day. Not bad, really, when you consider that young couples "wanting to enter the market" were paying at least $350,000 for just a little more leg room and a back-alley view of Chinatown, if that was their district of choice – meals *not* included.

Ryan had also sobered up by now. His older sister, Irene Samuels, had sent him a couple of letters from Prince George. "I know you are innocent and I pray for you every day," one of them said just above her signature. That gave him hope. An Aboriginal elder visited him weekly. His soft-spoken, curly-haired and bespectacled lawyer, a middle-aged man named Curtis Rice, visited him less often.

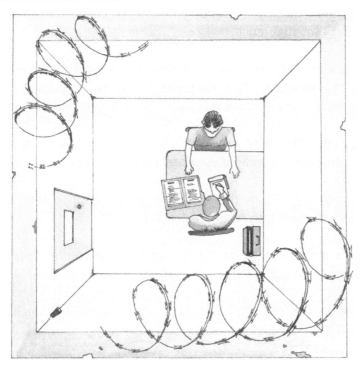

"Here you go," Mr. Rice said at the outset of a visit in late June. He handed Ryan a couple of graphic novels.

"Oh, thank you so much, sir. I really appreciate these."

A small table separated the men. Their chairs were bolted to the floor.

"Are they good enough?"

"They look great."

"Well, good then. You've got to keep your mind healthy while you're here," Rice said.

"I try. These will help. They will definitely help."

"Your sister told me that you are a pretty fine artist; a carver. I don't know much about aboriginal art, but it's beautiful when I see it. I'll say that much.

"My uncle Donny. He taught me a few things. So did Wendell, my cousin," Ryan said. "He's real good. I think he's in Quesnel now, or Williams Lake. I'm not too sure. He's got a girlfriend there."

"Well I thought we should meet again, to go over some of what you can expect to hear at your preliminary inquiry."

"My sister's gonna be there, with some of my supporters, from home. She said they're gonna protest."

"That's good, as long as she behaves in the courtroom. The sheriffs won't stand for any disruptions inside."

"I told her that too. It's bad enough as is. I don't want the judge turnin' 'gainst me, you know?"

"He won't. Don't worry."

"Did you find out about that guy?"

"The Bridges guy? Slim Jimmy or whatever?"

Ryan nodded.

"Yeah. A little bit."

Ryan's eyes widened, and he sat forward.

"Apparently he belongs to some kind of political group. Radicals from the East End. A bunch of angry kids, I think. Twenty year olds or something. Really intense about the environment, that kind of thing. They call themselves The Resistance and they hated Don Dickerson. They're against all the condos going up in Vancouver. They'd rather have gardens." Mr. Rice raised an eyebrow.

"Does he have an alibi?"

"Actually, not really. Not an airtight one, in any case."

"But they're lookin in to it?"

Mr. Rice shrugged. "I expect so. I'll follow it up."

"And what about those phone calls that lady made?"

"Denise?"

"Yeah. The ones to that guy, before the murder."

"And after," Curtis added.

"Yeah. What have they found out?"

Curtis sighed, then shook his head. Ryan sat back in his chair.

"Nothing, really," Curtis said. "They've both been interviewed.

She said she called Kimbel to let him know Don was real dirty for wanting to divorce her, and his statement paired-up with hers. I've read it. So what more can they do? Wiretap em?"

Ryan's eyes opened wider. They were thirsty for more.

"Sure, the circumstances are suspicious," Curtis conceded. "I told you the guy was up for influence peddling charges a few years ago, but those got stayed and I don't know why. He's not the most credible son-of-a-bitch around, I'll say that much, but really, Ryan, unless the police have some good reason to believe that George Kimbel and Denise actually plotted Don's murder over the phone, as opposed to just bitch about the guy, well, then, we've got nothing to work with."

"So what do you think? What are my chances?"

Mr. Rice hesitated before saying, "To be honest, I still think they're pretty good. I'll make sure the police give me everything they have on this Slim Jimmy guy. Maybe I can get some money for a private investigator, but I highly doubt it. We'll probably have to wait until the trial. Just bring the whole issue up in front of the jury. Hope it causes them to have some serious doubts. Remember, Ryan, that's all we need here. Reasonable doubt."

Ryan shifted in his seat.

"Stay optimistic in here," Mr. Rice encouraged. "There's lots to work with, even without this Resistance stuff. There's the motorbike tracks, the theatre tickets. It looks like a classic crime of passion, if you ask me."

"But the police think *I* did it just because I got fired."

"And because you had the knife – no small detail," Mr. Rice added.

Ryan shook his head vigorously before saying, "But I didn't do it. I didn't do it. I swear to the Creator, to the Being on High, I did not do it. I was just fuckin' drinkin' too much."

"Well I know I've asked you this before, Ryan – and you know I don't doubt you for a moment – but..."

"I didn't black out. I did not black out. I fell asleep in the park, earlier. After that I was fine."

Mr. Rice had no reply so Ryan sighed deeply, then asked, "What about those motorbike treads? Anything new?"

"Well, maybe. There is a guy in that Resistance group, an associate of Slim Jimmy's. He rides a bike, so I've learned."

"A motorbike?"

Mr. Rice nodded.

"So it could be him."

"It could be," Rice affirmed, "but the police believe you did it. They think you're a liar, plain and simple. They think *you* were accompanied to the garage by a getaway driver, on a motorbike, and you've got a motive, as far as they're concerned."

Ryan chuckled, even though there was nothing funny about his predicament, at least as far as he was concerned. It was dire and he suffered with the weight of it every day he spent stuck in his ten-by-ten condo. But for him the image of an associate and himself pulling into Don Dickerson's garage on a motorbike to commit cold-blooded murder had a cartoon-like quality, so he impulsively laughed at it, just like he did as a kid whenever Foghorn J. Leghorn belittled Henery Hawk for thinking he was a chickenhawk. As a child he watched that cartoon on Saturday mornings. He liked it a lot.

An old birch tree stood like a knobby, arthritic sentinel outside the living room window of Hannah's new south-facing abode: a small two bedroom suite on the third floor of an early 20th century heritage building. Six hundred square feet located just west of Granville Street, on 14th Avenue. "Heritage" took the form of a parquet living room floor and such features as cast iron radiators, skeleton key holes in brass doorknob plates, and a porcelain-plated, single-tub kitchen sink.

Hannah could not explain it if she tried, but she had impulsively taken Ryan Ghostkeeper's carving off Frank's bathroom wall and put it in "my" room, meaning the room that would be mine when I graduated from the "womb," which is just baby talk for my very first room.

Hannah had never been a loner but she was suddenly feeling a little plaintive and anxious about everything – about me, Don and Frank, her job, the move – so she reached out to Cactus Delaine for a friendly ear, and a low-key house warming.

"Sounds pretty serious, woman. Are you all right?"

The two friends were talking by cellphone.

"Yeah. I'm fine. Thank you," Hannah said. "But I do want to get some shit off my chest."

"Well I've got some bad news," Cactus informed her. "My grandma passed."

"Oh sweetheart. I'm so sorry."

"It's okay. It's actually okay. I told you before, I wanted her suffering to end."

"But still."

"I know, I know, but I'm not gonna get all mournful. I'm gonna do what gran would want, like go on this month's ride, the biggest of the year. Gran would want no less than to see me puttin' power to the pedal! There'll be thousands this time. No shit. Maybe, five, six, seven thousand of us."

"Oh my god. That sounds fun, but do you promise? I could talk to you afterward, with a bottle of wine later, at my new place?"

"Okay, sure, but I might not stay too long. Is that all right?"

"Of course."

"I've got more to tell you anyway," Cactus said. "I'll save it for the ride. Look for me at the art gallery, just like before. I'll be wearing a new pink tank top. I got it for four bucks on Main."

Hannah chuckled. "Okay."

The women found each other near the LED clock that was counting down the days, hours, minutes and seconds remaining to the 2010 Olympic Games. Charlie Menz grinned when he walked his bike past it. It made him think of the larger than life sign on the Edsel Ford Freeway, the one that looked like an odometer, except that it counted the number of cars being produced in Detroit, minute by minute.

Whoa. There's that guy again, Charlie thought when he saw James Bridges talking to Hurdy Gurdy, who laughed at something he said. After watching them for a minute Charlie surmised, *She seems nice enough. Maybe they're an item.*

The ride itself went without a hitch. Hannah found it as equally exhilarating and calming as the first time she did it, though her heart raced a little when she and Cactus acted as corkers at

Broadway and Commercial Street. Surprisingly, the drivers didn't get angry at them for blocking traffic there, but rather whistled at the unusually pleasant scenery. When Charlie passed by that same spot he rubbernecked, as he was sure he recognized Hannah from Ouisi. He almost swerved into a couple of cyclists.

Just slow down, move right out of the way, and wait till she gets back into the flow. Or go over there right now and say 'hi'. He watched her from a standstill as she stood there, her bicycle frame between her legs, chatting with Cactus, a woman he did not recognize.

C'mon. Don't be chicken. She'll be nice…

He put his right foot on the pedal and pressed, and like a fish that has just been released into the river after being beached, measured and photographed, he meandered confusedly toward Hannah. Only a few metres away, however, he lost his nerve and returned full speed into the thick of the school. *I shouldn't interrupt her conversation,* he rationalized. In point of fact, however, he chickened out and never did create another opportunity to say Hello during the ride.

By sunset the two women had cut out from the pack, cycled to a liquor store, and peddled south on Granville Street to Hannah's apartment.

"So, what's up. I'm all ears," Cactus said after Hannah had poured them each a glass of red wine. Cactus was perched on a love seat with broad, comfortable arms. Hannah was poised on a fat armchair, at an obtuse angle from her guest.

"Well, it's a couple of things. I'm really nervous about telling you, okay? Can you swear to secrecy?"

"Uh…okay. I'll be your priest." Cactus smiled.

Hannah took in a deep breath from her belly. "You know that Dickerson guy who got murdered, the guy you hated?"

"Sure."

Hannah exhaled from her stomach, as her yoga classes had taught her to do.

"Well...please, please don't judge me – don't judge me here, but I, I had sex with him."

Cactus looked at her friend with the eyes of an owl.

"I know you're probably disgusted with me and I understand. I've never wanted you to know."

Cactus said nothing.

"I was drunk," Hannah pointed out, "and feeling a little high about myself, I guess. You might find it hard to believe, but Don made me feel beautiful – *really* beautiful, and special, like I deserved to be treated like a lady. Frank never did that."

Cactus sipped her wine. *Please say something,* Hannah internally pleaded, but she said, "Please don't get the wrong impression. I could do without Don's money, seriously, but he lavished *attention* on me. I was tired of competing with Frank's motorbike, or a hockey game. I was tired of making dinner for him. I think I fell for being treated like a princess – again."

Hannah slumped. "I don't know why, and I don't really care why at the moment, because the whole thing has ended disastrously," she added.

"But that wasn't your fault," Cactus said, referring to Don's murder.

"Uh, no...It wasn't. But I haven't even told you everything yet."

Cactus looked intently at Hannah as her friend tilted her glass.

"We didn't use protection," the hostess revealed.

"Oh – shit."

Hannah softly shook her head and straightened her lips.

"So what, then? He gave you a v – ?"

Hannah shook her head again, but demonstrably so this time.

"Oh my god, you're – "

Hannah nodded. "Three months already."

Cactus reached out and clasped her friend's hand.

"Does Frank know?"

"Yes." Hannah looked into her lap. "That's pretty much why I'm living *here*. He knows, but he doesn't know who the father is."

"Jesus Murphy," Cactus exclaimed. "You *are* in some kind of shit stew, sister." She let go of Hannah's hand and sat back.

"Tell me about it."

"What are you gonna do?"

Hannah shrugged and said, "I don't know. Take one day at a time. Do yoga, breathe deeply, try to stay calm, take one day at a time."

"And pass the wine," Cactus added.

Hannah smiled, and refilled her guest's glass.

"You know what I was telling you about my grandma, right?" Cactus said.

Hannah folded her legs up to her stomach. "Yes, and I'm very sorry. Don't feel like you have to stay here, if you don't want, but you're welcome to stay as long as you need if you want some company."

"I'm all right. Really," Cactus said. "What I wanted to tell you is I've come into an inheritance…"

Cactus took a sip from her drink before saying, "My gran was pretty wealthy. She came from this family of strong women, really strong women, big in politics. Her own gran fought alongside the famous five, for women's representation in the senate. Do you know about them?"

Hannah shook her head.

"My goodness, girl, did you ever go to school?"

"I was never taught that," Hannah said, bringing her feet under her buttocks in her chair.

"And you grew up on a farm, right?" Cactus asked.

Hannah nodded, not sure of how that was relevant.

"Well Katy, my gran, was a bastard child. Her dad fucked off somewhere and her mom married for money. She told me I saw great gran a few times when I young, three or something, but I don't really remember. Anyway, she got the family home – gran, that is, but when she got really sick she wasn't just gonna hand it over to mom or my uncle Lyle. My mom's mixed up, as you know, and gran never trusted Lyle. Rightfully so if you ask me. He's always in debt, even though he makes lots of dough selling insurance. Ha! Gran wouldn't even buy her life insurance from her own son. He either spends too much, or makes bad investments, or gambles, or whatever, and his wife spends money like she's Joan Rivers, without the lifts."

Both Cactus and Hannah smiled.

"They might fight me, for the home," Cactus continued, "but too bad, it's right there in black ink I've been told. Grandma wanted me to have it because she liked my backbone, that's what mom once told me – and she trusts that I won't sell it away to get rich."

"Is your mom getting anything?"

"She'll be fine. The estate is sizable, there's insurance, and whatever else."

Hannah sat forward. "So are you just going to move in? Is it that simple?"

"I guess, but it's going to be really weird, and I'm not too sure if I could stomach it. I couldn't fill a single room with the things I own."

"Will the place stay furnished?"

Cactus shrugged. "Probably. I don't know what's gonna happen with all the stuff. But who's kidding who? I don't belong in Shaughnessy. I can't picture myself there. It's the richest of the rich – snob central. All I know is the Drive."

"I imagine you would have a hefty property tax, wouldn't you?"

"Oh yeah. There's that, but I'm assuming it's covered by the will or whatever."

"What do you think you'll do?"

"I haven't really had time to think about it, but an idea *has* crossed my mind, and it's pretty wild. Literally, it's pretty wild." Cactus's eyes were abuzz.

Hannah sat straight. "Like what?"

"Like bringing a little of Commercial Street to my new backyard."

Hannah thought for a few seconds as Cactus stared at her with a devious grin.

"I really don't know yet," Cactus intervened. "But it's a big space, a lot of green, a lot of room. Far too much for just one person to enjoy."

Hannah's eyes showed surprise.

"Let's just say there'll be a special meeting of The Resistance convening soon. You're welcome to come if you like."

3rd Quarter 2008

"Condo King Murderer in Court Tomorrow" ran *The Province*'s headline. "Condo Giant Preliminary Inquiry Begins" ran the *Vancouver Sun*'s. It was the first week of August, and ears were burning with curiosity.

"The justice system is racist." "Free Ryan Ghostkeeper." Ryan's sister, Irene, and a half-dozen or so First Nations sympathizers held such sentiments on placards outside of "222," the Provincial Court on Main Street. The number referred to the address, not the headache tablet, though I'm sure the lawyers, cops and judges inside kept a ready supply of the latter to get them through the day.

The small courtroom was packed like Coho in the Lower Fraser this time of year and necks were stretched eagerly, like herons' at low tide. Just what would the Aboriginal man who had been charged with stabbing Donald Dickerson look like in person? His mug shot had already been widely circulated by the press but citizens wanted to see the real McCoy.

Denise got to observe the action from the front row of the public gallery, in reserved seating. Next to her a Victims Services worker sat with a ready supply of tissue, in case the widow needed to sponge up tears.

When Denise first laid eyes on Ryan, as he entered into a box from a door on the side of the courtroom, a slight shiver ran up her spine. The young man was tall and handsome, with short and neatly combed blue-black hair. He wore a chocolate brown, button down shirt over red cotton, prison-issue pants. Like an experienced theatre actor, his eyes looked into the gallery without appearing to focus on any particular individual.

A Crown prosecutor with male-pattern baldness introduced himself as Lewis Chaulk and Curtis

Rice introduced himself "as counsel on behalf of the accused, Mr. Ghostkeeper."

Chaulk asked for an order excluding witnesses, but with Rice's consent, Denise Dickerson was allowed to stay. Both parties expected her to be a minor witness at the trial.

After giving the judge a quick summary of the Crown's case, Chaulk called some of the police officers and paramedics who attended the scene, and then moved onto the coroner. The professionals did not take long to confirm that Don Dickerson was found lying dead in a small pool of his own blood, in the parking garage of Yaletown condominium, having been stabbed three times in the chest. Cause of death: loss of blood. Two of the stab wounds penetrated Dee Dee's heart. One penetrated with great force the paper grocery bag he was carrying, ripping right through its contents and causing Don to drop it, so the pathologist opined.

A couple of tins of caviar avoided calamity, as did a small Camembert wheel, but a box of rosemary and thyme wheat crackers was split open, and a 300 millilitre container of pitted black olives spilled onto the floor. An upright stock of celery went unscathed, though a 1.25 litre bottle of organic guava juice smashed on impact with the cement foundation.

In cross-examination Rice asked the blood-spatter expert about the trail of blood that led from the garage into the alley.

"It took the form of a motorcycle tread, did it not?" he asked.

"It appears that way, sir."

"And that tread was discernible for about 8 metres into the alley, was it not?"

"That's my recollection, sir."

A police officer told the judge and the gallery that Mr. Dickerson had two tickets in his pocket for an 8:30 pm concert that evening.

The civilian witnesses followed the professionals. Mrs. Lepont, the postal worker who first discovered the corpse, described the shocking scene in vivid terms, shaking as she did, both from the recollection of the horrible death and from the stress of being in a witness box. After her Leonard Jordan provided his recollections. He was tending bar at the Yaletown Brew Pub, just a couple of blocks down the street from where Donald Dickerson was murdered.

"That's when I told him to leave," Jordan told the judge.

"And remind me: what time was that, again?" Rice asked.

"About ten minutes to nine."

"And you know that because you exchange floats at 9 o'clock, and it was just moments before that?"

"That's right."

"And why did you tell Mr. Ghostkeeper to leave?"

"Nobody tries to sell stolen property on my premises, sir."

"Stolen?" Ryan's lawyer paused before adding, "Why do you say that?"

The bartender shrugged.

"Well, was it stolen?"

The Crown stood up to object, so Rice sat down.

"Your Honour, how can the witness possibly answer that question?"

"I don't think that Mr. Rice actually – actually, forget that. I'll hear from Mr. Jordan," the judge said.

Chaulk sat back down and Rice stood up.

"Why did you think the knife was stolen?" he asked the witness again.

"I *don't* know, but why would someone come into a bar and try to sell a knife that he owned?" Jordan reasoned.

"Why not?" Rice asked. "Not everyone has the same cash flow that you likely have at the end of the night."

Chaulk got ready to object again, so Rice said, "Let's face it, Mr. Jordan, you assumed that Mr. Ghostkeeper had stolen the knife because in your mind he looked like the kind of guy who would steal a knife, didn't he?"

Jordan shrugged again before saying, "Yeah, I guess you could say that."

"Because in your mind, he's an Indian – right?"

Jordan paused, sat back and said, "I'll admit. It crossed my – "

Chaulk stood up again and said, "Your Honour…"

The judge interrupted him and asked, "Mr. Rice, where is this going?"

"I took a guess and I was right," Ryan's lawyer replied. "How quickly First Nations people are stereotyped in this society will be an important consideration when it comes to selecting the jury."

"You can worry about your jury later, but all this circumstantial evidence we've received so far, it's inconsequential? Is that what you want me to believe?" the judge probed.

Rice sighed. "I guess, yes, that is what I'm saying, your Honour."

"Let's leave stereotypes out of the present inquiry and move on to more material matters, please, Mr. Rice."

Another bartender testified after Jordan. Terrell Sims was working at The Yale the evening Big Dick was killed. How could he forget? Charlie Musselwhite was in the house, older than sand but blowing harp like no one's business.

"That's him. There. He was the man in the hard hat," he said, pointing to Ryan.

"Now tell us what he was doing," Chaulk said.

"He was just standing around the pool table, drinking beer."

Ryan had already told Sergeant Woolly that he went to The Yale after getting kicked out of the other bar, the one in Yaletown. "It was another place to shoot pool," he had told her. Both lawyers knew this.

"Anything unusual or out of the ordinary about his…"

Rice quickly stood up to object. "Your Honour, I'd ask my friend not to lead," he said. The judge nodded and Rice sat down.

"Mr. Sims, please tell his Honour what you saw," the Crown continued.

"Like I said, he bought a beer from me and I noticed that he was waitin' for his turn at the table."

"Did you ever see him play?"

"No I did not. It just looked like he got frustrated, impatient-like."

"Why do you say that?"

"He got kind of belligerent at some guy. I saw it. He either saw something..."

"Which guy? The accused or the other guy?" the Crown asked.

"The other guy – the white dude – he reacted to something, pretty strongly, and came straight toward me."

"Yes."

"And that guy there..." – Sims pointed to Ghostkeeper again – "he just bolted. I saw the back of him, his helmet, leaving the premises."

"And then what happened?"

"The white dude told me that that guy said he had a knife." Sims had pointed to Ghostkeeper yet again.

"Are we actually going to see the knife?" the judge asked.

"No, your Honour," Chaulk acknowledged. Then he asked Sims to continue.

"I asked the white guy if he saw the knife and he said No. I then asked him what the beef was about. He said he got accused of jumping the queue by that guy," again pointing to Ghostkeeper. "I said, 'So you're funny too...'"

"That's fine, Mr. Sims," Chaulk interjected, but Rice stood up and said, "No, Your Honour. I'd like to hear this."

Chaulk rolled his eyes, then stood up and said to his witness, "All right, Mr. Sims, explain yourself."

"Well, I just didn't like the guy, the white guy. I thought that fellow there" – Sims nodded at Ryan – "probably put his quarters down, y'know, and was waitin' his turn for a stick, and then this white guy and his friends butted in. The white guy was uppity, so when he told me something about jumpin the queue I just made a joke, y'know what I mean? They were playin' pool. It was a pun, that's all."

A paused ensued while smiles appeared on a few faces in the public gallery. Even Rice smiled tightly.

Constable Rarru testified about arresting Ghostkeeper and searching his suite at the Portland Hotel. He had found cutlery but no knife matching the description provided by Jordan.

Even so, a DNA specialist subsequently testified that Ghostkeeper had traces of blood on the cuff of his jean jacket, the very jacket he was wearing when he was arrested. Her opinion was that the DNA profile of that blood matched the victim's own blood – that there was a one in a seven billion chance that the blood on Ghostkeeper's jacket was from a source other than Don Dickerson.

Chaulk did not call Sergeant Woolly to testify about the statement Ghostkeeper gave her following his arrest. Ryan had denied having any involvement in Dickerson's murder so Chaulk viewed his statement as "self-serving" and therefore inadmissible. Chaulk figured that if Rice really wanted the judge to hear Ghostkeeper's bullshit to Wolychenski at this stage of the proceedings, then Rice could call Ghostkeeper to the stand. Not likely, he knew.

Indeed, the accused man desired strongly to testify but Rice advised him that there was no point in doing so – to save his testimony for the trial, when it mattered. Rice advised him, "If you had an alibi, then sure, I'd say tell your story at this point, but you don't, so save your explanation for trial."

In his final submissions to the judge Chaulk stressed the cumulative, incriminating effect of the circumstantial evidence against the accused man, as well as evidence of a vengeful motive. Chaulk said, "Mr. Ghostkeeper decided that he would take revenge on the very man who owned the company from which he was fired that morning. He had become a drug addict. He was now destitute and desperate, and he decided to get even."

Rice emphasized the countervailing details.

"Mr. Ghostkeeper simply could not have created those tracks," he urged, referring to the bloody motorbike tread patterns leaving the scene.

"They were plainly left by the killer, who acted alone," he contended desperately. "And whoever that was, it was not this accused." Rice pointed to his client. "There is no evidence that Mr. Ghostkeeper was going from bar to bar that night on a motorbike. He would have had to wear a proper helmet, for starters. And a licence, et cetera et cetera. It's obvious the investigation into this matter has been far from diligent," he continued. "It's been guided by tunnel vision, pure and simple. There is no smoking gun here. My friend can't even produce the murder weapon. The prosecution and police have turned a blind eye to alternate suspects. We mustn't forget, Mr. Dickerson was found with two concert tickets in his pockets and his wife was in Toronto at the time."

The judge interrupted to ask, "Are you suggesting, Mr. Rice, that this was a crime of passion?"

"That's exactly right," the lawyer replied, causing the judge to make a peevish face.

"Either moral passion, or political passion. It was planned, plotted out," Mr. Rice continued. "With the greatest of respect to the deceased, he had his detractors. Mr. Ghostkeeper was inebriated at the time. It just doesn't make sense that in such a state, apparently without any motive, he would manage to get a motorbike under the security gate and stab Mr. Dickerson without taking his money, or credit cards, or anything like that, and get back out again undetected."

When Rice finished his submissions the judge sat back in his chair, looked to the ceiling for a couple of silent minutes, then returned his gaze to the accused man and said,

"I will confess, Mr. Ghostkeeper, that all this evidence leaves me a little confused as to precisely what happened in that parking garage, but unfortunately for you I am entitled to be a little perplexed and to commit you to stand trial at the same time. The Crown does not have to convince me of your guilt beyond a reasonable doubt. Far from it.

"Now, you may or may not be familiar with the Bard, but there's a line from Macbeth, Act II, Scene II, if my memory serves me correctly, in which the newly anointed Thane of Cawdor – the one who had just stabbed the sleeping King Duncan to death, wonders aloud if an entire ocean could clean the blood from his hands. It is something like, 'Will all Neptune's ocean wash this blood from etcetera etcetera.' It doesn't really matter. I am not presuming that you killed Mr. Dickerson, Mr. Ghostkeeper – you are presumed innocent – but the evidence of his blood on your cuffs speaks as loudly to me as your involvement in his death as it surely did to the ignoble Macbeth, and it is on that basis that I feel compelled to commit you to stand trial."

♪ ♪ ♪

I've heard say that God is in the details, possibly even in the Bard's quill, but it was precisely those details that left the conscientious Sergeant Woolly doubtful.

"Fuckin 'eh," Constable Sorenson said to her upon hearing the news that Ryan Ghostkeeper had been committed to stand trial. The duo was in their cruiser, driving along West Broadway.

"Watch your language," Woolly said. She was behind the wheel.

"Do the crime, do the time," Sorenson added.

"I don't know," Sergeant Woolly said. "I'm having second thoughts."

"What?" Sorenson turned in his seat and looked directly at his partner.

"Don't you find those tire tracks at least a bit troubling?" she asked, watching the road.

"Not really." Sorenson shrugged. "He had the guy's goddamn blood on his coat. If you ask me, he had a get-away partner who bailed on him. End of story."

"But it doesn't make sense. If Ryan did it for revenge, why would anyone else want to get involved? No money was stolen. No credit cards."

Sorenson looked out his window as the cruiser passed the corner of Granville Street and Broadway, site of the old Aristocrat restaurant.

"And those tickets," Woolly pressed. "Maybe he was having an affair and his wife knew it."

"Oh come on." Sorenson looked at Woolly with a chafed expression. "Now you're speculating, pure and simple."

"I don't agree. Have you looked into every one of their bank accounts?"

"Oh gawd." Sorenson turned to his senior with consternation in his eyes. "You mean Don and Denise's, right?"

Woolly nodded.

"Yes, I believe we have, and with a fine tooth comb, but if you insist, I'll put someone back on it."

"Do that," Woolly ordered, without taking her eyes of the road. "And I think we should looker harder into those tread marks," she added.

"But he's already been…"

"I don't care," Woolly interrupted. "I'm not 100% sure Ryan's our man, and you know we'll get raked over the coals at trial if this part of the investigation is not thorough – if we don't eliminate possible suspects. Rice is no slouch. I can hear him now. Standing in front of the jury and accusing us of negligence."

"Tunnel vision. The defence of the desperate," Sorenson said in a sarcastic tone.

"It's all because of that public inquiry," Woolly noted.

"But come on," Sorenson pleaded. "Do you really believe this guy? That he just stumbled across the knife – just by accident, about five minutes after Don was killed – and then sold it for a few lines of coke?"

"Why not?" Woolly glanced at Sorenson. "Why not? He's consistent about that much. He recalls that much. I trust him more than Bridges, with his cheap story about the movies." She returned both eyes to the road.

"You heard from the employees. They've seen him there," Sorenson reminded her.

"No. Not quite. He's a regular, they said. They couldn't place him for that night." After a pause Woolly said, "And talk about having a motive. That kid wears his hatred like a badge of honour. And his friend Derek has a motorbike."

"But Derek was with his girlfriend," Sorenson replied.

"At the Brickhouse, so they say; again, with no confirmed alibi," Woolly retorted.

Sorenson sighed deeply before saying, "It's out of our hands," and she knew what he meant. It was in the hands of Lewis Chaulk.

"Maybe so," Woolly said, "but I'm going to look further into those tire treads, to cover that angle off, properly, and do whatever follow up that entails."

Sorenson cast her a wary look.

🚲 🚲 🚲

A *Wall Street Journal* article announced on September 17th that Americans were facing their worst crisis since the dirty thirties and that the light at the end of the tunnel was not yet visible.[1]

It must have been pretty scary times. Dark and scary, I'm sure. The free-market's Frankenstein had broken loose from his man-made chains and was terrorizing Floridians in XXL tees.

---

[1] Jon Hilsenrath, Serena Ng and Damian Paletta, "Worst Crisis Since '30s, With No End Yet in Sight", *Wall Street Journal* Septembr 17, 2008.

Tough Tiddlywinks

A Godzilla liberated by total Wall Street deregulation was stomping across Arizona, crushing sun-tanned golfers, their cries of "fore" silenced by foreclosure stakes driven straight into the heart of their American dreams turned nightmares. And to top it all off, a flood warning was in effect – of biblical proportions.

The Federal Reserve had to bail out the American International Group just to keep millions of starry-eyed suckers from drowning. But make no mistake, the entire global economic order was on the verge of collapsing. Catastrophe was nigh.

At least I was still safe and warm inside my little amnion sleeping bag when my mom accompanied Cactus and Slim Jimmy to Cactus's new Shaughnessy estate. The trio arrived on bicycles. Cactus pointed a fob at the locked wrought iron fence and commanded, "open sesame."

A neighbour from across the street watched the gates to 1620 Angus Drive separate. She had seen Cactus before and simply accepted that Ms. McLellan, the woman across the street who had recently passed away, had a wayward granddaughter. But this current situation made her nervous. After all, the home was now empty. It had been for months. So what was the granddaughter doing with the disheveled young man in a ratty green military-style jacket, black jeans and boots? And the well-groomed woman. Who was she? A realtor, perhaps? But all three were on bikes. No one wore a helmet.

She quickly telephoned Margaret Churchill-Booth, the Director of ASHEPOND, meaning The Association of Shaughnessy Estates Property Owners & New Developments.

"CeeBee," as Churchill-Booth was affably known among close associates, was perched on an exquisite rosewood settee, Victoria style circa 1900, in her expansive living room. A hot cup of tea was at hand on the oval rosewood coffee table in front of her, and a perfect intensity of afternoon light reached through a broad bay window to an array of envelopes. She was perusing her mail.

"Seriously?" she asked, upon hearing the neighbour's description of the visitation, or possible trespass.

"I'll swing by and say hello."

She jumped in her Range Rover, drove three blocks to 1620, and strode through the open gate like a baseball coach with a beef about an ump's call.

"Hello there!" she called out. The trio turned around to see the source of the greeting as they were ambling toward the back yard, talking to one another.

"Uh, hello," Cactus replied. She waited for the woman to get within talking distance before asking, "Are you lost?" Hannah and Slim Jimmy casually stood by. Slim smirked.

"My name is Margaret Churchill-Booth," CeeBee said, extending her hand. Cactus shook it. Margaret gave her and her friends the once-over and smiled nervously.

"I hope you can forgive my intrusion, but I am the Director of ASHEPOND, the association of members of this wonderful neighbourhood."

Cactus gave a sardonic look, catching Hannah's eye as she did. Hannah worked hard to suppress a grin. Jimmy turned away to meander upon the grounds.

"I saw that your gate was open, and the property has been vacant for some time," CeeBee continued. "Are you relatives, of…"

"I was her granddaughter," Cactus replied.

"Oh, my sincerest condolences Miss…"

"Miss Cactus. This here is Hannah…"

Hannah reached out and shook the Director's hand.

"And that guy there is James, co-founder of The Resistance. Have you heard –"

"Oh I see," CeeBee said, cutting off the young woman and barely glancing in Slim Jimmy's direction.

She fixed her attention on Hannah and asked, "Well, are you the realtor, ma'am?"

Hannah smiled and cast a knowing glance at Cactus.

"No one's selling anything," Cactus said. "I own this place. She's my friend. We're all here to have a look-see. And you're treh –"

"Oh, my goodness. It was not my intention to, well…" CeeBee found herself at a loss for words.

Hannah had begun to shift her weight, from side to side. The Director could not tell whether the size of her belly was causing her discomfort or whether she had some untoward purpose for being on the property.

"So if you don't mind," Cactus said in a firm but congenial tone, "my friends and I would like to…"

"Yes of course. It's really lovely property, isn't it?" CeeBee commented. She could no longer see Slim Jimmy. "I'll be on my way, then. I just wanted to introduce myself, so you could put a face to the association."

"Thank you. I've got the face and it was nice to meet you," Cactus said.

"And you too," CeeBee said with a pinched smile. "I'm sure we'll be seeing each other around."

"I'm sure we will."

Hands were shaken once more before CeeBee turned around and walked away.

When she got to the bicycles laying across the paving-stone driveway she turned around and shouted out to Cactus, "Excuse me, miss!"

Cactus stopped and looked, as did Hannah. "Have you read the property owners' rules and regulations?" CeeBee asked aloud. Cactus looked at Hannah, shrugged and yelled back, "No. Not yet."

"They're online, or I can get you a hardcopy if you like!"

"I'll read em later," was the distant reply.

So CeeBee left and Slim Jimmy appeared behind Cactus and Hannah to give the old dowager the finger.

"This place is fucking mental," he said. "It could fit 15, 20 tents on the grounds alone – and then there's a tennis court."

"Yeah," Cactus said, with her mind still on the white-haired busybody who she had just met. "Let's go inside, shall we?"

The Resistance was never a club to follow others' regulations. So it was that colourful pup tents and their pauper inhabitants began to occupy the sprawling grounds of Cactus's new home over the following weeks. Inspired by an emerging, mobile tent-city movement in Sacramento, California, Cactus invited Vancouver's impecunious, homeless and committed cyclists to live on her property on the condition that they abide by basic ground rules. No violations of municipal noise by-laws and no criminal behavior, including the smoking of mary jane.

The media latched onto the development like a liberal arts student to post-modernism (the latter meant so much less reading).

"We're all part of one big circle here, one big wheel," Hurdy Gurdy told a male reporter, "and every wheel needs a hub."

He retorted, "I take it you're the spokesperson," much to the guffaws of those gathered around.

Churchill-Booth and surrounding Shaughnessy residents were furious. The Director penned pointed missives on ASHEPOND letterhead, one after the other, ramping up the threat of legal action. She served these to whoever on the grounds would come forward to take them. There was always a taker.

One letter read:

The Association of Shaughnessy Estates Property Owners & New Developments

September 30, 2008

Cactus Delaine
1620 Angus Drive
Vancouver, B.C.

Dear Ms. Delaine,

Re: The Communal Residency at 1620 Angus Drive – Notice of Possible Legal Action

We, The Association of Shaughnessy Estates Property Owners & New Developments (hereinafter "ASHEPOND"), have made all reasonable attempts to engage you in meaningful dialogue about our concerns relating to the campground that has taken root at 1620 Angus Drive. With the exception of yourself, we are all agreed that this encampment seriously degrades the property values attached to Shaughnessy Estates. The degradation takes several forms, including but not restricted to the following:

i. The proliferation of tents and bicycles upon these grounds is an eyesore to the Shaughnessy community.

ii. Several of the settlement residents enter and exit at all hours by bicycle, thus posing a traffic hazard to us, for whom the automobile is an affordable, normal and quite proper means of transportation.

iii. The front gates to your Estate are not locked during the day or evening, thus presenting a security risk to the adjoining properties.

iv. Several of the inhabitants remain on the grounds without regularly attending to a place of employment, thus putting our possessions at a heightened risk of theft.

As you surely must know, the encampment has attracted an undue number of sight-seers and journalists, and is making it difficult for Angus Drive residents to get to and from work without being questioned about whatever it is your people think they are doing. This constitutes a clear nuisance, in our view.

ASHEPOND has taken all reasonable means to persuade you, the owner of the above-noted property, to dismantle "the settlement," as one woman there, a Miss Hurdy Gurdy, refers to it. For all intents and purposes you have ignored our concerns to date, and when by proper means we have asked the inhabitants themselves to leave the area, we have been met by defiance, obscene gestures, or indifference.

We therefore have no other recourse but to ask you one final time to clean up this blight in our neighbourhood or we shall commence an action against you for breach of your contractual obligations as a residence Association member, for nuisance, and for diminishing the enjoyment of our properties.

We should not have to point out that the Shaughnessy postal code is in a class of its own. ASHEPOND is strongly committed to maintaining this esteem and asks you therefore to give this letter your most serious attention.

Sincerely,

M. Churchill-Booth

Margaret Churchill-Booth
Director of the Board

Cactus pedaled each of ASHEPOND's letters to Sasha Večerkavic, a fellow cyclist and freshly-called lawyer who wrote formal responses *pro bono*. An adolescent of the Velvet Revolution, Ms. Večerkavic firmly believed that universal human rights reigned supreme, not only in her native Czech Republic, but in Canada, where she had lived for the last 16 years.

Soon enough, however, high principles stood to be tested at the B.C. Supreme Court, a venue tactically chosen by ASHEPOND, the plaintiff, whose membership had deep enough pockets to afford a suit at the high court, and who could justify a damage claim of more than $25,000, or at least an injunction. Its experts were prepared to testify that property values in Shaughnessy had dropped about 10% since the tent-site took hold.

The decaying B.C. Civil Liberties Association parachuted in to lend Cactus a much-needed helping hand, and to cloak her case in righteousness. Even so, the presiding judge, The Honourable Mr. Justice Brandon Warwick, had no difficulty concluding that the occupation posed a health threat to the neighbourhood and was a nuisance at common law. After all, he had many friends living in Shaughnessy, and over a happy-hour highball here and charity dinner there some of these fine folks confided to him their sense of displeasure with the whole situation. Mr. Justice Warwick ordered Cactus to have her community gone from the grounds of 1620 Angus Drive within 48 hours.

"Injunction Ruling Puts Stop to Shaughnessy Settlement" was the next morning's headline in a local paper.

"Yes, you've got to go, and peaceably so," Cactus told her many guests. "Please don't get arrested over this. Sasha will appeal the injunction, so we just have to let her do her thing, please. Let's be positive. I'll get you back here soon."

🚲

4th Quarter 2008

Pumpkin sales were brisk but October 2008 was shaping up to be the slowest month of the year for Vancouver condo sales. николь, Don Dickerson's most ambitious project, had gone into receivership, but The Manna was alive and well, above ground, and nearing completion when Sergeant Woolly and Constable Sorenson pulled their unmarked cruiser alongside the curb at West Broadway and Oak. A gleaming canary yellow motorcycle was parked a few stalls ahead. "Go ahead," Woolly said, so her partner took several pictures of it with a digital camera. The crime fighters had agreed that a warrant was not necessary. The bike was in public view.

Woolly and Sorenson then entered the gate of the condo site and climbed the stairs to the pre-fab office on stilts. Both were in uniform. The door was open and inside a short, burly man with a few wood shavings in his curly hair held court with a couple of twenty-something strongmen. The latter wore ochre-hued canvas overalls, hardhats, framing hammers, and the candied promise on their faces of a paycheque every other Friday.

The older guy stopped talking when he saw the officers.

"Pardon me, gentlemen, I'm looking for the foreman," Woolly said without waiting for formalities.

"You're lookin' right at him, officer," the older fellow said.

"Okay, sir. I'd like to speak to Frank Belleveau for a minute, if he's working here," Woolly said.

"Oh. Frank. Okay. He's uh..." The foreman walked to the front window of the trailer and drew Woolly's attention to a hollow unit in the development, at ground level. A man could be seen standing at a table in there, drawing a couple of workers' attention to some plans. A single bulb was lit overhead and welding sparks sprayed from a dark corner nearby. Metal stud wall frames were already in place and white plumbing pipes were exposed. A truck stacked with drywall was parked nearby.

"The fellow to the left there. That's Frank," the foreman said.

"Thank you," Woolly said. The site boss then pulled a couple of hard hats off a shelf and handed them to the officers.

"Regulations," he said.

Woolly and Sorenson nodded, put on the required helmets and walked over to Frank's workspace.

"Mr. Belleveau?" Sergeant Woolly asked, stepping onto a cold cement floor.

"Yeah. That's me. What can I do you for?" Frank asked. (His imperfect knowledge of English was not the reason for this hackneyed reversal of preposition and pronoun. He had first heard this phrasing at his mechanic's shop, from the English speaking owner. After asking Hannah about it, Frank decided to use it every now and then.)

"We're wondering if we can have a moment with you, in private? My name is Sergeant Wolychenski and this is Constable Sorenson. We're with the Vancouver Police Department."

Frank cast a mystified look at his assistants and blushed.

"Uh, sure. Why not?"

"All right. Come along then," Woolly said, and Frank followed the officers off the site.

"You're a biker, aren't you, Mr. Belleveau?" Woolly asked as they approached the cruiser. She and Sorenson took off their yellow helmets.

"Uh..." Frank stopped and stiffened, then took off his helmet. "What do you mean by that?"

"You ride a motorcycle, don't you?" Sorenson asked.

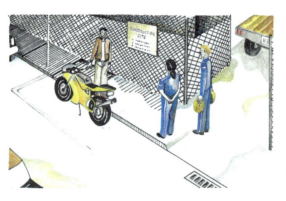

"Oh, yeah." Frank relaxed his shoulders. "That's my girl right there." Pointing to his Ducati.

"How many CCs does she pack?" Sorenson asked.

"Seven fifty." Frank smirked, keeping one eye on Sorenson.

"In case you're late for work?" Sorenson quipped.

"Never." Frank grinned. He folded well-built arms across his formidable chest.

Woolly leaned against the back, passenger side door of the cruiser. "How long have you been working for Don?" she asked.

"Uh...a few years now, I'd say." Frank looked skyward, apparently doing the math. "Yeah. That's about right. Tree years, going on four."

"Not on this site," Sorenson remarked.

"No. Oh no. This one's only been up and running since, uh...well...April of last year. It is anudder CanCon job, though."

"So how long have you known Don Dickerson, then?" Woolly asked.

"Oh, about...Ay. Wait a minute." Frank looked at Woolly and her partner a couple of times, in rapid succession. "If you guys showed up here to dig around about that, just say so. I thought a guy was on trial for that, so don't play games with me."

"Okay. Fair enough. That is why we're here, Mr. Belleveau," Woolly said casually, folding her arms across her stomach. "You're right. There is a man in custody, facing trial for Don's murder, but we are interested in a piece of evidence that doesn't make a lot of sense to us. That's why we're here."

Woolly looked intently into Frank's eyes. Frank shrugged, put his hands in his front pockets, and made an impish shape with his lips.

"We're interested in a tread pattern from a motorbike, one that was left at the scene," Sorenson said.

Frank strained not to look at his bike.

"We've been hunting down every slick that has that pattern for weeks," Woolly continued. "There's a lot of them, unfortunately. So we've been spending all our time these days talking to folks such as yourself, folks who have bikes with Diablo tires. Diablo Corsos, is that right?"

"Yeah. Corso threes." Frank looked toward his bike, then back at Woolly.

"So we ask everyone a few easy questions, like where they were the night Don was killed, for starters. And if they weren't at the scene..."

"Then they don't have to die?" Frank interjected. A devilish smile burst across his face, which turned crimson red, and he started chuckling. Woolly looked at Sorenson with a raised brow.

"I'm just kidding," Frank said. "Goodness. I'm kidding. That's Johnny Cash. Don't you guys listen to music?"

Woolly furrowed her brow. Dots of sweat formed on Frank's temples.

"We're here to ask you, Mr. Belleveau, if you want to tell us where you were on Friday night, the 28th of March. That's all," Woolly said, "but," she quickly added, just to keep Frank from speaking yet, "you don't have to. We're just making inquiries. You have no obligation to assist us. I want you to know that."

"So what if I don't?" he asked.

"Then we won't know where you were on Friday evening, March 28th. It's your business. That's all."

Frank pinched his Adam's apple and nodded.

"So maybe we'll come back later," Woolly added. "There's a lot more Pirelli Diablo Corso IIIs out there. Wet radials. 120 width in the front. 180 in the back. 70 aspect ratio in the front. 55 in the back. 17 inch diameter front and back. Transversal grooves. I've been at it so long I've got it memorized. I don't know. It's just that we haven't met any other riders who actually worked for Dickerson."

"The night Don got offed by that Indian I was sitting at home, drinking beer, watching a western – a cowboy movie. I remember hearing about the murder the next day."

"So you were watching a movie at eight p.m. on a Friday night?"

"That's right. A DVD I rented earlier that day. You can ask my ex," Frank said.

"Your ex?"

"That's right. A woman I was living with at de time. My fiancée, Hannah Verso."

"Was she watching the movie too?"

"She came home during the movie."

"And where was she?"

"Working late."

"On a Friday night?"

"Yeah. So what? It was tax time."

"How do we get a hold of her?" Sorenson asked.

Frank swallowed emptily and told the officers Hannah's new phone number. "Go ahead," he said. "Call her. She'll tell you exactly where she found me that night. Sitting in a chair, drinking, watching Burt Reynolds. He shouldn't be in cowboy movies."

Woolly pushed herself off the car and handed Frank her hard hat. Sorenson handed his over too, then walked around the back of the cruiser to the driver-side door. Frank put his own helmet back on.

"Okay, Mr. Belleveau. Thanks for your time," the Sergeant said. "If for whatever reason we need to talk again, can we find you here?" she asked.

"Yeah. Sure." Frank looked at the site and swung his arms up casually, helmets in hand. "It's not gonna' be done anytime soon, as you can see," he said. "At least not without breaking code," he added after a pause, grinning.

🚲 🚲 🚲

Sergeant Wolychenski and Constable Sorenson followed up on Frank's invitation and phoned Hannah at her new apartment. She was out, so they left a voice message.

"Hey, nice to see you back," Charlie said to Hannah. "I thought that whole mess would have scared you away for good."

Charlie had just perched himself on a bar stool at Ouisi. Hannah was seated at a deuce across the floor, chewing a chunk of veggie burger. She blushed and waived, then said, "Ah...no, but that was an awful day, that's for sure."

"I take it you live in the neighbourhood?" Charlie asked.

"Yes, actually. On 14th, in a building just west of here. What about you?"

"I'm in Strathcona."

"Oh." Hannah knew little about that area, except that Chinatown bordered it or was actually in it.

Suddenly Victor came through the door.

"Hey," Charlie said. Victor nodded, first at Charlie, then Hannah, and the two men shook hands before Victor lifted himself onto a barstool.

"My co-dependent has arrived," Charlie said to Hannah. He turned toward the bar to order a beer but stopped, twisted back, and stepped off his stool. "I didn't get your name before, ma'am," he said, approaching Hannah, "but I'm Charlie, just in case you forgot, and that fellow there's Victor. I think I did mention that."

Hannah put her hand in front of her mouth as she was swallowing some food. After a few seconds she said, "Pardon me, I'm Hannah."

"If I may be so bold, would you care to join us?"

Hannah shrugged and said, "Oh. Okay. Thank you."

She brought her unfinished meal and pint of beer to the bar and sat next to Charlie.

"Please, help yourself to some fries," she offered him and Victor, but both men graciously declined.

"Well, then, my American avengers, at least tell me something about yourselves," Hannah said, before taking another bite from her burger.

"I don't want to speak for the traitor – " Hannah looked at Victor, who winked back – "but I'm from Detroit," Charlie said.

"Which makes him almost Canadian," Victor quipped.

"Or British, or even French, depending upon where you like to start your imperialist history," Charlie remarked.

Hannah's eyes reflected confusion.

"You're not from the U.S.?" she asked Victor.

"I am, ma'am. I'm a transplant from Oregon. Portland."

"But a communist," Charlie piped up. Victor chuckled again. "That's why he lives here now."

Hannah remained in the dark.

"Forgive him,' Victor explained. "Charlie is so old-fashioned for such a man of the world. You don't have to be a communist to be run out of the States anymore. Just a socialist." That comment raised a couple pairs of eyebrows at a nearby table.

"Don't be fooled," Charlie urged Hannah playfully. "A rose by any other name would still smell the same."

Still confused, Hannah said, "Okay then. So you're from Portland, and you're from Detroit, but what do you guys do here in Vancouver?"

"I came to school here. Now I'm a teacher," Charlie said. "And the old man here" – Charlie looked at Victor and grinned – "well, he makes pictures for a living."

"You're a director?"

Victor smiled. "No ma'am. A painter."

"Ohh, sorry."

"Oh, no need to apologize."

"Oh but you should, Victor. It's the Canadian thing to do," Charlie said, winking at Hannah. She smiled.

"What about you though," Charlie asked the stranger, longing to know if she was in a relationship. "How do you pay the rent?"

"Well, that's actually a little complicated at the moment."

Charlie looked slightly askance at Victor, who raised an eyebrow.

"Whoa there, don't be thinking dirty thoughts," Hannah said. "I'm a bookkeeper. I do accounts for a development company, but I've been laid off for the moment."

"Because of the market?" Victor asked.

"Yeah. Sort of." Hannah ingested the last chunk of her burger.

"What do you think about that whole tenting thing that was happening up there?" Victor asked Hannah, nodding southward, in the direction of Cactus's Shaughnessy home. It was only about six blocks from where they were seated.

Hannah blushed, and swallowed, suddenly stuck in her own thoughts.

"You know that girl, don't you?" Charlie asked. "I've seen you at the critical mass ride with her."

"You've been to critical mass?" Hannah replied.

"Yeah, and I saw you there, with that girl who owns that property up there. I actually saw you cork with her. Impressive."

"You should have said hi. That woman's a friend of mine. Cactus."

"She's in the news a lot," Charlie said. "She's pretty intense."

"Yeah. She's really into politics, but she's got a great heart. I met her at a party a while back. She loves cycling and hey, she got me into it."

"I actually hope she wins her appeal," Charlie admitted. "It's a good cause." He downed a mouthful of beer before saying, "there's a place just like Shaughnessy where I'm from, called Indian Village if you can believe that."

Victor grinned.

"But no teepees, I take it?" Hannah asked, going along with the groove.

"Not even one American Indian. Just whites and blacks. Real wealthy, though," Charlie replied.

Hannah did not know what to say.

After a pause Ruby, the bartender, asked her, "Do you mind me asking when you're due?"

"Mid-November." Hannah put her right hand on her protruding belly and rubbed it gently.

"I would have never guessed. You're so fit," Ruby remarked.

"Oh. Thank you." Hannah's face turned pink. "I like exercising...

and yoga. I'm sure the bicycling helps a little."

"Are you going on the next ride?" Charlie asked.

"Ah, I doubt it. I don't really like to bike when it gets cold...and dark. I know that's sucky but...but to be honest, I probably won't go again until the spring."

"Well I just had my bike stolen anyway – at Simon Fraser if you can believe it – so I won't be going on a ride until I get a new one."

"That's terrible," Hannah said.

Victor pretended to play a violin and Ruby winked.

"Thanks guys," Charlie said sarcastically. "I appreciate your support."

"Well you can borrow mine if you're not too embarrassed."

"Thank you, but that's okay. It's not the colour. I don't want to ride a cruiser, but I'll find a new bike, thanks."

"Ah, if you like, I'll ask my friend Cactus if she can help you. I mean, she can probably find a used bike," Hannah clarified, "but a good one, and probably a cheap one, if that's what you like. That's her style."

"Sounds great. Very much appreciated," Charlie replied.

"But I should get going," Hannah said. "It's been a pleasure meeting both of you. I'll be back, I'm sure. The veggie burger's great. I'm definitely going to tell Cactus about it. She's a vegetarian."

Hannah reached into her handbag, pulled out a twenty and gave it to Ruby. "You can keep the change," she said before stepping down from her stool and shaking Victor and Charlie's hands goodbye.

Charlie strained to follow the contours of her figure out the door without Victor or Ruby noticing.

"Me thinks he likes," the bartender said to Victor as the door swung closed.

Ain't too proud to beg, are you, Mr. Motown?" Victor chided his friend.

🚲 🚲 🚲

When they arrived at her door later that evening Hannah was wearing a printed baby blue summer dress. A baby doll, some call it. An empire waist to others. Many women wore them during Napolean's reign. Lucky little piece of shortcake that guy was. The dress hugged Hannah's fulsome breasts and flowed generously over her torso and hips, stopping about midway down her thigh.

"Please come in," she said.

Woolly and Sorenson stepped onto the parquet floor of the living room. Hannah's bicycle leaned against a radiator.

"Please. Have a seat." Hannah ushered her visitors to her sofa. She sat in a fat, green-olive-toned armchair across from the police and clasped her hands in the fold of her thighs, lady-like, just to keep Sorenson's thoughts on track.

"So Miss...uh..."

"Just call me Hannah, please."

"Do you mind, Hannah, if Constable Sorenson takes some notes of our interview here?"

"Oh no." Hannah looked at Sorenson. "Please, do what you have to do," she said with a smile.

"Okay then," Woolly began. "As I mentioned on the phone, Hannah, we've been investigating for some time the murder of Donald Dickerson, a man your fiancé used to work for."

"But a man's already in jail for that, no?"

Sorenson glanced uncomfortably at Woolly.

"That's true," the Sergeant said. "But we're just looking into some further details of the case – some forensic details, as I mentioned on the phone."

"Okay. Yes."

"They involve a tire tread pattern, one that happens to be similar to the kind of tire that Frank Belleveau has on his bike."

Hannah looked apprehensively at the officers.

"Don't worry, ma'am. There are a lot of bikes on the road with these tires, I can assure you," Sergeant Woolly said.

Hannah nodded and formed a tight smile.

"But we spoke to Frank, as I mentioned on the phone."

Hannah removed one hand from her hem and petted the broad arm of her chair.

"And asked him about his whereabouts on the night of Don Dickerson's murder."

Hannah looked awry at the female cop, then returned her hand to the hem of her dress and fidgeted with it.

"He told us that he was at home the night Mr. Dickerson was killed, and that's why we're here. To ask what you recall of that night."

Hannah cleared her throat and looked at both officers before saying, "Uh, yes, that's right. I had come home and he was sitting in the living room. The t.v. was on and he had been watching it, obviously. I was tired, and didn't pay attention to whatever program or show was on."

"Do you have any idea, however vague, what kind of show was on?" Woolly asked.

"Well it was a Western, that's for sure. I remember the outfits, rifles shooting, the typical stuff."

"What time was it when you arrived? Do you remember?" Woolly continued.

"Uh…" Hannah cleared her throat again. "I think it was about nine o'clock. Shortly before then," she replied.

"So you'd been out?"

"Yeah," Hannah replied. She had difficulty looking Woolly in the eye. "I worked late that night at the office. I was behind with tax stuff."

"Oh. You're in accounting?"

"I do books, yeah, but I'm an office administrator too."

"Where do you work?"

"I'm unemployed right now but at that time I worked at Nirvana, a condo site."

"Oh. I see. Is that the one near Tinseltown, that big cinema in..."

Hannah nodded before Woolly said, "Chinatown. That one looks like it's gonna' be big."

"Actually, it's in receivership," Hannah said.

"Oh. Did you work for Don before that time?"

"Yes. I briefly did the books out of his office on Hamilton Street."

Sorenson eyeballed his partner, a rookie reflex that Hannah witnessed and Woolly ignored.

"I was preparing the numbers for his employees' T-4s," Hannah continued. "And I was just generally helping run the office. It was quite hectic actually."

Woolly brought her hand to her chin and rubbed her index finger back and forth across closed lips. Hannah unclasped her hands and pushed them across her thighs as if she were kneading dough. Sorenson cast Hannah a phony smile.

"When did you stop working for Don, if I may ask?" Woolly asked.

"You mean his company, right?"

Woolly and Sorenson traded glances.

"Yes. CanCon," Woolly confirmed.

"In April." Hannah pushed her hands into the fold of her lap again.

"May I ask why?"

Hannah shifted in her seat, crossed one leg over the other, and rested her forearms across her shins. "Frank and I were starting to quarrel, at home I mean, and though we didn't really work together – he was on site at THE MANNA and I was at NIRVANA – our personal affairs spilled into our work. Or at least they did for me, and I thought I should leave the company."

She looked at her questioners nervously. They remained silent, stone faced.

"You see," she continued, "I got pregnant and I didn't want to tell Frank right away because I knew it would be a problem. A *big* one. We'd talked about it lots since we moved in together and Frank had made it abundantly clear that he wasn't ready – yet. Always 'yet.' 'Not yet, not yet,' he'd say. But I knew I wanted the baby, and I was having second-thoughts about our relationship. Uh..." Hannah shifted in her seat again. "Do you really need to know any of this, or...?"

Woolly hesitated before saying, "It's your call, really. You've been helpful so far."

Everyone went silent for a half-minute, thinking their own thoughts, before Woolly reassured Hannah that she need not speak to the police if she did not want to. Woolly added, "but I am curious to know if Frank is the father of your child there." She nodded toward Hannah's stomach.

Hannah had already guessed that her situation, as freshly disclosed to the police, made this question inevitable. "I'm not sure," she replied, without sounding haughty or evasive.

"You're not sure you want to tell us, or you're not sure – "

"I'm not sure he's the father, but I assume he is." This time Hannah's tone did have an edge to it.

"But you're living separate and apart from Frank right now, right?" Woolly asked.

"Yes. I moved out."

"And you're not currently working, you said?"

"Well, I just finished some modelling work, for Pacific Tides Trust."

"Hey." Sorenson sat forward. "*You're* the woman on their ad, aren't you?"

Hannah blushed and nodded.

A few seconds of silence ensued before Woolly said, "Hannah, we know that Frank has an assault conviction back in Quebec, about five years ago. I've seen the photos. He beat a woman pretty hard. It's our bread and butter to know these things. So if you left Frank because he's hitting you, or abusing you, or frightening you in any way, just tell us, okay?"

Hannah shivered and goose bumps appeared on her arms. "I didn't," she said. "He got a little out of control once, but that was a while ago. I just don't want to live with him anymore. I don't know what to think these days. I want to have my baby, in peace, where I can think out my options."

Hannah loosely hugged herself as the expression "my options" rang loudly in Woolly's ears.

"When are you due?" the Sergeant asked.

"Mid-November."

"Congratulations."

"Thank you."

"Well then...I think Clyde and I have enough for today. I'm really thankful for your time, Hannah. Really. We have to cover all our bases and not everyone's so cooperative, but you've been great – and I really wish you the best next month." Woolly eyed Hannah's belly and winked.

Everyone stood up, Sorenson stifling a yawn.

"Here's my card," the Sergeant offered Hannah. "Call me if you *do* have any problems with Frank."

"Okay, but everything's fine. Really."

As Woolly descended the

stairs of Hannah's apartment she told Sorenson, "I have a funny feeling that this case won't break open until Miss Hannah has her baby."

"Why's that?" her partner wondered.

"She's not pregnant with Frank's baby. I'm sure of it. She's pregnant with Dickerson's."

"Oh Jesus." Sorenson rolled his eyes, stopped at the bottom of the stairs, and, at nearly six inches taller than his senior partner, he turned, tilted his head, and looked her in the eye. "I know you'll want to slap me for this," he said, "but no women's intuition on this file, please, Sarge. Let's stick to the evidence."

"Oh, oh, oh. Oh would I love to slap you, Clyde," Woolly said, her neck tilted skyward, "but I wouldn't feel anything. Don't ask me why." Then she shrugged and said, "just my women's intuition," as the partners proceeded into the fresh air.

It is hardly surprising that kids love Halloween, that one day of the year they get to make Jack-o-Lanterns, dress up like warlocks and devils and ghosts, walk around the neighbourhood after dinner and demand candy from strangers. If I were a conspiracy theorist, which I'm not, I would be inclined to believe that the whole ritual was invented by dentists.

Charlie Menz liked Halloween too. As a teacher he never failed to use the occasion to digress from his course syllabus, to give a history lesson, an economics lecture, and a piece of autobiography all rolled up into one.

"It was the birth of the Reformation, the *Reformationstag*," he told the class gathered inside the mountain Quadrangle. He put air quotations around the German word, just like Jesus did around "the meek," I'm sure, when he spoke about inheriting land on the Mount of Beatitudes.

"That's right. It's the same day, about 500 years ago, that Martin Luther nailed his 95 *Theses* to the door of All Saints' Church. All Saints' Eve, some call it, but it's Halloween just the same. And why did he do it?" instructor Menz asked his students.

No one ventured a guess.

"Because he knew the Pope was more into developing real estate than instructing on the faith. Julius wanted a huge new basilica, and it required financing. So he found himself a big group of investors, suckers really, who paid him for 'indulgences' – not things like Belgian truffles, silk ties, or derivatives..."

A few students chuckled.

"...but cheap ways to avoid punishment for their transgressions."

Charlie paused before asking, "Any other momentous events that took place on Halloween?"

Again, his students stared at him blankly. Even confusion and consternation showed on some faces.

"What about 1763? Any takers?" A couple of students shook their heads.

"It was Halloween of that year when Pontiac, the great Chief of the Ottawas, got an important missive from Louis Dequindre. Dequindre's letter informed Pontiac that a French commandant stationed nearby, a fellow named Neyon de Villiers, could not help him recapture Fort Detroit from the British. You see, the French had lost the fort to British soldiers three years earlier, shortly after crazy King George's troops surprised the hell out of General Montcalm's men on the Plains of Abraham. Now that, of course, was no small moment in your country's history, or mine, really.

"Pontiac and Montcalm were close, really close, so the Ottawas Chief wanted to give Wolfe a good pounding. I'm sure he wanted to take a few scalps as well, but he really wanted Fort Detroit back, both for his own people and for the French – *les habitants*. He had already been trying to establish a pan-Indian confederacy cuz he wanted to stop British imperialism. But with Dequindre's Halloween letter he knew the jig was up, so he lifted the siege, promised to bury the hatchets of his people, and left to the Maumee River."

Two friends at the back of the lecture theatre made drinking plans for later, via Facebook. Charlie said, "The historians say he 'sued for peace,' whatever that means. What probably happened is that he entered into a settlement, and in exchange for laying down his tomahawk he was promised that a city and an American automobile would soon be named after him."

A few smiles appeared on the faces before him, so he ran with it.

"That was the tradition back then. It's why Chrysler makes a Grand Cherokee and why you can go across North America in a Winnebago. The Apaches, I'm sure, had a lot more leverage. They got a whole war helicopter named after them."

The last comment evoked hearty chuckles from a handful of students.

"And what about that old fort anyway? It's my hometown, and it was a pretty hot piece of real estate in its day, even without an indoor swimming pool, plumbing, or electricity. Tonight, though – right now, as I'm standing here, and you're all sitting there – it's on fire. Seriously."

Eyes widened. Doubtful expressions were cast.

"I'll show you," Charlie said. The friends on Facebook stopped typing as Charlie pulled down a wide screen from the ceiling, turned on a couple of switches at his lectern, and clicked on a pre-set website. Live video footage of a Devil's Night house fire was suddenly projected onto the front wall of the classroom. Firemen were in the foreground, working their big hoses. People from all over Michigan had gathered in Motor City to watch hundreds of homes burn down to a crisp.

"Who's to say that great things haven't been born from flames?" he asked when the clip was over.

"Such as?" a student asked.

"The devil of capitalism," Charlie retorted, garnering a few groans.

"I thought that was Adam Smith," one student ventured.

"That's what economists will have you believe, but they're wrong, again. Does anybody know about the great fire of London?"

Charlie noticed a couple of yawns. No one put up their hand. One of the two students who had paused their Facebook planning for the Detroit footage sent out a tweet, "Detroit's on fire tonight. Teacher's not. Boring as an ice flow."

Charlie explained, "In 1666, on a September night, a fire spread from a bakery through the city, being whipped up by the wind. The inferno lasted three days. It ruined hundreds and hundreds of acres of property, and of course St. Paul's Cathedral. So, you might ask, what has this got to do with the father of capitalism?"

A student typed into his laptop, "Teacher's a definite pyro."

Charlie got no audible response so he just continued along.

"When a city burns down people need somewhere new to live, right?"

He could see a few heads nod.

"So you need real estate – and let's get more precise, you need a real estate developer."

Now the teacher could see a few smiles among his students. "But whose gonna pay to have their homes rebuilt?" he asked.

"The insurance companies," one student quickly proposed.

"In 1666?" Menz asked.

That same student shrugged.

"Well, enter the son of Praise-God Barbon."

A few wrinkled faces and smiles appeared across the room.

"His short name was Nicholas, but he was christened 'If-Jesus-hadn't-died-for-thee-thou-wouldst-be-damned Barbon.'"

Now there were a lot of wide grins in the room.

"No kidding. The original Son of a Preacher man, this guy was, but he was also the first guy to introduce fire insurance to London, *and* he developed large tracts of real estate there. He was a big capitalist, a big free-marketer, long before Smith put his pen to the topic. He wrote *A Discourse on Trade* and my favourite, *Apology for the Builder*. Imagine, a book called *Apology for the Builder*. It's beautiful."

Most of the students were getting antsy, wondering how their teacher could have digressed so far from the evening's original topic – vertical urban farming – to arson, religion, and capitalism.

"But anyway. There you have it. My home town's on fire tonight," Charlie said. "Not the whole town, of course, but lots of homes. We call it Devil's Night."

Standing in front of that captive audience, maybe Charlie felt an obligation to "print the legend," as they say, because we don't in fact call it Devil's Night anymore. To show respect for all the good Samaritans and guardian angels who patrol the streets and prevent fires, we now call it Angel's Night. Perhaps I prefer to accentuate the positive, but I love Halloween precisely because the next day good things like angels really do come down from the sky. Linus van Pelt may wait for the Great Pumpkin, but the souls of dead people, men, women and children alike – they come down to earth too. The children, *los angelitos*, are actually the first to arrive. They show up on November 1st.

REMEMBRANCE DAY, or Armistice Day if you're more technically inclined, passed with its usual solemnity, grey speeches, bagpipes and bugles. I don't want to disparage the event, but I don't really understand why Americans remember all those World War I casualties on November 11 but not the arrival of the Mayflower at Provincetown Harbor in 1620. I know it was bad-timing, being a Saturday, the Sabbath. After weeks at sea the beleaguered Puritans had to wait a day to unpack, but it was the Saturday, November 11, I'm pretty sure, when the Brave New World officially kick-started, when the New Jerusalem was seeded.

Fast-forward nearly four centuries and I find myself about to be pushed into this earthly paradise, whether I like it or not. By now we can safely call it a Brave Old World, like a resilient beater on a used car lot – it burns oil, it has a rusted undercarriage and a leaky radiator, but it still turns over. The next owner will surely get some nasty surprises.

That's right. Hannah's sudden contractions paled in intensity to those being felt across global financial markets. Seven angels blew seven trumpets, the wicked three-piece warriors of Wall Street broke the Seventh Seal, and the floodgates gave way to a torrent of foreclosures and job losses, just like the Book of Revelation prophesied. Excess liquidity was drowning the markets. Even the big banks started to capsize. CEOs worked hard to keep their ships and yachts upright, as Master Jones and his crew did for the Mayflower, but these modern, topsider stewards were not adept. It was now time for them to take a page from the sea-sick Pilgrim's playbook, to get down on bended knee, and to pray.

As with every epic voyage on the silver screen, these genuflections were heeded just in the nick of time. A saviour was returning from a faraway time and place. An archangel trumpeted it so.

But this time big change, possibly revolution, was in the offing. A second advent, an era of fiscal responsibility, was nigh. So many idols needed rescuing: the sacred cow, the Golden Fleece, the Holy Grail, and above all the Holy Trinity – GM, Ford and Chrysler.

After riding for two years across the country, plains, prairies, and Ozarks, battling foe after foe, and building a sweeping groundswell of grassroots support along the way, this mortal cynosure managed finally to conquer Ohio, Virginia, Pennsylvania and even Florida, to answer the prayers of everyone who had lived beyond their means, bought on credit, and lost their variable-mortgaged homes in the great, cataclysmic flood. To centenarians he looked a lot like Socrates Potter – not Beatrix or Harry – and under his deft métier judgment and punishment would surely follow. It was time to eject the money-changers from the temple, yet again. Indeed, the world was about to witness hardship and pain the likes of which it had not witnessed since the Great Irish Potato Famine, or even the great dust storm of 1935. Ordinary people everywhere now faced life with potentially fewer automobiles, smaller television screens, cheaper restaurant dinners, and lower credit lines. The question on everyone's minds had become, Is such a life worth living?

"Sure," Ryan Ghostkeeper replied when his cellmate asked him that very question.

Ryan grew up on Nak'azdli Reserve #1, on the southeastern shore of Stuart Lake, so it became known after Simon Fraser, James McDougall and John Stuart portaged and packed their way around the area for the North West Company in the early 19th century. To Ryan's own people, the K'oo Dene or more widely, the 'uda ukelh – the people who travel by boat in the morning – the lake was Nak'al Bun or Nak'azdli Lake.

Reserve #1 was just a stone's throw from Fort St. James, once the Stuart Lake trading post, and not much more than an hour's drive from Prince George. Though Ryan was born and raised near enough to the namesakes of foreign Saints and Princes – even Mount Pope Provincial Park rose to the north – his own home was once the site of a bloody battle, between his people and other tribes, where the Nak'azdli River funnels into the lake. That lake just happens to be the home of Early Stuart Sockeye salmon fries and juveniles, before they make their long voyage to the Pacific Ocean.

One evening when Ryan was still a fry, just a six-year-old boy, he was awoken from his dreams by yelling and banging in the living room of his home. By now he recognized the sound of violence. Although he was scared he ventured as far as his doorway to see what was transpiring. Through a narrow slit in the open door he watched his parents slap, kick, swing at and throw one another, but he did not notice right away that his father had already been stabbed in the chest, three times. The dripping blood was difficult to see against the navy blue sweatshirt his dad wore, especially in the dimly lit living room.

Ryan had witnessed his parents engage in similar behaviour before but he did not understand what intoxication was. He had no idea how violence might be the product of a mind affected by alcohol, as he had no experience with the substance.

His drunken father managed to regain some control, enough to squeeze his soused mother's wrist and dislodge the steak knife that had wounded him, but he was staggering.

"You fuckin two-timer. Bashtard. Cocksucker," his mother barked out when the knife fell from her hand, and she socked her husband in the side of the face with an unrestrained left. The force of the blow toppled him to the floor, behind the sofa, out of Ryan's view.

His mother swayed a little before plunking herself down on the sofa, then she saw the crack in the door, and Ryan staring through it.

"Go to bed," she demanded in a husky and imposing drunkard's drawl. "He'sh a fuckin two-timer. Right Darrell? Are you fucking listening to me?" she asked her husband, turning her head enough to face his listless back.

Ryan had returned to his bed, as directed, his heart racing. His mother stopped looking at Darrell and laid her head against the sofa. After staring blankly at the ceiling for a few seconds her eyes closed and she passed out. She was too intoxicated to consider that her husband might be bleeding to death, which he did about four minutes later.

Ryan was raised thereafter by his uncle Donny and his aunt Agnes, both non-drinkers, who did their best to help the young boy cope with the violent disappearance of his parents. Among other things, Donny taught his nephew how to make traditional wood carvings and drawings. Ryan enjoyed these arts and became modestly adept at them.

Life with Donny and Agnes was satisfying, even therapeutic, to Ryan for a few years, but as the boy entered his early teen years, and puberty, he succumbed to the influence of adolescent rounders, older kids in his community who were looking for new drinking friends and recruits into their petty criminal ways. Ryan was an easy target. He lacked self-esteem, court-ordered psychology reports would later conclude. This was especially so whenever he returned with his uncle and aunt from Burnaby's

Prison for Women, where his mother was serving a lengthy sentence for manslaughter.

So yes, Ryan had pondered his cellmate's question before, when feeling crippled by his criminal record, drowning in seemingly insurmountable alcoholism, or waking up in remand. He struggled most intensely with the question when his mother passed away, only a couple of years after returning from prison. She had contracted HIV while inside.

Ryan's heart still pumped hard enough to push him through the occasional brick wall of despair he encountered. That's why he could readily say to his cellmate, "Sure," this life is worth living. He was determined not to suffer a fate like his mother's, just as he had resolved not to blame anyone else for his situation. In fact, Ryan was not prepared to blame any human being for his current predicament.

"I'm only in here," he told his mate, "because of those damned coyotes. I seen them follow somethin' down to the water so I checked it out, but I should've known better."

He had told Woolly and other officers exactly that when he was interrogated, but they chastised him for being untruthful and conniving.

"They were a sign I was on the wrong path," he explained to his cellie. "I should've gone back, 'round the other way, then I would've never ended up in that stupid alley."

"Because that's where you found the knife, according to you," the fellow replied.

"It's the truth," Ryan said.

"And you didn't notice that it had blood on it?"

Ryan shrugged and said, "I was pretty drunk."

His cellmate shook his head. "You're actually gonna tell that story to the judge?"

"Yeah." Ryan shrugged again. "It's the truth."

"But you got no alibi, man...right?"

"Just the coyotes, and my own word."

"Well take it from me," his mate advised, "your coyotes count for shit, and so does your own word in this fuckin' system. There's no justice in this fuckin' system, man. No justice at all. It's just a fuckin' racket for lawyers and judges. That's all."

The fellow then swung onto his back and laid down on his bed, so Ryan did the same, but more slowly.

About 9:00 pm on November, 22, 2008, Hannah phoned a taxi cab to whisk her to the BC Women's Hospital. When she arrived she was too far advanced in her cervical dilatation to get to the delivery room, so she squatted in the emergency room lobby amidst a gaggle of assistants.

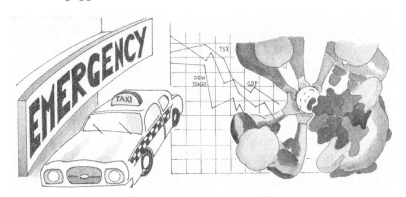

My own precious housing bubble popped right there as I fell

into awaiting hands, but I didn't drop as far as the stock market did. Oh boy. Mom's cervix may have expanded from seven centimetres to ten, in mere hours, but the Dow industrials fell 150 points almost as quickly. The S&P/TSX composite index dropped even more, plummeting 370 points, or 3.5%, to close at 10,574.98. Nasdaq sank too: 38.44 points to 1847.69. The threads on Bay Street were unraveling like my umbilical cord. The soles along Wall Street were splitting. The belts on Main Street were tightening, but my mom was in exhausted bliss.

Amelia Erica Verso, so my birth certificate read. Mother: Hannah Rosetta Verso. Father: Unknown. But that last part wasn't really true.

Frank came to see me the next day, pulling up a chair to the bed, telling Hannah "Congratulations!" and saying I looked adorable. He even encouraged Hannah to reconsider marrying him, right there on the spot, while my baby lips were glommed to a nipple. Sure enough, Hannah said No, so before leaving the hospital Frank gave a bucal swab at the lab, just to cover off the whole paternity issue.

Little did Frank or Hannah know that in a nearby operating theatre Denise Dickerson was undergoing a C-section. Just imagine, I was about to have my own baby sister. Well, okay, my own baby *half*-sister, but still, who's to complain? Before I could barely open my eyes I already had something in common with someone my age. Consanguinity. Just saying it makes me feel good. Denise christened the little tyke "Laura Lynn." Her birth certificate read, Father: Donald Roy Dickerson (deceased).

In the ensuing weeks and months Hannah showed me off to anyone and everyone on south Granville who cared to walk up close and make a fuss. Many passers-by did, usually wiggling their index finger in front of my face and asking me how old I was. I just lay there all snuggled in a sling, usually under an umbrella. Cactus adored me.

But be careful what you wish for. That's a wise warning to dreamers. Only a week or so after I was born Bing Crosby started dreaming of a white Christmas.

Hannah had to hear him sing about that dream in pretty much every store she shopped at. I'm sure a lot of Vancouverites hoped for a snowy Yuletide too, and they got it. Boy, did

they get it. The snow fell, and fell, and fell, more than it did on the Atlantic Coast. Flights got cancelled. Cars were buried and the streets were slick. Salt was added to the sidewalks, but insult was added to injury when the newspapers reported that Canada

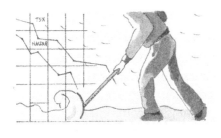

registered its first trade deficit in 30 years. Oh boy how the sky was falling. Retail sales plunged 5% across the provinces. It's hard to say whether consumers had just become a little too Scottish with their savings, even at Christmas time, or whether they just couldn't manœuvre to the

malls because of all the snow. Suddenly everyone was cursing the white Christmas and I'm sure more than a few people wanted to bust Bing in the chops whenever they heard him croon that cheesy song.

1st Quarter 2009

The New Year ushered in around the world with less fanfare than usual, given the sad state of the global economy. I was confined to the plastic bars of my cradle, like a chimpanzee at the zoo, or like Ryan Ghostkeeper, as he chaulked up his ninth month in the pre-trial jail. He did not join the others to watch the televised Times Square crowd count backwards from ten, or to listen to the dreary Scots tune play as streamers prettied urban skies. No, he drew pictures and imagined the day he would get to tell his side of the story to a judge, about how it all happened after he got fired from THE MANNA site.

Much to the dismay of ASHEPOND, in early January a ragtag congregation of homeless people, cyclists, and activists eagerly returned to the neighbourhood. An appeal judge in chambers had lifted the injunction against the community Cactus had established at 1620 Angus Drive. "It was the right thing for the court to do," Miss Veçerkavic told reporters. "It is a temporary measure, until the matter can be dealt with on its merits," a drawn CeeBee pointed out. "I remain confident that the law is on our side here," she added.

Sergeant Woolly seized the opportunity to further the interests of her peripheral investigation into Big Dick's murder. She sent boyish-looking Constable Tom Blundell into the commune to befriend James Bridges and, with any luck, pull information from him about the crime. Blundell would of course be acting in an undercover capacity, pretending to be a radical, left-leaning cyclist.

"I lost my shirt," Charlie Menz told Ruby, who was on shift at Ouisi, leaning against her side of the bar. "Almost all my RRSPs tanked."

"But the market went up today," Victor Pavlenko said, without looking up from his newspaper.

"What a relief," Charlie said cynically.

"So don't you think now is the perfect time for you to go out there and get a new shirt," Ruby commented playfully.

"A new what?" Charlie asked.

Victor lowered his paper slightly. "A new shirt."

Charlie leaned back and inspected his shirt. "Is it *that* bad?"

I was just takin' the piss," Ruby said, and Hannah smiled, having caught the banter as she walked through the bar's entranceway.

"C'mon. You said it, so you must've been thinkin' it," Charlie replied, just like one kid in a schoolyard to another.

Hannah had seen Charlie in his blue plaid shirt before, so worn and thin it had a silvery lustre. She couldn't imagine the man shopping for clothes.

Victor lowered his paper to look at Hannah.

"No paparazzi?" he asked. His tone was light.

Hannah reflexively shook her head, then paused, looked at Charlie and Ruby with a taut smile, and shrugged.

The cat was out of the bag. Charlie had biked past a Pacific Tides Trust billboard and recognized Hannah as the model. Naturally he had told Victor to check it out.

"What'll it be, darling? The usual?" Ruby asked.

"Yes please, but two."

"Whoa…A big appetite already?" Ruby said, indirectly referring to me.

Hannah smiled, handed Ruby a twenty dollar bill, and said, "The other one's for the real celebrity, actually. She's with Erica, at my place. I thought I'd just bomb over quickly and get us a bite, to take out."

"You guys are both vegetarians, right?" Charlie asked.

"Cactus is, but not me, not religiously, anyway." Hannah took some change from Ruby.

Victor chuckled and lowered his paper to the bar. "I should hope, madam," he said, "that you are no member of any such sect. Religious devotion is dangerous at the best of times, but to take an oath against the consumption of Canadian bacon, or beef au jus, if that's your cancer, is surely as unnatural as swearing off all knowledge that is carnal, is it not?"

Charlie was looking bemusedly at his friend. Hannah's eyes searched for some kind of explanation from either Charlie or Ruby. The barmaid just smiled and shook her head. Victor had the biggest smile of all.

"I confess, I couldn't do it," Charlie said. "I love burgers too much."

"But I thought you liked the veggie burgers here. You recommended I try one," Hannah said.

"Uh, yeah, but that doesn't mean I don't like a good all-beef patty."

"Seeking converts already?" Victor asked Hannah.

She rolled her eyes. "For somebody who's supposed to be reading the paper, you've sure got your attention elsewhere," she said playfully.

"A good veggie burger debate beats the Arts and Culture section any day," Victor said.

"Ahh, listen to you," Charlie said.

Victor grinned.

"He's featured today, in the Arts section," Charlie said to Hannah. "Here." Victor handed his newspaper to his friend and Charlie opened it up to a page showing Victor and one of his paintings. Hannah looked past Charlie's shoulder.

"Wow. Look at you," she said, casting Victor a big smile. "Your painting looks beautiful."

"You can see them if you like, at the gallery," Charlie said to Hannah, stating the obvious.

"I would really like that," she replied.

"Well the opening is March 27th. That's a Friday. I'd be more than happy to see you and your friend there, too, the vegetarian, if she likes," Victor offered.

"Here you go," Ruby said, handing a brown paper bag to Hannah from the other side of the bar.

Hannah thanked Ruby then turned to Victor and said, "Uh, sure. I'll let her know. It sounds great. Anyway, I've got to get back to my little one. I'll be in here again soon enough, and you," she said to Victor, "make sure you try one of these." She pointed to her bag. "They're great. They're not going to kill you."

"I don't know," he said with a glint in his eye. "I'm agnostic, by the way."

✌✌✌

By February the global economic meltdown, not to be confused with global warming, a mere trifle in comparison, was in full swing and showed no signs of abating. Pontiac the city went into receivership. Pontiac car sales declined almost 100% from the previous February.

Indeed, the seventh trumpet had clearly sounded and the seven angels hearkened with their poisonous vials. One by one the angels emptied these into the sea, the rivers, and the valleys. The wrath of God was evident everywhere. Frankenstein and Godzilla were still trampling the planet uninhibited. Ocean levels were rising. Forest and prairies were ablaze. But this was nothing yet. Six million Americans had foreclosed over the course of the last year. Five million Americans were on employment insurance, and the banks had to be propped up on stilts with hundreds of millions of tax dollars. Government helmsmen around the world threw their drowning citizens lifejackets called "stimulus" packages, unexpectedly causing panic among Viagra® shareholders.

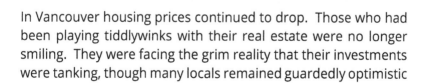

In Vancouver housing prices continued to drop. Those who had been playing tiddlywinks with their real estate were no longer smiling. They were facing the grim reality that their investments were tanking, though many locals remained guardedly optimistic of a turn-around, what with the 2010 Olympic Winter Games on the horizon.

Denise Dickerson was one such optimist. After pooling much of the largesse Donald had left her, she packed up the Yaletown penthouse, which she had sold just at the peak of the bubble, and moved to Bever*lee* – the Canadian version. She chose a modest 5,000 square foot dwelling in the British Properties, a bungalow with an indoor swimming pool and unobstructed view of Vancouver, and even Mount Baker on a clear day. Density was Don's thing, not hers.

Denise drew on a cigarette – an old habit she had resurrected, even with her new baby nearby – as her sister spoke to her from Cabbage Town.

"I know you you're tired of hearing it, Denise, but you should have divorced Don years ago," Louise told her. "I always thought he couldn't be trusted and I tried to tell you so in my own way."

Denise stared out her expansive living room window. "I wish you would have been more direct," she said to her sister.

Louise sighed. "Like I said, I tried now and then – so did Bernie – but you always defended him, like he was royalty or something. But there's no point dwelling on it. If you want us to come, we'll come. I've already told you that, and we mean it, both of us."

Denise looked up at her ceiling, hauled on her dart again, and said, "I'll think about it. I just don't know if I want to make a fuss or not."

She was referring to the one year anniversary of Don's death.

"Of course if you want to come here, you're welcome to do that. You know that," Louise said, and after a pause added, "We'd love to see Little L."

"I don't think I wanna put her on a plane right now. It might be too much for her. Besides, I've always hated crying babies on planes."

"Oh my. How considerate is that? Can't you leave her with Christina?"

"I don't know. I'll think about it. How about I get back to you in a few days."

"Well don't wait too long. Give us time to get reasonably priced tickets, if you can talk of such things anymore."

"Okay. Give my love to Bernie. Bye bye."

🚲 🚲 🚲

It was nearing quickly – the first anniversary of Big Dick's demise – and the realty tycoon lay no less deserving of formal commemoration than other great historical figures who had been cut down to size in the month of March.

Julius Caesar was the obvious one. He wasn't sufficiently wary of the full moon or the ambitions of his competitors. But there was King Eddie in England too. A nasty Queen named Etheldritha – sounds like an ingredient of anti-freeze, if you ask me – aided in his assassination. It must have been easy, though, because he got stabbed while sitting on a horse. Too bad. According to some, Edward was a real saint, even a martyr, for trying to save his Church.

Although the same could not be said about His Majesty Mr. Dickerson, Louise decided to fly out to Vancouver anyway, along with Bernard, to commemorate the anniversary.

The sisters were sitting at a granite topped bar in Denise's kitchen. The weekly Entertainment section of the paper was spread out in front of them, and Denise pointed to a quarter page advertisement for a vernissage at Modus, a posh gallery on 3rd Avenue, just south of Granville Island, near defunct railroad tracks.

"Why don't we go?" Louise asked.

"That's what I was thinking," Denise said. "I need to fill some of the wall space in this place."

Louise cut away a sliver of Camembert and placed it on a cracker, then picked a pitted Calamata olive from a dish and balanced it on the cheese before lifting the hors d'oeuvre to her mouth. Her lipstick print adorned the rim of a glass of Chardonnay.

"Your office needs a piece," Bernard remarked from a swivel chair in the den. He was down the hall, a good ten yards away from the sisters, searching restaurants on the Internet. The sun had almost set, and through the wall of glass in front of him he could see the entire cityscape of Vancouver beginning to glow. "I can see a really nice piece going over the printer here," he called out.

"Trading in Derivatives…Sounds peculiar," Louise said to herself.

"I wonder if he knew Don," Denise wondered aloud.

"Do you want me to Google the guy?" Bernard asked.

"Great idea," Louise replied.

"How do you spell his last name?"

"Let's see here. Pavlenko. P-a-v-l-e-n-k-o," Louise shouted down the hallway.

"It sounds like that psychologist, the one that did those tricks with the dog," Denise surmised.

"Oh." Louise chuckled. "You mean Pavlov."

"That's it." Denise took a sip of wine then said, "I hope the guy doesn't paint salivating dogs." The sisters chuckled.

"His stuff is good," Bernard called out. "Why don't you come and have a look?"

Louise rolled her eyes at the thought of having to get down from her stool. "That's all right. We trust your judgment."

"Oh God, I don't know about that," Denise said.

Louise looked her sister straight in the eyes, feigning great offence at the suggestion.

"You know, that awful sculpture thingy from London," Denise whispered.

Louise guffawed, then said, loud enough for Bernard to hear, "That's right. What were you thinking in London, Bernie?"

"Hey, that was a sound investment. What would you know?"

Louise winked at Denise and sliced herself another sliver of cheese.

"Maybe I'll meet someone rich and famous," Denise said with a playful lift of her eyelid.

"Hey hey hey. Easy there, sister. Don't get ahead of yourself.

We're here to pay that bank machine some respect."

Suddenly the sound of infantile bleating from Laura Lynn's bedroom stopped the ducks from quacking. Louise's eyes lit up. Denise shook her head gently before saying, "Let's go get 'er."

Both women crossed an expansive and polished living room hardwood floor. The interior lights of the room were off but exterior lights cut diagonally through the wall-to-wall plate glass and showed up the floor polish, as well as the tinted-glass top of a capacious, artfully shaped coffee table.

"Christina?" Denise called out calmly.

"I'm here, madam," a young woman from the Philippines announced. She emerged into sight from the dark.

"Louise wants to hold her for a few minutes first."

"No problem," Christina said.

At the door to Laura Lynn's bedroom Denise flicked the switch then approached the crib. Louise followed on her heels, with Christina behind.

Denise made a soothing sound and said, "Momma's here, sweetheart, and so is auntie Lou."

Denise picked up her child, who immediately calmed down, and gave her a kiss on her forehead. "There there, here's auntie," she said before handing her carefully to her sister. The three women smiled at one another.

Little L squawked a bit as Louise rubbed and patted her back.

"Can you give her a bottle?" Denise asked Christina. "We've got to be going."

"Of course."

So Louise handed Laura Lynn back to the nanny.

"Are you ladies ready to roll?" Bernard asked when the sisters appeared from the unlit hallway.

"What have we decided?" his wife quickly rejoined.

"Let's go to the Wedgewood," Denise suggested. "Just for a drink or two. Don always liked that place."

"And after the opening?" her sister wondered.

"Vij's. You'll love it," Denise proposed.

"Oh, sure. The Indian place you mentioned. Should we make a reservation?"

"No. They don't make them. First come, first serve," Denise informed her sister.

Bernie jingled his keys and said, "Then enough talk, please. I'm hungry enough as it is."

"Okay okay. Drink up, sis," Louise urged her sister.

Hannah and Cactus arrived at Victor's opening reception earlier than Denise and her relatives. Hannah had almost declined to show, as she had to find a babysitter, who turned out to be Frank.

"There he is," Hannah said to her friend, once inside. She could see Victor's profile as the star of the hour spoke to a few people. Small groups of other guests mulled in front of the various paintings throughout the gallery. Admirers and critics alike held glasses of wine, pointed and opined.

Cactus went to the bar, one of those long church bazaar tables draped in white linen, holding bottles of red, lines of glasses, and ice buckets of white wine and beer.

Hannah read the title of Victor's show printed across the top of one wall – *Trading in Derivatives: A History of Supply and Demand in Oil*. She did not know anything about art, so she believed, and presumed that the others around her did. Thus she was self-conscious as she crossed the floor toward the first painting that caught her eye.

It instantly conjured up a childhood memory. Mountain ridges and hills in the background followed the lines of a graph. A storm was coming from the upper left hand corner, and toward the right a partly deflated hot air balloon appeared to be falling behind the hills. A field of wheat was in the foreground and a few children were running through the stalks, apparently captivated by the falling balloon.

She recalled being in the kitchen, in Kelowna, some 25 years ago, when she was 10 or 11, and asking her mom if she could have a ride in a hot air balloon. It would be too dangerous, her mother told her, so she asked her father, who was watching television. He said the same thing and told her about the Hindenburg crash. When he finished that story he said it would be too expensive anyway. *He didn't know the cost of renting a balloon,* she now thought to herself, staring at Victor's painting. *That's what he always said when he didn't want to do something, or buy something...though he did get me that book afterward, with the beautiful pictures...Where is that thing anyway?*

"What do you think?"

Hannah's shoulders popped back and her heart nearly pumped through her ribs. She turned around and Cactus handed her a glass of red wine.

"Jesus, girl. You gave me a fright."

"It's called Inflation," Cactus pointed out.

"Huh?"

"Inflation. That's what he called it. Being ironic, I guess."

Cactus stepped in front of the adjacent painting, surveyed it for about ten seconds, then put her face up to the label. She read, "Twist and Shout, Oil canvas, 4' x 4', $8,000.00," as Hannah studied the image of a middle-aged man sitting comfortably on an old-fashioned porch in an armchair, smoking a pipe and reading the *Financial Times.*

I can't believe the detail, Hannah thought. She brought her face closer to the newsprint. 1930, she read.

The background was a desolate stretch of land, some telephone poles and lines receding to a vanishing point. A distant tornado appeared to be receding. *Or is it approaching?* she wondered.

"You didn't tell me you were such an art freak," Cactus said, waiting by impatiently.

"I'm not. I just want to appreciate what Victor does. That's all."

Hannah turned to survey the crowd, then said, "Hey, there he is, talking to Charlie, and Ruby too."

"Your friends?"

"Yeah, from the bar or whatever. I told you about 'em. Let's go say Hi. I'll introduce you to Victor."

Hannah and Cactus crossed the floor toward a small assemblage around Victor.

"Oh hi," Charlie said when he turned around and saw Hannah. She had tugged on the back of his shirt. "This is Cactus," Hannah said, and the teacher and the activist shook hands. "And this is Ruby," who also shook Cactus's hand.

Victor winked when he saw Hannah but did not stop talking to his admirers. "She's an MP, a conservative from Calgary," he said. "I can't remember her name but she was at a bar in Ottawa with her friend. At some point this drunk at the next table stood up and I'm not kidding, he dropped his pants right there and then… and then his underwear, right in full view of anyone who could see, I guess." Charlie grinned. Ruby was smirking.

Victor took a sip of his wine and winked again at Hannah before saying, "So the woman yells out, or someone did, I guess, 'What *the hell* are you doing?' and he says, 'Isn't it obvious? I'm tabling my stimulus package!'"

Ruby chuckled loudly and a big smile flashed across Charlie's face. Hannah cast Cactus a confused look.

"But that's not even the end of the story," Victor continued. "The crazy thing is that the prankster was charged with indecent exposure but he got off – no pun intended – because playing a joke is a legitimate defence!"

"Oh for Christ's sake. He must have had a pretty small package," Ruby said, with a glimmer in her eye.

Charlie groaned but a few others in the group burst out laughing.

Hannah grinned but didn't get the joke. Cactus just smiled and shrugged.

Victor caught Hannah's eye. "Thank you for coming," he said with sincerity.

"My pleasure. This is Cactus," who then shook Victor's hand. "I really like your paintings," Hannah remarked.

"Well thank you most kindly." Victor looked Cactus in the eye and said, "You're the vegetarian, right?" He was mindful not to refer to her celebrity status in Shaughnessy.

"Right you are."

"Well I finally convinced him to try one of the veggie burgers, and it obviously didn't kill him," Charlie said.

"But never again," Victor said. "I assure you, I'm back on the beef."

"Oh oh. Be careful now, Victor. You'll be in for a fight," Hannah said, knowing Cactus's sparkplug nature.

"Nah. Not here. Not tonight," Cactus said. "We're on your territory, but I would like to get another glass of red and look at more of your paintings."

"All right, but don't feel obliged, to look that is," Victor remarked affably. "Drinking and gossiping are de rigueur at these functions. Most of these people don't give a flea's fart about the art. They just want things to match."

Hannah rolled her eyes. "That's what you might think," she said, "but I'm going to look at more of your paintings too."

Hannah, Cactus and Charlie left Victor's coterie just as Denise Dickerson, Louise and their designated driver, Bernard, entered the gallery. The sisters were tipsy, rose-hued, and animated.

Louise headed for the wine bar, so Denise clasped Bernard's hand and pulled it gently in the direction of the east wall of paintings.

"Come with me. We've got some shopping to do," she said.

After running her eyes over a few pieces and checking out prices she asked Bernard, "So what do you think?"

"I don't know. They're, uh, interesting, I'll say that much," Bernard answered.

"Here darling," Louise said, handing her sister a glass of Pinot Noir. She gave Bernard a sparkling water.

"What do you think? Can you see any of these going in my living room?" Denise asked her.

"Let's look at the lot of them, first," Louise decided. "You don't want to be impulse buying here."

"Art's a big investment," Bernard reminded his sister-in-law.

"Well..." Denise turned around and looked at the other paintings in the gallery from a distance. "They all look to be pretty much the same to me."

"But let's go take a close-up look," Louise encouraged.

"Of course," Bernard agreed.

The trio moved along to a panel of Victor's paintings just as Hannah, Cactus and Charlie stopped at the bar for reinforcements. Charlie and Cactus were enthusiastically discussing the ASHEPOND conflict in Shaughnessy.

"Have either of you ever heard of Hazen Pingree?" Charlie ventured.

Cactus giggled and asked, "Hazen what?"

"Hazen Pingree. P-i-n-g-r-e-e."

"That's him, there. The greying guy, with the glasses," Louise said to Denise, pointing to Victor.

Hannah did not notice Louise or Denise's presence, as she was listening intently to what Charlie was saying. Neither Denise nor Louise recognized her, either.

"He was the mayor of Detroit, just before the turn of the century, when we, I mean Americans, were in yet another one of our recessions. He came up with this idea of growing potatoes on lots that weren't being developed."

Louise looked Denise in her lightly intoxicated eyes and asked, "Are you sure you want to do this?"

"We could do that," Cactus said. "There's still lots of space in the backyard. Or we could dig up the tennis court!"

Denise swallowed the last pool of wine in her glass and nodded.

"Why not?" Charlie wondered aloud, looking at Hannah.

"Then let's go," Louise said.

"Sure," Hannah replied to Charlie, unsurely.

Bernard ineffectually protested with a shake of his head before following the sisters to the artist.

"Excuse me sir," Louise said to Victor, who was talking to a couple at that moment. "I understand you're the artist here?"

"Uh, yes, that's me."

"Well my sister, Denise..."

Denise nodded at Victor and he smiled back.

"...would like to buy one of your paintings."

"Oh...that's wonderful. Which, uh..."

"I'd like that one right there," Denise said, pointing to a 3' by 3' canvas on the wall to his right.

"It's called Demand and Supply," Louise said.

"Oh yes."

"Her ex-husband's answer to everything," Louise quipped under her breath.

"I can see the colours working very well with the aubergine in my den."

Victor's pleasant face turned dour.

"I think so too," Bernard said. "You could use something above the printer."

Victor winced. "The?...Excuse me," he said. He could see Hannah chatting with Cactus and Charlie, and walked toward them.

"But sir!" Denise called out, following on his heels. "Where do I go to..."

Suddenly she stopped talking, and walking, for there she was, her nemesis with the beautiful smile, lashes and curves. Hannah had turned around to say hi to Victor.

Denise went stiff like a gopher in the cross-hairs.

Everyone in the gallery turned to see the source of the outburst. Victor then turned back to Hannah, whose big eyes showed fear, and knowledge.

Sensing a potential repeat of the Ouisi attack, Charlie stepped in front of Hannah and said, "Listen lady, get your ass out of here before I have it thrown out."

As a security guard approached, Louise clasped her sister's left arm, from behind. "Let it go," she whispered into Denise's ear, before casting Charlie and Hannah a dirty glance.

"Not a problem," Denise snapped. She turned to Victor and waved her finger at him. "If these are your friends, I don't want your lousy painting!" she said.

"Okay okay," Louise said softly to her sister. She tugged slightly on her arm and Denise fell back slightly on her heel. Victor moved forward to stabilize her.

"Fuck off," Denise slurred, "and get that whore out of my face." She threw her wine glass hard against the floor and cast Louise a look that said, 'This is fucking unreal!'

The security officer stepped forward to address Denise but she turned to Louise and said, "C'mon. Let's go."

Louise caught Bernard's eyes and nodded, then the Torontonians skulked their way out of the gallery, Denise in tow.

When the door was closed behind them Victor said to his patrons, "It's okay everyone. You got an unexpected bonus tonight. I didn't know there would be performance art, so my assistant will come around shortly with a hat. Be generous. It's important to keep the arts alive."

A few nervous guests chuckled. A caterer started to sweep up the broken glass.

"Sorry," Hannah said to Victor. "She hates me."

"Evidently," Victor acknowledged. "But pay her no mind. She has an aubergine den."

"Fuck. I was ready to clock her," Cactus added.

"No no no, I... Maybe we should get going," Hannah suggested. "Frank's been sitting long enough."

That wasn't entirely true. Frank had actually agreed to babysit me until midnight, but Hannah was embarrassed and ashamed by her encounter with Denise. She simply wanted to leave the gallery.

Victor left his friends to mingle with others.

"How are you gals getting home?" Charlie asked.

"We'll probably just walk, eh?" Cactus replied, looking at Hannah. Cactus had left her bicycle at Hannah's apartment.

Hannah nodded.

"Actually," Cactus said on second thought, "I might go to the Railway Club. A good band's playing there tonight: So Funking Uptight."

"I've heard of them. Yeah," Charlie said.

Cactus looked at Hannah with a sparkle in her eye. "You sure you've got to be home?" she asked. "These guys are supposed to be real good."

"Oh, all right, but we can't stay too long," Hannah resolved.

"That suits me fine," said Charlie. "We'll go for a set and I'll get you guys a cab home, if you like."

Hannah looked at Cactus, who nodded. "Okay. But let's get going then," Hannah urged.

🚲 🚲 🚲

2nd Quarter 2009

In the early morning of April 1, 2009, as Ryan Ghostkeeper lay on his side, on a tightly-packed mattress atop his slab of bed, he had a vivid dream.

He had finished most of his dinner and was now sitting on his bed, in his cell, watching a male coyote lick a plate of food clean. Another coyote, a mother, was lying in the corner of the cell on Ryan's prison-issue blanket. A litter of pups sucked on her teats.

When the male lifted his head Ryan looked into his eyes, put his hands warmly around the animal's neck and asked, "What do you know, bro? How are we gonna get her out of this place?" The male coyote looked at the mother and her pups for a few seconds, then turned to Ryan.

"Oh. I see," Ryan said, for he had read the male's eyes as saying that the mother had earlier found and swallowed a key to the cell. Ryan only had to wait for her to defecate, and the key to her and her family's rescue would be right there, like a diamond in the rough.

Footsteps approached unexpectedly and Ryan heard the click of the key unlocking his cell door. What *now*? he wondered as the door opened and a crack of light expanded across his walls.

A youngish man wearing a red baseball hat, a black hoodie and blue jeans appeared but instantly retreated behind the door at the sound of the male coyote's threatening growl.

"It's okay, buddy," Ryan said to the animal. He brought the coyote's head to his thigh and patted his ribs.

"Mr. Ghostkeeper, I am a police officer," the visitor said.

"What do you want?" Ryan asked.

"I've got great news for you, really."

"What is it?"

"Time for you to go home."

"Seriously?"

"I'm telling you God's truth."

"Then come in," Ryan said. "My friend here won't hurt you." Ryan turned to his companion and said, "Be nice now. This man is welcome here."

The cop entered. He had short, thick, wavy red hair and a five o'clock shadow. He was smiling.

"Lookie here. Nice dogs," he said, seeing the peaceful family scene.

"They're letting me go?" Ryan asked.

"Yeah. You wouldn't believe it. I just got a confession from the guy who killed Don Dickerson."

A surge of excitement caused Ryan to stand up instantly. The male coyote looked up at him and whined with happy anticipation.

"In a church confessional, if you can believe it. We had it wired. The guy thought I was a priest. You know. He broke down and said his guilty conscience had become too much to bear. Goof. I told him what his penance was and arrested him as soon as he stepped out of the booth."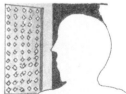

Ryan moved forward to hug the officer but was suddenly awoken by a baton tapping against his cell door, for real this time. His dream was over. He shifted in his bed. So did his cellmate.

"Ryan, wake up. I've got great news for you," a prison guard said.

Ryan opened his eyes again and turned his upper body weight onto his elbow.

"Fuck off," his cellmate said sleepily, to no one in particular.

The guard stepped. "Get up. This is a big day for you."

"What's up?" Ryan asked. His cellmate sat up and looked at the guard with a squint.

"They're letting you out today," the guard said.

"What?"

"Just what I said. You're a free man. Come on. Get up."

Fuck, Ryan thought. *Dreams do come true.*

He stood up and excitedly pulled his canvas pants over his legs, almost falling onto the ground. His cellie put his pants and shirt on with little emotion, and said "Fuckin 'eh."

"I can't believe it," Ryan said.

"You've got to have breakfast first, with everyone else," the guard said.

"No problem!"

Ryan and his mate followed the guard to the cafeteria. Prisoners were already in queue for their pancakes. Some had assembled at their tables and were securing their rations of orange juice. Another routine day in the life of institutionalized men was about to begin, and Ryan was not sorry for one minute to be leaving.

"Why are you so fuckin' happy?" one inmate asked when Ryan sat across from him.

"'Cause I'm going home today."

"You ain't fuckin' outta here today. Don't kid yourself," the inmate said, then he stuffed some pancake into his mouth.

Ryan looked around. Everything seemed normal, just as it was every other morning, but several prisoners suddenly looked up or turned their attention  to a sparkler flickering away on top of a muffin. An inmate was carrying the little cake on a plate, from the kitchen area, toward Ryan. He had already received permission to use the "one-off" sparkler, having promised not to use it violently, and having accepted that extra officers would be monitoring the ceremony. Such officers were now filtering into the cafeteria.

A big smile curved across Ryan's face. "I told you," he said to the inmate across from him.

When the inmate set down the muffin, its sparkler fizzling out, he said to Ryan, "It's your lucky day. Make a wish."

A guard retrieved the sparkler and walked away.

Ryan did not make a wish. He closed his eyes, prayed to the

Supreme Being and thanked it for bringing salvation to him. When he opened his eyes several inmates smiled and yelled out, "April Fools, fucker!" Ryan looked around, wildly. Some of his fellow cons erupted into laughter. His native brothers raised their shoulders, showing confusion.

Ryan stood up and grabbed the dastardly messenger by the neck. He squeezed hard and pummeled the fellow in the face, breaking his jaw. Other inmates jumped Ryan and a brawl ensued between Native and non-Native inmates. The guards took about fifteen minutes to get the situation under control. By then Ryan had suffered a severe beating to his head and ribs. He was subsequently charged with "assault causing" (bodily harm) for the damage he inflicted on the muffin prankster.

"C'est un possoin d'Avril – an April Fool's prank."

That's what Frank Belleveau told two attractive women at Kits Bar that very evening, right after telling them about Charles of Lorraine's infamous jail escape during the 30 Years war.

"Imagine dat," he said. "Dressed like farmers, de Duke and his wife just walked right out of dare. They even told the guards but those dummies did not do anything 'cuz it was April first. They thought it was just a prank."

Frank flashed a big smile and both women reciprocated, a fair-skinned, red-headed young woman named Jane, and Judy, her darker-toned, Italian-looking friend. All three were seated at a table in the busy bar, a notorious meat-market. Young and beautiful men and women, mostly university students, but also those professionals in their mid- to late-30s, like Frank, came to survey the scenery.

Tonight he was trolling for action. He had gone months without sinking his fly but was now thinking, *tonight's gonna be the night* – his line might just pull in one of the two rainbow trout smiling in front of him. The redhead had invited him to the table after chatting with him at the bar. When he laid eyes on her friend he happily accepted. Pretty face, brown eyes, jet black hair, *nice tits*, he thought – but not necessarily in that order.

Judy Costanza was a hard-body type, less curvy than Hannah, and Frank made most of his eye contact with her. She seemed amused by his accented observations – about the Quebecker, for example, who told the waitress to make it snappy because "ee" was parked twice outside, meaning double-parked. Judy chuckled at this and other examples of "Franglais" that Frank had to offer. Sometimes she lightly tapped his hand when making a point of her own. Good, he thought. Body language was important. She was physically comfortable with him.

When Jane stepped out to answer a cell phone call, Frank boldly took the opportunity to ask Judy for her number.

"Ahh...I don't...No," she said, looking toward the door, as if seeking her friend's assistance.

"Oh, okay. You think I'm not an onnest guy." Frank slumped against his chair back, deflated.

"Well, no. It's not..." Still no sign of Jane.

"Oh come on, Ju-dee. I'm a decent guy, hard-working. I'm just asking for one date, just...."

"Okay okay. Give me your number."

Frank provided his phone number, watching as Judy typed it into her iPhone. "Will you really phone me?" he asked as soon as she was finished.

"Sure. Yeah...Probably, okay?" she said nervously as Jane approached the table.

"I look forward to it," Frank said, immediately smiling.

Charlie Menz did not have as much as Frank in most departments: permanent residency status only, a rented room on Victoria Street, an outdated laptop computer, and a few low-paying teaching contracts in urban planning, one at Douglas College and two at Simon Fraser University. But he did share one attribute with Frank that most other mortal men lacked: the nuts to ask Hannah Verso out for a coffee.

"It's like your reserves. Your native reserves, on the prairies," he said to her over a coffee on West Broadway, just north of the hospital. "I drove by a couple of those in Alberta when I was coming out here. Jesus. They look like some of the neighbourhoods in Detroit, but nicer, if you can believe that. These are decrepit communities and houses I'm talking about.

Completely barren, burnt right out. Ramshackled. Some of them look like abandoned farm houses, which is why I guess they've got all these start-up farm projects going on."

"In the city?

"Yeah. Right smack in the city, but it doesn't look like a city. That's what I'm sayin'."

"Detroit doesn't look like a city?"

"Well, in the downtown, of course, but not the residential areas. There are vacant blocks everywhere, in the East Side, North, even West as you get further from downtown. Wasteland, everywhere."

"That's where you grew up?" she asked.

"No. I grew up in Birmingham."

"In England?"

"No no, I'm talking about a boring, wealthy suburb of Detroit. I moved out when I finished high school, to midtown. I wanted to study city planning and design. I actually wanted to live in Detroit, if you can believe it, so I went to Wayne State." Charlie paused, then asked, "How is it?" in reference to the carrot cake Hannah was eating.

She nodded, then swallowed and said, "Just fine. Would you like to try it?"

"Sure," he said, so Hannah handed him her fork. He carved off a slice and shoveled it in. "It is good – fresh," he remarked. After rinsing it down with a sip of coffee, he said, "In my fourth year I wrote an essay entitled The Real American Revolution. It actually got published – a professor encouraged me to do it – so I went to graduate school."

Hannah's eyes lifted. "You're an author?"

"Uh, yeah, but not like you're thinkin. My article was for academics. It's in a journal."

"Like a magazine?"

"Uh...I guess, but a magazine for geeks."

Charlie smiled. So did Hannah. "So you wrote about the American revolution?" she asked.

"Yeah. I just didn't think there was anything interesting about Americans beating the British, y'know, in 1776. We got political independence, sure, but so what? Now we've got financial dependence, on China and other places. We're resource dependent all over the place, so we're not much better off than where we started, if you ask me. Besides, the Brits weren't all that bad. Hell. You guys didn't complain, and you're doin just fine."

Hannah didn't quite know what Charlie was talking about, though she had listened to Frank disparage the British enough times to sense that Charlie didn't have the full picture, or wasn't giving her it. "Les maudits anglais," Frank would sometimes say.

"My essay argued that the real revolution began right in the heart of Motor City, and that the very reasons America became great are the exact same reasons for its demise."

Hannah scraped the remaining icing and cake off her plate with her fork. "What do you mean, its demise?" she asked.

"Well. Just take Detroit. Its citizens are starving, *en masse.*"

Hannah cast him a look of disbelief.

"I'm not kidding," he said. "In the heartland of the richest country in the world, lots of people are starving. And like I said, there's acres of dilapidated properties."

"Maybe you need a politician like that guy you were telling us about, the guy who planted all the potatoes."

"Oh yeah, Pingree. Absolutely. There is a lot of that going on, actually. Detroit's probably at the forefront of this type of urban innovation in North America, but any city could do it. We all did it, well, lots of Americans did it during World Word II – to stave off food shortages caused by rationing. They were called Victory Gardens back then."

"Wow. Victory Gardens. That's wonderful," Hannah said, smiling. "I've seen a couple of community gardens here," she noted, "and Cactus is trying to do her thing."

"Oh I know. Vancouver's starting to get this happening," Charlie conceded. "But it's all too little, too late, wouldn't you say?"

"Why do you say that?"

"Because you're going the same way here as Detroit did, and L.A., with their massive freeways. Expand, expand, expand – create an automobile dependency – and devour farmland in the process."

"But what are we supposed to do? The population's getting bigger, isn't it?"

Charlie shook his head in frustration. *It's not because the population's getting bigger.* He wanted to say that Don Dickerson was on the right track, that multi-use buildings even high-rises had to be the wave of the future, but he knew a lot better than to resurrect that dead horse.

"It is," he replied, "but that's not the problem."

"Why did you come to Canada?" Hannah asked.

"I got a scholarship, from UBC, to do a doctorate in urban planning. When I checked out the campus I liked it, so I came, but I never did finish my degree."

"Why not?"

"Well, I'm not so sure I want to –" Charlie shifted in his seat and looked away for a few seconds.

"Oh. I'm sorry if I –"

"It's all right. It's all right. I – I just have a tendency sometimes to get a little down. I hit a low period at UBC."

Hannah looked into her cup of latté then lifted it up for a sip.

"I couldn't get inspired," Charlie said, lightening his tone. "I don't know why exactly, but it wasn't the first time I found myself in trouble like that."

"What do you mean – trouble?"

"With my mind. I've had this recurrent thought, ever since I was a teenager, really – that maybe there's no point in striving toward anything; that maybe I shouldn't care about doing anything good for society – do you know what I mean?"

Hannah's eyes had widened. She gently shook her head in the negative.

"I just think sometimes I should stop trying to do anything meaningful, that's all, because it's kind of a delusional goal. It's way easier just to live in the moment; to eat when you want to eat; to drink when you want to drink; even to have sex when you want to have sex."

He blushed when he said that last part. So did Hannah.

"Now maybe you're thinkin' that sounds horrible," Charlie continued, "like that's not a good way to be, and you might be right if you thought that, but I'm not so sure. I've never figured out what I've been put on this earth to do – to enjoy myself, or to help other people, and – "

"But can't you be both ways?" Hannah interjected.

"I don't think so, and this is my recurring dilemma. Or let me put it this way: If I take life seriously, then I inevitably get depressed, because life is depressing when you take it seriously – whether it be shootings of innocent people, the state of the environment, poverty, hunger, yah da yah da yah da. And I can't change any of that. Neither can you. So what's the alternative? To accept the mess we've created for ourselves, and I don't know, act as if it's not right before our eyes: to have fun, to party, to gorge ourselves? That's what I see all around me in this city, so why don't I just join in?"

Charlie shrugged his shoulders after saying that.

"But you've helped Cactus out, with that potatoes idea, and that's doing something important, I think." Hannah reached across the table, looked Charlie in the eye, and clasped his wrist.

A tingle went up his spine and colour rushed to his cheeks. He hesitated before saying, "I sometimes think I'm all fucked up just because I'm a Pisces."

Hannah chuckled, then he blushed.

"I've been told a little about that stuff here and there – I know it's a lot of hocus-pocus – but it seems pretty much on the money, for me, at least."

"So what are Pisces like?" Hannah asked.

"Lost souls. Perpetually caught between two worlds. Poets at heart, romantics, artists, whatever, but we won't unchain ourselves from reality. We accept reality just as much as we long for it to be different."

"You're fish," Hannah added gently.

"Yeah. Fish out of water…Out of the smelly Detroit River, in my case," he said with a smirk. "But what about you?" he asked. "Do you fit your sign, whatever that is?"

Hannah smiled. "I think so. Can you guess it?"

Charlie shook his head. "I have no idea," he said, "but I don't think you're a Pisces."

"I don't seem like a lost soul to you?"

"Nope. Not from what I can tell. You seem like you've got your shit together pretty much, if you can pardon the expression."

Hannah kept smiling. "I'm a Libra," she said. "And yeah, I think I pretty much fit the sign – the scales."

"So you're fair, is that the idea?"

Hannah nodded. "And other things."

"Like what?"

"Uh...well, we're supposed to be smart, and sensitive, and, well, graceful."

"That's a Libra?"

"Pretty much. I honestly don't know that much about astrology."

Hannah had a sip of her latté.

"Are you from here?" Charlie asked.

"From Vancouver?"

"Yeah. Don't take offence, but you look Brazilian or something like that."

"I'm Canadian. I was actually born in Kelowna, shortly after my parents moved here, to Canada. My mom's from Portugal. My father's Dutch. They came here in the 60s, like a lot of Portuguese people."

"But your dad is Dutch?"

"Yes. He was the son of a farmer, and he liked to fish. He met my mom during a trip he took through Portugal, a vacation, fishing up the coast, from Lagos up to Lisbon. He was with some friends and they were out for dinner one night, in Lisbon I guess, and he saw my mom. She was out with her own friends. She's very pretty. And, well, my dad must have had some nerve, asking her group to join his, but they did, and the rest is history as they say."

"Could they even speak each another's language?"

Hannah chuckled. "Not really, but mom says he was really charming. He carried a harmonica around with him and he's good. He can play some serious blues."

"So what? They got married?"

"Yeah. In Lisbon. Dad left the family farm and moved there. It was the honourable thing for him to do."

"And then they came to Canada?"

"Yeah. They went to the Okanagan and worked on orchards for a while. Mom got work as a chambermaid, but it didn't take dad long to get his own farm running."

"And you were born in?"

"Hey. We girls don't just announce that stuff."

Charlie grinned. "Okay. X that one," he said. "But when did you move here?"

"A few years after high school. I followed a boyfriend. He got a scholarship to go to UBC – just like you, but his was to play hockey."

"Wow. He must have been good."

"He was. He was a big, tough guy, like most of my boyfriends."

Charlie furrowed his brow.

"I don't know," Hannah said. "Those have always been the guys who ask me out. I guess I like the feeling of security they give me..."

"But – " Charlie anticipated.

"But, yeah." She chuckled, then said, "there's always a but, isn't there?"

Charlie smiled, shrugged, then looked at his watch and said, "Don't you need to be getting back? It's three o'clock."

"Oh yeah. You're right. Thank you."

Hannah did indeed have to return to her apartment, as she had left me with Cactus and promised to be no more than an hour.

Not surprisingly, Frank wanted my mom to know that he had found himself a new girlfriend.

"I met her at the bar," he told her over the phone.

Hannah paused before saying, "Funny how history repeats itself."

Frank chuckled. "What's that expression you English have?" he asked. "You can take de man out of de boy, but..."

"But you can't get either of 'em to piss sitting down."

Frank laughed. "She said I looked like a cop, and she had a thing for cops," he said. Hannah rolled her eyes and paused before asking, "So is she pretty?"

"Han*nah*. You know you don't need to ask that."

Hannah rolled her eyes, again. "What does she do?" she asked.

"To be honest, I didn't quite understand it, but something to do with advertising."

"Well that's good. She makes her own money."

"Of course, but she won't have to spend it."

"Come on now. You're such a bullshitter."

"Eh!"

"Oh give me a break, Frank. That's exactly what you told me, if I remember correctly, but you were a little tighter with your purse strings than you like to imagine."

Frank was chuckling.

"I don't know what's so funny," Hannah said, "but I'm happy to hear you in such a good mood for a change. I hope it works out, but I should get going…"

"Oh, do you have someone special in your life now too?"

"Uh, sorta, kind of, sorta…but not really, no. I've just gotta get to work, and make sure Erica is ready for Cactus."

"All right. I'll get going, but I'll let you know how things go."

"Of course. You don't have to be a stranger."

"Thank you. Salut."

"See ya."

Hannah hung up the phone and came to my crib. I was lying awake, squinting at my mobile, which wasn't actually mobile at the time. It was stationary. Words can be so tricky at times.

↖↑↪

Frank met up again with Judy Costanza, the athletic-looking gal from the bar. They were downtown at Rick's, a thin-crust slice of licensed real estate just off Georgia and Hornby. The sun was almost ready to pack it in for the day, as was Judy. She had waited nearly a half hour before Frank arrived.

"You came," she said when he approached her booth. "I was starting to think..."

Frank stopped and opened his arms. "Of course I came," he interrupted. "Why wouldn't I come?" He glanced around the bar.

"Ah...for starters, you were a little drunk when you asked for my number, if you can remember?"

"Of course I remember. Sure, I was drunk, but that wouldn't stop me from carrying through with my word, Ju-dee."

"Well you're here now, and I can stop thinking about being stood up..."

"I'm sorry for being late," he said. "I had a bit of trouble starting my bike." Frank slid into the booth, across from his date. "You look great," he remarked.

"You're lookin' fine yourself."

"Do I still look like a cop?"

"Yeah. You do, so grow your hair a little and maybe I'll change my mind."

A pretty, smiling waitress approached and took their drink order. Frank eyed her up and down. When she left Judy said, "Do you have an eye for all the ladies, Frank?"

"Not all of dem. Not monsters."

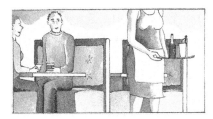

"Monsters?"

"You know what I mean. The scary ones. C'mon. Admit it. Some women are prettier than others. No big deal."

Judy stared blankly at Frank. He pronounced "others" as "udders," so however one sliced it, Judy thought, his comment required explanation.

"What's the big deal?" he asked after a few seconds silence.

"It's not a big deal. Just don't call women 'monsters.' It's not kind."

"All right, but I bet you never put any homely ones in your tv ads? Right? That's what you do, don't you? Make commercials?"

"Sure. Well I used to, but it's been a while since I've had any decent work. The business has gone south."

"Tell me about it. We've had contracts that have just gone nowhere. All kinds of sites around here have stopped building. Construction costs have gone up too high. Developers' money has dried up. Pre-sale buyers are going mental."

The waitress set down a Rye and Coke for Frank and a Sour Apple martini for Judy. "Can we just run a tab?" Frank asked.

"Sure," she said. The waitress turned away and Frank made a point of not looking at her butt.

"Cheers," he said, raising his glass. Judy responded in kind, then said, "I guess it's pretty bad everywhere, but I'm sure getting sick of hearing about the car industry. That's all we ever hear about. Three billion here. Ten billion there." She let out an impulsive chuckle and then remarked, "Christ,  we used to say 'money doesn't grow on trees.' Apparently it does if you're in the business of making shitty cars."

"So what do you do now?" Frank asked.

"It depends, really. I started up a business where I spruce up homes before they go on the market. Staging. It's so so. I work with some of the decorating people I know. It was going well while the market was hot, but even that's dead now."

Judy paused and sipped on her martini.

"I'm helping out my sister right now. Her common law, a real bastard, he took off with her car and left her high and dry."

"Oh shit."

"Just last week. They had a fight over breakfast. He complained that the coffee was too weak, the bacon too dry, that kind of thing, if you can believe it, and then just scooped up her keys and drove away."

Frank shook his head knowingly. "I think they have bigger problems than coffee and bacon," he said.

"Yeah. Exactly. But no one knows where he went. Dianne called the police and they told her they got bigger fish to fry. 'He'll come back,' they told her. Pffff. They're just lazy, if you ask me, and right now Dianne is managing her two little girls by herself, getting them to the bus and getting to work on the bus herself. It's a real pain so I'm helping her out, giving rides from school when I can, and helping with after-school supervision, that kind of thing."

"He sounds like a prick," Frank said.

"Tell me about it. If I ever get my hands on him I'll throttle him within an inch of his life."

Judy tensed her arms and held her hands about six inches apart, her fingers poised for the imaginary squeeze. *This chick has a couple of big guns*, Frank thought as he slid his drink down the hatch.

"Can I get you another one?" the waitress asked. Frank had not seen her approach. "Sure. Uh, a double, please." He looked at Judy. "No thanks. I'm good for now," she said.

When the waitress turned her back Judy said to Frank, "Take it easy, man. The night is young."

"Okay. You got me a little revved up there."

"Well it's serious. I want to find Roy and bash his brains in."

"Roy?"

"That's his name."

"Where do you think he is?"

"I don't know. Why? Are you in an adventurous mood?" A mischievous, almost coy smile formed across Judy's face. It was sexy, and heightened Frank's attraction to the stranger across from him.

"Rye and Coke, two shots," the waitress said, setting down Frank's drink. Frank looked up at her and could not stifle a grin. The waitress eyed Judy's empty glass.

"C'mon, let's order one more round – for the road," Frank urged her.

"All right. I can have one," Judy replied.

The waitress left and Judy said to Frank, "I take it that's a yes?"

Frank grinned again and said, "Sure. So where are we going?"

"I don't know. We could go to Burnaby. Roy could be hiding out there, with relatives. I know where they live. They're scumbags just like him. But he could be in the Interior – Kamloops, or around Lake Shuswap – cocaine central. He's probably gone back to using, so that's where I think he is – that's his community."

"In the Shuswap?"

"That's where it all started for him," Judy said, "but he'll probably come back pretty soon, with his tail between his legs. He always does."

"So what are you saying? You want to go to Burnaby tonight to spy on Roy's relatives? Just the two of us?"

That's exactly what I'm saying, Judy thought. "I'll do the driving. It'll be fun," she said.

After they had finished their drinks Judy took her Sarasota orange Firebird and Quebeçois companion along East Hastings Street and into the sleepy hollow of Burnaby. After turning south on Delta Avenue then East onto Union she slowed down. Simple, one story homes set back from the sidewalk by modest front lawns and young trees lined both sides of the street. Madonna's pulsating tunes filled the car's interior, giving it a dance club vibe. Frank was feeling buzzed.

"What are you gonna' do if you find him?" he asked.

"I'll call him out."

"Aren't you frightened to just show up, without notice? What if he gets aggressive?"

"If ee gets aggressive," Judy said, again with a mischievous smile, "that's where you come in."

"What?"

"What do you think I invited you along for? Your good looks?"

"A man can hope," Frank replied with a knowing smile.

Jesus, no lack of confidence in this guy, Judy thought, but she couldn't disagree with his self-estimation. He was handsome. "You're not yellow, are you?" she asked.

"Yellow?"

"Chicken."

"*Tabarnak*. No, but…"

"I can handle myself," Judy interrupted, amicably. "You're just back-up." Then she turned into a quiet, dark, residential street, cutting the volume on her stereo and slowing down.

"If I don't see the car," Judy said, "let's call it a night."

"You don't want to go for another drink?" Frank ventured.

Judy smirked upon hearing an "udder" drink. "Nah. Not tonight," she said. "I've got too much to do tomorrow, but I'll give you a ride back to your car."

Frank sighed.

"What does it look like?" he asked.

"It's a new Forester. A Subaru wagon. Green."

"I'm not familiar with those."

"Just look for a shiny, compact wagon. I'll recognize it, but y'know, I'm not seein' it. There's his driveway, right there," she said, pointing to a driveway on Frank's right. "That's his brother's piece of shit."

The Firebird rolled by a lightweight Ford pick-up, which Frank thought was a nice truck, but he saw no point in disagreeing with his date.

"I don't see it anywhere," she said before turning up the stereo and picking up her pace.

The duo returned west along East Hastings, under the muted beams of street lamps.

When Judy arrived at Ric's and parked, Frank turned to her and said, "So you're not inviting me over?"

"Whoa there. Not quite so fast. I'm not that kind of girl," she replied.

"Okay. All right. But I'm not just a muscle guy for you, am I?" Frank's tone had a pinch of insecurity to it.

Judy reached over and cupped Frank's chin with her left hand. "Don't be silly," she said. "I didn't take your number because I needed an enforcer. That's not it, but I was a bit drunk the other night, okay? Let's take it easy. I like you, but every time I moved too fast with a guy I've been burned. I've got trust issues. I'm telling you that right now."

Frank turned his mind to thoughts of Hannah. He was pining to feel the warmth of a woman's naked body next to his, and the fact that he would unexpectedly be left cold for a night brought memories of making love to

Hannah into bitter relief.

"Where's your car?" Judy asked.

"I don't have one. I ride a bike, remember?"

"Oh yeah, but you're not biking home tonight, are you? Please tell me you don't drink and drive, Frank."

"Well, I could drive my bike tonight, I know dat, but if you insist, maybe I shouldn't. Maybe I should get a ride home from you?"

"Where do you live?"

"Just over the Cambie bridge. Not too far, I promise."

"Well, only if you promise me that you'll never even consider riding your motorbike after you've been drinking."

"Oh Judee." Frank sighed. "I swear. I give you my word."

⚡ ↓ ⚡

Judy phoned Frank a few days later, mid-week, and offered to take him to Anton's, a cheap pasta restaurant at the easternmost end of East Hastings Street, or at the westernmost base of Burnaby Mountain, whichever way one wanted to look at it. Anton's was a bit of a local spectacle. It drew diners with really big appetites and general penchants for 'trying their luck' to its tables by offering meals *gratis* to those who could completely finish their servings. Of course, to minimize this possibility the servings were gargantuan – bigger than IHOP stacks – and whatever the conversation around the checkered cloths might be, one thing was for certain: no patron ever ventured to ruin another's bloated pleasure by mentioning starving children in

Africa.

"Why there?" Frank asked. "I can never eat the full meal."

"But it's fun," she said. "I love standing in that silly line-up."

"All right. Let's do it."

Judy looked just as sexy as she did on the weekend, as far as Frank was concerned. She wore a pony tail and large hoop earrings, and her taut biceps were exposed. Had she not accentuated her breasts in a sporty black top, Frank might have felt a little sexually confused.

While he piled in a mound of baby clam pasta Judy informed him that Roy had returned her sister's car just a couple of days ago, and that she herself, Judy, had come close to turning him in – or "shoving his head into a running engine fan."

Frank sat back.

"What?" she asked.

"Why do you talk like that?" He wiped spaghetti sauce off his lips.

"Like what?"

"Like you would shove someone's head into a running fan."

"'Cuz I'd really do it. That's why."

Frank cast his date a doubtful look, then lightly shook his head.

"I did not know I was dining with such a wildcat," he said before plunging his fork back into his spaghetti.

"I stand up for myself, Frank. It's more than I can say for a lot of people, men especially."

Judy watched with amazement as Frank managed, mouthful by mouthful and in between idle talk to make the monumental serving of pasta before him disappear into his intestines. The effort was not pretty – almost concerning, Judy thought – but Frank was determined to impress his date.

She just shook her head, grinned and said "cheapskate" when Frank sat back in his chair and extended his arms, clearly to say, 'Look at me. I did it.' Other patrons definitely looked.

"Oh come on," he said in a lightly pleading tone; smiling, but urging his date to give credit where credit was due.

"All right, fat boy. You're a real champ," she told him, and in truth she was impressed. Such an unrehearsed act of gluttony took serious determination.

Upon leaving Anton's Judy and Frank continued on to the Pat Pub, a blue-collar watering hole and micro-brewery just west of Main Street on East Hastings Street. The bar itself occupied the ground level of a cheap hotel, The Patricia – thus "The Pat" pub. Patrons walked into the smell of old carpet, stale cigarette smoke, and artificial air freshener. The dart board was popular but there was never more than 10 tables full on the floor, even on a Friday night – except when Jelly Roll Morton used to play there 90 years ago. On this night, an amateurish band, three guitarists and a drummer played 70s Billboard hits loud enough to make every conversation one-sided.

"You what?" Frank asked, leaning in closer to Judy's ear.

"Just what I said." She turned her head toward him.

"You deal?" he asked in whispered disbelief.

"Just a little," she said. "A girl's gotta' make ends meet somehow. We're in a recession here, as you've noticed."

Frank shook his head but with drunken eyes lifted his glass. Judy met it with a childlike smile.

"Whadd'ya say?" she asked, looking her date coyly in the eyes. "Do you want a little piece of the action?"

"Are you serious?"

She closed her eyes and nodded.

Frank turned his head and watched the bassist pluck away to "Sweet Home, Alabama."

Sweet home, he mused. He imagined his kitchen in Ste. Foy, with his mother and sister and himself standing around drinking coffee, his mom's long grey hair, her delicate fingers holding a cigarette, and then he felt Judy's hand on his.

"Let's dance."

He looked her in her dark eyes – *noisette*, in his native tongue – so different from Hannah's. "Okay," he said, "but I'm warning you. I'm a shitty dancer."

"Look around," Judy said. "There's no one Dancing with the Stars here."

Frank worked off a little anxiety and carbs on the small, parquet dance floor. He had the prettiest and fittest partner on the floor, he was sure about that, but he felt clumsy in the face of her limber moves. After four or five songs she obliged his request to sit down and drink more beer. With a fresh one at hand he told Judy about his family in Québec and his mother's death, and she disclosed that her father beat her as a child. "Me and my sister," she confided. When he heard that he twitched, for he too had struck the opposite sex – Hannah and a previous girlfriend. He reached out to Judy's arm, to show sympathy, but she just flexed it and said, "Why do you think I've got such big guns?"

"You're serious?" he replied, with a hint of doubt in his voice.

She was smiling. She knew he was impressed but she just shrugged it off. He sat back as she said, "Pretty much. I had to get tough because my sister sure wasn't going to. I was stronger than her anyway, so I would intervene and things sometimes got ugly, but it was really in high school that I first started lifting. I thought it was cool. It allowed me to vent a lot of frustration."

"Well, they look good," Frank said. "Your pipes, that is."

"Do you want an arm wrestle?" Judy asked playfully.

"Hell no. I don't want to be beat by a woman, at least not here, in public."

"So maybe later?" was the flirtatious response, accompanied by a wink.

"Now you're talking."

After Frank drank another beer Judy gave him a ride home. At the curb across from his house Frank leaned over to give his date a kiss but she drew her head back.

"Ju-deeee," Frank whined. "I thought you..."

"Hey hey hey. Just slow down, okay?"

"But...but...you said." Frank was searching Judy's chocolate brown eyes for an explanation, but she kept them vacant.

"When I drink I can get a bit carried away," she offered.

"What?...Dis is your big trust issue, right?" he wanted to know. Judy remained still.

"You've asked me to hunt down an asshole thief, then to sell dope with you, and you can't agree to a kiss?"

Frank sat back in his seat, dropped his shoulders, and continued to look the driver in the eyes.

"It's just a kiss, Judy. I think you're gorgeous. You gave me a great time tonight. You're hot as hell so I want to kiss you. What's the big deal?"

Judy looked him straight in the eyes, without blinking, then he sighed and said, "Okay, if it helps you, okay, I'll ask around. I'm sure there's many of de guys on the site who'll be interested."

Judy leaned forward, put her hands on both sides of Frank's face, and looked him closely in the eyes before giving him a sensual kiss. Frank reached out with his right arm and put it around her back. In this awkward position, with the Firebird's centre console between them, they kept their lips pressed together for a minute before Judy gently pulled back and said, "Okay. Okay. Enough. I'm sorry, Frank, but no more tonight, okay? I'm so glad you came out with me. Truly. I'm serious. You're – you're bellisimo. Truly. But let's pick this up later, next week. Okay?"

Frank's eyes showed disappointment.

"C'mon, Frank. We got lots of time for this. I gotta go slow, okay? I won't let you down. Let's just take our time."

Frank groaned. "So when - when next week?"

"Uh, I dunno'. Probably next weekend. I'll phone mid-week if that's all right. I might have something for you."

Frank shrugged and stared at the gearshift. "Sure," he sulkily agreed. Then he got out of the car, looked back in through the passenger window, and gestured for Judy to call him.

ಠಠಠ

The mood was more cheerful among the residents at 1620 Angus Drive. After all, June was Bike Month, a celebration of what many members of Cactus's co-op, including those in the Resistance, regarded as the healthiest religion in the world. June was also the one month of the year when the true believers, and the exhibitionists, got a lawful opportunity to bare more than just their souls to their two-wheeled deity.

"C'mahhhnnn. You'll love it," Cactus urged Hannah over the phone. "We're all going."

"I don't think so," Hannah said. She was in her fat arm chair. Charlie sat on the sofa across from her, thumbing through a magazine.

"You got nuthin' to be squeamish about, sister. You've got the sweetest goods around: no question about that."

"I'm not a nudist, though." Hannah glanced at Charlie with a raised brow and a smile. He looked up from the magazine with a wrinkled grin.

"So wear body paint, panties, a bra," Cactus suggested. "Not everyone goes full-on skin."

"That's okay. I'm just too shy, but I am for sure going to come to the ride at the end of the month."

"All right. Suit yourself, but make sure you invite Charlie, okay?"

"Well, he's right here actually - fully clothed. Do you want me to ask him right now?"

"Fer sure."

Hannah turned to Charlie and said, "Cactus is inviting you to join the naked bike ride with her this Saturday."

"Is she gonna get naked?" he asked.

"I assume so."

"Tell her, uh No, but I'll definitely watch from the sidelines."

"Seriously?"

"You kidding," Charlie retorted. "Why would I miss a chance to see Cactus naked?"

Hannah eyes blossomed in a playful expression of shock. "Did you hear that?" she asked her friend.

"What?"

"Charlie has declined your offer, but he's going to be on the sidelines. He's really excited to finally see you naked."

"Pervert, pervert, pervert."

Both women chuckled.

Cactus got off the phone and returned outside, where her motley crew of sodbusters was tended lovingly to tubers of their own. The Angus Drive potato patch and vegetable garden were coming along swimmingly, and Cactus had announced to the media that the surplus harvest (after residents had stored their fill) would be distributed among the East Side's needy.

Even the mole in the area had recently sought cover elsewhere. "Tommy," a.k.a. Constable Tom Blundell, had learned a lot about gardening but not much about Slim Jimmy and his friend Derek's possible involvement in the Dickerson murder. He had actually met Derek and got around to talking about motorbikes.

"Slim tells me you have a bike too," he had said to his new acquaintance.

"*Did* have."

"Ah shit. That's a bummer. What did you have?"

"A Ninja, 650R."

"Oh shit. That's a nice bike. What did you do – convert?" Blundell patted the centre bar of Derek's bicycle when he asked that.

"Actually. No," Derek said. "You remember when that Dickerson guy got killed?" he asked.

"Yeah, sure. Who doesn't?"

"Well the cops got on my case about it, because of Slim and his fuckin' stupid website. I couldn't convince 'em I had nothing to do with it, so I sold it to a guy – out of sight out of mind, best policy – and fuck, wouldn't you know, I bumped into him a few months ago, on the Drive."

Blundell tipped his head.

"In a cast – a fuckin leg cast, and a crutch – so I had to ask him, y'know, not really sure if I wanted the answer but, if you know what I mean..."

Blundell nodded.

"Yeah, right," Derek said, "I asked him, 'How's the bike?'"

"And..."

"Sure enough. He crashed it."

"Better him than you," Blundell added. *But very shitty for us*, he knew.

Blundell dutifully updated Woolly, who readily conferred with Sorenson, who quickly asked, "Who cares?"

"I care," she said. "That bike was a two-seater. He told me that himself. And we can't positively say he was not there. We can't pin him down, we can't pin Bridges down, and it looks like a joint hit."

"Unless it wasn't."

"I know, I know. You think I'm wasting my time. You're convinced it's Ryan. Frank's tires proved inconclusive. Denise was clearly in T.O."

"Forget her. She didn't love him enough to want him dead," Sorenson said.

"Oh oh oh says the divorced man of...what is it now, five years?"

Sorenson grinned.

"He was ready to divorce her for Miss Pretty," Woolly pressed.

"So what? The plain fact is, everything points to Ryan, but for some goddamn reason you're soft on him."

"I believe him, that's why."

"Well his trial's coming right up. You'll get a chance to see just what a jury of his peers believes."

"His peers?" Woolly asked. "Who's the soft one now? Do you really think you're gonna see twelve unemployed Natives from Hastings and Main judging his fate?"

★⚖★

True to his word, Charlie made a point of watching the naked bike ride snake around Broadway and Main on the last Saturday in June. He wasn't especially enchanted by the numerous nutsacks that floated by, but the sight of Cactus's splendid form, adorned merely by pasties and a bit of body paint, was worth the wait. Naturally he felt a little ashamed and a tad perverted while secretly staring at his friend's naked friend, but like Frank Belleveau, he wasn't getting any real satisfaction of his own.

3rd Quarter 2009

That is why he took up Victor's invitation to visit Portland, not to see his ex-pat friend's art hang at Powell's, the big one on Burnside, or to revel in the myriad bike lanes and varieties of street-cart foods in the post-60s mecca, but because Cactus and Hannah had accepted the invitation as well.

The Can-Am friends ambled, ate and drank at such famous establishments as Belmont Station, the Horse Brass and the Rogue. Charlie worked hard to keep his behavior toward Hannah platonic, and was successful in doing so, even though he, Hannah, Cactus and I all shared a downtown hotel suite. Mom and I slept in one double bed. Cactus had the second one all to herself. And Charlie got a cot. Victor stayed with a cousin.

"They're sore. That's all I'll say," Charlie confided to Victor at the Horse Brass one afternoon as Hannah, Cactus and I toured the retro shops of South East Hawthorne, Cactus's favourite community. Charlie was referring to the blue patina of his genitals, colloquially speaking.

"I'm not kidding you. It's hard enough sleeping two feet away from Hannah, but Cactus is no slouch herself, and they both walk around freely in their underwear as they get ready for bed. At least Hannah wears a pajama top, but Cactus pulls her bra off just before she gets under the covers."

"They're comfortable around you. A good sign," Victor suggested.

"Maybe so, but I'm tellin' you. They're sore."

Victor chuckled. "You can stay with me if you want, and instead of getting to see a couple of sets of nice tits, you can see my old man pair – I'm almost ready for a bra myself..."

"Would you like Cactus's?" Charlie quipped.

4th Quarter 2009

Ryan Ghostkeeper's trial was the long-anticipated event of the harvest's end, like the latest Twilight premiere. Woolly had her apprehensions, but the general public was eager to see the young man charged with doing in the density king finally get his comeuppance. The courtroom was full.

"I was in Toronto at the time," Denise informed the jury from the witness box. One could see her stylish black button-up sweater, white blouse with a big collar and pearls. She ran the loop smoothly through her fingers after answering her questions.

She testified that she had left the morning of March 28 to visit her sister and her sister's husband. "I'm very close with them," she added, though Lewis Chaulk, the Crown prosecutor, did not ask about the intensity of her family bonds. He walked her through her evening in Toronto, and established that Don and her marriage had developed a few cracks over the years. Then it was Curtis Rice's turn to probe into Denise's personal life.

"So your husband did not invite you to a jazz concert on Friday, March 28th, Mrs. Dickerson?" he asked.

"No. He did not."

"But you know now that he had two tickets for a concert at the Vogue, for 8:00 pm. Correct?"

"Yes. Correct."

"And just to be clear, one of those wasn't for you. Is that correct?"

"That's right. I already said I went to the Princess of Wales theatre that evening."

"But did he tell you that he had two tickets for the Vogue before you went to Toronto?"

"No he did not."

"And you have no idea who the tickets were for, do you?"

"That's right. I have no idea."

"But you do know *now*, don't you, Mrs. Dickerson, that the deceased was contemplating a divorce from you only a week before he was killed."

Denise nodded ruefully, averting the eyes of the jurors.

"You have to say Yes or No, ma'am, for the record."

"Yes, I know that." Denise looked at Louise, sitting in the gallery. Louise closed her eyes and nodded discreetly in a gesture of support.

"So when did you learn that – that your husband wanted to divorce you?"

Denise paused, cleared her throat, and said, "I learned after Don was murdered that he asked his lawyer to file for divorce, but he hadn't yet served me with any papers. That's what I have learned after the fact, but my husband had told me to my face before I went to Toronto that he was leaving me. That was a few days before he was killed, a Tuesday or Wednesday evening, I think."

"Why did he initiate a divorce, as far as you know, Ms. Dickerson?" Rice asked.

"I guess he had been seeing another woman."

"Are you guessing, ma'am, or do you know this?"

"I know this now."

"Well what was her name?"

Denise cleared her throat again. "Hannah Verso, I believe."

"Hannah Verso?"

"Yes."

"Do you know who she is?"

"I do now, but I didn't at the time."

"And who is she?"

Lewis Chaulk stood up and asked to know the relevance of the question.

"I am entitled to establish an alternate suspect," Mr. Rice replied, thus causing a number of gasps across the gallery. Ryan turned in the prisoner's box to see the reaction.

Chaulk asked for the jury and Ms. Dickerson to be temporarily excused from the courtroom, a wish the judge granted.

"The alternate suspect must be viable," Mr. Chaulk then contended, "and my friend must establish a reasonable foundation for suggesting that someone else committed the crime charged."

So Mr. Rice did his best. "It's plain, m'Lord, that the deceased had two tickets for a special VSO concert the night he was killed.

No one interviewed by the police was invited to the concert as Mr. Dickerson's guest. His widow has no idea who the intended guest was, so it a reasonable and proper inference that it was someone who Mr. Dickerson wished to keep secret from her."

The judge sat forward.

"It is also plain that, just shortly before he was killed, Mr. Dickerson put divorce proceedings in motion. This was done, obviously, behind his wife's back. Now I was just about to ask who this Verso woman is when my friend objected. I can tell you, m'Lord, that at the time Mr. Dickerson was killed, Ms. Verso lived with a man named Frank Belleveau, a contractor who worked for Mr. Dickerson."

"So what?" the judge wanted to know.

"So you have heard evidence about these motorcycle tire prints that make a path leaving the scene. The Crown theorizes that they were left by an accomplice – an accomplice to my client, that is. My friend may ask the jury to draw that inference, but you have not heard yet that Mr. Frank Belleveau was Hannah Verso's fiancé at the time, and he rode a motorbike to and from work every day."

"And you are suggesting they match?"

"Consistent in generalities, but inconclusive, m'Lord."

The judge's eyes enlarged. "Mr. Chaulk?"

"Your Lordship, my friend is correct," the prosecutor replied. "Mr. Belleveau does own a motorbike. The tire marks left at the scene could be from his bike, but that's a very long bow, if not speculation. There's easily another 5,000 pairs of those tires on the streets of the Lower Mainland…"

"And Mr. Dickerson was thinking of leaving his wife for Ms. Verso?"

Chaulk scratched the side of his head before replying, "That's the evidence. I can't dispute it."

"And you're not calling Ms. – this Ms. Verso…"

Chaulk shifted on his feet.

"Or even Mr. – What was his name?"

"Mr. Belleveau, m'Lord, and No, with great respect I'm not obliged to call every witness the police interviewed. My friend can call Ms. Verso or her ex if he wants to."

"And just to be clear here," the judge interrupted, "Mr. Ghostkeeper does not have an alibi. Is that correct?"

"Not that I know of," Chaulk answered, "and of course if there is one, I should have been notified of it by now."

"Mr. Rice?"

Curtis stood up and paused before saying, "That's right, m'Lord.

I haven't given notice of an alibi defence, and I haven't decided whether I am going to call Ms. Verso. She's been interviewed and she does admit to having been Mr. Dickerson's intended date for the VSO concert…"

Members of the public gallery turned to one another with wide eyes.

"So she was invited to a concert by her boss and his wife didn't know about it. We've already heard about their dysfunctional relationship, so we can reasonably infer Mr. Dickerson was having a tryst with her."

"But you're not intending to call this Mr…"

"Belleveau?"

"Yes. Mr. Belleveau."

"I shouldn't have to call him," Rice argued. "The Crown should, so I can cross-examine him."

Mr. Chaulk tossed his pen onto the pad of paper in front of him and pushed back his rolling chair.

"You've got something to say Mr. Chaulk?" the judge probed.

The prosecutor stood up and said "Ms. Verso gives Mr. Belleveau a near airtight alibi. He was at home and watching TV by the time she arrived, shortly after leaving the theatre. He's been interviewed and his recollection lines up with hers. They're both credible witnesses. Perhaps my friend wants to make something of the tire treads because they were consistent with those on Frank's bike." Chaulk used air quotation marks when he said "consistent with" and explained, "but 'consistent with' does not mean 'identical to.'"

"If my friend *really* wants to make an issue of this," Chaulk continued, "then we'll call 50 witnesses from the Lower Mainland whose bikes have that exact same model of tire. I don't think we want to go down that road."

Mr. Chaulk sat back down and Mr. Rice stood up.

"I can't prove decisively that Belleveau was involved," Rice conceded, but he argued that "in the name of fairness my friend should have to put these important relationships to the jury. They are part of the narrative and they may well cast reasonable doubt upon my client. Mr. Ghostkeeper is entitled of course to the benefit of any such doubt properly raised."

The judge sighed before deciding that Rice should be allowed to question Denise Dickerson further about my mom, so the widow returned, brusquely, once the jury had taken their seats.

"Ms. Dickerson," Mr. Rice continued, "before we took a break I was asking you about Ms. Hannah Verso. Can you please tell the jury who she is."

"Well, when my husband was killed, she was the girlfriend of a man who worked for my husband, a contractor named Frank Belleveau."

"Thank you," Mr. Rice said. "And what do you know about Mr. Frank Belleveau?"

Denise looked at the jury, then the judge, and shrugged before saying, "Not much really. He worked for my Don, and Don did mention him every now and then. Sometimes he called him the Frenchie."

"Can you elaborate upon that for the jury?"

"Well, I don't know. Like Don would say things like, that Frankie, he's a solid worker, a dependable worker, for a Frenchie. But he did like him, I think. He found him trustworthy."

"Did you know if Frank and Hannah had children, before your husband was killed, I mean?"

"Uh, Don never mentioned anything like that to me. I can't say."

"And what about you? You told us earlier that you had a daughter."

"Ah, yes sir. That's true."

"And her birthdate is?"

"She was born November 22, 2008."

"So she was conceived, uh, oh, in March. So shortly before your husband was killed?"

Denise looked aghast at the judge, the jury, and the gallery, and ran her right hand firmly across her pearls. "Yes. She was."

"Did Mr. Dickerson know of this fact?"

"Why…no, he did not." Denise let out a burst of tears, but grabbed a tissue and got them under control.

Half the jurors sat forward as others shifted in their seats.

"Is it Mr. Dickerson's child?"

The jurors awaited her answer with bated breath.

"I…well, yes, I'm sure it is."

"And how can you be sure?"

"Is this relevant?" Chaulk asked, having stood up.

Rice, having sat down, popped up to say, "Of course it is, m'Lord. If her daughter is not Mr. Dickerson's daughter, then someone else was obviously in the picture at the material time – a fact that has never been disclosed to me."

"And if another man was involved? You're suggesting a motive?" the judge put to Rice.

"Of course."

"I'm satisfied the question is relevant, Mr. Rice. You may continue."

"So pardon me, Ms. Dickerson, but again, can you please tell His

Lordship and the jury how you can be sure that Mr. Dickerson was the biological father of your daughter?"

"Shortly before he was murdered…" Denise's voice trembled and she wiped an eye dry. "I had been in Arizona, with my sister Louise, and upon my return from our time-share there my husband and I had, well, we were intimate."

"And so that was, do you know the day of the week, the month?"

"It was a Sunday. I know that because that is when I got home from Arizona, and I was, well, I was a little surprised that Don was so eager to, well, be intimate, you know, because we had fallen a little apart in that regard."

"Well please do tell us if you had had any sexual relations outside your marriage – and I mean, of course, just around that time, Mrs. Dickerson?"

"No. No I did not."

"You're sure of that?"

"Yes I am."

"And so it was a Sunday, when? In late February? Early March?"

Denise looked to the ceiling for a few seconds before answering. "It must have been somewhere around the first week of March."

"And may I ask you, Mrs. Dickerson, who George Kimbel is?"

She grasped her pearls and stroked them, then she cleared her throat and glanced quickly around the courtroom before saying, "Yes I do."

"He wasn't somebody who particularly liked your husband, was he?"

"No. They had their differences. That is for sure."

"Did you like him?"

The witness flushed and glanced around the courtroom again.

"I haven't seen him here today, if that's who you're looking for," Rice said sarcastically.

Denise said nothing, so Ryan's lawyer asked her again, "Did you like him?"

"Not in the way I'm sure you're suggesting, but he's not a bad man, despite what the media would have everyone believe. I've bumped into him a few times over the years, at industry parties. He's always been kind to me."

"Because you phoned him, right? Just two days before he was murdered, didn't you, Mrs. Dickerson?"

She swallowed. "Yes I did. I phoned him the day after Don said he was leaving. I don't really know why. I wanted to let him know, y'know, everyone thinks you're the dishonest one, but you're not. It's my husband who can't be trusted. The guy everyone thinks is so honest. I was confused, I guess. I just wanted to vent or something."

"But he called you too, didn't he? After the murder?"

"Yes he did." This time Denise answered more quickly, with more strength in her tone. "A lot of people phoned me then, sir, to send condolences. Mr. Kimbel's call was no different than the others. He might have had his professional differences with Don, but he was human enough to look past them, so I'm not sure what you're insinuating here."

That wasn't entirely true. Denise had a pretty good idea of what Rice was insinuating with that last line of cross-examination, but Rice decided to go no further with it. He simply did not have enough hard evidence to support a theory that Denise Dickerson had asked or even paid George Kimbel to take care of the fornicating Density King once and for all.

※※※

Denise was allowed to step down from the witness stand the next morning, to watch the rest of the show. The witnesses who appeared at the preliminary inquiry took their rightful turns in the box again. Over a week passed by in this fashion, with jurors fading in and out of attentiveness depending upon the materiality of the evidence, whether it was accompanied by visual aids (always preferable), and how much serotonin their lunch choices produced.

"And that, m'Lord, and ladies and gentlemen of the jury, is the Crown's case," Chaulk said, as soon as his last witness exited the courtroom. He plumped down in his seat, the taxing burden of conducting a high-profile murder case temporarily off his shoulders.

The jurors looked expectantly to and fro – to the judge, to the lawyers, at themselves. They had become accustomed to being led on a leash by the judge, the paid dog-walker. Now they sat dutifully at the curb, waiting for the next tug to pull them safely through traffic, if there was going to be more traffic. They simply did not know.

"Mr. Rice?" the judge said, and Mr. Rice stood up.

"Yes, m'Lord. Mr. Ghostkeeper will take the witness stand."

Eyes widened all across the courtroom.

From the instant Ryan Ghostkeeper stepped from the prisoner box, flanked by security, and entered the witness stand, wherein he solemnly affirmed to tell the truth, the whole truth, and nothing but the truth, the jurors attended to his every word and gesture as if they had ringside seats at Ali and Foreman's Kinshasa swing dance in '74.

"They fired me," he told Rice, after answering some preliminary questions about his roots on Nak'azdli Reserve #1.

"I was drunk. I won't deny that here. This one guy, he could smell it: the liquor on my breath. So I got reported."

"So what happened next," Rice wanted to know.

"I apologized to the supervisor. I told him I relapsed, but he said too bad. I was a lia*bi*lity."

"And then what?"

"He asked me to leave."

"Did you get paid?"

"A hundred forty dollars."

"In cash, or a cheque, or..."

"By cheque. I had to go to Cheque Mates."

"Where was that at?"

"On Broadway. At Oak there."

"Then where did you go?"

From there he went to the liquor store beside the Fairview Pub and bought a bottle of Canadian Club Rye whisky – "C.C.," he told the judge. He sipped on that as he ambled along West Broadway toward Main Street, and north from there.

"I just kept walkin' – ended up at the bus terminal. Y'know, the train station," Ryan told the jury.

"At Main and Terminal?"

"Yeah. At Main Street."

"And what did you do there?"

"I couldn't buy any drugs. No one was sellin' at the Skytrain, around there, so I just crossed the street and sat down."

"Where did you sit down?"

"Under a tree."

"But where?"

"On the grass, in front of the station."

"The Skytrain or the real train station?"

"The real station, where the trains come."

"Oh. And then what did you do?"

"I fell asleep."

"What were you wearing?"

"My jacket. My boots. My hard hat. I was still wearin' that."

Ryan grinned, evoking a couple of taut smiles from the jury.

"When did you wake up?"

"I d'know. I had no watch. I still don't."

"Was it evening?"

"Like dark?"

"Okay. Was it light out or dark?"

"The sun was almost set – someone stole my booze."

"What was that? Someone..."

"Stole my booze," Ryan reiterated.

"So what did you do?"

"I got up, put my hard hat on. It fell off when I was sleepin."

A couple of jurors grinned.

"I was really hungry, so I walked across the street, to where the Skytrain is. I bought pizza."

"At the Skytrain?"

"No. At the pizza place near there, kind'a behind there, on Main Street. I bought three slices of Hawaiian, my favourite, and I ate them there. I drank a root beer too, I think."

"And then where did you go?"

"Well, I was startin' to get my legs, eh? I walked toward the big golf ball."

"The..."

"The big golf ball. Your great ball of science."

"Oh, you mean Science World."

"Yeah. Our science world, it's a circle too, but not like that one. It's not a..."

"That's all right, Mr. Ghostkeeper," Rice interjected. "Just keep to, to what you did."

Ryan stared at the Cambie Street bridge, at the red and white lights, criss-crossing, as he recalled. The north side was more lit up than the south. That's where all the action was. Downtown.

Ryan was right about that. The bars and clubs were filling up, and Hannah Verso was in the washroom of a Yaletown café, changing into the dress that she would wear to the Toots Thielemans concert, but Ryan didn't tell the court that. He had no idea what Hannah was doing, or that Don Dickerson was at Meinhardt's grocery store on Granville Street, looking forward to a drink, just to relax his nerves before seeing his beautiful date.

Don was expecting Hannah to look hotter than any other woman at the concert, and he couldn't wait to lay his eyes on her, sit next to her, and put his arm around her for everyone else to see. For that matter, his wife was already half-cut at an after-theatre party on King Street West, in Toronto, with Louise and Bernard. She had her eyes on an eligible bachelor in a Hugo Boss blazer, anointed by Ralph Lauren cologne, with a Porsche Boxster across the street.

"A couple of coyotes caught my attention," Ryan told the jury. "They bolted across the path, about 10, 15 metres in front of me. They seemed to be chasing something, so I followed 'em. My cousins," he added, prompting a half-dozen jurors to scribble on their pads.

"Yes," Rice said, prompting his client to continue.

"But then I lost sight of them. They vanished, somewhere near the bank. I waited and watched for a few minutes, and then heard voices say, 'Go north. Go back home.' The coyotes told me that, so I listened."

Some jurors looked askance. Others continued to make hurried notes.

"Actually, I continued west for a few minutes," Ryan explained, "then I turned north 'til I got to Yaletown. I was real thirsty, like a sea sponge, my uncle used to say.

"I took the alley. You never know what you'll find there," Ryan testified. "Clothes. Chairs. I found a nice lamp once. Sure enough, I noticed somethin' shiny that night too."

Ryan went toward the object, bent over and picked up a knife by the handle. "Blood," he murmured under his breath, but looking around he saw no trail of blood leading from the spot. He told the jury that, and by pointing to a spot on a blown-up overhead photo of the alley, he confirmed that he was standing only metres from a parking garage entrance.

"That's the parking garage in which you stabbed Mr. Dickerson, isn't it Mr. Ghostkeeper," Chaulk charged when it was his turn. Ryan had photos of the crime scene in front of him.

"No sir."

"No? That's not the man who had you fired that very morning?"

"Well, the foreman told me I was fired. Maybe he was ordered from above. I'm not sure," Ryan said.

"C'mon, Mr. Ghostkeeper. It was the last straw wasn't it? As far as you were concerned, he had it coming. You got even with him right there and then."

"No sir. I got drunk. That's all."

"And then you found a knife in an alley, just metres from the scene in those pictures – the ones in front of you. That's what you want the jury to believe?"

"Yes sir," Ryan replied.

The lawyers had already agreed that the trace of blood found on Ryan Ghostkeeper's sleeve matched Don Dickerson's DNA. There was a one in bazzilion chance that it was from someone else.

"What were the lighting conditions like?" Chaulk continued.

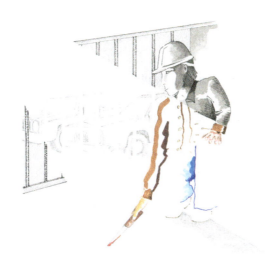

"It was those security-type lights."

"A motion detector?"

"Yeah. That's it."

"You set off the motion detector?"

Ryan shrugged. "I guess."

"You mean your motorbike set it off – right?"

Ryan looked at the jurors and said, "No. I don't know how to ride a motorbike."

"But you had a friend who did, right? An accomplice?"

Ryan shook his head softly and said, "No sir." Then he looked at the judge and said, "I was all alone that night, until I got to the bar."

"Let's keep to the alley for the moment, Mr. Ghostkeeper," Chaulk said.

"Yes sir."

"Tell us what you did with that knife again?"

Ryan ran his finger across the blade.

"And you noticed it had blood on it? That's what you told this court this morning, correct?"

"That is right, sir. I wasn't sure it was blood. I was drunk. I wasn't thinking."

"You just picked it up and what? Did you inspect it? Take a close look at it?"

"No. I cleaned it on my sleeve. It was sharp. Nice."

"Oh I'm sure it was. It was steel – stainless steel, would you agree."

"I don't know. It looked new."

Ryan then squinted into the night sky, mindful of the Being Up on High, and slipped the knife into his jacket pocket before finding himself a watering hole across the street.

At the Yaletown Pub, attended that evening as usual by financiers, television writers, advertising producers, and other upwardly mobile men in golf shirts, blazers and gold watches, with one eye always on the ladies, Ryan caused a stir. Not only was his attire unwelcome, especially his hard hat, which he wore, but he tried to sell the knife he had found. A patron complained to the bartender – "that's all it took" – and Ryan was told to leave, just like what happened to him at work that morning. So he gulped his beer, followed the bartender's orders, and threaded his way to the Yale, with cash still in his pockets. His testimony about waiting to play pool at the Yale meshed with the picture Terrell Sims, the bartender, had already painted for the jury.

When Ryan left the blues bar he proceeded along Granville Street to another bar. He did not encounter anyone, or any animals, en route, he testified, and Chaulk never asked him about Hannah Verso, who in fact passed right by the accused man. She had just used the washroom of a fast-food eatery to change from her evening dress back into the clothes she had worn at work. She was headed toward the Granville Street bridge, in a hurry to get home, to take a bath. Lost in her own thoughts, she paid no mind to the tall Native man wearing a construction helmet who almost bumped shoulders with her.

"So you say you entered another bar. That's what you recall doing next?" Chaulk asked.

"Yes, sir."

"Oakley's, right?"

"I guess so, sir. I only learned that later, though, from the police."

"And that's where you sold the knife?"

"Yes, sir."

"To a young man wearing a black baseball hat, so you say?"

"Yes. I think it had some silver writin' or somethin' on it, like I said."

"And he gave you what? You say $10.00 for it, and some cocaine?"

"Yes, sir."

"Did he offer the cocaine, or did you ask for it?"

"I showed him the knife and told him I was sellin' it. He offered cocaine. I asked him for $10 plus some of his coke. We did a couple lines in the bathroom." The brows of a few jurors wrinkled at that evidence. The judge just kept scribbling away.

"Which you did off the top of the toilet tank; that's what you *recall*, right?"

"That's what I *did*, sir."

"And then he left, and you have never seen him since?"

"No sir. Uh, I mean yes sir. I have not seen him again, but I told you, I told the police what he looked like. He was wearing a heavy metal t-shirt. I guess they can't find him."

"Or he never existed, right, Mr. Ghostkeeper? You didn't sell the knife to anyone: you discarded it somewhere, where it would not be found by the police?"

Ryan was shaking his head in the negative. "That's not right. I did sell it to that guy," he countered. "He had a lightning bolt on his neck. I remember seein' that."

"A tattoo?"

Ryan shook his head in frustration before saying, "of course."

"Then let me back up for a minute here," Chaulk asked in an aggressive tone. He stepped back from the lectern and paused, drawing the jury in to his own sense of frustration and disbelief. "You had drunk how much whiskey since, when was that again, about one o'clock in the afternoon?"

"Yes sir."

"But how much? How much of your bottle did you drink before it was stolen?"

"A lot of it."

"What's a lot? A third? A half? Two thirds?"

"I drank almost all of it, sir."

"I suggest that you were pretty intoxicated for the rest of the day. Do you disagree?"

"No, sir. I mean, sorry, yes sir."

"The coyotes you saw. The ones who spoke to you and told you what direction to go, that was an intoxicated illusion; a hallucination, no?"

"No, sir. It happened. I heard em. I wasn't that drunk."

"Coyotes talk in your world, Mr. Ghostkeeper?"

"Uh, to me, they do."

"You didn't like being fired, did you Mr. Ghostkeeper?" Chaulk pressed.

"I'm used to it."

"But that wasn't my question."

"I'm used to being fired. To answer your question, I was disappointed because I tried to stop drinkin. I failed, again, and I lost my job, again. My whole life I've been 'dicted. But I've been sober now for months and months."

Chaulk had to restrain himself from saying 'because you've been incarcerated all that time', a serious no-no in a jury trial. Instead, he said, "I want to suggest to you, Mr. Ghostkeeper, that this time you were really angry at your boss, just because you had worked so very hard to overcome your addiction. Do you disagree?" Chaulk eyed the jury and gave them a look of smug confidence.

"I – I think I know what you are saying, sir. I was a bit upset with my boss, sure, but I was really angry at myself. I can't blame my boss for my 'diction."

The Crown socked away with more questions, but his to-and-fro with Mr. Ghostkeeper was like Foreman trying to KO Ali in his rope-a-dope. Chaulk tired out without ever landing one on the chin.

When Ryan was released from the witness stand, he walked modestly toward the prisoner's box, a sliver of a smile upon his face, and he sat down.

Curtis Rice had grappled throughout the entire trial with the question of whether to subpoena Hannah Verso, but finally he decided against doing so. To call her to the witness stand could backfire, and would not necessarily produce any more information than he had already obtained from Denise – that she, Ms. Verso, had become Don's recent lover and rationale for divorce. But to turn to the jury and ask it to find that Frank Belleveau was aware of this, and murdered Don because of her betrayal – would the jury buy it or would they turn on him for the suggestion? Would the defence seem too desperate? He decided not to take the chance.

Although Ryan was coloured and the jury was all white – like separate laundry loads, I guess – he did not fare quite so poorly as Tom Robinson did in that old black and white movie starring Gregory Peck. Times have changed since the Great Depression, though not much, and the jurors were slower to decide Ryan's fate than they were for Tom Robinson, that unfortunate Negro with the broken left arm. That's what they called him in the movie: a Negro. I loved it when Mr. Peck's character, Atticus Finch, told the jury that a Negro had the temerity to feel sorry for a white woman. Imagine that.

In Ryan's case seven men and five women deliberated over the evidence for three nights and almost four full days. They slept over at the Day's Inn because they were sequestered, a big word for a big situation, and when they finally filed into the courtroom, one by one, with solemn expressions on their faces, anxiety was high all around.

The judge turned to the lawyers and the public and said, "It has come to my attention that the jury, despite their most strenuous efforts, cannot reach a unanimous verdict, so in the circumstances I must declare a mistrial and consequently order a new trial."

Rice turned in his chair and looked at Ryan with a raised eyebrow. The strangest feeling shot up the young man's spine, the most confusing combination of relief, heaviness and elation. He had not been convicted of murder. He would not be going to jail for life, yet. He remained in theory an innocent man, a free man, but how he longed to be released from the remand centre.

With Louise holding her sister's hand firmly, Denise appeared stricken. After all that, after all the hype, the public airing of her dirty laundry, the many days spent listening to tedious evidence, all of it just one big waste of time. She could have been golfing in Phoenix or playing the slots in Sin City. "His lawyer was good," Bernard said to her under his breath.

🚲 🚲 🚲

Charlie was doing only slightly better than Frank in the ever-predictable single man's attempt to charm a woman through lies or truth, pontification or humour, just enough to drop her defences and with those, hopefully, at least her brassiere, and in a perfect world, her underpants.

Charlie's potion lay perhaps in his genuine neurosis or "sensitivity," a kind of personality pollen that attracted women with a nose for sweet and soft petals. It had little or no power, of course, over those drawn to the oilier aroma of capital gains or the salty scent of a pugilist's armpit. These were women for whom a "sweat shop" was no problem if they could afford the membership and one of the personal trainers employed there. These women had never heard their man complain about the glass ceiling for female employees. After all, wouldn't every man love such a thing? How perfect for looking up skirts.

But for some women, even women like Hannah, who had rubbed against body-checkers and cheque-writers alike, men with smooth skin and delicate bones could be appealing. These women wanted their love to be more than half a tennis score.

Okay, so Charlie wasn't *that* sensitive. He liked hockey too – hackey, as he called – or at least the Red Wings. But things were starting to look up for him, in the woman's skirt department, that is. Since his trip to Portland he figured he had almost seen it all. No, he had never been to the Moulin Rouge, the Crazy Horse, or even Chez Paris, in Montreal, but he had seen Hannah's lush bumps and limber curves in nothing but underwear at the Holiday Inn.

How could he be so lucky? he wondered. He had not told her how beautiful she was. He had not bought her flowers. He had not even taken her to an expensive restaurant.

"You don't think he's gay, do you?" Hannah asked Cactus one rainy mid-October afternoon. They were on Granville Street. Hannah was pushing me in a plastic-moulded pram toward Angus Drive. I was protected by a transparent cover while Cactus carried a big umbrella for herself and Hannah.

"No," Cactus said with confidence. "He doesn't spend enough money on his clothes."

Hannah looked at Cactus with surprise in her eyes. Her friend just grinned and after a pause said, "I'm kidding. Jesus, woman. A guy like Charlie, I don't know. He's a great guy, like he's really helped out with the communal garden idea, and he helped me find a good lawyer, but I don't know. When it comes to women he's a chicken, if you ask me. He likes you, no question about it. He likes you so much I bet he's too scared to make the first move. He thinks that'll scare *you* away. What an idiot."

Hannah chuckled.

"Anyway, that's my guess, and for another forty dollars," Cactus said, holding out her left hand, palm up, "I'll psychoanalyze one of your parents. Who will it be?"

Cactus winked and Hannah smiled.

About a week before Samhain and the arrival of the Great Pumpkin, 80 years ago, Americans experienced two of the darkest days in their history. They were so dark they seemed black, so they became known as Black Thursday and Black Tuesday – October 24th and 29th, respectively. Frankenstein had arrived in lower Manhattan, ticker tape endlessly spilling out of his ribs, as if he had been disemboweled. Investment trusts and common stocks liquidated out his back door like diarrhea. His menacing face and outstretched arms caused everyone in the marketplace to panic and sell, sell, sell at any cost. Grown men in expensive business suits jumped out of skyscraper windows. Well-heeled, bloated bodies were fished out of the Hudson River.

How fitting, how rich, that the man-made monstrosity should have appeared just days before Halloween, like nasty Mr. Ewell in that Gregory Peck movie, when he terrified Jem and Scout on their way home from the school party. The giant clodhopper had returned this October too. Adults had to look over their shoulders. Consumer confidence remained low, as did trading in commodities and investment securities. Sure, America had *technically* pulled itself out of the recession over the last quarter, but with 15 million people still unemployed, no one was going to start playing tiddlywinks yet.

Rather than buy and sell real estate, Detroiters had simply resumed their past time of burning it down. Charlie was telling Hannah all about Devil's Night – he still called it that – as they walked toward her bedroom in the early evening of October 30. The sun had just finished casting sepia light through the windows.

"...So you get these citizen patrols, locals, carrying shotguns..."

The bedroom light was turned off, the room was generally dark, and Hannah left it that way. "Come in," she ushered when Charlie stopped at the door. *I'm gonna start a fire right here,* she thought, and said, "I don't want you to think I'm not interested in what you're saying, but let me interrupt for one second. I just want to show you something." She felt awkward, having never had to play such a trick on a man before.

She went around to the far side of the bed and looked out her bedroom window into the blue-black of the evening sky. Charlie was now just inside the door. After taking a deep breath Hannah lifted off her sweater, then turned around and looked at her guest. He could barely discern her facial features and the outline of her figure. She unclasped her brassiere, now revealing largely shadowed mounds.

Charlie was struck dumb so after a pause Hannah said, "You were saying?" Then she pushed her jeans down to her ankles and pulled them off. When she stood up Charlie said, "Jesus... uh..."

Hannah inched her knickers down past her hips, exposing her

professionally-trimmed vulnerability, all for Charlie's eyes only, and that is when, like any neurotic male, even one from Detroit, Charlie had to ask, "Hannah, are you sure you want to do this?"

She grinned, fondly thinking of Cactus's remark, "what an idiot," then reached into her bedside drawer, pulled out a condom she had put there a few days earlier, and held it up in reply.

She was sure.

* * *

A handsome and very famous American president once said that a rising tide lifts all boats, but I would dare to say that the metaphor had become inappropriate for the current times. Rising tides around the world were scaling to dangerous levels. The English town of Cockermouth got flooded right out, including the home of the late great Mr. William Wordsworth himself. Not to worry, though. Even if the master's words were not inscribed by indelible ink, they were probably underwritten against all acts of God. The point is, however, you don't want to lift boats too high.

Frank did not own a boat, but his spirits were rising. To his happy surprise, Judy Costanza phoned him up again, to ask him on another date and possibly engage him in a small business venture.

"Don't be frightened," she told him over drinks at the Biltmore hotel, a second-rate inn at the crossroads of 12th Avenue and Kingsway, once "Vancouver Road," the historic route that took all the king's men and all the king's horses from New Westminster to the port of Vancouver. Its tall, pink neon sign was bold, but the lighting inside was dim. The couple sat in a red pleather booth across the floor from an empty and worn black stage.

"I've been doing this in times of need for a few years now. My sources are reliable. I've never had any kind of trouble, and tonight I just need you for muscle."

"But Judy, you said...?"

Judy flexed her left bicep, thus displaying a prominent vein. "Unless you'd prefer it to be the other way around," she said.

"No, I don't..."

Judy interrupted to say, "I've got a small package to deliver to someone in Port Moody and I want you to come with me. If all goes well, and it will, I'm sure, I'll get some cash and we'll..."

"What are you delivering?" Frank asked. His tone was anxious, worried.

"Just a bit of kush – to make ends meet."

"Kush?"

"Weed. A bit of marijuana, Frank. It's nothing, seriously."

Frank sat back in his seat and looked across the table – at the stranger facing him. His mind was racing.

"I'm getting the sense that there is more to you than you have told me about," he ventured.

Judy shrugged. "We've all got a little more to ourselves than we let on, don't we?" she asked.

Frank said nothing.

"It's called getting to know each other," his date added. "It's a process. We've only gone out a couple of times. We met in a bar. We're getting to know each other. I hardly know anything about you, and yet I'm trusting you to come on a small delivery with me, to act as a little security, and for a pretty penny, too. You could turn me in, and yet you're the one getting all nervous."

Frank remained mute.

"C'mon Frank. Relax," Judy urged, smiling. "Let's go do this thing and then have ourselves a fun evening out."

Frank let out a long sigh and said, "Okay. Fuck. Why not?"

So after finishing another drink Judy drove him along the Burrard Inlet all the way out to Port Moody.

"That's pretty...de lights," Frank commented en route, in reference to the residential and industrial lights across the water.

"I guess it is," Judy replied, keeping her eyes on the road.

They arrived at a stretch of two-story beach-style homes, just north of St. John's Street, not too far from the train station. The neighbourhood was plain: lower-middle income.

Judy parked, got out of her car and walked up the pathway onto a porch, Frank in tow. Interior lights were on and Frank could see plainly into a room. Three or four men were perched on the edges of their seats, drinking beer and watching the television. Suddenly a couple of them jerked back and groaned. Frank assumed they were watching a tight hockey game.

Judy rang the doorbell. A tall, well-built and clean-cut fellow came to the door, smugly eyed Frank up-and-down, surveyed the scene around the front yard, and accepted a package Judy offered him. He was a couple inches taller than Frank, but not as thick in the chest.

"You brought meat?" he asked.

Judy nodded and he shook his head disapprovingly.

"When will you learn that trust is the name of this game?" he asked.

"When I'm prepared to lose the game. Can I go now?" she requested.

The man pulled an envelope out of his back pocket and handed it to her.

"Cheers," she said before turning around to leave. Frank followed her to the car.

"Your meat doesn't look too bad," the buyer said.

Once he was inside the car, Frank remarked, "You were right. That was easy."

"I told you so, but you never know. It's better to be safe than sorry."

Judy reached into the envelope she was given and pulled out two $100 bills.

"Here you go. I told you I would pay you well."

"Are you kidding?" Frank asked.

"No I'm not, but you have to keep your mouth shut. Can you do that?"

Frank had not yet reached for the bills. "But I didn't do anything," he said.

"Yes you did. With you there, he wasn't going to get stupid. You earned your share, so please, lighten up, and let's go spend a little."

"*Tabarnak*," Frank said under his breath. The fact that he had disparaged the sacred "tabernacle" was lost on his companion.

Judy drove him back into Vancouver.

"Do you like Sangria?" she asked him en route.

"Yeah. I do. I like the fruit."

"Then I know where we're going."

"Where's that?"

"To my neighbourhood."

Judy drove to The Latin Quarter, a small, warm and lively Spanish restaurant on Commercial Drive, where the food was exquisite and the live mariachi music energizing. Along the way she passed a CanCon development at Venables. A security fence was erected around a row of small businesses.

"I'll be working there soon," Frank informed her.

"Don't say that out loud around here. It's not too popular in this neck of the woods."

"What's there not to like? You've got a new – "

"So what? This neighbourhood doesn't want new. We're Italian. The old is fine by us. Did you see that dance hall we just passed?"

Frank looked over his shoulder. "Ass-tow...Astorino's?"

"I've been to three or four wedding parties there. A *total* blast."

Inside the busy restaurant Frank and Judy continued to learn about one another while drinking Sangria and being serenaded. After hearing about Judy's Italian heritage Frank mentioned Hannah, an "ex" having Portuguese blood. "She never brought me to a place like this," he said, "but she had no class."

Frank then told Judy that Hannah cheated on him, he was sure, when he was visiting his sick mother in Quebec. "Imagine that," he said, not mentioning Hannah's child.

"Do you know who the guy was?"

Frank looked at Judy blankly for a few seconds before saying, "I think it was my boss."

"Oh shit."

Judy paused and looked Frank directly in the eye. "Tell me you don't work for the guy anymore, do you?"

Frank put his right hand on the back of his neck and gripped it, as if were tight and needed a massage, then he looked intently into Judy's eyes before saying, "Not anymore."

"Did you have words with him?" Judy asked.

Frank shook his head lightly, then said, "No, I never did." He lowered his voice and added, "The guy was killed before I had the chance."

Judy made a face in disbelief. "Are you serious?" she asked.

Frank nodded. "It was that prick Dickerson, Don Dickerson, the guy who got stabbed by that autochthon, I mean that Indian."

Judy screwed up her face again. "I thought he was getting another trial."

Frank shrugged. "He is. He's got himself a good lawyer – probably at our fuckin' expense."

"No doubt," Judy remarked. "So how do you feel?"

"About that guy?"

"No, about being cheated on."

"Do you have to ask?" Frank said. "You're the one with trust issues," he reminded her.

"All right, all right. Stupid question."

Judy reached across the table and tweaked Frank's cheek. "It sounds like Hannah doesn't know what she lost," she added, then then she reached her foot out and tapped Frank's toes a couple of times. A warm feeling welled in the man's loins and Frank's thoughts turned away from the past, toward the future – the very near future. With expectations of warmer feelings to come yet, he happily consumed almost a full pitcher of sangria. He even danced a little before last call.

When everyone was diplomatically ushered out of the restaurant Frank asked Judy if he could stay at her place.

"I don't think that would be a good idea," she replied.

"Please, Judy, don't treat me like this," he pleaded. You brought me great music, beautiful drink, and you expect me not to want you."

"You're just drunk again." Her tone was matter-of-fact, but not unkind.

"No I'm not. I feel great."

"This feels great," Judy replied. She had lifted her palms and face to the light rain that was falling. When she returned her focus to Frank, his expression was serious and his hands were dug into the front pockets of his leather bomber jacket.

"All right," she said, "but we better go to your place, and don't get any ideas. I'm not saying I'll spend the night."

"*Tabarnak*. Tu es trop difficile."

"Whatever that means," Judy replied.

When they got to Frank's place, Judy did allow her suitor to get a little off his chest while they sat on the sofa, but not too much. I am no baseball expert but he easily got to first base. She pitched him a curve ball, which he hit into shallow right field. That was the passionate kissing part, but he kept trying to steal second by getting his hands under her brassiere. She finally gave in and let him feel her all over there, but "No no no," she insisted, when he gripped the zipper on her pants.

"Judeee," he moaned. "My balls are killing me."

"Then go do what you've got to do, because I'm not there yet. I've told you that already."

"But you don't understand!"

"No. You don't understand."

"Okay okay," Frank said. "Let's not go any further tonight. You are welcome to stay de night."

"No Frank. I know men. I'm not sleeping over."

"I'll sleep here," Frank offered, pointing to the sofa cushion next to him.

"Oh, a real gentleman after all."

Frank chuckled. "Yeah, I guess. You've got the wrong impression of me. I'll take the sofa, if that is what you want. Hell, they do it in the movies."

Judy pushed Frank down, onto his back, and leaned over him. Then she kissed him a few times before saying, "I'll sleep here. It's not long enough for you."

🚲 ⏺ ⏺

When Frank awoke the next morning – Sunday, November 22, I need to point out – Judy was already gone. Frank was seriously disappointed. The only spoor she left was the scent of her perfume on his undershirt. Chanel No. 5, no less. What a coy little fox that Judy was turning out to be.

But who really cares about what Judy and Frank were doing or thinking that morning. I just said it was November 22nd, which means I was officially one year old. The Seven Sisters were most certainly smiling upon me again, all the way from outer space. After all, Subaru sales were ascending right through the roof and whoa, Canada's federal debt – that too had skyrocketed – to a half trillion dollars, an all-time high. I bet my government had to wash a lot of dishes to pay off that whopper of a bill.

Mom held a small party for me in her apartment. She blew up a lot of balloons, hung some pink and baby blue streamers, and with Cactus's help made a lemon cake smothered in white frosting. The cake was round and had a fat #1 candle stuck in the centre. Everyone was invited over for 4:00 in the afternoon. Cake, coffee, wine or whatever else people wanted to drink or eat was on offer. Jimmy and Hurdy Gurdy came. So did the Americans. Charlie arrived early and made a habit of putting his arm around my mom's hip every time she got close to him. She didn't seem to mind.

Victor brought me a small oil painting.

"Oh my, that's wonderful," mom said, holding it out in front of her. The background was light purplish, bluish and rosy in tone. In the foreground, simple shapes of different coloured fish passed each other. Hannah knelt down and said, "Look, lovely."

I put my finger on one of the fish, which brought smiles and "aahhs" among the guests.

"Let's put it on her wall right now," Hannah suggested. Victor looked at Charlie, then shrugged. "Why not?"

Hannah got a hammer and a nail from her tool box below the kitchen sink, Victor poured himself another glass of red wine, then Hannah returned to my room. Cactus carried me in. Everyone except Victor offered their own opinions as to how high to hang the painting, and where, relative to the centre of the room it looked best, but Hannah had the last word. She hung it front and centre across from the foot of my crib. A round of applause went up, then Hannah said, "Okay everyone. Job well done. Let's have cake and coffee."

The guests gathered around a table in the living room. Mom lifted me up and out toward the candle, but I couldn't blow that thing out. She tried to show me how to blow and the guests laughed at my paltry efforts – *with* me, I hope, not *at* me. How was I supposed to know what to do? I was only one year old.

Frank showed up after everyone had eaten cake, and Charlie stopped putting his arm around my mom's waist.

"This is for you, sweetheart." Frank squatted down and presented me with a squeeze toy, a bean-stuffed cow that made an electronic "Mooooo" sound when I held it tight. I liked squeezing it, which meant that I ignored my stuffed goat for a while.

"So, how's it going?" mom asked Frank in the kitchen.

He shrugged and took a sip of a beer Hannah handed him.

"You still seeing that lady – uh…"

"Judy?"

"Yeah. Sorry."

Frank shrugged again.

"You don't know?" Hannah asked.

"It's going good, but I think she's a tease."

Frank reached into a bowl of cashews and popped a few in his mouth.

"Mooooo," went my squeezed cow.

"I guess we're taking it slow. That's how she wants it," Frank told his ex.

"Well, that sounds good, but how do you want it?"

"I'm fine, actually. I like her, but how are you doing? You're like – ey." Frank stopped what he was about to say, having just noticed Ryan's carving on the kitchen wall, above a small table.

"You finally decided to put it up. It's about time, you thief." He grinned. "I was going to ask for it back – for posterity, as you English call it."

"Well, he's innocent now," Hannah explained.

"Oh oh oh, not yet."

"The stupid pigs still think I had something to do with it! Fuckin assholes," Slim Jimmy called out.

"Language!" Hannah admonished.

"Mooooo." I did it again.

Charlie walked into the kitchen. Frank turned slightly on a heel and smiled.

 "Ah, l'American – l'homme de Detroit," he said.

"C'est correct, l'homme *Dé* troit, from Fort Pontchartrain du Dé troit, if one wants to get really technical about it."

"Ey. Fuck off. Quoi sais-tu aux Français?"

"Hey hey hey. Language!" Hannah pleaded.

"Not much," Charlie said. "But the Brits did kick your ass on the Plains *and* in Montreal a year later. And then you let a bunch of American militiamen seize your beloved fort…"

"What de?"

"But most important, 'cuz I know this is what really eats you," Charlie said, "it's that the Joe is sitting on your old French stockade."

"Fuck that," Frank said. "You – "

"C'mon, man," Charlie interrupted with a wide grin. "You Quebeckers love your Habs but you've got nothing on the Wings and you know it."

"Go Canucks!" Victor chimed in from the living room.

"Try 24 Stanley Cups to, uh, what? You guys got, uh, 10 or something?" Frank asked.

"Yeah, that's right – one of them last year and four of them since you last got one, uh whenever that was."

"93."

"Oh yeah, against Hollywood."

"Fuck you."

"Stopping talking like that, both of you," Hannah chided.

"Mooooo."

"They fucking throw uh, le poulpe on dee ice, those guys."

"The what?" Victor inquired from the living room.

"Le poulpe, uh…"

"Octopus," Charlie clarified, his cheeks now tinted vermillion.

"Jesus," Victor interrupted again, "I first thought you said poop – that they threw poop on the ice – and now you're saying it's not poop, it's octopi?"

"What are you guys talking about?" Cactus wanted to know as she entered the kitchen.

Charlie shook his head lightly and said, "Detroiters have a stupid habit – well they used to, but it's illegal now – someone would throw an octopus onto the ice during a Red Wings game."

"But what *for*?" Cactus asked. She and Hannah wore looks of consternation and disapproval.

"I don't know why it started," Charlie said, "but it has to do with how many games it takes to get into the finals. Eight."

"Oh fuck. I've heard everything now," Cactus said.

"Okay okay, everyone, can we all just go a little easier on the language?" Hannah pleaded as Cactus opened the fridge.

"Mooooo."

Cactus retrieved a few beers by their necks, for her and her friends, and Frank said, "Fine. I'm sorry. Let's change de subject then."

Cactus left the kitchen with her drinks, and when she was out of earshot Frank said to Hannah and Charlie, "Like when are you two going to stop associating with those idiots in Shaughnessy. That thing's an embarrassment."

"No it's not. It's an important --"

Hannah interrupted Charlie, saying, "Let's not talk about it here."

"Why don't she just sell it? She'd be an instant millionaire," Frank said, nodding in the general direction of Cactus.

"I said let's not talk about it here. It's Erica's birthday. Let's lighten up. I need to get back to my guests."

Hannah walked out of the kitchen. Charlie opened the fridge.

"She cheated on me, in case she hasn't told you that yet," Frank said to Charlie's back.

"She did tell me." Charlie turned around, now with a beer in hand, and faced Frank. "We all make mistakes," he added.

"She's a gold digger. Une poule-de-luxe. That's what she is."

"No she's not. She made a mistake. That's all. It wasn't about money."

"Then what *was* it about, man?" Frank asked, raising his voice a little. Hannah heard it and returned to the kitchen.

"Enough, you guys. Please!" She looked Frank straight in the eye. "Either chill out or take off, okay? We're having a party here."

"All right, all right. I'm just tryin' to make a little conversation with your new friend."

Cactus came through the door. "Hey pretty momma. Hate to break up the fun, but I'm gonna get going. I'm going to a movie at seven."

"Which one?" Frank asked.

"Tell No One." Cactus chugged back her beer.

"What's that."

"A French movie. I don't know. A thriller. It's got great reviews."

"Maybe I should go with you. Help explain la traduction," Frank suggested facetiously.

"Some other time, Frankie boy. Some other time." Cactus looked at Hannah, set down her bottle, took a deep breath, then said, "Okay. I've got to get going. It was a real slice."

The two women embraced.

"Mooooo."

"Hey you little sweetheart," Cactus called out to me. Victor was entertaining me in the living room.

Cactus hugged Charlie, then looked at Frank and said, "You're not getting one." Everyone in the kitchen, including Frank, laughed, and then Cactus and Frank hugged each other. Cactus had a lot of love for friends.

She returned to the living area and lifted me up, saying, "I gotta' go, sweetheart." She also squeezed my new cow a couple of times. That made me smile.

"We should get going too," Hurdy said to Jimmy.

Cactus put me down and left.

"So soon?" Victor asked. He picked an olive from a dish, put it in his mouth, then reached for a bottle of red and tilted it back. It was empty.

"I don't think we should leave the site for too long," Hurdy said. "You never know what kind of trouble those Shaughnessy freaks will stir up next."

"Just build a trap," Victor offered as the others entered from the kitchen.

"Yeah, always set a trap," Frank said. "De kind that go snap."

Hannah rolled her eyes and looked at Charlie. "Who invited him, anyway?" she asked.

Charlie shrugged and lifted his hands up, as if to say, 'Don't ask me.' Frank just grinned.

When all the guests were gone mom brought me into my bedroom, retrieved my little goat from my crib and handed her to me, then brought me up close to Victor's painting. "Look at all the pretty fishing passing by," she said. I held out the goat and pressed her against one of the fish. "Ah, you like orange," mom said. Then she brought me back to my crib, tucked me in and said, "Sweet dreams, sweetheart," before turning out the lights.

I squeezed my new cow a few times, and mom said, "Shhhh. Just go to sleep, honey."

My stuffed goat and birthday cow would have to wait for Saint Nicholas to bring them more barnyard friends, but Woolly got a present well in advance of the annual extra-terrestrial sleigh ride.

One of Sorenson's unrelenting underlings found the bank account, and a critical withdrawal.

"I just decided to look under her maiden name – Laylock," the digger explained to his seniors' gummy faces. "She's had the account forever, well before she met Don."

"Five thousand dollars?" Woolly asked.

"Exactly. On the afternoon of the 26th. Two days before the murder."

༈

"Oh I see. You snooped into my *own* financial affairs, after all I've been through. I don't know what to say. Seriously. You're thorough, at least. I give you that much."

Such was Denise's disheartened response to Woolly upon receiving the news that her $5,000 withdrawal before leaving for Toronto had been discovered. The police gave Denise the choice of attending the police station or being interviewed at her own home. Denise chose the latter.

"Coffee?" she offered her guests, on a silver platter – literally.

How could they decline?

Each officer took their cup and saucer in hand, without kid gloves this time, and sat down on an impressive leather sofa. Denise sat across from the officers. Her complexion was rosy and her eyes alert, so Woolly observed.

It took a while, but after several pointed questions Denise admitted to having given the money to "a competitor."

"Mr. Kimbel," she added, after more prodding.

"So you were not honest with us…"

"Or with the court," Sorenson interjected.

"When you said you phoned him just to bitch about your husband," Woolly concluded.

"Those weren't my words," Denise corrected.

"Do you know what perjury is?" Sorenson asked.

"Yes I do, sir, but put yourself in my position, if you can imagine it for just a minute."

Both cops waited keenly for more.

"I suspected my husband of cheating on me, as you already know, and I was going to Toronto, so I hired a fellow…"

"Mr. Kimbel," Sorenson interjected.

"Yes. That's right. I did hire George. I hired him to follow my husband's movements."

"For five thousand dollars?" Woolly inquired politely.

"Why not? I didn't know what the going rate was."

"There's Yellow Pages for private detectives – or Google," Sorenson said.

"So what. I knew George, and I knew he needed money."

Denise looked in both officers' eyes before admitting, "And I guess there was a little malice there. I liked the idea of George possibly catching Don in the shit."

"Catching Don in the shit?" Sorenson repeated with incredulity in his voice.

Denise sighed. "Call it what you will, sir, but when Don was killed I knew I would be a prime suspect if you guys learned about my deal with George. I'm not naïve."

"But you hired Don for what exactly?" Woolly asked.

"For what *exactly*?" A prickle went up Denise's spine. "I just told you. To spy on Don, but nothing more."

"How long were you going to be in Toronto?" Woolly clarified.

"A week, but I asked him to start Friday."

Sorenson took a verbatim note of this revelation, Denise looked at Woolly for a signal to continue or not, and Woolly lightly nodded.

"I showed him our windows, from the front. I didn't give him the keys," Denise added quickly. Sorenson was scribbling rapidly.

"He was just to follow Donald home from work and watch the

windows."

"And where is Mr. Kimbel these days?" Woolly asked, an investigative weariness in her voice.

Denise shrugged and said, "It beats me."

"Do you have his number?" Sorenson pressed, again glancing up from his notes.

"Of course."

Denise put her coffee on the tray, stood up, and went to her kitchen.

Both officers eyed each other and slurped back some room-temperature coffee. Sorenson then pretended to pull an arrow from a quiver and set it in a bow. He pointed it toward the invisible prey but stopped as soon as she re-entered the room, reading out Kimbel's cell phone number. Sorenson was flush, but Denise didn't notice.

By December 1st 2009 it was official. The recession was over, in Canada at least. The third quarter actually showed economic growth for the first time in a year. GDP expanded at 0.4%. Piddly, perhaps, but a drop in the bucket is better than no matches for a fire.

Inside the Ouisi Charlie was decrying the auctioning off of the Silverdome, an entire football stadium, in Pontiac – "You mean your decaying Coliseum, right? The one where the Lions used to feed on Saints and Vikings while thousands of drunken fans cheered on. That one?" That's how Victor put it, maybe a bit insensitively, but even for people like him, for people uninterested in sports, or for people concerned about crumbling empires, the economy remained the predominant topic of liquid-lunch conversations. Frank and Judy were discussing a labour issue at that very moment, upstairs in Joe Fortes restaurant, across the bridge from Charlie and Victor.

The downtowners were dressed sportily, but neatly, and had already finished a bottle of white and a pricy burger each with a fries-salad combo. Their unused cutlery gleamed. Bulging patrons around them clacked away in tailor-made threads while servers with Janus smiles and elegant arms dutifully fawned over their whims. At this upscale establishment late lunches were normal, boastful write-offs for whichever silk tie convened them.

"I've got some more work," Judy offered.

Frank looked to the ceiling and back to his date. "What's with the work? I've already got a job," he said, then he leaned across the table and added under his breath, "a legal one."

Judy reached out her hand, which Frank readily grasped, and she looked at her potential accomplice seductively. She inhaled from her belly and exhaled slowly, all the while maintaining eye-to-eye.

"I'm gonna' admit something to you and I don't know how you're going to take it..."

Oh shit, Frank thought. Here it comes. *Another confused lesbian.*

"I'm not just an unemployed stager," she confided.

Thank God, Frank thought.

"And I'm a little more than a part-time weed dealer," she said in a near whisper, having leaned forward.

Frank raised an eyebrow and she sat back.

"I'm a little more involved."

"With those guys?"

She nodded and sat forward again.

"It didn't exactly seem small time," Frank revealed.

"Well, that guy who came to the door is pretty low level. I work with a few guys who supply a pretty broad clientele."

Frank retracted his hand and slumped back in his chair. His antennae stiffened.

"You might just wanna walk away now, 'cuz I was just kind of feeling you out that night, to...to see if you were willing, willing to put yourself in a little danger, if you know what I mean?"

Frank folded his arms across his slouched chest. His eyes were fixed on Judy's.

"If it matters to you, you passed."

"So?"

"So we can always use new..."

"Meat?" Frank asked.

Judy shrugged, paused, then asked, "And what I am to you?"

Frank sat up and said "Don't even think that."

"Well that's not a word I use, and no, you're not just 'meat' to me, Frank. You're talent, as far as I can tell, and we can always use new talent. We're not amateurs."

Frank shrugged his shoulders. "What de fuck?" he said under his breath. "I'm not a criminal, Judy. I don't know what you're thinking here."

"Okay. Okay. Maybe I was wrong – in thinkin' you might come around – but don't hate me, okay Frank? I'm sorry. I really am."

Judy paused before saying in a hushed voice, "When we first met in Kits I saw an opportunity, and I acted on it. I did it because you looked streetwise, tough maybe – you told me you rode a Ducati for Christ sake – and I thought you were handsome. I'm just sayin'." She bit her lip and conceded, "and I guess you were charming. That's not part of the job's prerequisite, but it mattered to me, if you know what I mean."

Frank was thinking about how great it was to feel her up the last time they were together, and how he was still dissatisfied with the incompletion of his ultimate goal.

"So was it all just a plan?" he asked. "I could make out with you a bit, as long as I helped you out?"

Judy reached her hand across the table again and clasped his.

"No Frank. Not at all. I've been totally honest there, okay? I told you. I've got some man issues right now 'cuz I've been in one too many abusive relationships. I'm not the best judge of men. I'm learning. I just wanna' take it easy. I wish you could respect that."

Frank gave Judy's hand a light squeeze and said, "Okay. But I'm having a hard time with that because I haven't been with a woman for a while, and I've told you many times now, you're hot, so it's only natural I'm hurting a little."

Judy flushed, chuckled and then looked up at the ceiling, so Frank squeezed her hand again. She looked at him and said, "So I don't know what you wanna' do now. I like you. That's clear, but I've got this little secret goin' on and I don't know if it's gonna' work. I tend to go with guys who play the same game. You know what I mean. So it might be better if we end it here, right here, I hate to say," she said, tapping the edge of the table, "unless you're willing to walk a little on the wild side."

Frank sat back in his chair again and sighed.

"Remember, there is a lot of cash to be made here. A lot. If you get interested, the next job will be really easy, a bigger payoff than the last."

Frank was in a conundrum.

Puis je fais comme si je ne l'ai jamais recontrée?

He didn't totally regret meeting her, especially after hitting that double into right field after dancing and drinking at The Latin Quarter. But maybe now he should walk away and forget about her. Or he could carefully walk the tight-rope she was offering him, helping her out with a few illegal ventures on the expectation of finally rounding third base and sliding into home.

The waitress appeared and he ordered a beer. "Hey, that's your turd," Judy quipped. Frank let out a chuckle as she declined a glass of Chardonnay.

"It's my second," Frank said, still smiling at her joke.

"But you've already had wine."

"I can handle another beer," he said emphatically.

"Okay. All right. I was just thinking about that poor Native guy who showed up drunk on your site. They were talking about him on the radio. He's still in jail."

"So?"

Judy stretched herself forward, put her right hand above her mouth for secrecy, and said, "I mean, everyone knows being drunk on a work site is pretty friggin' dangerous, but who would have expected that guy to off his boss, just for firing him." She then pulled back from the table and chuckled a little mischievously.

Frank grinned. "You have a dark streak in you, lady."

"And you don't?" she queried.

"Ah, Ju-dee," he replied, exhaling as if he had become impatient with the turn in the conversation. "What's the next job you've got lined up?"

"Muscle again, but hold on here," she quickly urged, as Frank had screwed up his face. "The odds are you won't have to do anything. We've got ourselves a breach of trust and we're gonna' take care of it. That's all. You understand that, don't you?"

"Uh, I'm not sure what you mean."

"You've been screwed around before, haven't you?" she asked.

"You mean Hannah?"

"Duhh...It pissed you off, right?"

"Uh..."

The waitress appeared and set down Frank's beer. He thanked her and started filling his glass.

When the waitress was out of earshot Judy said, "Don't be macho. It really hurt, didn't it?"

"Sure. Yeah. It did."

"And you wanted to hurt someone right back, right?"

Frank didn't reply.

"What? Are you just a big pushover?" Judy asked.

"No, but..."

"Well we get even when someone screws around on us," Judy made clear.

"What are you going to do?"

"Teach someone a lesson. The hard way, so don't get all soft. He'll walk away on his own two feet, a little worse for wear, a little smarter too, I assure you, but the problem will be solved, and you don't have to do nothin' but wait outside and keep watch."

Three flabby businessmen pulled out chairs at a nearby table. Frank saw them make knowing eye contact with one another, about Judy, Frank correctly presumed. That was okay, Frank thought, until the tallest of them, a paunchy, balding fellow with a glistening forehead and slip of sweat between his hairy nose and purplish lips, tried to sneak an extra peak. Frank looked him directly in the eyes – challenging him to continue – and the fellow quickly looked away.

"Where?" Frank asked in a lowered voice.

"Poco Inn, on Lougheed."

"When?"

"Tomorrow night – at seven o'clock. Come to my place first and I'll give you a ride. You don't want to show up on your bike. The less there is to identify you, the better. Capisci?"

"Do you want to, to maybe, uh, go out for a few drinks after? It's a…"

"Of course. I'll even introduce you to a couple of my associates." Judy chuckled after she said "associates." "We can have a couple beers with them – they're not bad guys actually," she noted, "and then you and I could go for dinner or something."

Frank liked the thought of the "something" part.

❅❅❅

How better to get into the holiday spirit than to situate Santa's North Pole right in the heart of Shaughnessy Estates? It took some convincing, but Hannah and Charlie finally got soft and agreed to contribute funds to Cactus's Yuletide project. By the first week of December bright, multi-coloured Christmas lights adorned the grounds of 1620 Angus Drive, even lining some of the tents that were still pitched, despite the rain. A giant inflated snowman smiled at passers-by, and a similar zeppelin of Santa Claus and his reindeer stretched in mid-air from two oak trees. The coach house had become "Santa's Workshop," as the large plastic red-and-white sign above the door announced.

Children loved the spectacle, but Margaret Churchill-Booth viewed it as a direct affront to the sophisticated décor that typically adorned the district this time of year. Her challenge, which she put to the board and their lawyer, was to "bring down this mockery" without appearing to be "uncharitable or unChristian."

The local media was unsure of who to support this time around. With the Olympic Games barely two months away, reporters were discouraged from presenting images of class-conflict. They were to present Vancouver in its best possible light. The Shaughnessy feud itself would reflect poorly on the city, but the wonderful floating images, so symbolic of generosity, goodwill, and innocence, those were surely worth telecasting around the world.

"She's threatening to serve me with another suit. Something

about violating some goddamn residency adornment and hydro-electric rules – an 'ordinance' it says here." Cactus showed Hannah the letter from ASHEPOND.

I was trying my damnedest to pull some plastic shapes off a big plastic ring on the handle of my jolly jumper.

"It's just another threat. Can't Sasha deal with it?"

"Well sure, but that doesn't mean the crusty old bag won't get a temporary injunction. She's up to here with our shit," Cactus said, holding her right hand horizontally far above her head.

Charlie entered the apartment with a bag of groceries. He said hello, put the food in the kitchen, and returned to the living room. Hannah gave him a light kiss before he sat down next to Cactus on the love seat. The women gave him a replay of their preceding discussion and he nodded along for a couple of minutes, but then he threw up his hands and said, "Well, if you want my opinion, I'm plain sick of her. Bring 'em all inside."

Cactus slumped her shoulders. "Uh, you know we can't…"

Charlie shook his head sternly and said, "We can't what?" Neither Cactus nor Hannah replied so he continued. "Let her fight you in the goddamn court of public opinion. It's Christmas for Christ's sake. You've got the media on side. Those people shouldn't be getting so wet anyway. They could get sick."

"I know that," Cactus said, "but…"

"But if they go inside, they'll be warm, and if they stay outside and get sick, it'll be on her fuckin' head!" Charlie declared.

Hannah added, "Remember why your gran gave you that place. Because you do the right thing, that's why, and you fight for it. You're a real inspiration. At least to me you are."

"Ahh. You guys seriously think I should just give her the big F.O.?"

Hannah looked at Charlie. She nodded when he did. Cactus reached out and gave her friends an affectionate hug. The trio agreed that the existing tenters could move inside the mansion and the coach house. This was a momentous decision because the friends were well aware of the historical prohibition against multiple-family living in single Shaughnessy estate homes. External blight was one thing. They understood that. But to violate regulations about life *inside* the buildings on the property? This was a whole new aggression.

The elderly woman living across the street from 1620 Angus Drive phoned Margaret Churchill-Booth as soon as she saw the tents wither and their inhabitants take up occupancy inside the home. Cee Bee thought she had died and gone to heaven.

"They've finally done it!" she exclaimed to the troops, all dutifully gathered in her spacious living room, though now at ease, a few drinking coffee, a couple sipping tea, others nursing Sherry.

The General held a well-worn copy of the Regulations out front of her. "Their move was in clear violation of Rule 27(1): No residence of Shaughnessy Estates shall be occupied by more than one family at a time, except in accordance with Rule 48(1) and (2)."

The latter rule simply allowed for exceptions in cases of pre-approved multi-family dwellings and for visitations of friends or relatives of periods no longer than three weeks at a time. The troops were smiling.

"So I propose a motion that Ms. Delaine be asked to appear before the Board, whereupon we ask her to cease and desist in the violation now occurring. And then...uh, well, first, does anyone want to forward that motion?"

A lanky, stooped, and retired UBC business professor promptly raised his hand.

"Dermott forwards the motion," Churchill-Booth noted. "Anyone to second it?"

A younger, shorter fellow who developed ATM software for a living raised his hand.

"Thanks Jim. All in favour?"

Everyone raised their hands, then Dermott turned to Jim and raised his Sherry glass, which Jim carefully tapped with a coffee cup.

"Miss Napoleon has finally arrived at her Waterloo," Churchill-Booth could not resist saying.

But had she?

Cactus refused to pull out the campers from inside her home, which had now become the clandestine headquarters of The Resistance. Accordingly, she found herself at the receiving end of another lawsuit. This time, however, a senior lawyer wanting a piece of the David and Goliath limelight decided to go to battle for Cactus.

"I know he's an asshole, but he could be perfect," Charlie told Hannah over supper.

"What's wrong with Sasha?" Hannah lifted a spoonful of hot, pre-packaged carrot soup to her mouth and blew on it. I was in a highchair, making contemporary art on my tray with my fingers, mushed broccoli and mashed potatoes.

"Nothing. She's great, but two heads can be better than one, and I'm not kidding, I overheard this very guy at the bar a couple of weeks ago, bitching and moaning about the whole lez-gay marriage thing. He went on and on, y'know: why should lezzes or gays have a right to marry?"

"Mm-hmm," mom uttered before ingesting another spoonful of soup.

"He was goin' on about some big legal decision by your Supreme Court – about lezzes and gays having a right to a civil marriage. He kept calling them that: lezzes, dykes. 'The family's not what it used to be,' the guy said, mocking the Supreme Court's thinking. 'The traditional family is a thing of the past? Bullshit. Discriminatory? Bullshit.' That's what he was saying.

"I didn't quite understand everything he was talking about," Charlie continued. "Well, the traditional family part: one man, one woman, two kids and a car, that I got. They say it's based on religion, this guy said, but no, it's based in nature, he insisted."

"Aren't you going to eat your soup? It must be cold by now."

"I'll get to it in a sec."

Hannah got up, pulled me out of my high chair and took me to the sink, where she cleaned me off.

"He said, 'Look, if a family's no longer a wife, a dad, two kids, et cetera, then why stop there? Why not bring in the dog, or the cat? Why not let a man have a civil marriage to a dog. Give matrimonial rights, benefits, property rights and all that kind of stuff to a dog?'"

"Okay okay," Hannah interrupted. She had seated herself at the table again and was bouncing me gently on her knee, hoping to keep me in a good mood, as it was getting close to my bed time. "I'm sorry. I just don't see what you're getting at," she told Charlie.

"Well the guy's a lawyer."

"Yeah. Obviously, but what..."

"But he's got an axe to grind, and now he's got the perfect grindstone."

"I'm really sorry, Charlie. You probably think I'm stupid but I just don't..."

"Look sweetheart. Cactus is being sued for having too many families under one roof and he'd be the perfect guy to go to court and argue that the plaintiffs or whoever are wrong. Cactus doesn't have more than one family living at Angus Drive, because what is one family anymore? According to this lawyer, we don't really know. There's no traditional family anymore. So who is to say that the commune – or The Resistance – or all those homeless people livin' inside are not simply one big happy or not so happy family? You can't discriminate against them by viewing them in terms of the traditional family. That's my point. This guy could help Cactus defeat that Churchill-Booth bitch."

Hannah's emotions were all mixed up, but she did feel warm while keeping me balanced. After a moment's thought she looked at Charlie with big eyes.

"I don't know what it is about you," she said, "but I think I'm lucky I walked into the Ouisi that day."

Charlie blushed as he ate another spoonful of lukewarm soup.

※·⚜·※

Bing Crosby and his nostalgic wishes for a White Christmas had already returned to the airwaves of grocery stores, retail outlets and downtown elevators by the time Frank met up with Judy again. On Friday night, December 11, Frank stood right outside the window of Room #108 at the Poco Inn while Judy waited nearby in her car.

Tough Tiddlywinks

Frank heard tight-lipped conversation between three different voices, then he heard slapping. A man whined. Frank put his ear closer to the wall but stepped back quickly when he heard the sound of knuckles making hard contact with a body. Something or somebody crashed into furniture and after about two or three minutes – Frank wasn't looking at his watch – two men emerged without a scratch. They nodded at him and proceeded straight to their own car.

The room's door was open slightly so Frank peered inside. A man was duct-taped to a chair that had been tipped or pushed over. His back was to Frank and he was struggling to break free. Frank stepped back and returned to Judy.

"Hey, dipshit, did that scumbag see you?" she asked when he got in the car.

"Uh, no. He did not see me at all."

"Rule number one," she said, "don't enter a scene like that unless we okay it. Capisci? That lump of shit could have identified you, and you don't want that, but here, you're services were greatly appreciated."

Frank accepted an envelope Judy handed him. He poked inside and counted five $100 bills.

"All dis for dat?"

"That," she emphasized, "was very important to us, so be happy, and let's go and celebrate."

Inside the Firebird Frank stuck his neck out, literally, in order to give Judy a kiss. Her perfume and the fragrance of her hair fanned his desire. She turned and allowed him to plant his lips on hers, so he reached his arm around her seatbelt and pressed himself closer. After a minute she said, "All right love, let's leave some of this 'til later. I told those guys we would meet 'em at the Biltmore, so let's get over there."

Frank recognized the two fellows who had emerged from the motel right away. They were seated at a corner table drinking beer. One of them suddenly bolted back in his chair and laughed out loud. He wore a slick leather jacket and had greased-back hair. When he caught his breath he said, "Horseshoes up their ass. That's all it was. They played like crap."

"I don't agree," his companion said. He wore a Canucks baseball hat pressed firmly over short brown curly hair.

Judy and Frank arrived at the table. "Alphonse," Judy said to the fellow in the leather jacket, "I'd like you to meet Frank, Frank Belleveau." The men shook hands.

"And however tempted you might be, don't ever call him the Fonz," Judy warned Frank.

"She's right," Alphonse confirmed. "I don't like that."

The other fellow stood up, shook Frank's hand, and said, "I'm Bryce."

Judy and Frank pulled out chairs and sat down. There were already two clean, empty glasses on the table, and a half-full pitcher of beer.

"Let me guess," Judy said, filling the extra glasses for herself and Frank, "you guys are already on your second pitcher and all you've talked about is last night's Thrashers game."

"You a fan?" Bryce asked Frank.

"Of the Canucks?"

"Heyyy. Who else?"

"Try the Habs."

"Oh oh oh. A man with backbone," Alphonse said.

"Or frog legs," Bryce said, winking at his accomplice.

Frank nevertheless turned to Judy and asked, "Is this for real?"

"What?"

Frank turned to Bryce and said, "This bullshit."

Bryce said, "Hey hey hey, man, I was just kidding. It was a stupid joke. Forget it. Judy said you were a tough guy."

A waitress passed by and Bryce signaled for another pitcher.

"So you from Montreal?" Alphonse asked.

"No. East of there. Québec City."

"So you've seen the Nordiques?"

"I seen a few games, but Quebeckers still root for the Habs."

"We were talking about how much some of these guys get paid," Bryce said.

"Imagine," said Alphonse, "two grand a game for some of these schmucks. That's 2,000 bucks an hour."

"Not an hour," Bryce reminded him, just as the waitress put down the second pitcher of beer. Judy began to top up glasses.

"Okay, so whatever, the top guy plays 40 minutes..." Alphonse conceded.

"Well you guys just paid me $500 for 10 minutes work, which is about exactly the same, so I don't know what you're complaining about," Frank remarked. "I can't shoot, or score," he added.

Alphonse grinned and said, "Not bad. I figgered you right," then he turned to Bryce and said "Like I said, the man's got backbone." Alphonse faced Frank again and said, "but we're not payin' youse to shoot *anybody*."

"Though we do need you to help us score," Bryce added.

Frank looked at Judy, who gave him an impish look and took a sip of beer. His eyes asked her for more than that, so when she set her glass back down she told him in a friendly voice, "It's your call."

"What's your driving record like? And don't bullshit me," Alphonse quickly added, "because I can check it out for myself if I want."

Frank stiffened in his chair a little. "Here, in BC, it's real good. Back home, not so bad."

"Well I need a driver, a driver I can trust."

Frank looked at Judy again and said, "You can't do it?"

She tilted her brow toward Alphonse and said to Frank, "It's a special trip and he's a chauvinist. He doesn't want me to drive."

Bryce refilled everyone's glasses and as he did he said, "We want you to drive a van back from Penticton for us..."

"What's in it?" Frank wanted to know.

"Cigarettes."

Frank leaned toward Bryce and Alphonse and said, "I won't deliver dope, so don't bullshit *me*."

Alphonse put up his hands as if to say, "ease off," then said, "You have my word, Frank. I said cigarettes, so it's cigarettes." He immediately said after that, *sotto voce*, "They're duty-free."

"But not supposed to be, if you know what we mean," Bryce added.

Frank cast Judy a look of apprehension.

Alphonse said, "Mr. – what is it again?"

"Belleveau."

"Well Mr. Belleveau, I don't know how much of a businessman you are, but in classical economics, the supply of goods governs the market. Supply even creates demand. That's why we're all encouraged to be entrepreneurs – to invent a printing press, your television, the Internet, your gas-powered leaf-blower, your Post-Its, Jesus, your fuckin' plastic covers for bananas, and – and this."

Alphonse picked his BlackBerry up from the table, held it out, and tilted it back and forth in front of Frank, Bryce and Judy. "Where would I be without this little baby, huh?" he asked. "Where would any of us be?"

"It's obviously why we have opposable thumbs," Judy quipped. "God knew we'd invent the BlackBerry one day. It was part of his grand design, no?" she added. Alphonse rolled his eyes as Bryce groaned.

"We wouldn't be able to compete. Simple as that," Alphonse said. "We *need* these now. What was once desire" – he paused for effect – "is now need. What was once desire is now need. That's how the system is supposed to work, to transform innovation into need, but there's a flaw, you see. The classical theory pictures lots of small guys, like mackerel, inventing their shit and competing freely against one another, not two or three killer whales, merging together and killing the competition. We're not supposed to have monopolies, right?"

Bryce nodded. "But any businessman in his right mind"– Alphonse tapped his own temple a couple of times when he said that – "would rather join forces, outmuscle the competition, not go toe-to-toe against others of equal strength. Everyone of youse can figure that out, right?" Alphonse looked around the group, indifferent as to how they really felt about his speech. "It's a no brainer, I'm telling you. It's just that no one wants to admit it, cause then it's not free enterprise, right? But whether its legal cigarettes, or stolen cigarettes, or legal drugs, or illegal drugs, legal guns or illegal guns, it's all the same. You've gotta outmuscle the competition or absorb it, and that's exactly what we're doin' tomorrow." Alphonse now looked Frank in the eye.

"I got it I got it. Enough already," Judy said, looking at Alphonse. "You're not organized crime – *we're* not a gang. We're just another unwanted box store. If Wal-Mart can do it, then so can we. I got it. I really got it. Now drink up everyone. I need my beauty sleep."

"What's the matter, Frank? I make you nervous?" Alphonse asked. "Because you're lookin' at her more than youze lookin at me, and I thought I was the pretty one here." Alphonse grinned after saying that, and Judy smiled. Frank did too, but ambivalently so.

"It's just a drive for Christ sake, from Penticton to Vancouver," Alphonse said. "Five. Six hours. You just gotta keep your eyes on the road, not on her. Maybe that'll be too tricky. Whadd'ya say?"

"How much?" Frank looked at Judy after he said that.

"Three Gs. Each," Alphonse replied.

"I want to sleep on it."

"You do that, and set your alarm. We leave early in the morning."

1st Quarter 2010

Who would have figured? The American economy, that determined little engine that could, finally managed to push forward by the end of the first decade of the second millennium, more than two years since the deepest recession in its history, barring of course the really Great Depression. But who would have imagined that the big-eyed caboose could have ever rolled uphill on burning shovel loads of socialism? I know. Such toxic stuff, worse than coal and other four-letter words. It was actually making some otherwise very hardy people very ill. The principled descendants of Puritans were among those most affected. They decided that their best remedy was a natural one – tea, of all things – so tea parties started springing up across states, even in public, rain or shine. English Breakfast was banned from the menu, but cups of peppermint, orange pekoe, and chamomile were sipped freely as attendees voiced displeasure with Uncle Sam, their very own Mad Hatter.

Frank Belleveau would not be caught dead at a tea party. He preferred his beers and bars too much. So after a long morning's drive over the precipitous but magnificently picturesque Coquihalla highway – in a rental car, no less – a waitress served him a draught at Slack Alice's, the "premiere" exotic dance lounge in Penticton, B.C. One pasty stripper was working the meagre lunchtime audience, swinging herself athletically around a pole and performing splits on a pink faux-fur mat. Sensual, beckoning words from a Sinead O'Connor hit poured through the speakers.

A television screen behind Frank, set up high in a corner, showed live news footage of rescue workers scouring the rubble left by a 7.0 magnitude earthquake in Haiti. It had hit near Port-au-Prince two days before. Searchers were on desperate missions to save whoever might still be breathing. The naked dancer caught glimpses of the footage when she twirled or slinked to face the nearly empty barroom.

Frank was growing impatient. Judy had phoned him earlier to say she was being debriefed by the guys in possession of the van. They had come from Dawson Creek. She ordered Frank to have no more than one beer while he waited, and said she would be there shortly. *Hurry up*, he thought. When he had arrived he noticed a sheriff's van in his rear view. It pulled into an adjoining parking lot, for the provincial court building, so he realized when he got out of his rental. Now a fresh stripper was about to perform, but he didn't care. His geographical proximity to handcuffs had him wanting just to get home.

Judy arrived as the peeler was playing peek-a-boo with Frank through a triangular window she created between her pudendum and her knees, which were on a soft blue rug. Her bare buttocks were in the air, facing the barroom.

"Hey, I think I took yoga with her once. Let's go," Judy said.

Frank grinned and swallowed back his beer.

En route to Vancouver, just after they passed Merritt, Frank saw a charcoal four-door behind him. It looked just like an unmarked cruiser, with the GPS units on the roof.

"I think we're being followed," he told his navigator.

"Then just stay calm, and if they pull you over, let me do the talking."

Frank tensed up.

"You want a cigarette?" Judy kidded, just to relax him.

"It's not funny. We're knee deep in some serious shit here."

"Don't worry about it," she said.

As Frank ascended a hill the cruiser pulled up alongside him. Frank tried to keep his eyes on the road but did peak quickly to his left. The male in the passenger seat was wearing shades. Frank could not see the driver, who accelerated a little. The passenger then put his forearm out the window and pretended to point a handgun at Frank. Frank tensed up again, just as the passenger smiled and pretended to pull the trigger.

"Fuck me. Did you see that?" Frank asked Judy. The cruiser sped ahead. "That guy just pretended to shoot me."

Judy chuckled. "Don't worry about it. I think it was Chuck. The Fonz knows him, personally."

"Those cops were dirty?" Frank's eyes showed genuine consternation.

"Jesus, Frank, where have you been your whole life? You've never heard of dirty cops?"

"I just. Fuck..." Frank shook his head, but kept his eyes on the road.

"We've got 'em on the payroll," Judy remarked.

～～～～

"Incroyable," Frank remarked, a bottle of bubbly in hand.

The smugglers were now in Frank's living room. Frank was seated in his favourite armchair, the one Hannah found him in when she returned early from The Vogue. Judy was seated on the chair's arm to Frank's left. She had just thrown an elasticized roll of bills onto the coffee table, next to a paper bag of Chinese take-out. The outer denom on the roll was a hundred. Frank could see that much.

"No, Frank. They're real. All thirty of them," Judy assured him. "My friends value your assistance that highly. You can see they make a lot of money and guys like you help 'em do it. It's hard to find someone with cojones. You've obviously got 'em."

"But three G's for driving a truck? C'mon!"

Judy smirked at Frank's pronunciation: "tree gees."

Frank popped open the champagne anyway. What else was there to do with it? Then he and Judy dug into Chinese food, but that's when Judy made a confession – a big one.

"I haven't been very honest with you from the get-go," she said.

"That I know already," Frank replied. "So what's new?"

"Well, I haven't held down a regular job for years. This job we did this afternoon. It was no small potatoes, as you can probably guess."

"I don't consider three grand for moving illegal cigarettes small potatoes."

"But you did it."

Frank poured himself more champagne. "I'm not myself lately," he explained. "I lost my mother last year and I have not spoken to my father since. He's such a prick, a health inspector, for farms. He bothers farmers about their poultry, and their pigs, and shit like that. When he divorced my mom she had to go to court for support. He didn't even want to share custody. Can you believe that? A father doesn't want to see his own kids. It would cut into his travelling time, mom said he told the judge. I'm sure that made the judge mad, because he would have known. My dad just wanted to travel around from farm to farm, screwing other women along the way." Judy grinned at "udder women."

"So trust, honesty, loyalty – those things mean a lot to you?" she asked.

"Of course."

Judy paused for a few seconds, then asked, "Was he a drunk? Your dad?"

"No."

"Mine is. Antonio makes his own wine and drinks it like cherry cola. Come to think of it, his doesn't taste much different."

Frank chuckled, then asked, "Does he grow, uh, l'ail?"

"Uh..." Judy tilted her right ear toward Frank. "I didn't catch that," she said.

"*L'ail*. It's uh, you know, for cooking, in de bulb, like that." He drew a small, bulbous outline and stem in the air with his hand.

"Oh. Garlic."

"That's it. Does your father grow that?"

"Heyy. Who's getting a little stereotypical here? Did your dad make maple sugar, or syrup, or whatever?"

Frank chuckled, looked toward the ceiling and said, "I do remember going on a couple of those tours, in the trees, with my family." Then he turned his attention back to Judy and said, "but I don't want to talk about them right now. It makes me uncomfortable."

"No problem. I understand. If it makes any sense, the guys you've met – Bryce, Alphonse – they've become like brothers to me, like an extended family. They watch out for me, and they make a shit-pile of money."

"Committing crime. So what?"

"Jesus, Frank. I never guessed you'd be such a pussy. You just made three thousand delivering tax-free cancer sticks to the needy. It seems like everyone wants to rip off the government but you."

Frank shrugged.

Judy shook her head and said, "C'mon, man. The way things are goin', it'll be more acceptable in a couple of years to smoke marijuana than cigs. You wanna' bet on it?"

Frank grinned and said, "No thanks. I am not a betting man."

Judy smiled and said, "Well then, when it happens just remember: you heard it from me first. Cigs will be illegal and kush'll be regulated. In the meantime I'm gonna make some real dough on the black market. Y'know, there are dirty dancers in this city, just like the one you were admiring today, and escorts, who'll make as much money as you made today, in one evening. Some lawyers make that much in a morning. So what's the problem?"

Frank shrugged again and had a glug of champagne.

"If it matters to you at all, Bryce and the guys really are willing to bring you in, if you know what I mean?

"Bring me in?"

"Well, just like I was talking about – about family. Those guys are fairly well-connected."

"I have figured that out by now."

"All right, but I'm just letting you know, if you want to get a little more deeply involved you can make a lot more than a few G's here and a few G's there."

"Sure sure, Judy. I hear you. I really do."

"Okay then. Sorry. I'll stop talking shop. You want to get a little more personal instead?"

She looked him in the eye and nodded toward the stairs.

"Now you're talking my language. Should we bring this?" Frank asked, holding up the bottle of bubbly.

"Of course."

Beyond the bedroom walls the moon was large and low. Judy curtailed its beam with small twists of the rods that lowered the shutters as Frank watched from an armchair. She passed by him, set her glass on top of the dresser that Hannah once used, and began to undress, top first. 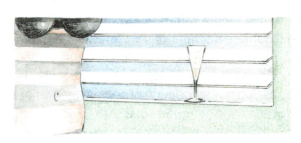 Frank stared at her firm cappuccino-coloured breasts pressed into a black bra.

"I've told you," she said, after sitting on his bed and beginning to unbutton her pants, "you don't have to do any of this stuff you've been doing for me. It's been getting me and my friends through the recession, but that's our business. I'm here tonight because I want to be with you, not them."

Frank leaned forward, pulled the right roll of bills from his back pocket, and held it in his right hand. "I – I – I just don't..."

Judy pushed her jeans off her feet and reclined on the bed. She was now wearing only her underwear. "I'm getting a little cold," she said. "Do you mind if I get under the covers?"

"*Es*-ti. Of course not." Frank's profane reference to the host, the wafer – Christ's body – was lost in translation on Judy. "But..." he was about to say.

"But what, Frank? You wanna keep talking now? Is that what you wanna do?"

Frank set the money on the window ledge as Judy maneuvered herself under the sheets and a duvet, before propping herself up on Frank's pillows.

"You know what I want to do. I wanna be in there, right next to you. You know that, but..." Frank flipped off his right shoe.

"Frank, if you think you're taking a risk with all this stuff, you should know that I've been hearing things about you that cause me some concern."

"Oh yeah. Like what?" Frank flipped off his other shoe.

"Well, this is probably not the best time, so please..."

"No. I want to hear it," Frank said.

"Well, it's just that Bryce and Alphonse told me to be wary about you, because you were investigated for that Dickerson murder.

Isn't that right?"

Frank paused for a few seconds before dropping his pants.

"You seriously think I had something to do with that?"

"Not me, okay? You don't need to get excited here, all right? It's just Bryce and Alphonse. They say there's people who know you've been questioned by the police, about that murder."

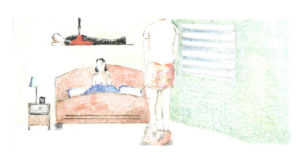

"Well, yeah. Sure. I was questioned, but that was all. It was routine stuff. They wanted to know about my motorbike because treads or something were at the scene." Frank was unbuttoning his shirt. "I worked for Don," he continued, "so they interviewed me, but I told them exactly what I was doing at the time he was killed. I was watching a movie."

"What movie?"

"Whoa! So now you're going to interrogate me?" Frank was now standing at the foot of the bed, naked except for his jockey shorts.

"Don't be silly. I was just wondering what kind of movies you like. I don't know that much about you, except that you can hold your liquor, and..."

"And I'm willing to commit crimes for a beautiful woman. It's pretty pathetic, don't you think?"

Frank shook his head, kneeled onto the bed, and got settled

under the covers. Judy put her arms around him and gave him a passionate kiss, which flooded his flagging self-esteem with adrenaline and dopamine. "Are you saying I'm not worth it?" she whispered before pulling away a little.

Frank grinned and pulled her toward him again. The wayward Catholics then had a fun and sweaty romp. Yet again Judy did not let Frank slide into home base, but she did relieve the pressure he was feeling by taking his matter into her own hands, so to speak.

☞ ☯ ☞

"Make Love, Not War!" So hippies and beatniks used to say. (Now they just ask for change with a capital C).

But so too was the underlying message of the majority decision in *Association of Shaughnessy Estates Property Owners and New Developments v. Cactus Blossom Delaine*, delivered the morning of January 26, just two weeks before the start of the 2010 Winter Olympics.

Madam Justice Yvonne Bruberger, a woman almost two-decades younger than Margaret Churchill-Booth, but of similar pedigree, refused to conclude that the communal occupation of 1620 Angus Drive violated the Shaughnessy Official Development Plan or any other regulation or law on the books.

In her written reasons Her Ladyship rejected all four arguments that the ASHEPOND lawyer had advanced for upholding the trial court's eviction order.

First, she ruled that the Angus Drive "manor" – the word she used – remained a single family dwelling, contrary to ASHEPOND's pleadings, which had been amended to address the recent indoor occupation. No renovations had been undertaken to convert the residence or sub-divide it to accommodate multiple tenants. In Bruberger's words:

There is nothing in the Rules or the Development Plan that expressly forbids camping on the lawns of an owner's residence or inside, and it cannot properly be inferred that any such intent was contemplated by these regulations. A fair application of the *expressio unius est exclusio alterius* rule does not lead to an unpalatable or unreasonable conclusion in the circumstances. If ASHEPOND wants to amend its rules in an attempt to remedy this situation, that is for them to do, but I cannot say, and I do not hereby pretend to say, that such a rule would survive judicial scrutiny. A woman's home remains her castle at common law. Who the defendant chooses to allow to pitch tents within the walls of her property is her decision, subject to considerations I now address.

I. The Public Health Issue

The plaintiff contends that the occupants of 1620 Angus Drive pose a health risk to the members of ASHEPOND and surrounding community. It says the situation is sufficiently unsanitary as to require eviction. The lower court so found but with great respect I cannot agree. The evidence establishes clearly that the occupants have lawful access to the washroom facilities of the primary residence and coach house, and that they use these appropriately. Public health officials have attended the grounds more than once since the occupation began, at the request of the plaintiff, and have failed to identify a health concern sufficient to support the plaintiff's contention that the campers and in-door occupants are in contravention of the ASHEPOND Rules.

II. The Drug Issue

The plaintiff alleges that the occupancy has brought illicit drugs into its neighbourhood. If this allegation were to be substantiated then of course the defendant might have more than a civil problem on her hands. The lower court was of the view that the allegation was indeed substantiated, but here too I must disagree. The evidence that I accept is that police have attended to the grounds of 1620 Angus Drive on a few occasions, with warrants in hand, because neighbours have insisted that they have seen drug transactions taking place among occupants, and because they could smell the distinctive aroma of cannabis drifting from the premises. Every time the police arrived and made lawful searches, however, no illicit substances whatsoever were found. The lower court findings in this regard were unreasonable.

III. The Nuisance Claim

The plaintiff has contended further that the occupancy itself and the behaviour of the occupants are both a nuisance at law, and have eroded the proper use and enjoyment of the property of surrounding neighbours. Again, despite the lower court acceptance of this view, I cannot agree. The weight of the evidence plainly established that the playing of musical instruments, even amplified at times by human pedaling of stationary bicycles, ended by 9:00 pm every night of the week. Police attended to the premises on several occasions due to complaints by neighbours. They heard nothing upon arrival or even as they neared their arrival that could cause a reasonably tolerant neighbour to complain, in their view.

The defendant herself has argued, quite properly, that she is often subjected to the sounds of gas-powered lawn mowers and leaf blowers throughout the day, as well as the whirr of electronic weed-whackers. She testified to the frequency with which lawn maintenance and landscaping trucks arrived in the neighbourhood, and to having to endure the pollution spewed from the exhaust of their gas-powered equipment.

IV. The Multi-Family Prohibition

Finally, to return to the complaint that the ASHEPOND Rules do not permit 'multi-family' dwellings without proper New Development approval, I am inclined to agree with the defendant that the definition of "family" in the common law of this province and country has expanded significantly over the past few years. A family is no longer confined to a heterosexual husband and wife and the children born from or adopted into that union. It includes various relationships between adult men and women, regardless of their sexual orientation, and the offspring produced by these relationships.

Though I would hesitate to say that the sky has become the limit in this regard, or that technology is the sole culprit, I do find that it would be inconsistent with the *Charter of Rights and Freedoms* to conclude that the conglomerate of cycle enthusiasts who have pitched tents on the lawns of 1620 Angus Drive are not a "family," legally speaking. The same logic applies to the fact that some of the individuals have moved inside for the winter months. The *Charter*, especially the equality clause, must be given a generous interpretation. If bi-sexuals can form a family, so can bi-cyclists.

Finally, it must be noted that the plaintiff has not helped its own cause in these proceedings by referring to the occupants of 1620 Angus Drive in its pleadings as communists, lay-abouts and vagabonds. One expects more respectful treatment of historically disadvantaged groups in Canadian courts of law.

"We will definitely appeal, by right!" Margaret Churchill-Booth replied to a scrum of reporters outside the courthouse. They were on Smithe Street, underneath a concrete walkway.

"What about the image such a move would create, for your association?" one reporter asked.

CeeBee looked at him with offended wonder. "I don't know what image you are talking about, sir. ASHEPOND is not a charity. It's a residency association, doing what is entirely proper to maintain the most valuable real estate in this city. I'm sorry if that fact displeases some – I really am – but Shaughnessy is not the place where one comes for social housing. It never has been. There are lots of places for city council to house these people." CeeBee flitted her right hand toward City Hall and said, "God knows I pay enough taxes for them to get on with it."

The message on the other side of the courthouse, the Nelson Street side, was less taxed. "It's a great day for justice," Thornton T. Drammel told journalists. A small "c" celebrity in his own right, having been an offensive star for the Giants, Drammel was the lawyer Charlie managed to track down and introduce to Cactus. He and Sasha Veçerkavic were surrounded by a throng of exuberant young people, cyclists and social activists, all raising fists of solidarity and shouting variously, "Cactus! Cactus! Vive la Resistance! Power to the Pedal!" and similar sentiments.

Hannah was more reserved, though she was happy for her friend. Television cameras were rolling and she did not want to be caught on film or appear on the evening news. She did not want Frank to see her. She did not want Denise Dickerson to see her. Charlie Menz motioned to give her a warm embrace, but she gently resisted.

Her meandering eyes had caught a tattoo shop across the street and suddenly she was ruminating about them – tattoos. She had often toyed with the idea. Almost all of Cactus's friends had them, as did Frank. Maybe it's time she got inked. She imagined herself with a beautiful but modest drawing somewhere on her skin – a flower, perhaps, or a saying, near a shoulder blade. Somewhere hidden, discreet. Somewhere private. She wasn't as bold as Cactus, Hurdy Gurdy and the others. And then she noticed a cartoon tortoise painted on the side of a parked car. "Tortoise Home Insurance – The best protection around," the slogan read, and her thoughts turned to the plaque in her kitchen – to the raven, the paddle, the canoe – then to Frank, and to Ryan Ghostkeeper. How was that young fellow holding up? she wondered.

"Hannah?" Drammel called out. "We're going to The Winking Judge, a pub on Smithe. It's just around the corner. Will you join us?"

"Uh." Hannah hesitated. "No thanks, Thornton. I'm going to get back to my baby girl."

   🚲 🚲 🚲

Mr. Kimbel had finally returned from a "vacation," as he put it, in Costa Rica, and attended the Main Street police detachment in Vancouver, upon Sergeant Woolly's request.

In a small interview room equipped with audio and video recording equipment, Woolly extracted more details of the fallen realtor's involvement with Denise Dickerson shortly before and after her husband's murder.

"You both withheld information from us. She has already made that clear. You could be charged with obstruction."

Kimbel nodded and looked at the floor.

"What do you have to say about this?" Woolly asked in a raised voice.

Kimbel looked at his interrogator with sheepish eyes.

"Look at me," Woolly said, pointing to her own eyes, "and tell me you didn't take money to murder the man you were so envious of, by many accounts."

The freshly-tanned "person-of-interest," to use the proper police designation, faced Woolly and said, "I did not kill Mr. Dickerson, ma'am. That was never the plan. I was supposed to track him and take pictures if I saw him with another woman."

"So did you take any?"

Kimbel pursed his mouth and shook his head gently. "On the day Don was murdered," he said, "I followed him from his office.

He went to a grocery store, the fancy one there on Granville. Meinhardt's. I waited outside. From there he drove over the Granville Street bridge and went to his condo in Yaletown."

"How do you know that?"

"Denise gave me that address. She even showed me where the place was, where the windows of their condo were, and everything. That was on Thursday. We did that in my car. I was to watch their front windows and report – that's all – so when he pulled into the alley on Friday I knew there was no point in following him."

"Was he with anyone?"

"In his car?"

Woolly nodded.

"No. Not that I saw."

"So he turned down the alley, at where?"

"Off Hamilton there. Mainland, whatever it's called. I get screwed up in Yaletown. All those half-streets and one-ways. He pulled into the alley right behind his condo. I can assure you."

"And then what? You took your position out front – or what?"

"I watched, and I waited out front, but no lights came on."

"Did you see anyone in a hardhat in the area?"

"No I did not, ma'am."

"Did you see anyone on a yellow motorbike nearby?"

"No I did not." Kimbel shook his head gently after his reply.

"But you heard sirens, right? Police cars? Fire engines? Please tell me you're not deaf as well as blind, Mr. Kimbel."

Kimbel was now looking at the floor. After a breath and without looking up he said, "I heard them, and I saw them, and I decided not to stick around." Then he looked up at Woolly, paused, and said, "Whatever it was, I didn't see anything, and I didn't wanna have to explain anything to you guys – to your fellow officers, I mean. The binoculars and camera themselves would have made me pretty suspicious."

"So you and Denise just kept this little scheme to yourselves all this time, hoping it would never come to light – all while a young man has been in custody and faced trial for first degree murder?"

Kimbel shrugged, looked his interrogator in the eye, and said, "I guess that's right." He did not blanch, technically speaking, because the copper tone of his face remained unchanged, but the perspiration beads sprouting across his body reflected the sickness he felt.

"What did you do with the five grand?"

"I kept it."

Woolly stared at Kimbel with a show of resigned displeasure. Her judgmental and tired gaze, however, was not directed specifically at him. It was for all the persons who had sat in that chair and had such difficulty seeing past their own noses. After fifteen seconds or so Kimbel said, "I'm sorry, ma'am. I needed the money. Denise didn't. We were in a recession."

Woolly rolled her chair away from the realtor. As he stood up to say his adieu, he remarked, "it seems we still are."

No kidding. If the thousands of international gold-seekers who flocked to the cloudy slopes and trails around Vancouver in February and March were any indication, the global economy was lacklustre. Even so, the 2010 Winter Olympic Games and the Paralympic Games came and went with no expense or cheer considered excessive. These contests were seven years in the making, after all, and Canadians were determined to keep a much greater share of the purse from the Americans than they did in the 1850s, the last great gold rush to occur in B.C. (Who said people have short memories?)

Those rascally Canadians, once so proud to be second best – once internationally reputed for their modesty – now so determined to best their athletic nemeses to the south and to "Own the Podium." They ended up actually fulfilling their proprietary ambitions. Fourteen gold medals! More than any other country, including the U.S.! Wow. And that overtime goal by Crosby could just turn out to be the defining moment of Canadian history, more so than when Roy Brown shot down the Red Baron (if in fact he did that); or when the Bill of Rights was enacted in 1960; or when national Medicare legislation arrived six years later; or when Mike Bossy tipped in that shot from Paul Coffee at the Saddledome in 1984, in overtime, to send the Soviets packing.

"Can you believe we saw that?" Denise said to Bernie, once her Escalade had broken free of the massive crowd dancing around GM Place.

"I could *not* believe the angle," Bernie piped up.

"I still can't believe I had my head turned," Louise pined. "Those fucking louts next to me. All the way from Winnipeg, they were so damn proud to announce. If I didn't keep my eye on them half the time, I *know* they would have spilt beer on me."

"I offered to change seats, love," Bernie reminded her.

"It's okay. It's okay. We spent $400 a head and I missed the winning goal. Let's get a drink."

Charlie Menz and Victor Pavlenko watched the game at the Ouisi. Charlie got heckled because he refused to conceal his desire for the Americans to win. As soon as Crosby scored the winner a couple of patrons poured beer over his head – Charlie's, not Sidney's.

"Okay okay," the Detroiter pleaded, his hands above his head. "You guys win. We're not worthy." He was tipsy and having fun with it all, as was Victor.

Law-abiding citizens across the whole Lower Mainland ordered rounds upon rounds of drinks, correct in the belief that their hangovers would not be met with professional admonition. Excitement had to be constrained, however, at the Surrey pre-trial detention centre. That's where Ryan Ghostkeeper watched the golden wrist shot from a communal television room. The sober inmates naturally shouted with glee at the goal but were dispatched to their respective cells minutes thereafter. Ryan was happy for Canada, but his stomach was tight. His second trial was only two and a half months away.

2nd Quarter 2010

As with every jail sentence, all great parties must come to an end, one way or another. Vancouverites moaned to radio jockeys, television hosts and print journalists about their post-Olympics hangovers, even genuine depression, once the flame was finally snuffed. This malaise was not unlike the general feeling of Americans toward their bruised and battered economy. Millions were still unemployed, consumer confidence was shaken badly, housing starts were way down, delinquencies were way up, and foreclosures were at an unprecedented high. A lot of banks owned a lot of vacant homes (or thought they did).

At least the rough-and-tumble, no-holds-barred NHL playoffs had arrived to distract unemployed and underemployed men and fathers from fears of homelessness, hunger, repossession, and other forms of emasculation. I'm sure that that big-bearded economist who said religion was the peyote of the masses had never seen a Bruins or Blackhawks post-season smackdown. The Red Wings made it to the show this year, so Charlie Menz was happy. The Canucks did too – the annual carrot on the stick team. Even the Habs made it, which surprised many observers, but not Frank Belleveau, a true believer.

He and thousands of others watched the first couple of games around the league with great enthusiasm, but the general mood was unexpectedly and rudely interrupted by breaking news that an oil rig in the Gulf of Mexico had exploded and was leaking oil at an unprecedented rate. Initially the situation appeared to be a horrible accident, but maybe it was part of a Grand Master plan.

"AND I stood upon the sand of the sea, and saw a beast rise up out of the sea, having seven heads and ten horns, and upon his horns ten crowns, and upon his heads the name of blasphemy."

Judy read that passage to Frank from his sofa. He was seated across from her in his armchair, his feet on the coffee table, still wishing she would either leave him alone for good or give herself to him entirely. The pair's relationship had effectively chilled over the last couple of months as Frank had grown highly impatient with Judy's unwillingness to go all the way. He had decided to look for love elsewhere – primarily on Plenty of Fish – but she was there on this afternoon to enlist Frank's services yet again. As a way of warming him up to her visit, Judy had decided to play a game: Which of the two Catholics knew the scripture best?

"I don't know of any oil rig named Blasphemy," Frank said.

"Come on. Don't stall. Give it to me...What's the book?" Judy asked him.

"I give up."

"Loser. It's Revelation, Chapter 13:1."

Frank shrugged, then said, "But beware of false prophets."

"Oh, nice one, but easy," she said. She had not even passed him his Bible this time. "Matthew, Chapter 7."

"*Tabarnak*. You've actually read that thing?"

"Of course I did. It's not just the good book. It is a good book. Here's one you should know: A corrupt tree bringeth forth evil fruit."

"Oh yeah. Don't tell me." Frank rapped his forehead with his knuckles a couple of times. "It's either the New Testament, the Book of Gospel, or it's Genesis," he guessed.

"Genesis?"

"Yeah."

"And you're a Nimrod," Judy quipped. An intense grin shaped her face.

"Hey. What the...?" Frank sat forward, putting his feet on the floor.

"No no no. Seriously," she said. "A mighty hunter. That's what I meant." She was suppressing a strong urge to laugh.

Frank remained uptight, staying focused on the question. "I meant with Eve there," he explained, "listening to the snake, eating da pomme from de tree of knowledge. It's a poisoned fruit, right? That's what makes them realize they are naked. That's why I said Genesis."

Judy's smile receded. She paused and said, "I've never thought of it that way, but you know what? Not bad. Not bad at all. I'll give you half a point because the passage in fact comes almost right after the one you read to me: Matthew, Chapter 7."

Frank groaned, then put his feet back on the table and reclined, his hands clasped together on his stomach.

"I take it I win?" she asked.

"Yeah. You win. You should have been a Sunday school teacher. I know I would have studied harder. I'm gonna' get a beer." And he got up from his chair.

"Well, when you get back it's time to talk a little business, if that's all right?"

Frank was stepping into the kitchen. He put up his hand and waved, to indicate Yes, but without enthusiasm.

"I can promise you $10,000 for this one," she said, raising her voice just enough for him to hear from the kitchen. That number caught him a little by surprise. It was the most she had put on offer to date and it was sorely tempting. Frank's construction contracts had dwindled, as had Vancouver's real estate market generally, and economists were expressing real fears of the global economy sinking further yet.

"C'mon. You've heard of Robin Hood, haven't you?" Judy goaded as Frank stepped into the living room, beer in hand.

He chuckled. "I didn't know the poor needed pot."

"Sure they do. Some don't, for sure, but it's the principle of the thing," she urged.

"Let me think about it, okay? I'm serious. I'm interested. I just want a little time."

Four days later Frank found it invigorating to follow Judy, Bryce and Alphonse into a wealthy suburban home in Richmond, right through the front door, after Bryce so brazenly and professionally picked the lot – all before sunset. All four associates descended unmasked, with garbage bags in hand, into a basement paradise of pot. They loaded up with dozens of plants. Frank and Judy took one trunk-load of crops themselves, and Frank could not stop grinning all the way back to Judy's place.

"You were right," he admitted, "it does feel good to steal from criminals."

"Have I convinced you, then? This is more fun than the nine-to-five any day, isn't it?"

"Ju-*dee*," Frank said in an admonishing tone.

"I know you're reluctant to join us full time, but come on. Just think about how easy that was."

Frank shook his head, smirked and said, "That was a blast, no question, but that's it, Judy. Please. I'm done. *Tout fini*."

His partner cast him a look of genuine surprise before returning her eyes to the road.

"You promised me ten grand, so I'll take it, but I'm movin' on, okay."

"Yeah. Internet dating. How's that going?"

Frank did not reply.

"Well, I'm guessing that at least you've been laid a lot."

That suggestion, which was not inaccurate, nonetheless perturbed Frank. He screwed up his face.

"I know you've given up on me, Frank, but all I asked was for you to wait until I was ready. And now I am."

Frank looked straight at her.

"I'm ready," she repeated, and her eyes met his for an instant.

"Don't shit me, Judy," Frank said. "You teased me long enough, and enough is enough. I don't want to play that broken record anymore."

"Well I never meant to tease you. I was perfectly honest with you. I needed time, and now I've had it. I'll admit it, I don't like the thought of you doing all that Internet dating."

Judy took her hands off the wheel quickly to put air quotes

around "dating."

"Variety *is* dee spice of life, Judy, but I'll admit, it's becoming a little, uh – what do you..."

"Tedious?" Judy offered.

"Yeah. That's it."

"So what are you saying? Do you understand what I'm offering?" Judy asked.

"I think so. So where do you want to go?"

"To my place first. I wanna put on somethin' special. Then we'll go out and have some fun."

"Some fun?"

"Yeah. I understand what that word means to you, and I promise: we will have some fun tonight."

🚲 🚲 🚲

Judy lived up to her promise.

She first took Frank to her place and stuffed the sacks of marijuana in her bedroom closet. She then mixed a couple of Alexanders. "What's that?" Frank asked as she did so, a worried look on his face. She told him and he sniffed the concoction before tasting it.

"Not bad. A woman's drink," he said.

Judy allowed him to take his martini glassful into the bedroom, where she changed into a low-cut, pink veneer blouse, white hip-hugging slacks and high-heeled shoes. She then applied her war paint in the en suite washroom as Frank reclined on her bed and sipped away.

"You know, Frank," she said into her mirror while carefully applying eyeliner, "I sometimes can't help think about that poor kid going to trial again."

"What kid?"

"You know, that Indian fellow on trial for killing your boss. The trial begins in just over a couple of weeks. "

Frank rolled his eyes. "He's not a kid. He's a grown man and he did something terrible."

"You think so?"

"Sure. Why not?"

"Well...the jury didn't convict him the first time."

"Yeah, but these things happen. God knows what angles his lawyer played."

Judy came to the doorway, put her arms out, and said, "What do you think of these angles?"

"Hoochie mama. I likes, I likes. So let's go and have a few drinks, and stop worrying about that fuckin' guy. I want to get back here and watch you take that all off again."

"Jesus. Do you think you can wait? Judy asked sarcastically.

"I don't know. I'll try."

So the Italian and her Québécois escort first went to Crush, on Granville Street, and had a few martini varietals, but not before a round of professionally-mixed Alexanders, Judy insisted. The booze made the couple feel younger than they really were, so they walked a few blocks to Au Bar on Seymour, to mingle and sparkle and twist their hips in sync with the other bodies on display. By 2:00 am the volume of the DJ's mixing, distorting and scratching had almost rendered them deaf. Unable to keep up with the kids, they departed in a cab.

Frank was feeling a little fuzzy. Judy was clearer, but tipsy.

When the taxi stopped at Judy's place Frank told the driver, from the back seat, "She'll get it. She's a big time criminal. She steals weed from people's homes, so don't mess around with her."

"And he likes to smoke it," Judy added, winking at the driver and handing him a $20 bill. "You can keep the change."

Judy felt increasingly anxious as she led Frank along her outdoor walkway, into her apartment building, through her front door, and within a few minutes, into her bedroom. She did not turn on the ceiling light but rather went to the corner of the room, not far from the head of her bed, and switched on a lava lamp. Bright yellow globs slowly began to well up through translucent orange syrup.

"What do you think?" she asked her guest.

"I like that," he replied indifferently. He was more interested in seeing her get undressed.

"Because I'm wondering if you want to record this, or not?"

Frank stopped in mid-motion. He had almost pulled his shirt over his head, but his eyes were still concealed. Judy began to unbutton her blouse and after a few seconds Frank lifted his shirt over his face and asked, "Are you kidding?"

"It'll be our first time. I just thought you might want to save the moment," she replied. Then she tossed her blouse on a chair and unzipped her slacks, exposing pretty pink underwear.

"I thought you had trust issues." Frank stumbled slightly when he said that. He was trying to pull his jeans off his legs.

"I do. I'm not letting *you* have the tape. It's *my* camera. My tape."

"I don't know." Frank drew out the word "know", then said, "let's forget about that. Let's just do it."

"All right. You win."

Judy unclipped her bra, pulled down her panties, and got under her bed covers. Frank slid over and put his arm over her shoulder. They lay chest to chest, face to face, smiling, with their legs warmly overlapped. Frank brought his free hand onto Judy's breast and she felt him become stiff as the Pope's crozier.

Judy stick-handled Frank for a minute before sitting up, straddling him, and bringing him carefully inside her. Frank moaned and she let him feel blissful for a few seconds. She gyrated ever so slowly before lifting herself off his point of interest. When she did he furrowed his brow in confusion.

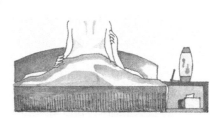

"Oh Judy. What now?" he asked.

"Here's what, and I am going to say this once and only once." Judy leaned forward and let her nipples lightly sweep across her lover's chest. Before straightening up again she kissed him.

"I don't believe you, Frank, when you say you had nothing to do with Don Dickerson's murder, and that scares me."

"But..."

Judy quickly put her right hand over Frank's mouth and the left one around his member. The latter had temporarily lost its resolve so she gently brought it back to attention, then she removed her hand from Frank's mouth and continued:

"I have sources who tell me it was you who actually knifed Don Dickerson, because you were mad as hell that that millionaire prick stole your fiancée while you were away, in Québec, dealing with your mom or whatever."

Frank said nothing and she could feel him wilt again, despite her committed grip.

"I know you're scared. I know you've been harboring this secret for over a year. Who wouldn't? But you need to know, I'm precisely the person you can tell this to, and *should* tell this to. You should have figured that out already. The last thing I'm ever gonna do is squeal. Look at what you've got on me – B & E's, smuggling contraband, grow rips, assisting gangsters for God's sake. But seriously, and more important, I don't give a shit about Dickerson – the Density King. What a laugh. He was a scumbag, and if you ask me, you did society a favour if it really *was* you who offed him."

Judy put her hand over Frank's mouth again, leaned forward and pressed her breasts to his. Gently but firmly she pulled on his joystick. The L.E.D. clock said 3:10 am. To the side a big yellow bubble was rising to the top. Frank still felt fuzzy. In fact, all the booze he had consumed was only now having an intoxicating effect.

"So tell me, Frank," she whispered into his ear, "tell me the truth so I know I can trust you, so I can love you, really love you, here and now, knowing for sure that you're not like all the others." She removed her hand from his mouth, arched her back, and tucked both arms below her breasts.

After a couple of seconds Frank said, "Let me inside then, and I'll tell you what you've been dying to hear. Let me inside you so I know I can trust *you*."

Judy lowered herself over Frank's dogged bone. She slowly and firmly rocked and Frank felt good again, really good, though he was having difficulty getting to the pinnacle.

"I did do it," he uttered. "I have no idea how anyone could have figured that out, but yeah, I did do it."

Judy rocked a little bit faster as, to her surprise, these words tickled her, right on her private pink button. Her body started to quiver. Frank too was on the cusp of beating his battle with alcohol fatigue.

"That's all you had to say," Judy noted, grimacing slightly. "The truth. That's all I wanted."

Frank finally let loose, just as Judy's own body experienced a pulsating eruption of its own.

Oh Santa Maria. Santa Maria! she uttered privately, her neck tilted toward the dark ceiling. Restraining tears she glanced down at Frank, her body still tingling. His eyes were closed, his body apparently spent. He selfishly preferred sleep at this point to any kind of discussion of what had just transpired. *Si diavolo*, his lover thought, but she was euphoric, even amorous. She had finally landed her man where she wanted him, a man for whose charm and dark side – whose machismo – she had  unwittingly fallen; but having done so, she knew that her career as a police officer was now over. She had solved the case – a very difficult and important one at that – but on Monday she would be fired for the way she did it, just as sure as the sockeye dies after spawning.

❋❋❋

Naturally, as it was for Romeo and Juliet, the joyous moon of Frank and Judy's consummation was soon eclipsed by the icy break of day, but no lark or nightingale chirped a pleasing cadence to arouse them. Rather, a bothersome crow squawked obnoxiously from a nearby power line.

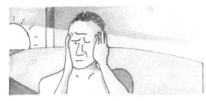

"Oh, je suis magané," were the first words Frank muttered upon awakening. He tried with great difficulty to open his eyes.

Judy had barely slept. "C'est quoi, monsieur?" she asked, whimsically showing Frank her limited knowledge of French.

With his eyes closed, Frank smiled.

"Je suis magané. I'm wrecked. I got a bad hangover," he explained.

"I'll make some orange juice – or I've got some tomato juice, whatever you like."

"I just want to go back to sleep."

"Why not? But I'm getting up," she said, sitting up on the bed. "I'm restless, and I've got a lot to do today."

Frank rolled over on to his side. Judy stood up, got a baby blue terry robe from the back of her door and put it on.

"Are you going to turn me in?" Frank asked, barely awake and in a tone that suggested indifference, or that he already knew the answer – that no, she would not betray him.

"You fool," she said affectionately, before leaving the bedroom for a shower.

Truth be told, as the water splashed over

her tired body and the foam of lavender-scented shampoo slid down her skin from her hair, she was wracked with indecision.

There was absolutely no question that she would have to reveal the fruits of her undercover efforts to her superiors and the matter would go directly to the Chief of Police for disciplinary action – possibly outright dismissal from the force. That prospect was daunting enough, but just as dazzling, if not more, was the genuine possibility that Frank's confession amounted to a hill of beans, that it was unreliable, and would not be admissible as evidence against him in a court of law.

The fruit of the poisoned tree. Matthew, Chapter 7. Police know the principle well. Evidence obtained from a tainted or corrupt police investigation is often excluded from criminal trials.

Ohhh, she murmured. The water drummed against her neck.

All police officers know that an induced confession is a troublesome one. That's the guiding rule, not to hold out to suspects the promise of some favour or advantage in exchange for information. No tit for tat.

Judy could not stifle a smile when that expression came to her. *I certainly gave him the tit,* she mused before stepping out from the tub and taking a towel off her rack.

Was it worth it all? she seriously wondered. *What would Sergeant Wolychenski think? She didn't ask me to go that far.*

Judy watched herself in the mirror, stroking a comb through her hair. Then she put on her terry robe again, stepped into her bedroom and stared at the face upon her pillow, lost to the unconscious zone.

Maybe it isn't too late. Alphonse. Bryce. They don't need to know, yet, how I got you to talk. They just need to know that you did talk, that you spilled the beans, albeit under the influence. They can take that to Dan. He'll think up something...

Judy stepped a couple feet closer.

You fool. Look at you. I've seen her – her picture in the paper. Her face on the billboard. Molto caldo. And you let her get away. So you took it out on Big Dick, not her, and then you ran into me. I'm flattered just to think I compared.

Frank stirred slightly but did not awaken, so Judy went softly to the kitchen and prepared a small pot of espresso.

They'll probably use me one more time, just to lead you to them, or maybe not. Maybe they'll find you themselves. But once you find out that I told them, that's...that's...

Judy pulled a knife from her cutlery drawer, took a slice from a butter chunk on a saucer, and put it in a fry pan on her stove. She turned on the burner.

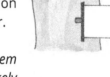

Unless I can just convince you to tell them what you told me, but that's not likely gonna' happen.

She pulled out a half loaf of bread from the freezer in her fridge.

Maybe I should just forget the whole thing. Don't tell anyone. Pretend it didn't happen. Who really needs to know, anyway?

She pried a couple of slices off a frozen loaf with her knife, before returning the hind end to its frosty lair. Then she opened the fridge and picked a couple of eggs from the rack.

But you won't shut up. She had turned on her heels now and was pointing the knife in the direction of her open bedroom door. *You'll tell someone. Probably her, of all people. And then I'm really fucked. It'll become public. Who am I kidding? I'm fucked already.*

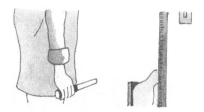

Turning back to her stove, Judy quickly tapped the eggs on the side of the fry pan and dropped the goo and yokes in the pan. The espresso maker bubbled up.

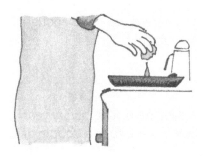

The strong, attractive scent caused to her close her eyes for a few seconds.

Two weeks. They've got just two weeks, she thought, pouring the morning elixir into a cup.

May 24. Not even three weeks away.

She took a sip, twitched, and sat down at her small, square kitchen table. The start date of his second trial was etched in her mind. She pictured Ryan vividly from the one afternoon she attended his trial to

watch the videotapes of his police statements. His back was to hers as he watched himself on the monitor, until the court took a break and he turned around to see his supporters. He had short cropped hair. A thin, sprouting moustache. Weathered but determined eyes. And a striped dress shirt his lawyer had bought him. A sober, handsome young Native man.

Fucking innocent, and over a year in shackles!

She got up, but not to flip the eggs. Rather, she turned off the burner and sat back down. A well of anguish pulsed upward, from her stomach, from her core. Her torso convulsed and she laid her head on the table, pushing her coffee cup out of the way with one hand. With her head embraced by both arms she wept, tears washing over her cheeks and her ribs jutting back and forth like a choking dog. The sound of her moaning was loud enough to wake the collared hound in the other room.

🚲 🚲 🚲

On May 11th Vancouverites went into deep mourning. Every year the burial took place around this time, give or take a couple of weeks. The Canucks had just been left for dead, like road kill, again, except that they hadn't been squashed on the road. The desperados were careened on home ice by an American team with more local boys on it than Vancouver's own, and the latter – the Blackhawks – would get the thrill of hoisting the Cup a few weeks later.

The weather wasn't helping to lift spirits. Like an important package expected from Canada Post, the perennial early spring had been delayed at a climatic substation somewhere untraceable.

It took a few days, but Judy decided to roll the dice and carry her deception and betrayal of Frank even further than she had already done. She had no choice, she felt. After having spent the night in his bed, being sexually intimate, she was now seated on the living room sofa. Frank was standing in the middle of the room, drinking a coffee, and casually watching the scenery outside his window.

"I tell you, man, there's no time limit to when the police can stop investigating you," she told him. "If that Indian is acquitted, there's a real good chance they'll come after you. You're on their radar, but that puts us at risk."

"And how's that?" Frank asked, a slice of contempt to his tone.

"You've been hanging out with us for months now. They know that. They keep tabs on people like me, surveillance, Frank. If they're interested in you, they'll come digging around my backyard too, and Bryce's, and Alphonse's. They'll ask us about you, and we've all gotta be on the same page. We gotta know the truth in order to bury it properly."

Frank looked at Judy doubtfully.

"We're guilty by association, Frank, but you don't need to worry. We can make these problems go away."

"Oh, and how's that?" Frank asked, as if he wanted an explanation for a sensational magic trick.

"You saw it with your own eyes," Judy quickly reminded him. "These guys are in with dirty cops, but not only cops. They know judges too."

"Fuck that. I don't believe that," Frank said disdainfully.

"Do believe me. They're well connected."

Frank shook his head and set his coffee down.

"Don't you think it's just a little amazing that you've committed, I don't know, six or seven serious crimes with me by now, and there's not been one whiff of an investigation or suspicion cast on you, me or any of us?"

Frank thought about this, his brows knit.

"It's time to sober up, Frank. We're all very well connected. You as well as I. Now you need to tell Big Dan how you killed Dickerson. Dan's our boss. He'll protect you for good, I can promise you that."

Frank said nothing.

After a half-minute of silence Judy grew impatient and said, "Dan doesn't know anything yet, so I'm gonna tell you how to sell this to him, all right?"

Frank picked up his coffee, took a sip, made a face, then put the cup back down.

"So that's it?" Frank asked. "You tell me what to say to this guy, Dan – Big Dan? – and I meet him somewhere, spill my beans, and that's it?"

"That's right."

"Have you ever met him?" Frank asked.

"Yes I have, and I can assure you, they don't call him big for nuthin."

Frank knit his brows again and reached for his coffee, even knowing it would be cold.

It was.

After swallowing a mouthful anyway, Frank said, "But I don't want anything to do with these fucking people after this, is that clear?"

"I know, I know," Judy said. "Maybe you'll reconsider after you meet Dan. Seriously. He's an impressive guy. You'll like him,

I know it, but if you don't, and you want out, then I'll walk away too. I promise you, Frank, I wanna be with you, but you've just got to understand right now that it's too late for us to keep your shit between us. You need Dan's protection and his guys need to know about your shit so they can protect themselves from nosy cops."

"Fuck this," Frank blurted.

Judy got up from the sofa and slung her arms loosely around Frank's neck. "Jesus, love, don't sweat it," she urged, looking her new ragazzo warmly in the eyes. "It'll all go smooth as gelato."

Frank tilted his head back, away from Judy, and gazed at the ceiling.

Three days later Frank sat across from Big Dan (wonderfully played by RCMP Sergeant Daniel Martelli) in a tenth floor suite at the Inn at the Quay, in New Westminster, and explained how he killed Don Dickerson more than two years earlier.

"He came at you?" Martelli asked, for the second time. He just wanted to make sure, squeezed in as he was to the suite's only Barcalounger. At six feet three inches and 240 pounds – some fat, some muscle – he intimidated Frank, though his manner was affable. He was in fact reclined as he listened to Frank, his legs crossed casually over one another, and the souls of his cowboy boots facing the confessor. Big rings adorned his fingers. His suit was elephant grey, his shirt purple and tie baby-blue. He was nursing a beer. Frank had one too.

"That's the truth. I swear it. I only went there to threaten him."

"And how did you know he would be there?"

"I suspected that he had a plan with my fiancée. She told me a big story about being out with girls from work, but one of them phoned earlier, asking for her. I knew where the prick lived, so I went there, on my bike, and I waited. I know his car, and it wasn't long before he pulled in, to his garage, his underground, you know what I mean?"

Martelli nodded and Frank had a swig of beer before continuing. Three other RCMP officers were watching the whole interview through a one-way window between Martelli's suite and theirs. The police rented these rooms for precisely such occasions. The monitoring room was currently set up with audio-visual equipment. If necessary, the officers could call Martelli on his cellphone and direct him to ask specific questions. Martelli was more or less in the dark about the file, by design. His colleagues wanted to hear as much detail as possible directly from Frank.

"So we confronted each other" – each otter, to Martelli's ear. "He was carrying a bag of groceries and he put it on the trunk of his Mercedes. Just like that." Frank made the motion. "Then I told him I wanted to talk but he told me I was a loser, a *cuckold*. He told me to fuck off. So I took a swing but I grazed him only. He must've ducked. He kneed me in the groin and hit me twice. Pow, pow, and I went down, on one knee."

Martelli nodded again, and sipped his beer.

"That's when I pulled out my knife. I wasn't going to take a beating like that, but I never meant to kill him, I assure you that. Just wanted to stop him."

Frank sat forward on the sofa. "I saw what I had done, so I fled. I was scared, so I can't remember what I did with the knife. I'm sure I just threw that somewhere."

An officer next door phoned Martelli and asked him to press Frank a little about the grocery bag.

"Mmm-hmm. Mmm-hmm." Dan clipped his phone shut, then said to Frank, "Just my old lady, she keeps a short leash, but I'm curious: after this guy put down the grocery bag, he fought you, then you stabbed him. I take it the groceries were still on the hood of the car?"

Frank paused to think.

"I mean. The guy didn't fight you with a bag of groceries in his hand, did he?" the undercover Sergeant pressed.

"No no," Frank said. "They got knocked off in the fight, or they slid down or something, because yeah, a juice bottle broke. I remember that now."

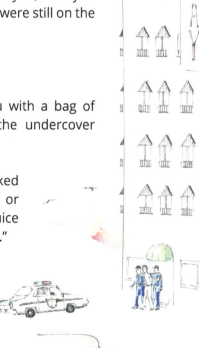

When the covert monitors were sure they had heard enough – enough to charge Frank with Don's murder and make it stick – they phoned the Sergeant next door and told him to call off the questioning. Martelli pretended to be annoyed by yet another interruption, but took the call, answered it as if it was entirely unrelated to what was transpiring in the suite, and hung up.

"Well I don't know how you feel about all that," he said to Frank, "but I'm impressed. Real impressed. You've made the heat look like a bunch of old women on this one. And hell, so what if that injun goes down? He would have done life on the installment plan anyway. Lots of 'em do."

Martelli shook his head, pushed forward in his recliner, and put his empty bottle on the floor.

"Drugs. Booze. They're fuckin' hooked. And everyone blames the white man," he said, getting up from his chair.

Frank stood up as well.

"The boys say you don't wanna keep up our line of work. Are you sure?"

Frank shrugged nervously.

"We hate to lose a good man, so I'm in no hurry to give you your walking slip. You've done no wrong by us and I'll do no wrong by you. You've got my word. This little discussion here will never leave this room."

Martelli extended his large hand, which Frank shook, then escorted his guest to the door.

As Frank rode the elevator down to the lobby he felt a peculiar, uneasy sense of relief, of anxiety, of guilt even, for he had followed Judy's advice and lied a little to Big Dan, a well-connected mobster, so he believed.

"There were no witnesses, none whatsoever," she had urged him to remember. "If you tell him Don provoked you, taunted you, belittled your manhood, he'll never know the difference. And what does it matter to those guys, anyway? They're not cops," she had told him. "They just want to protect you and themselves."

Frank pushed open the front doors of the Inn at the Quay and was startled to hear his name called out over a megaphone. "What de?" He could hear the words "under arrest" and he now saw three police cars in the parking lot, doors open, officers staring at him, guns drawn. He stopped in his tracks and was immediately handcuffed by two officers who had snuck up from inside the lobby.

"Qu'est que...?"

"Mr. Belleveau, you are under arrest for the murder of Donald Dickerson. You have the right to remain silent, and anything you say can be used as evidence against you in a court of law. Do you understand, sir?"

Frank glowered at the officer, said "Yeah. I do," then hung his head and allowed himself to be led to an awaiting cruiser.

🚲 🚲 🚲

Frank's guilty plea two weeks later was naturally front page news, but he pleaded to manslaughter, not murder, and got a sweet sentencing deal, just as Judy had predicted. On the strength of the hotel confession the Crown would have some difficulty proving "beyond a reasonable doubt" that Frank wasn't provoked, or even that he intended to kill the adulterous Density King, especially when jurors learned that Don had betrayed the accused's trust by pursuing his fiancée so aggressively.

Sure, the police suspected that Frank probably lied to Sergeant Martelli about the grocery bag. They believed the victim was holding the bag when he got stabbed, which he was, but they couldn't prove it with certainty.

Moreover, the optics of the investigation inclined the police and the Crown toward the deal they struck with Frank. There could be no question that if Frank went to trial his lawyer would tell the jury exactly how his client's confession was elicited. The jury would not only hear about the fictitious crimes Frank aided and abetted with undercover police, and the large sums of cash he was paid for doing so. They would also learn about the sexual intimacy he shared with Corporal Jovita Costanza.

As the serpent foresaw, the Crown was more than content to keep the corrupting image of Frank and Jovita's (aka Judy's) intertwined nakedness hidden from public view. Frank agreed to an eight year prison term for manslaughter and Corporal Costanza was placed on paid leave. Frank would likely serve about four or five years, after which time he could return to the dusty earth to begin tilling it anew. By then the child that was just taking root in Jovita's belly would be four or five years old. Jovita was a good Catholic girl, after all, who accepted the natural consequences of biting into tasty fruit.

The camera flashes nearly blinded Ryan Ghostkeeper as he left the Surrey pre-trial centre a free man. Curtis Rice was by his side, to give him a ride into Vancouver, where he was scheduled to give a live radio interview on the CBC.

"Mr. Ghostkeeper. How does it feel after all those months?"

"It feels good. Real good," he replied.

Once he was in the studio he told the interviewer, calmly, "What I don't understand, is why the police, and the Crown, didn't believe me. I told them I was innocent, but no one believed me."

"But there was a circumstantial case, was there not?"

"But I don't understand. What circumstances?"

"You were found with the murder weapon. Isn't that true?"

"You are right there. I found the murder weapon, but I told the police that. I just found it. I tried to sell it. Nobody would believe me. Not even the Crown."

"Do you think your race had anything to do with the fact that police suspected you, despite your protestation of innocence?"

"Of course it does!" Slim Jimmy shouted. He was seated on a picnic table on the front yard of 1620 Angus Drive, taking a break from gardening. A battery-powered radio broadcast Ryan's interview across the yard, loud enough to reach the ears of the few other gardenhands who were on their knees, weeding or gathering green beans, or working hoes or small shovels, digging up carrots and potatoes.

"You mean did they suspect me because I'm Indian?" Ryan queried.

"Yes," the interviewer confirmed.

"Oh, maybe. I don't know. There's a lot of us in jail there. I've been in jail before. So I guess they do suspect us a lot."

"What are you going to do now, after so long in jail?"

"Come live with us!" Cactus shouted out. She was picking green beans.

"Oh, my aunt's waytin to take me to her place," Ryan said, "to go for dinner somewhere, I guess. I'm sure I'll see some cousins there."

"Come live with us! Come live with us!" the Angus Drive gardeners shouted in unison.

"Do you know if your lawyer is planning on taking any action, to address the fact that you were wrongly imprisoned for so many months?" the interviewer continued.

"I fuckin' hope so," Slim Jimmy said from the picnic table.

"I don't know about that," Ryan replied. "I don't know what he can do. You'll have to ask him."

"Ryan, I am sorry for your unfortunate experience with the justice system, and I wish you the best," the reporter concluded.

"Thank you."

"Good bye."

"Good bye."

"Come live with us! Come live with us!" the gardeners shouted out again.

In late June a plan was approved in Detroit that would see thousands of neglected houses in the city systematically demolished over four years. Wilting, dilapidated boxes that once concealed family secrets and fortified American dreams would be forcibly flattened, but this time there would be no steamrollers and pavers on the near horizon. There would be no I-75 to extinguish the black vitality of Paradise Valley. In a city four times the square area of Vancouver, with a population shrinking toward Vancouver's own, creating density would not be the challenge. The new Paradise – the Brave New World – would have to be imagined differently, but the Sedentary Old World, the Old World of Shaughnessy Estates, built solidly on the soil of a Pacific West Coast rainforest, could stay just the same. So the Supreme Court of Canada ordered before it took its summer break. ASHEPOND had won its appeal, "confirming that private property rights remain every bit as strong today as they were when our forefathers built this fair land." That's exactly what Margaret Churchill-Booth told reporters at a press conference.

The tents, bicycles and impecunious joie de vivre on the grounds of 1620 Angus Drive quickly disappeared, mostly to resurface in East Van.

Hannah Verso had already taken refuge in her 14th Avenue fort. After Frank admitted to having killed Don Dickerson, unscrupulous reporters did their homework and put the word out that Hannah was the most likely femme fatale. Media soldiers now stood outside and at the ready

with their video camera bayonets.

Hannah was used to her physical appearance being the subject of comment, but now her private shame was on front-page display.

"I'm a fucking awful person!" she bawled, curled up in the foetal position on her bed, her eyes bloodshot from continual sobbing.

"Hey hey hey," Cactus uttered softly and soothingly. She lay behind her friend, spooning her, as Hannah sniffled and snorted into a handkerchief. "You're no such thing," Cactus said.

The light of the summer sun penetrated Hannah's blinds.

"She's got a sister. Did you know that?" Hannah asked.

"A...what?"

"Don's wife. Denise. She's got a daughter, you know. Born when Erica was." Tears streamed down Hannah's face. She sniffled.

"That's two, two little girls who will never know their father."

"C'mon. You don't know that the other kid is Don's." Cactus's tone remained soothing.

"Well I'm sure it is."

Cactus did not know what to think about that.

"Do you think you'll go?" she asked, after a pause.

"I don't know. I'm scared, I guess."

Again, Cactus didn't know what to think. She had never been to Detroit.

"But he'll be *with* you," she said, referring to Charlie. "It's his hometown. I'd love to go, if you ask me."

"I'm thinking about it," Hannah said. Her body had calmed a little, being in Cactus's embrace.

"Anyways, please please please come with me on the June ride. I know there's people out there just dyin' to photograph you, to make your life miserable, but you've got to ignore them. They can fuck right off. You can't let them keep you in here, wrapped up in a cocoon."

"I don't know, really. I'm so sick and tired of people staring and pointing fingers. I prefer to stay inside."

"But Jesus, sister, you've got to get out! No one at the ride is gonna poke fun at you. They like you. You've supported the Resistance, though I shouldn't be telling you that."

"Think of all the people we'll pass who will recognize me."

"They will not! Get a grip."

⚥ ⚥ ⚥

Charlie had also encouraged Hannah to participate in the critical mass ride.

"We'll all go together, of course. You too," he said, looking at me.

Hannah eventually acquiesced, and on Friday, June 25th at 5:45 pm, we all rolled onto the north grounds of the Art Gallery.

Hannah towed me in a bright orange bike trailer with a patch on it that Cactus had given me:

The pack was rumoured to be six thousand in number that day, and during the ride, whenever Hannah glanced behind her, to check on me or smile for Charlie's phone camera, she could not see the end of the shiny spokes and rubber and smiling faces.

There were the usual honks in support along the way, just as the occasional irate driver blared his horn at an intersection blocked by corkers. Hannah stayed behind a fellow with a battery-powered CD player or radio or something attached to his bike carrier. He was playing a lot of old time favourites, Motown and disco hits, all of which lifted Hannah's spirits and took her mind away from recent events.

Bit by bit, block by block, she found herself closer and closer to the front of the pack. Coming out of the downtown core, heading west along Georgia Street, the cyclists directly in front of her were quickly veering right and left to make the walls that would protect the group from oncoming traffic. Suddenly she and the music man were at the very front of the pack. She got a small anxiety attack when she saw a few cars approaching from the north. She had only corked once, with Cactus, and she relied on Cactus's courage to do so, but now she had to do it. She swerved and stopped in front of a shiny black import luxury car that was approaching the street from West Pender. Charlie was close behind, as were a couple of other cyclists.

The driver of the import pressed on his horn, which prompted the cyclist with the sound system to turn up the volume. Hannah looked at the black-haired driver and raised her hands in the air, in resignation. Like a swarm of locusts, the cyclists swept by, though a couple more joined Hannah and Charlie, to show solidarity. The driver got out of his car and yelled, "Get the fuck out of the way or I'll drive right fuckin' into you people!"

"Take it easy, man," one corker said. "Just relax. There's nothing you can do about it," another explained. "Look," Charlie urged, fanning his arm in the direction of the passing cyclists, "there's thousands of people comin' through here. You're just going to have to wait."

"Get the fuck out of the way!" the driver repeated, getting back into his driver seat. His face was purple and bloated.

Hannah looked at Charlie with widened eyes. Charlie shrugged and threw up his hands.

The driver bolted forward a couple of feet, until his bumper came within about six inches of Hannah, who quickly tried to get out the way, but other corkers stood fast and even aggressively moved closer to the black car. Hannah was now stuck right in front.

"Fuck. Get 'yer bike out of there, Hannah!" Charlie pleaded.

"I can't!"

"Don't worry, guys," the sound-box cyclist said. "He'd have to be a fuckin' nut bar to drive further."

But just then the black car's engine revved. Hannah and the others instantly turned their heads to look. The vehicle surged forward. "Oh my – stop! STOP! STOHHHPPP!" Hannah screamed as the bumper and grill slammed into her leg, knocking her and her bike over. "Someone help me! Please, please stop!" she begged.

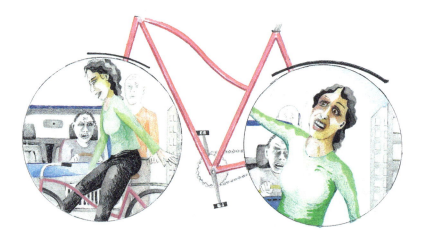

Surrounding cyclists pounded on the aggressor's car and shouted for the irate driver to stop. Some lost their balance and tipped over in a loose domino effect. Charlie yelled out Hannah's name, but her voice faltered as she suddenly found herself winded, prone, and in numbing pain. Her bicycle frame was sandwiched between her lower legs. "Please, please god! Stop!" she cried out.

Cyclists continued to shout and pummel the determined vehicle with fists and ready objects, silencing Hannah's own cries and terror as the front bumper and undercarriage proceeded over her. The driver had lost his mind, to road rage in the extreme.

In a desperate attempt to shield herself Hannah raised one arm as best as she could. Charlie pulled on it, but to no avail. She was pinned hard to her bike, just as the latter was now pinned tight below the car's chassis. The vehicle pushed on, bending Hannahs' bike entirely and pressing it across her flesh and bones.

She screamed until her voice gave out.

The odor of engine oil was now upon her, as was the prospect of death. Seconds later she blacked out.

The driver toppled four other cyclists, including Charlie, before stopping. Fellow riders screamed and scrambled for safety. The driver got out of his car and waved his arms and fists around in the air. "See what you fucking caused? You fucking selfish pricks!" he shouted. "You all think you own the road!" Three cyclists tackled him to the ground and struggled with all their might to keep him pinned. Two cops who had been on bikes worked hard to restrain cyclists from beating the driver into unconsciousness.

My little orange chariot had been turned on its side and I was crying. Charlie pulled me out. Shaking, he handed me to a stranger, then tried to phone 9-1-1 on his cell phone but his fingers were too jittery. Others had already made the call.

A few cyclists and a bicycle cop carefully pushed the black vehicle back to reveal Hannah, limp and bloody. "Jesus Christ," Charlie moaned before ducking down to pull the bike out from her legs.

"You fucking murderer!" one woman shouted at the driver, who had just been formally arrested. Many in the crowd were yelling at him.

Charlie quickly lifted Hannah's head and put his fingers across her neck. She still had a pulse.

"Wake up, sweetheart. Wake up!" Charlie begged. Two of the bicycle police knelt down beside him.

"We'll take care of her from here. An ambulance is on its way," one of them said.

Charlie reluctantly stood up and looked around. Everyone was gawking. A couple of cyclists in the throng shouted at passing cars, "This is what you do!" "This is what we are up against!" Many of those closest to Hannah's body were visibly shaking and crying. Some cyclists were texting or lifting their cell phone cameras in the air, hoping to capture the action for their Facebook pages. Charlie was trembling. Tears streamed down his cheeks. The young lady who was holding me gave me back to Charlie. He hugged me really tight. Though he did not know it, Hannah had suffered a skull fracture and concussion, her jaw had been broken, her ribs were crushed, and a lung had been punctured. An approaching siren could be heard.

News of the maelstrom was broadcast almost instantly, and for the next couple of days my mom lay on her back, mostly in an operating theatre, in critical condition, hooked up to an oxygen mask, I.V. and machines that measured her respiration and brain functioning.

As much as Hannah's parents and Charlie and Cactus wanted to be by her side, they were only allowed to see her a few minutes each day. Hannah's mom and dad offered to take me to Kelowna, if need be.

For the time being, however, they were staying in a downtown hotel, not too far from Hannah's apartment, where Charlie and Cactus were taking care of me.

Come to think of it, the Sockeye were trying to get through Hell's Gate right about then, struggling with all their might against a powerful current just to get to Stuart Lake. Like them, my mom's fate depended on some kind of primordial blueprint for success, the equivalent of a cosmological coin toss.

On the second day my mom was in the hospital Frank phoned, collect, from jail. He cried and cried and said that if Hannah died or did not recover fully he would kill that fucker when he got to prison.

On the third day after the accident a surgeon with a five o'clock shadow came into the hospital waiting room. Hannah's mom and dad were there. Charlie and Cactus were not. They were pushing me in a stroller along 10th Avenue, en route to West Broadway, to get some lunch for everyone.

Hannah's mom and dad looked at each other with apprehension in their eyes, and about four minutes later, in the privacy of a small doctor's office, the surgeon told them the worst, that my mom's heart had stopped about twenty-five minutes earlier.

That meant my mom's spirit was already off the ground and in the sky, ascending like a colourful kite at the tail end of a child's fingers, even as Cactus was ordering soup and sandwiches for everyone, to go.

The doctor had closed her eyes by the time we returned, but I got to see mom with her eyes open later that year, just as I do every year around my favourite holiday. In case you have already forgotten, that's Halloween, the most important time of the year. Well, that and the Day of the Dead, when mom's ghost comes back to earth for a visit. That's also when I come back to Vancouver with Charlie and his new girlfriend, who's really good to me. I take a week off my studies in history at Wayne State and come home to catch up with mom, to visit Cactus, and Victor, and even Frank and Jovita and their kids.

Source Material

Friedrich Nietzsche, The Gay Science, trans. by Walter Kaufmann (N.Y.: Random House, 1974) at p.181.

Jon Hilsenrath, Serena Ng and Damian Paletta, "Worst Crisis Since '30s, With No End Yet in Sight", Wall Street Journal September 17, 2008.

Carrier Sekani Tribal Council, Aboriginal Interests & Use Study on the Enbridge Gateway Pipeline (An Assessment of the Impacts of the Proposed Enbridge Gateway Pipeline on the Carrier Sekani First Nations, May 2006), Section 2.0 - 2.1, pp.8-11. www.carriersekani.ca/images/docs/enbridge/AIUS%20 COMPLETE%20FINAL%20inc%20maps.pdf

First Voices, Nak'azdli Dakelh Community Portal (www.firstvoices.com/en/Nakazdli-Dakelh)

Gerry Clare, People of the Rocks: The Sekani of British Columbia as seen in the Journals of Mackenzie, Fraser, Harmon and Black (http://www.calverley.ca/Part01-FirstNations/01-033.html

Nak'azdli Band, www.nakazdli.ca/history.htm

Elizabeth Furniss, Changing Ways: Southern Carrier History, 1793 – 1940 (Quesnel, B.C.: Quesnel School District #28, 1993).

Elizabeth Furniss, Dakelh Keyoh: The Southern Carrier in Earlier Times (Quesnel, B.C.: Quesnel School District #28, 1993).

About the Author

When bills need to get paid Christopher Nowlin heads straight to an office, usually Gene Café on Main Street or Café Calabria on the Drive, in Vancouver. There he will prepare teaching lessons or legal analyses on his laptop (which is rarely on his lap), surrounded by the buzz of other decentralized bees, the clinking of cups and saucers, sharp blasts of steam and the gurgling of roiling milk, as well as the colourful to-and-fro of outside passers-by. Otherwise Chris is probably cursing the rain, trying to enjoy life on two wheels, or painting and drawing on two feet. To see his visual art and a list of his various legal essays please visit www.christophernowlin.com.

Chris is also the author of *Judging Obscenity: A Critical History of Expert Evidence* (non-fiction) and *To See the Sky* (fiction).